The Books Of The Wars

BY
MARK GESTON

THE BOOKS OF THE WARS

This is a work of fiction. All the characters and events portrayed in this book are fictional, and any resemblance to real people or incidents is purely coincidental.

A Baen Book

Baen Publishing Enterprises
P.O. Box 1403
Riverdale, NY 10471
www.baen.com

ISBN 10: 1-4165-9152-4
ISBN 13: 978-1-4165-9152-8

Cover art by Alan Pollack
Maps by Randy Asplund

First Baen printing, February 2009

Distributed by Simon & Schuster
1230 Avenue of the Americas
New York, NY 10020

Printed in the United States of America

10 9 8 7 6 5 4 3 2 1

PRAISE FOR THE SCIENCE FICTION OF MARK GESTON

" . . . reminiscent of the classic SF of Clifford D. Simak in its elegiac tone, especially his City series. . . ." —**David G. Hartwell**

"I like this book very much!"—**Gerald Jonas**, reviewing *The Siege of Wonder*, in *The New York Times Book Review*

"A remarkable work and especially potent . . . " —**Donald A. Wollheim** on *Out of the Mouth of the Dragon* in *The Universe Makers*

" . . . a book that would have been a 'classic' if it had been written in the 'good old days.' Standards are higher now, but it meets them head-on." —*Analog* reviewing *Lords of the Starship*

"Mark Geston's s-f novels are polished and literate. . . ." —*A Reader's Guide to Science Fiction*

" . . . Geston's novels are distinguished by his skillful style . . . examines the fine line between science and magic." —*The New Encyclopedia of Science Fiction*

" . . . up there with Zelazny's Amber series. Some of the passages and images are so vivid they will never leave you." —*SFFWorld.com*

"A weird, horrifying future of continuous flux, stasis and war. . . . Brilliant journey through a . . . world of misunderstood prophecy and inappropriate technology. . . ." —**David Pringle**, *The Ultimate Guide to Science Fiction*

"Grim and somber stories, with some fine imagery and a uniquely bitter ennui." —*Anatomy of Wonder 4*

CONTENTS

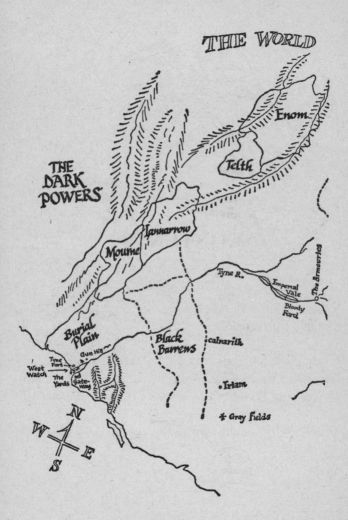

SURREAL SPLENDOR:
Three Novels by Mark S. Geston

1.

In 1991 John Douglas of Avon, a house I've never worked for, sent me for quote the bound proofs of Mark Geston's first new novel in over a decade. I knew John only well enough to say hi if we happened to be standing in front of a hotel at the same time.

I quoted enthusiastically.

Years later I ran into John (in front of a hotel) and asked him how he'd happened to send the proofs to me. There weren't, I'd have thought, many obvious clues that I'm a Geston fan.

John explained that he knew I'd started writing at about the time *Lords of the Starship* appeared. He assumed that *anybody* from that period would not only be familiar with Geston but be an enthusiastic fan.

He was certainly right about me.

2.

The Books of the Wars reprints three early Geston novels: *Lords of the Starship, Out of the Mouth of the Dragon,* and *The Siege of Wonder. Siege* is probably a self-standing novel, though nothing is quite as certain as it may first seem in these fictions. *Dragon* can be read as a sequel to *Lords*, but it need not be.

Dragon was the first of Geston's books that I read, while I was in Vietnam. We'll get back to that.

3.

You can read *The Books* as exercises in plotting. The plots aren't conventional, but they most certainly exist. The sweep and purpose of *Lords*, the recapitulation of the world by the viewpoint character's wanderings in *Dragon*, and the quest of *Siege* which leads to a mystery greater than the one it answers—all are perfectly structured in their different fashions.

You can read *The Books* for their gorgeous, detailed imagery—Faberge eggs in prose, if you will. I suspect much of the enormous critical impact they had when they were first published was due to the surreal majesty of their settings. As a few typical examples: the first sight from on high of the yard where the miles-long starship will be built; aircraft arrayed like worshippers under the stained glass of a great cathedral; or a great wizard escorted by shambling corpses in armor.

You can even read *The Books* for their characterizations. Though often cameos, they are real human beings who have their moments and pass on, as happens in real life. Because the ideas are so overwhelming a reader may ignore the individuals, but the author never does. Here a civilian, handed a sword and engulfed by battle; there a madwoman in a plague-swept ruin, speaking lucidly of what had happened and then dissolving into the laughter that is her only defense; or again, a precise military officer leading his unit into the heart of unreason in the calm certainty that his truth will prevail . . . all real, all vivid.

And if you have the sort of mind that I do, there's another reason you might want to read *The Books*.

4.

I prefaced a collection of my humorous stories by noting that the only kind of humor there is in a war zone is black humor—and there's no place I've been where I more needed the humor.

In the same context, these gorgeous, surreal novels are about hope.

5.

When I entered college in 1963, the Vietnam War was a squabble in a distant place. There'd been similar squabbles in my memory—rather a bad one in Lebanon, for example—but that had been with Eisenhower as president. Now our president was Kennedy and shortly Johnson; and perhaps more important, their Secretary of Defense was Robert S. McNamara, a technocrat and a monster.

By the time I got my undergraduate degree in 1967, Vietnam was a storm that had broken over America and the world, shredding society and bodies. Tens of thousands of Americans had died, and hundreds of thousands of Vietnamese.

The war was building without plan or purpose. Each previous failure was used as the reason for a further, greater, effort; which would fail in turn, as by then everybody knew it would fail.

General Westmoreland announced light at the end of the tunnel, shortly before the tunnel collapsed on him in the form of the Tet Offensive. Politicians lied—to themselves first, I believe, but to everyone else as well. And the war went on and would go on, and on. There was no end, and no hope.

6.

But I was a law student at Duke, deferred from the draft for so long as my grades were good enough to keep me in school. Grades weren't a problem—I made the law journal easily.

And then, as one of his last acts in office, Mr McNamara cancelled the deferments of graduate students. I was drafted along with nine other members of my hundred-man class (eight of us were on the law journal). The demographics of the armed services changed: a third of my basic training platoon had graduated from college. The army created courses that were only open to college grads. (I took one.)

One of my army buddies was getting his Ph.D. in Old English at Princeton. Two more were getting theirs at the University of Chicago: one in zoology, the other in physics. It wouldn't have been completely unfair to call us the best and the brightest America had to offer. Our government sent us to Vietnam.

I was helpless and hopeless, and the person I'd been in 1968 died in that muggy, endemically corrupt meat-grinder. The body that walked off the plane at Travis Air Force Base on January 13, 1971 had nothing inside it but anger.

7.

I don't know what Mark Geston intended in these novels (I hope to learn in his own introduction), but for me they perfectly capture the ambiance of the Vietnam War, both the way it was conducted and its effect on society. In *The Books*, however, there are things that I didn't have (though others must have): hope and purpose and dreams.

8.

The Books are founded in concrete reality. Physical descriptions are crisp and vivid. Geston's subject is society, not individual characters, but the characters he draws are just as real as his picture—for example—of a winged abomination preparing to stoop on a convoy of barges.

The political and social movements Geston describes are those of the present world (and of men for as far back as history penetrates). Sometimes the fictional motivations initially appear as surreal as the juxtapositions of physical realities (for example, armored horsemen with jet bombers), but the reader soon finds that *The Books* are self-consistent and completely logical.

The events themselves are the ordinary ones of the evening news, but Geston has imposed system. By looking for causes with a historian's eye rather than taking the (literally) ephemeral viewpoint of a journalist, he unveils Truth instead of just creating copy. Here is the fabric of everyday life, clothed in jewels and given a purpose greater than men or even Mankind.

The great and terribly destructive strivings of *The Books* are entered into for their own sakes. The dreams of the people involved are directed at particular results, but in every case the real result is different from and greater than the conscious intention of the participants: they seek a specific end, but what grows instead are realms of infinite possibility, spreading and pointing like thorn hedges.

9.

I said that *The Books* capture the ambiance of the Vietnam War for me. To be explicit, they display ruin, misery and failure.

And yet there *is* hope, there *is* purpose; there is reason to live, even if that reason is death. I couldn't escape the reality of death in Vietnam and Cambodia, but Mark Geston made it possible for me to believe that there might somehow be a purpose in such a world; that there might somehow be hope.

10.

What *I* found in these novels was hope in the midst of hopelessness. I found here the thing I couldn't find in my own heart, and which I desperately needed.

Dave Drake
david-drake.com

FIRES FAR AWAY

The three novels collected here were not originally designed as a unified trilogy. The thought of finishing one story at a time, let alone a novel, was daunting enough for me when I started. But completion of the first unexpectedly suggested the second, which may therefore be loosely considered a sequel. Both of them were written when I was in college, and things in the 1965–1968 timeframe supplied plenty of desperate energy to fuel their imaginings. A long break followed, but when I picked things up again with *The Siege of Wonder*, the appeal of violent histories distant enough to be myths and the incongruity of the pedestrian and the recognizable in direct conflict with the literally divine and magical in such settings was as strong as it had been before.

9

The first book is really a set of related stories about individuals who would inevitably succumb but who would first brace and equip themselves in evocative armor that, to me at least, recalled what had happened before, even if only in others' imaginations. These characters acted for wrong or even reprehensible reasons as often as they did for worthy ones, but they still moved forward against overpowering oppositions. I found it easier for me to describe these people if they were on the bridge of a heavy cruiser I knew to be the *Des Moines* (given the nom de guerre, *Havengore*, in the first two novels), or at the controls of bombers I could visualize as Heinkel 111s or B-52s. Pitting such machines and people, who vaguely hold the same ideas and values of the times in which they really existed, against dragons and demons and knights was and remains very appealing to me. It let me place historically validated courage and power, and suffering, firmly in realms of fantasy. The chance to assign a literal reality to these collisions, of the mortal against the immortal, ambition against self-destruction, and help them play out against each other was a great reason for the first book, and I found the idea appealing enough to come back to it afterward.

The stage setting for much of this was war, my acquaintance with which has been, by good fortune, entirely historical and literary. For reasons that had everything to do with an introverted nature instead of any precociousness, I began reading histories of real conflicts in grade school. I still have *The Rise and Fall of the Third Reich* I doggedly read in junior high school, realizing how little I was grasping. I have no idea where the appeal of such things came from, so I rationalize it as part of a larger fascination with modern history. Most of my reading remains history, not novels. The working title of my first book was, unsurprisingly, *A History of the Ship*. It was changed to *Lords of the Starship* by the editor at Ace Books, Don Wollheim, who was then riding high on his inspired introduction of *The Lord of the Rings* to American readers.

I read about people in modern wars, both real and imagined. A lot was really adventure, Alistair Maclean and C.S. Forester were favorites, but others were harsher, like James Jones, Nicholas Monserrat, and John Hersey. Of course, there was Eric Maria Remarque, but everyone in sophomore high school English *had* to read him.

I should further confess a melancholy that also began too early. It was and isn't anything paralytic but was the reason for some things that might not have happened as they did if I had not been so distracted. Tragic histories then awaited my imagination and offered confirmation if not relief. They possessed both grandeur and terrible ruin, which matched the way I read it had always been, and while the latter would *almost* always triumph, the former's doomed gallantry and aesthetic appeal was undeniable. Individual people fit uncomfortably into this outlook and I found it easier to understand them when they were already embarked on some great tide, rather than simply trying to understand each other.

I started sending short stories to the usual magazines in high school. A handwritten rejection letter from Avram Davidson, then the editor of the *The Magazine of Fantasy and Science Fiction*, in 1964 meant I was getting close.

Kenyon College in 1964–1968 was still a men's school and not a place of great social polish—as if any American college or university was or wanted to be in those tumultuous years. But Kenyon went out of its way to sidestep the collegiate avant-garde and do things as idiosyncratically as possible. It also possessed a great and genuine appreciation for undergraduate learning and a literary tradition that ran through John Crowe Ransom and Randall Jarrell. It was isolated and insular. It was a perfect place for my accumulated imaginings to find their way into stories and I wrote both *Lords of the Starship* and *Out of the Mouth of the Dragon* there. But by junior year, 1966–1967, the world outside was upended by the civil rights struggle and the Vietnam War. There was also the permanent droning of the Cold War in the background.

I admit the sense of despair and failure got a little out of control with *Out of the Mouth of the Dragon*. But it worked as a story and I am much prouder of its excesses now.

I returned to the idea of characters caught up in a great sweep of an irresistible history years later with *The Siege of Wonder* (the third book, *The Day Star*, was purposely gentler than its predecessors and does not fit the cycle collected here). Things take longer when you leave law school and have a regular job. Of the three in this collection, this one most depends on the prosecution of a declared war between two great camps: science on the one hand (this is not a swipe at the awful cover on the original hardcover edition) and magic, as real and literal as the other. I know it may not seem that way to the reader, but to my own perception, the side of science was the more attractive and tragically romantic because of its discoveries of limitations and mortality. Its enemy wizards could not afford such self-awareness.

J. R. R. Tolkien survived the worst of the Great War and, fantastical though his epic is, it was told from inside a maelstrom, and that shows in the humanity of many of his characters and the ferocious scale of what confronts them. Others who have endured war have the same kind of authenticity. I've tried to come close to them, writing as I have from the outside. I have no wish to get any closer.

—Mark S. Geston

Lords of the Starship

PREFACE

Historians, as a rule, are particularly fond of "golden ages." They delight in pointing out how those condemned to live in current times come out so poorly when compared to the august citizens of later days. But it seems that in the years immediately following the Dorian Restoration, even the darkest chroniclers could not contain their admiration for their own times; even more remarkably, they chose to write about it while it was going on, not waiting until we had fallen into the inevitable pit.

Because of this ebullience and of the massive writings that it prompted, we should be in a unique position to answer the question that is connected to all golden ages: why did they fail? It is, therefore, all the greater tragedy that it seems that there is really no sure way of even approaching the question; the libraries that have survived for our scrutiny contain vast numbers of works on history, sociology, and the like (but most are oddly deficient in works of science) which appear to be virtual carbon copies of each other. Almost all of them are brimming with confidence in their own age and an almost irrepressible optimism about the future. Their titles *(The Finest Age, Now Forever, Millennium of Gods, Present Perfect)* give mute testimony to the temper of the times . . . and further notice that the authors of these books were not crackpots or blind Utopians, but acknowledged authorities, men of substance and learning. Of a Fall we can find no mention; it is difficult enough to find mention of the mere possibility of decline.

But while explicit mention of the beginning of the end is absent, one can easily see that the number of works begins to slacken around 1483. The hopes echoed in writings published after that date are almost identical to previous works, but they are fiercer, more emphatic, more desperate in tone. This decline continues until there were simply no more books printed at all; exactly when this occurred it is impossible to tell because of the varying and usually inaccurate calendars employed in later days.

At first, one might suspect some monstrous plot designed to remove all pessimistic literature from the hands of the people, but we have enough evidence to surmise that almost no restrictions of this nature were ever imposed. It would seem that people had been so happy, so incredibly content that when things took a change for the worse, they could only ignore it. One can almost envision those last wretched authors fighting battles with their own minds that might have rivaled the chaos that was raging beneath their very windows. Their incessant denial of the obvious in favor of the broken memories of the past led, in many cases, to out and out insanity.

And then, one supposes, people just stopped writing and turned their attentions to darker things.

The age that followed this collapse, the one which we are in now, has been given many names, none of them really miserable enough: the Darkness, the Pit, the Black Years, Badtime, and so on. For the year 1483 was merely the beginning, when the first vital parts began to fail. Separating this date and the present, there lie an indeterminate number of years during which things not only failed but changed and sometimes even grew.

In man, the change consisted, I think, of a loss; of what I cannot say, but the results of it are the ghastly societies of our times.

In the World, the change was more visible, or it would be to a citizen of the First World, had he the misfortune to be alive now. Our World has been twisted, warped, and torn so utterly out of shape that it bears virtually no physical resemblance to the First World. The people and some of their stories linger on, but that is all. Just how this monstrous dislocation was accomplished is probably beyond human ken, but its fact is undeniable; the maps and statistics in First World volumes could not all be complete fabrication, yet none of them bears the slightest resemblance to any portion of the World today. . . .

Five pages here seem to be missing or censored out.

How can I sum up an uncalculated age of confusion and darkness in a few pages? I cannot. My mind reels and stumbles as each passing minute reminds me of yet another tragedy, another catastrophe that my readings have prodded from my imagination with their mindless optimism, and which my direct experience has more than confirmed the possibility of. I am sickened and humiliated that the fate of my race and my World should come to such a dreadful and apparently permanent juncture.

Fragment of a manuscript found during the opening of the Black Library at Calnarith.

I

Sir Henry Limpkin's head servant had brought him word of the proposed meeting at a little past midnight; he had been sitting in his study sometimes drowsing, but he had been fully awake when the man entered and thus did not fly into his customary rage. An Office of Reconstruction officer treasures his sleep as some do pearls, but tonight it was not to be had.

When he was told that General Toriman's batman had brought a summons to his residence, he had slipped out of his smoking jacket and into a warm sports coat even before the servant had returned with his greatcoat and boots.

A hansom cab was called, and Limpkin left as soon as it arrived at his doorstep, leaving word that Lady Limpkin was not to be disturbed and that she should not worry if he did not return by morning.

Normally it is about a twenty minute drive to General Toriman's castle on the slopes of Mount Royal, but the icy slush slowed the cab's horse considerably. In the half hour that it took to reach his destination, Limpkin had a chance to think, his concentration broken only by an occasional curse from the freezing driver above and the hard thump of the iron shod wheels hitting a pothole.

After some ten minutes of driving they came to the city walls, were identified, and passed through, leaving the North Gate behind. They took the seldom-used River Road that curves off to the northwest just past the northern extremity of the walls; after a bit of fast trotting, Limpkin could spot the lights of Caltroon against the hulking immensity of Mount Royal.

Limpkin dismissed the cab at the castle's main gate (being careful to generously tip the frozen driver) and rang for admittance. "Your business, sir?" called a voice from the high battlements. Limpkin looked up but all he could discern were three flagpoles: to the right, Toriman's personal flag with the family coat of arms; to the left, the regimental banner of the 42nd Imperial Hussars, Toriman's unit before he retired, with a tangle of battle streamers flying above it; and in the center, the black and silver of the Caroline Republic. "Sir Henry Limpkin to see General Toriman, as requested," he shouted at the bodiless voice.

A small door opened on Limpkin's left; a man appeared with a lantern and a polite, "Follow me, if you please, sir?"

Limpkin was led across the icy courtyard, through Caltroon's second wall, past the now lifeless formal gardens, and finally into the Great Keep.

Caltroon's history could be traced back almost seven hundred years to the time when it had been but a small, fortified outpost of a forgotten empire. Since then at least thirty nations and a hundred great men had added walls, fortifications, towers, and, five hundred years after Caltroon's birth, the Great Keep.

It was a place of great antiquity, where the inherited relics of a thousand defeated nations lay, where crossbowmen of Toriman's personal guard patrolled over stone-filled shafts, housing the rusting shells of ballistic missiles six centuries old. The Toriman coat of arms, brought from distant Mourne with its mailed fist and winged horse, hung beside those of the greatest men that ever strode the World in those pathetic days. Everywhere one looked, his eye would alight upon the beautiful or the awesome, never anything else. For it was an identifying characteristic of the masters of Caltroon that they should prize beauty, because their lives were so often devoid of it, and power, because without that they would soon have no life at all.

Limpkin thought of all this as he was led through the labyrinthine rooms and halls. The bloodied lance of the present and the pitted rifle of past ages hung between a piece of exquisite crystal sculpture from Bannon der-Main and an illuminated manuscript from the Black Library at Calnarith. But the dust was gathering on the beautiful and the powerful alike. The castle and its master were, by slow degrees, dying. *As am I*, thought Limpkin wearily, *as is the Caroline Republic, as is the World.* The lot of them would never actually fall, but the dust would simply keep on piling up until they were all buried.

Limpkin absently recalled that once, when he had had lunch with Toriman and several other officers and civilians from the War Office, he had remarked to the General that mankind seemed to have lost something a very long time ago. As to what it was or as to when it had disappeared, Limpkin could give no clue. And Toriman had turned to him and said that he often got the same feeling; perhaps the missing essence could be found? Perhaps. Toriman was credited with stranger feats, and Limpkin had received unofficial word that the General had been wandering around the western wastes for the past four and a half months; perhaps this meeting . . .

Limpkin quickly abandoned this line of thought as the servant opened a door and stood to one side. "The General is waiting for you in his study, sir," he murmured, and vanished into the shadows behind Limpkin.

General Toriman's study was a colossal room more reminiscent of the nave of a cathedral rather than the cozy, walnut paneled dens that one usually associates with gentlemen's studies. Its wall consisted of hardwood bookcases running the length of the room. Row upon row of finely bound volumes, richly inlaid map trays, and celestial globes of all sizes filled the walls and dotted the floors on either hand. The far wall was dominated by a huge walk-in fireplace; its fire, along with four wrought iron chandeliers, lighted the vast room with a warm, pulsating glow. Replicas of the three flags that Limpkin had seen flying from the walls stood by the fireplace, their brocaded insignia glowing in the rust-yellow light. And once again, the Toriman coat of arms, this time made of burnished steel and brass, hung directly above the mantle. The rest of the wall was paneled with a deeply stained mahogany.

As Limpkin walked into the cavernous room, he became aware of the floor: black and white checkered marble. Even a room as large as this one could have been made more pleasant by the vast quantity of books and artifacts at hand; the warm fire, the soft light and darkness, the smell of fine leathers, paper, and rare wood were all canceled out by that cold floor. Leaf through one of the volumes and a soft rustling would be heard; listen to the fire: a pleasant crackling. But walk upon the floor, with the regimental insignia of the Army graven into the black squares, and you put a frigid screen over the soft beauty of the place. Limpkin crossed the floor quickly, his steel-tipped traveling boots clanking harshly on the polished marble.

Toriman's desk was set directly in front of the fireplace; it was almost as impressive as the room itself. It was at least seventeen feet long, made of a single slab of rosewood; it was supported by four thin, almost delicate legs which, along with the border that hung down about five inches from the rosewood sheet, were richly carved and inlaid with mother-of-pearl. Complicated but not profuse gilt moldings ran around the desk.

Turned toward the fire was a rather large, high-backed chair; it too was done in rosewood with gilt embellishments. It was upholstered in black and gold brocade. General Toriman sat there, leafing through an ancient folio with the General's crest on the covers.

Toriman was old now, almost sixty-eight, and his face showed the reflected horror and misery of a lifetime spent on the battlefield. His hair, iron gray, was combed back severely and was remarkably thick for a man of his age. His face, with its interlacing network of lines and old scars, was a marvel of shadows; his deeply set eyes sat in two dark caves, betraying their presence only by an occasional glint as they caught the firelight. His sharp nose, solid jaw and almost lipless mouth completed the cold portrait.

As he rose to greet Limpkin, one could see that his marvelous physique of latter days had deteriorated only slightly; the General still carried his bulk with the brutal grace of an Imperial Hussar. Limpkin felt as if he had moved under a thunder cloud.

The two men were not the best of friends. Toriman had no real friends, but for the past ten years they had known each other fairly well. Toriman was the first to speak, apologizing for his dragging Limpkin out on such a beastly night, but he thought that he had come upon something which he and his Office should know about as soon as possible. He motioned toward another high-backed chair, this one not quite so large, which Limpkin pulled close by the fire. A servant brought in some wine, and the General produced a small walnut thermidor from amid the clutter of maps and documents on the desk.

When both men had settled down with their goblets and cigars, Toriman spoke. "Limpkin, I hope that you will forgive the faulty memory of an old man, but am I correct in saying that your job involves something to do with the development of the nation? I think you told me at a party once, but as I said . . . " Toriman touched a finger to his forehead; firelight glinted off a gold ring.

"Yes. 'Getting the country back on its feet' is the usual phrase. Although I am, at times, really quite confounded as to how I am to recreate a world that I know nothing about and one which might"—Limpkin's voice dropped slightly—"exist only in legend." He brightened a bit. "But, it's an easy job; most hopeless ones are. I can sit in my fine office on George Street and fire off no end of orders and plans. And the results? My dear Toriman, you can see as well as I that the Caroline Republic and the rest of the World is nothing more than a sometimes-freezing, sometimes-burning hell hole. It appears that it has, for all intents and purposes, always been so and will continue to be so, or worse, until some benevolent deity chooses to bring it to an end."

"You paint a discouragingly black picture."

"The model is black"—Limpkin paused—"a fact which the exploits of the 42nd Imperial Hussars and other elements of other armies have not helped."

Instead of being insulted Toriman only seemed to relax a little. "Correct, more or less; I offer no apologies and no excuses. Those days are dead now." Toriman drew thoughtfully on his cigar and stared into the fire. "But we can hardly allow the unalterable past to sully the plotting of a brighter future, can we?"

"Hardly. Please continue," breathed Limpkin, more relieved than anything else.

"Do you remember, once, several years ago, I had had lunch with you and several other officials? And do you remember that you had taken me aside and remarked that the trouble with the World lay not in its barren fields, but within the spirits of the men who inhabit them?"

"Yes, of course. As a matter of fact, I had been thinking of that very instance on the walk here."

"Good, fine. I have a report"—Toriman lifted a fat folder from the desk—"whose contents I will not bore you with." He dropped it with a slight smile. "In substance, though, it says almost exactly what you had suspected: something has been lost. Call it the ego, the will to power, or whatever you mean; we both know what I am talking about."

"Then I was right?" Limpkin asked a little incredulously.

"Oh, quite right. Now, don't go complimenting yourself," Toriman said, smiling, the firelight glittering off his shadow-cloaked eyes. "Many men have suspected it before. The trouble is that few could prove it and fewer still would admit it to themselves. I must confess that even I had some trouble in getting used to the idea that most of the people alive today are virtually emotional eunuchs.

"But that is true, as I said, of only most. I hope that I am not being overly vain in considering myself in the minority. And I hope that my estimation of you, Limpkin, is equally correct. But back to the report. . . ." Toriman picked up the folder once again and began leafing through it.

"This essence, which neither of us can precisely name, was probably lost long before any modern records were penned. But the legends, as far as I can tell, contain a great deal of truth. I have traveled much in the service of my country"—Limpkin thought he could detect a trace of disgust, but he chose to disregard it—"into many strange—the rabble would call them enchanted—lands and I have seen many of the relics that our fathers left behind. They are older than you or I can ever possibly imagine; their character strikes the people dumb with awe—which, of course, defines our whole problem right there. The Grayfields with its fleets of spectral aircraft, overgrown with fireweeds and vines, but as real as my hand. The Fortress at the mouth of the Tyne River—beside it even my ancient and mighty Caltroon appears to be a wooden lash-up built only yesterday."

Limpkin was amazed and somewhat frightened to find the myths of his provincial childhood suddenly acquiring awesome substance; but he also found an odd comfort in it. "Please go on."

Toriman looked into his eyes for an instant and nodded. "Go on? How far shall I go on? For every legend there are ten actual wonders. The hulks of great ships, aircraft, and machines litter the edges of the World, and not even the legends attempt to understand them."

"Just by way of curiosity, why have we not heard more of these things?"

Toriman shrugged. "Who can say? The World is an incredibly vast place, far outpacing the estimates of even the wisest geographers. It is easy for even works of the Tyne Fortress' magnitude to become lost in it.

"Our World, Limpkin, the civilized one, is but a small island. The ravages of a hundred thousand pogroms, wars, inquisitions, and 'rectifications of history' have further helped to erase any sure knowledge of the past. The might and power and skills have almost all been purged from the earth."

Limpkin nodded and then simply asked, "How did it happen?"

"What happen?"

"The end of the First Days."

"Oh? Not even the Black Libraries can tell us that, but I can make a guess as to how long ago it happened: three thousand years."

"Small wonder that traces of the old World are so hard to find. It must have been an incredible cataclysm."

"Perhaps. Some volumes in the Black Library at Calnarith hypothesize an Apocalypse of some sort, but these accounts are always submerged in so much religious rot—Second Comings and the like—as to be almost useless. But whether our loss in man occurred just before any Armageddon or, more likely, as the result of one, is irrelevant. The thing was lost and then all the horrible decline followed. Perhaps men just went to bed one night, and when they awoke they found that the night had stolen something from them.

"In some places the fall was rapid and absolute, as it is in the far west and south. In other places, here for instance, the fall was slow and agonizing. Hell, Limpkin, if I see aright, we are still sliding and won't stop until our lands are as sterile as the Black Barrens, our cities occupied by dry rot and worms, and our descendants the pets of lizards."

"And now it is you, my dear General, who is painting the black picture. Obviously, you have brought me here to present a scheme for relieving the blackness. What do you suggest?"

Toriman blew a smoke ring and lightly said, "Rebuild."

Limpkin had expected something a trifle more original. He let out a little laugh. "General, I realize that that is the way out but certain rather formidable obstacles stand in one's way."

"Overcome them." The General seemed to have sunk into a pocket of conceit arising from his very evident ignorance of the real state of the nation; Limpkin wondered, for the smallest of moments, if the man was going senile. Limpkin patiently pointed out, "My Office has been working on that problem for the past century and we have come no closer . . . "

"That is because you were not working with the right tools nor with the right technique," Toriman said amiably.

Limpkin was beginning to get upset. "Perhaps being always on the business of war, dashing across the country from one campaign to another, you have not been able to examine the land and the common people as closely as I have.

"I admit that, by comparison, the Caroline is in pretty fair shape; but what we are comparing it to . . . dammit, Toriman, stop grinning at me!"

"Sorry, Limpkin." But he kept his grin.

"The land is destitute; the collections of hovels that we call towns and cities are virtually ruled by juvenile gangs and vice lords; industry, such as it is, has maintained a steady 2.8–2.6% annual decline." He shot a frigid glance at Toriman. "And foreign wars ravage our fields, destroy our finest men, and bleed the state treasury white."

"Why?"

"What?"

"I asked, why haven't these faults, which I have already outlined (so you see I am not a total dunce), been corrected by your Office."

Limpkin was getting progressively more irritated. "We have tried. Didn't I tell you that? The cellars of the Office are glutted with copies of orders and directives to the Government, our own regional offices, to the people themselves; some of these orders are more than eighty years old! We've sent out every kind of order, used every kind of appeal, threat, or tactic that we could think of, but the letters go out and that is the last we ever hear of them. Send a man out and he comes back empty-handed or beaten to a pulp, depending upon the temperament of the people.

"Ah, the people! The bloody-damn, sacred people! Tell them that their very lives depend upon a dam or upon the repair of a city's walls and it's like talking down an empty well. It's almost as if the men were less than men, as if"—Limpkin lifted an eyebrow—"they had lost something." Toriman smiled briefly, his face a harlequin mask of shifting light. "All right then, once again we have come upon this fact. Now what?"

"First of all, my agitated friend, perhaps we should qualify ourselves by saying that this essence has not really been lost, but rather has been, ah, anesthetized by three millennia of simple hell. Acceptable?"

"It seems to be your conversation."

"All right, we don't have to go traipsing off into the Barrens or some other objectionable place looking for enchanted vials with this thing in them. All we have to do is awaken it in the citizenry."

"Ah, there you are. Just what my Office and its counterparts have been trying for years to find. With all due respect, General, you have told me nothing that I did not already suspect, and if you can offer nothing more original and concrete than these philosophical or psychological meanderings, then we can both count the night a failure."

Toriman took a puff on his cigar and then suddenly crushed it in an ebony ash tray on the desk. "Yes, quite right. We have had enough of cigar and brandy talk. Enjoyable, but time consuming." The General's voice shifted emphasis subtly. He heaved himself out of the chair and vanished into the shadows past the fireplace. He was back in a second, towing a wheeled frame with a map strung between its uprights. He pushed the chart in front of the fire so that the translucent vellum took on a three-dimensional aspect when view from the front.

Limpkin studied the map. To his right in the east was the Sea and the coastline of the World. He could recognize the Maritime Republics, New Svald, and the Dresau Islands off the Talbight Estuary. Above and below this, the seacoast was pockmarked by minor nations with progressively unfamiliar names (some of which, such as Truden and Dorn, he had previously thought of as existing only in children's tales).

He caught a reference point, the free city of Enador to the south of the Talbight Estuary, and followed the Donnigol Trace westward until it reached the southern extremity of the Caroline. Around his homeland were her neighbors and their sister nations; very comforting, but the eye could not help but notice that they comprised only a very small portion of the map.

Ignoring the smile of satisfaction that Toriman was wearing, Limpkin got up and unabashedly gawked at the illuminated chart. The fire behind it made it look as if the World were floating on a sea of molten glass. The cartography was flawless; mountains appeared to be in relief and the rivers seemed to flow with turquoise water. Many of the countries had their national standards painted under their names: the golden eagle of the House of Raud, the winged horse and mailed fist of Toriman's own Mourne, the four stars of Svald and the seven of New Svald, and the indecipherable rune-standard of the tribes which laid claim to the heraldry from Heaven and Earth and less savory realms and deposited them on this fantastic map.

Toriman eased back into his chair and began talking. Limpkin at once saw that his was to be a virtual lecture and the guise of dialogue would be discarded. Toriman began. "Limpkin, before you lies the concentrated knowledge of too many years spent in places that I and the other people who helped to make this map had no business being in. Rather like a partial outline of . . . "

"Hell," Limpkin meekly offered. Torman accepted it without notice and moved on.

" . . . of hell, although I must own that Purgatory seems like a better term; more varied, you know.

"The map itself represents an unknown percentage of the World. Beyond its precincts lie, one would suppose, more lands and seas and oceans, but of them we have not even legends. But for all intents and purposes, this map will be more than adequate." Toriman got up from his chair again and stood before the glimmering charts; he lit another cigar and used it like a pointer. "Now, here we are. Around us, of course, are ringed our neighboring states. Direct your attention, if you please, to our northernmost province, number 18, which goes by the name of Tarbormin, I believe. Up there, in those desolate high-lands, lies a lake, unnamed, from which springs a river, also unnamed. It flows down, out onto this plain"—tracing the course of an incredibly thin streak of blue with the glowing cigar—"where it crosses into our illustrious and thoroughly detestable sister state of Yuma.

"It continues across Yuma, having acquired a name, the Tyne, and quite a bit more water, past the Armories, and finally down into the Imperial Vale where it is lost to common knowledge.

"Once into the Vale, the Tyne becomes quite a large river. In one spot, Bloody Ford, it's almost a mile across. That name is mine, I'm afraid." Toriman's voice shifted slightly, away from the tone of absolute command. "The 42nd had been pursuing bandits and we were quite taken up in the chase until the half-men and their wild dogs set upon us." Toriman gazed off into the pulsating dark-ness for a moment and then returned his eyes to the map. "Forgive me, Limpkin, I will try to stick to essentials; but there are so many memories here, all either bitter or awesome ones, never beautiful, except for one." Again his eyes wandered, this time to the northern reaches of the World where the coastline dissolves into a shattered patchwork of fjords and inlets. The tight skin went slack about his face and his eye-pits fell to the cold marble floor. "Again, Limpkin, your pardon. This is almost turn-ing into an expedition into a life I would rather forget."

"A woman?" Limpkin questioned, hardly knowing he had said it.

"Yes," replied Toriman in a distracted manner. Limp-kin was mildly astounded that Toriman was capable of even approaching such a thing as affection.

"And now?"

"Dead, for this was in my youth, so very, very long ago; dead by my own hand, I suppose, but that was in the days when we still used the Plague as a tactical weapon." He. shook his head like a man rising from a heavy sleep. "The Tyne," he continued abruptly, the scarred skin again drawn tautly against the skull, the eyes flashing in their dark sockets; so sudden was the change that Limpkin instantly dropped the thought of questioning the General on a point: that the Caroline Army had never used the Plague as a weapon because of its unpredictability. "The Tyne exits the Imperial Vale here, after about six hundred miles, and curves southward until it finally reaches down to here." Toriman outlined an area near the bottom of the map. "It enters the Black Barrens where, through some ancient wizardry, or more likely radiation poisoning, the land is as sterile as an operating theater. Finally the Tyne flows into the sea, whose probing arm you can just see here along the bottom of the map; here we find our elusive goal.

"On the western side of the delta stands the Tyne Fortress, which I told you about earlier, and on the other bank, the eastern one, lie the Yards."

"Yards . . . ?" Once again Limpkin was totally in the dark.

Toriman looked slightly exasperated. "No legends? Curious, the people of western Yuma certainly have enough about it." Toriman resumed his seat and picked several sheets of paper from a folder. "Briefly, the Yards are an enigmatic, to say the least, expanse of concrete situated on the banks of the Tyne delta. I have no absolutely sure information on who might have built them, for what purpose, or anything along those lines; but I can guess that the Fortress and a rather curious structure several miles upriver called Gun Hill were constructed for its defense." The General looked at the papers on the desk for a moment. "Just as an aside of no significance, all the main armament of the Fortress and what is left of Gun Hill's battery are pointed west; but all of these affairs are of great antiquity so I shouldn't think that any menace they were supposed to combat is still alive.

"The Yards themselves are approximately four miles wide, five where they reach down to the Sea, and about nine miles long. Along the middle of this field, and running about ninety percent of its length, is a huge elevated ramp or slipway of truly titanic dimensions; this ramp runs into the Sea and drops off into an excavated trench leading to deep water. All about the Yards lie mile upon mile of rail track with what appear to be carriages for cranes still on them and in operating condition.

"There are huge storage caverns emplaced under the surface of the concrete, which are filled with more machinery and equipment; also, there are vast rooms apparently devoted to the design of—but more of that later.

"I spent quite some time in and around the Yards—I was almost killed when I strayed into one of the Fortress' minefields. One can still trace out what must have been a complex of roads leading away from the Yards and through what I think may be the remains of a town that surrounded them. Of these ruins, there is little except for a spectacular tower located in the middle of the Delta. Its name was Westwatch; once it might have been tied to the Yards and the Fortress by several large bridges, but this is almost pure speculation.

"So here we have four structures. The tower is but a hollow shell now, but its thousand foot height might have been used to watch for whatever the Fortress was supposed to fight. But it would be best to leave the Fortress alone, for I suspect that despite its fantastic age the equipment inside of it is still quite alive and eminently capable of accomplishing its purpose: killing. Then there is Gun Hill. Who can fathom it? Huge, incomprehensible machines which remind my military mind of nothing so much as the mounts for siege cannon." Toriman paused for a sip of wine.

"I am astounded," mumbled Limpkin in a dazed voice. "They must have been incredible men."

"If they were men at all. No, now don't look so surprised." Toriman's expression changed from one of complete command to one of perplexed doubt; the eyebrows arched and the lips were tightly pursed. The voice, usually so beautifully sure and commanding or reaching downward for some lost, gentle sorrow, was now halting and confused. "I know very little of those that built the Yards and the Fortress and I can only express a personal opinion of them: they were not"—the General stopped uneasily and searched for the words—"not of my kind of flesh and blood. They were *different*, Limpkin, and fanatically dedicated to ideals totally at odds with those I hold eternally sacred; I can only feel this, smell it in the wind that blows from Gun Hill or the Fortress, but I feel it as strongly as I feel the strength of Caltroon's walls. There is an essence inhabiting those ruins which I cannot help but feel would, if given physical substance, try to kill me. Lord, just talking about it brings a fear to my heart; can you feel it too, Limpkin?"

Limpkin said yes, he did, but in a guarded tone, for while he knew that anything Toriman could fear should have thrown him into a panic, all he could feel was a great deal of puzzlement at the General's reaction and an irrepressible sense of worshipful pride in hearing of the great buildings. It was almost as if he had been descended from the race that Toriman now said he hated. Limpkin thought it best to try to return the conversation to its original course. "But what has this to do with us? The builders are dead, they must be, for such great power in the hands of the living could hardly have escaped the World's notice."

Toriman brightened at this. "Quite right, Limpkin; just a personal opinion, but one which I think you will share more closely when you see the Yards for yourself. But even if you do not feel it as strongly as I when you look upon the land, you will feel a deep fear for the countries that surround it and us. And if not fear, then hate; the World is up to here with it. The World is your hell, my purgatory; it is a . . . "

" . . . prison," Limpkin again filled in unexpectedly; Toriman's mask-face broke into something really approaching a wide grin.

"Precisely. And when a man is unjustly condemned to a prison, what is his first desire?"

"Why, to escape, naturally."

"Again right. But in our case the prison, the World, is so escapeproof that the sheer weight of despair has weighed us down and killed hope itself. This is why that sleeping bit of motivation has never awakened. Even if it did, it would probably die of starvation. Despair, Limpkin, is the key. What we need is the antithesis of despair: hope."

"Obviously, but isn't this just . . . "

The General held up his hand. "From the brief sketch I have given you, what do the Yards sound like they were built for?"

Limpkin thought for a moment. "A shipyard?" he asked in a cracked voice.

Toriman's fear of a moment ago was now completely banished by this new factor. "Yes, quite, exactly. A shipyard, the obvious conclusion. And I will further confess to you that any ships that might have issued from the Yards did not sail upon any sea."

"Meaning?"

"The night sky . . . "

"A starship!" Limpkin almost screamed with rage that Toriman should climax his tale with such an absurdity. "Toriman, is this your great antithesis of fear? This?"

Again Toriman halted him with a gesture of the hand and a turning of the head. "I am dead serious. No proof, none at all, but this conclusion is inescapable."

"But no nation, not even the whole World, could have actually built . . . " Limpkin rolled his eyes at the mere thought of the size of such a ship.

"Why not? Someone built the Fortress and the Yards; remember, they were not crippled by the dead air of the World. Now, what I propose is that the Caroline build a duplicate; I have found quite a few fragmentary plans left, and the Yards' cellars are filled with parts. Make it the escape route, the way out of this vile prison."

"Escape to where, if I might ask?"

"That," said Toriman with a wave of his hand, "is a minor detail."

"I'm afraid, General, that I have been led into too many pits of ignorance by your convoluted manner of speaking. The idea of a starship lifting us all to a, hopefully, better world is certainly intriguing, if impossible."

"But the ship's primary purpose will not be one of simple transportation, but that of a Cause, the thing about which all the dormant hopes of our nation can crystallize.

"And here is the trick: the ship will betray the people for their own good. Here, look at this." Toriman unfolded one of the sheets he had removed from the folder. Standing up, he laid the report aside and spread the paper out on the desk. Limpkin also rose and saw on it a beautifully executed "artist's conception" of what must be Toriman's ship.

It was an overpowering thing; incredibly long and thin, it looked exactly as one might suppose a starship to look like. Its sharp, pointed nose hovered far above the flat expanse of the Yards; the body curved back, dolphin-like, to a pointed tail atop which grew a single vertical fin of unimagined height. The delta wings started about one-quarter of the way down the hull, slanting to a sharper angle as they grew, and finally ending in a straight dropoff at right angles to the ship.

"Beautiful, Toriman, just magnificent. The engineer who conceived of it had the soul of an artist," said Limpkin, half joking.

"This total plan was designed, as were most of the things for which we have no plans, by a psychologist. As a mere carrier of human freight, it would be a practical failure, but it is a lot more likely to capture the imagination of an illiterate peasant than a dun colored sphere."

"How large will, ah, would she be?"

Toriman turned to Limpkin. "She'll be about seven miles long, a third of a mile in diameter, and have a maximum wingspread of three and a half miles. The tail will rise about five-eighths of a mile above the hull." Toriman sipped some wine; Limpkin collapsed into his chair, trying to decide whether to laugh or pity Toriman. "Has it captured your imagination, Limpkin?" questioned Toriman solicitously.

Limpkin could only grimace. "Are you serious about this thing? Really? Even if those of the First or some other World could build it, this World hasn't a chance."

"I agree it is beyond us now, and perhaps it shall remain so forever, but this is a minor consideration. The real point here is that the original builders left enough material to start. We've even a set of engines, or what seems to be a set, sitting below the Yards." The General lit another cigar; Limpkin saw that the gold ring on his left hand had, predictably, the horse and hand crest on its face. "Here, then, is my plan. First, we must establish a route to the Yards; once Yuma is removed through a minor war, the Tyne River will serve us splendidly. Once the way to the Yards is open, the building of the ship may commence. I estimate that a proper schedule should allow for about two hundred and fifty years." Limpkin coughed lightly. "But of course the ship will never be completed.

"You see, Limpkin, the main, indeed the only purpose of the ship will be to become a rallying point about which the will to power may awaken and be nourished. And, here comes the tricky part.

"All the plans that I have shown you for the ship are completely theoretical. Even those that I found in the Yards have translated from their rune-language into our own on a very unsure basis. For all we know the ship might collapse of its own weight, or might blow up on takeoff, or—the possibilities are endless and this is why we must never allow the ship to be finished. The effort that will flow from the resurrected spirit of the people and directed at the ship to make it their escape hatch must be covertly rechanneled back into the body of the nation proper.

"Allow me to elaborate. You, man, today go out to one of our outlying villages and issue an order: build a dam here. Why? the people ask you. For your own better-ment, you answer, and for the growth and strength of mother Caroline. Yes sir, right away, sir, they answer. They will attack the stream immediately with gratifying fervor, until one of them notices the land about him. He and his father and his ancestors for a thousand years before him have worked that sterile soil, died of the plagues left in it from a hundred dark ages. Why build the dam? What good will it do? Nothing can touch this land, nothing can change the cast of the hell that he has been born into. And for mother Caroline? Was it mother Doria so many years ago? or mother Aberdeen? or . . . " Toriman shrugged. "The man is impermanent, the states transient, the efforts at improvement swallowed by the everlasting agony of the World; only the World exists and will continue to exist and to bend to it one's will appears to be beyond the power of God Himself.

"But a year later you return to the settlement; the spring floods have washed away the pathetic efforts of last year. You issue the same order. But this time when they ask you why, you will have a different answer: 'You, my beloved people, will build a dam for the ship. You will build it so that eight power lines may run into a far-off place called the Yards where this mighty mechanism is abuilding. A starship, a way out. I do not ask you to try to tame this hostile land, I only ask you to honestly work upon it so that we may someday leave it behind.' Then you will produce illustrated diagrams of the ship. Imagine their expressions, Limpkin, when you start to describe the dimensions of the ship in miles instead of mere feet. And then they will look about them, at the same land and a new thought will arise: escape from this World where before the only escape had been death.

"Your men must be skilled, Limpkin. They must speak like prophets and engrave this silver fantasy upon those torpid, withered brains. And if your Office is skillful, every time a peasant looks at the land his eyes will rise to the sky, and at night they will stand out under the stars for hours, dreaming of their new destiny; they will not make it, you must tell them that, nor will their sons, but someday their seed and their spirits will be freed from the shackles of this dismal prison.

" 'Where will my son's son go?' they will ask. It hardly matters what you answer. Use your ingenuity, but make sure the story is always the same. Legend has it that men, before the end of the First World, journeyed to the stars; pick a star, dream up a planet green and golden in the light of its young sun. Tell them that there are homes and factories and roads there, left behind and carefully preserved when the dying First World called its children home in a last effort to save itself. Paragon, Harbor, Home, name it whatever your Office chooses, but make it a paradise, and one as filled with man-made wonders as those of nature, for my psychologists tell me that if the people are told that their new world is ready for instant, comfortable occupation with a minimum of struggle, it will be all that more desirable. A world fit for the habitation of men, and nothing less.

"So the people will set to work with the monstrous shadow of the ship, graceful as a cormorant and powerful as an awakened god, casting the hideous Earth into servile darkness. But here is where the ship will begin her betrayal. The dam will be, if my and many others' estimation of human nature is correct, completed and the eight power lines will stretch to the southeast. Here is where your Office will move in. Only two lines will eventually reach the ship; the other six will be diverted into an area that truly needs them. Their places will be taken by empty dummy cables. And if anyone ever asks about any of this, simply tell them that it is 'for the ship.'

"As more and more of these efforts are diverted back into the nation, the land will become more bearable and more profitable. At first there will be a steadily ascending curve of work, then a zenith will be reached when the people finally begin to realize that the previously unyielding land has changed. As the land grows richer and richer, interest in the ship will taper off, for now the people's will to power will have awakened and fed upon a sufficient quantity of simple hope to allow it to live and grow.

"So you see that the ship's ultimate aim is to become a half-finished hulk. Her reality will be in her building, not in any never-to-be-taken trip into space.

"Who knows"—Toriman drew deeply on his cigar; firelight glinted off his golden ring—"perhaps someday, when the World has grown a great deal more like the First World, the ship will be completed. But then it will rise from the World in the spirit of adventure and not as a beaten fugitive."

For at least a minute neither man spoke. The General had outlined the battle plan and now his chosen lieutenant tried to digest its essentials. Another minute passed; Toriman's gaze drifted to the map and stopped over the tangled northern coastline. At last Limpkin spoke. "Seven miles long; seven miles long and three wide . . ."

Toriman chuckled with satisfaction. "Exactly, my good civil servant, seven *miles* long. Think of it! Seven *miles* by three *miles!* Think of it blotting out half the sky while thirty thousand feet up; see it rumbling down its ways to meet the Sea, for no runway possible could ever support its weight. And think, Limpkin, as will the people, of a day that will never come, when they will file into the cabins and leave the world behind them. Then the thunder, the Sea thrown into confusion, its surface boiling from the engines' breath. Slowly, very slowly at first, she will start to move; then faster with a tidal wave wake trailing aft. Then up into the air, the shock wave of compressed air traveling before her like a terrible herald, flattening mountains." Again the stillness.

Limpkin finally roused himself. "I find your scheme entirely impractical."

"We are in an impractical position."

"My mind refuses to accept the sheer size of the thing. But then my imagination takes over, with a vengeance in this case. Could we not just use the pretense of building the ship?"

"I admit that it would be more inexpensive, but no, I'm afraid that the ship must be built. Perhaps a man of your stature, one who has read some of the First World and now knows that the stories of its might are true, can be excited merely by the idea of the ship. But here we are trying to inspire the slow-minded, dull, witless people, and several generations of them at that. They must be able to go to the Yards and come back to their godforsaken villages and tell of the glory and power of the ship. The Yards are many leagues from here and you can be sure that with every step the pilgrim travels back toward his home, the ship will grow just that much more magnificent. The ship, the ship, the ship, this must be their only thought until the land begins to bend, as it must, to their will."

"The ship could easily become a god," intoned Limpkin as the thought grew in him.

"Only if she grows too fast. Only if she absorbs the imagination instead of merely capturing it. That is the job of your Office."

Limpkin now turned to the painting of the ship. "And her name?" he inquired, not raising his eyes.

"*Victory.*"

"*Victory, Victory . . .* " Limpkin repeated. "And I suppose that your psychologists dreamed that up too."

"Of course. That and much more." Toriman walked over to one of the thin map drawers that, twenty deep, ran along each wall; he flipped out the end of a blueprint and a sheet of mathematical notations, normal numbers and symbols ranged beside an apparently corresponding row of rune-figures. "The ship," said Toriman, gesturing at the rest of the library, "and the knowledge to build and sail her."

Limpkin sensed that the audience was over. He put on his coat and waited for a sign from Toriman. "I hope that I have not kept you too long, Limpkin. Here, I'll walk you to the gate." Toriman produced a fur-collared jacket with the silver piping of a field officer.

When they had reached the main courtyard, between the two walls, Limpkin could see that dawn was growing beyond the distant city. One of the general's carriages, complete with footmen and heavy chasseur escort, was waiting.

As Limpkin boarded the coach, he turned again to the east to see the clouds of a young snow storm already shrouding the sun. "A dark dawn," he observed with as much dignity as he could summon up at that early hour.

"Perhaps others will be brighter," Toriman rejoined. "Many others besides myself have had a hand in this plan, Limpkin. Many more able and knowing than either you or I shall ever be; we are not alone in this, and we never shall be."

A footman shut the door and the convoy rumbled out of Caltroon and down to the River Road.

About a mile from the castle, while adjusting his blanket and warming pan, Limpkin came upon a present from the General. It was a small model of the *Victory*, wrought from solid silver, and beautiful detailed. Limpkin held it up to the feeble light of dawn until they reached the city walls; *seven miles!*

II

For a week after that the work piled up on Limpkin's desk as the miniature *Victory* flew on a thousand imaginary voyages to a million different worlds. And at the end of each trip, when the great starship had been moored in a turquoise bay, a party was sent ashore only to find that the new world was the one they had left so many years ago, but changed into something fine and beautiful.

On the eighth day a messenger was sent from the Office of Reconstruction to notify Toriman that an appointment had been made for him and Limpkin with the King and Council.

But the messenger returned saying that the General had contracted a slight virus and his physician had insisted he stay in bed. In his place the General had sent twenty-eight carriages with the contents of his library on the ship in them. He also sent the keys to the Black Libraries at Dartmoor and Iriam; they had not been opened for a thousand years, for their contents had been adjudged by successive Churches to be too heretical and dangerous to be absorbed by the human mind.

Despite Toriman's absence, the audience with George XXVIII and his Council was successful, although Limpkin felt that he had not conveyed the grand scope of the design as well as he might have. In place of the General's commanding language he had used graphs and maps and charts. And when he left he noticed that several Councilors, as they waited for their carriages, glanced up at the night sky and quietly moved their lips.

III

Suddenly the Office of Reconstruction assumed a different character. The staff was reduced by about half, for after several millennia the words "security risk" had reentered the common tongue.

The Office itself was a pleasant pile of granite left over from when the Dorian flag had flown over Caltroon. But now an iron spike fence grew up on its lawn, separating it from George Street and the surrounding buildings. Guards armed amazingly enough with actual rifles and, perhaps even more amazing, in clean uniforms, stood at the new gate and patrolled the grounds.

A carriage shuttle with the War Office was established, for the upcoming war with Yuma would require a great deal of coordination between the two ministries.

Most of all Limpkin noticed that his staff, which had been told of the ship and its actual purpose, was actually exhibiting a near enthusiasm for their work; he almost yelled with surprise when he saw a clerk running down a corridor to catch a War Office coach.

But these were fairly intelligent people, members of a more or less elite and their activity could be the result only of the novelty of the whole scheme. Limpkin hoped that this estimation was wrong, and as time went on he thought he saw evidence that he was.

Every week a fat dispatch pouch arrived by mounted messenger from Caltroon with instructions in Toriman's handwriting; although it made Limpkin feel at times like a marionette, he followed them religiously. The first step was the manufacture of a war with Yuma.

IV

Later historians called it part of the "era of the Ship," but when the war started, only the innermost circles of the Government and some of the military knew of its eventual aim. It was begun in the south and centered around a small village by the name of Canbau, which sat at the intersection of three of the major trade routes in that area. The town's major industries were legal and illegal highway robbery, bars offering something politely labeled the Black Death, and bordellos. The Caroline garrison there synthesized the needed incident when it "found" a cargo of illegal armaments secreted away in a Yuma caravan.

The Caroline Republic demanded an apology for sending arms to revolutionaries operating in her mountains. The Yuma Foreign Office had the stupidity to note that this was the first mention of any sort of insurrection in the Caroline. Publicizing this as a deliberate evasion and an intolerable display of arrogance by Yuma, a force of Caroline cavalry was sent to plunder all Yuma caravans on the three roads. Yuma, still not seeing the point of the affair, protested first with several notes and then with the destruction of a Caroline irrigation dam which a hasty survey determined to be within Yuma's borders.

The Caroline's sense of justice and right being offended, an attack was launched from Canbau. One could almost hear the chuckling coming from the War

Office, the Office of Reconstruction, and Caltroon. Caroline mounted forces supported, it was rumored, by horse-drawn artillery of a very ancient vintage (and consequently, of a very high state of efficiency), swept westward. They reached the eastern border, wheeled, and drove northeast, diagonally across the country.

It was not a very bloody conflict, for in those days of fluid alliances, loyalty often depended upon which way the chips happened to be falling at the moment. One by one the towns of Yuma surrendered until, four months and one day after the first incident, the black and silver of the Caroline was run up the State House flagpole at Bannon der-Main, Yuma's capital. The only real battle developed in the north, a week after the formal truce. A group of die-hard patriots, crying God and Constitution, barricaded themselves in the Armories. There, emplaced in cliffs overlooking the Tyne, they managed to hold the entire Caroline expeditionary force at bay for a month.

Since the Caroline liked to preserve the image of a perfect war fought in a perfect way to a perfect victory, contemporary accounts of the battle at the Armories are generally sketchy. But there are songs about that place: the confidential war diaries of the units involved provide enough material for the construction of legends. The Tyne was supposed to have flowed red for a week and the peasants living in the surrounding regions now tell of a hideous battle between men and demigods.

There is now a small lake, fed by the Tyne, where the frontal galleries of the Armories used to be, and one has only to overturn a stone or clod of soil to find some blackened instrument of war.

The 42nd Imperial Hussars garnered another battle pennant. Toriman sent a wagon load of wine to the survivors and a shipment of fine coffins to the dead.

V

Another month passed. Limpkin had just returned from a victory parade and was going over arrangements for the opening of the Black Libraries. A man in Toriman's personal livery arrived and handed him a note. The General had died last night. In pursuance of his will, the body was immediately given the last rites and cremated.

Limpkin was shocked, first by the fact of the great man's death, and then by the almost fumbling haste with which the burial had been carried out. Had anyone been at the General's side when he expired? The man answered that there had been only his personal physician, a priest, and the commander of the household guard. It was they who interred the body and gave the sealed coffin over to be incinerated. Caltroon's guard had been disbanded that morning and many of them had already left for their old homes. The castle itself was closed and sealed.

Limpkin's first impulse was, of course, to go to Caltroon to try to divine some purpose in the shameful speed with which the General had been disposed of. He voiced his intentions to the messenger.

"Little point in that, sir." The man answered politely.

"Why? Has Caltroon been picked so clean that there is nothing of Toriman's left?"

"Yes, sir. It was all in the General's will; he said that we were to remove anything that was his and either destroy it or send it back to his family's house in Mourne." The man paused, looking embarrassed. "And now, if you'll excuse me, sir, I must be going, for my family's house is even more distant than the General's."

Limpkin dismissed him. He felt a sudden weight of responsibility crushing down upon him.

VI

Despite the General's sudden withdrawal as the guiding force behind the ship, Limpkin found his notes, the contents of the Libraries, and the new spirit of his colleagues most helpful. After the eventual success of the Yuma war, and the sending of a secret expedition to the Yards, Limpkin found that the next logical step would be to begin leaking word of the Myth of the Ship, as it has since been called, to the people. In this cause, Lady Limpkin held a ball at which certain "highly secret" bits of information were imparted to certain carefully selected gossips.

Within the week the story had penetrated the upper echelons of Caroline society. Within another week enough had filtered down to the lower classes to set the markets and bars abuzz with speculation. The ship became a bomber (curse her!); a missile to rid the supposedly fertile west of the Dark Powers; not a starship at all, but a boat to sail to the lost continent of Balbec; a pointless project that showed that George XXVIII had finally gone completely off his nut.

Limpkin followed his instructions and allowed the people to whip themselves into a frenzy of wild guessing. Matters were helped along, as per one of Toriman's directives, when Limpkin sent wagons through the streets, their towering loads tantalizingly draped with thin canvas. Then, as a final touch, Limpkin had a motor truck exhumed from Caltroon's vaults, set up with the help of some Black Library volumes, and run through the city in the dead of night. Of course the implied secrecy of the operation was belied by the fact that the vehicle's muffler had been removed and it took a most tortuous route from the Office of Reconstruction to the walls. On the flatbed trailer that the truck pulled sat an immense transformer, dating from the First World; its insides were rusted out, but a fresh coat of paint made the colossal mechanism appear quite impressive. This weird machine, coupled with the fact that there had not been a single self-propelled vehicle operating in those lands for two hundred years, sent the populace into a spasm of wonderment. Limpkin also sent the truck, this time with a chasseur escort, rumbling down many of the Caroline's main highways at appropriately odd hours.

Messengers were sent dashing about the nation bearing dispatch cases filled with blank paper. From centuries of torpor, even in war time, the Caroline responded to this synthetic atmosphere of crisis; only a very small elite knew of the hoax, but for the other 98% of the nation, the ship, the Second Coming, the new day, the world called Home were all at hand.

In the early spring, heralds came into every town of the Caroline and into the new Protectorate of Yuma. They carried notices of an assembly to be held in the capital three weeks hence, for George XXVIII had a message of paramount importance to convey to his people.

VII

Never before in the history of the World, or so the Caroline's publicists said, had such a multitude been gathered together in any one place for any purpose save war. Thousands upon thousands crowded into the city and camped out on the surrounding slopes. From every village in the land and from many of the Caroline's sister nations they came to hear what some said would be a hoax but what most believed would signal the beginning of the Third World.

Limpkin stood in his office on George Street, looking out upon the vast crowd; the mob started five or six blocks north, in Palace Park, and backed up past the Office of Reconstruction, finally thinning out by the War Office. The throng filled the five other streets that radiated in a semicircle away from Palace Park to a similar degree.

Townsmen and merchants on top of their carriages, cavalry officers, bright in their red and gold uniforms, rough teamsters in what passed for formal dress in that level of society, illiterate shepherds from the Randau Basin and befurred mountain folk from the north, sweating in their heavy cloaks. Prostitutes wiggling through the masses, doing a land office business; drunken brawls causing swirls of color in the ocean of heads and shoulders; the raucous yell of hawkers selling bad water and cut gin. A pity Toriman was not there to see it all.

Limpkin turned from the window and sat down at his desk; he picked up the model of the *Victory*. He did not go to the Park to hear His Majesty, for he already knew what he would say; Toriman had written the speech.

George would tell the Myth of the Ship with an eloquence that the General's psychologist had figured would not tax the meaner minds present, yet would lift the knowledgeable.

The wild cheering told him that George had appeared; the ghostly silence told him that the ship had been born.

VIII

The acceptance of the *Victory* project was successful beyond Limpkin's wildest expectations. The papers, even the non-official ones, caught on to the idea with a passion; the *Victory*, the *Victory* was all that one could hear in the streets.

A small silver star was added to the flag of the Caroline: *Home*.

IX

A few days after the announcement, Limpkin picked up Directive #975 from his desk and read the instructions of the dead General. "The physical position of the Yards presents something of a problem: the people could easily become estranged from the ship by the great distances involved, not only in miles but in tradition and feeling also. Interest could wane and fail.

"It is clear that an emotional, halfway station must be established until the ship itself acquires enough physical majesty to obviate its need. Somewhere in the wilderness between here and the Yards the flag of the Caroline must be raised in great and glorious conflict, for only an act of violence can be accomplished out there—such is the nature of the land. Our banner must be liberally smeared with the blood of heroes and enemies, the greater the heroes and the lower the villains the better. The more violent, the more vicious the fight, the greater the size of the monuments that will be raised. The more families cruelly broken, the longer will the bitter memories remain.

"So it appears that our only problem is finding a suitable location with suitable opponents. Allow me to suggest the Imperial Vale; it offers really detestable inhabitants who can be counted upon for a good fight, a beautifully hostile landscape and historical setting in which the heroics may find an appropriate backdrop; at any rate, the Tyne runs right through it and it must be cleaned out eventually, so why not now?"

There followed a short list calling for a moderately strong force of galleys to be sent, ostensibly to the Yards to begin preliminary work there; this expedition, in contrast to earlier ones, was to be made fully public.

At the end of the directive there was an assurance from the General to Limpkin that he and his men would make sure that a battle of the proper character would take place; Limpkin put it down, awed at the General's incredible foresight and praying that this admiration would not be ruined by the outcome of this adventure.

X

Philip Rome was as close to a civil engineer as any nation could have been expected to produce in those days.

In his youth he had dreamed of building a new and greater World, full of shining machines and great cities. But when he set out upon his career, he found that one may design the most wondrous and perfect machine imaginable, but that to build it properly was impossible. People just did not care if a gun exploded after five shots or after five thousand; the most inspired plan for a bridge was useless when it was hardly looked at during the building. The World abounded, more or less, in pure knowledge, but to effectively apply this knowledge in even the simplest manner was just beyond human capabilities.

So Rome's work decayed until he reached a state of slipshod quality in keeping with the rest of the World; a battle-ax design, but not too improved, had been his crowning achievement for the past five years.

But some of his early doodlings had come to the attention of the Office of Reconstruction; the man had some imagination, thus the Myth of the Ship would doubtlessly be enough to lure him into any sort of venture. Also, the man had lost virtually every shred of talent that he once had and was therefore expendable. Finally, he had a monstrous family that would recall his gallant sacrifice, should he be lost.

"Your Nation and the *Victory* have need of your abilities, Mr. Rome . . ." read the form letter.

Thus it happened that Rome found himself on a river boat convoy heading down the Tyne to the Yards. There were thirty galleys ranging in length from forty to a hundred and fifty feet long; they were following the buoys laid out by an advanced party that had preceded them by two days.

They had left the gaping hole in the Yuma mountains where the front of the Armories had been several days ago, had crossed through the Battle Plain west of Yuma and were now penetrating into the Imperial Vale. This canyon, hundreds of miles in length, was hot, sterile and dark. The vertical cliffs that rose almost a thousand feet from the floor of the canyon gave one a maddening feeling of imprisonment or even burial. If the World was a prison, then the Imperial Vale must surely have been its dungeons.

The stifling, fetid atmosphere, the large mud flats and numerous caves offered refuge for some of the most noxious life forms then existent. Mud snakes fifteen feet long and seven inches in diameter made water sports a decided rarity, and monitor lizards kept short expeditions to a minimum. Then there were the half-men. Despite the numerous ways of warping body and mind out of its proper shape that a thousand years of war-oriented science had produced, and despite the liberality with which these weapons were used, mutants were fairly rare in the World. If their own body did not hide some mechanism of self-destruction, then one could be fairly sure that the local populace would either kill or exile them, usually to the Imperial Vale. Of course, this applied only to those with aberrations of the body, all too often the mind mutants escaped the attentions of the municipal vigilance committees, contributing to the downfall of quite a few states. (Witness the nation of Arnheim, which in its final days based its political appointment system on the applicant's ability to murder the current office holder. The entire state went up in smoke when sixty percent of the population decided to run for the presidency.)

As the decades died, the sophisticated efficiency of gene-radiation bombs and mind gases gave way to the simplicity of the club and sword; a bit more messy, but you only killed individuals instead of the future. So the body mutants were driven off, mostly to the Imperial Vale, and the mind mutants pretty well took care of themselves.

At one time, now mercifully forgotten, the Vale teemed with those grotesque refugees, their frightful powers governed after a fashion by the few mind mutants that had also escaped there. There, it was whispered, you could find neo-humans worshiping everything from their own excrement to the mummified bodies of normal men. Some could fly, others could swim, many could do nothing but crawl. And out of the all of this, the most horrible thought was that every single one of those abominations had descended from people like yourself; the fact that humankind was capable of producing things like them drove many into a madness of their own.

Then the Vale was a more hospitable place; a jungle-like mat of vegetation hid the vile bodies from prying eyes on the cliffs above.

Eventually, though, the festering sore of the Vale grew too hideous and dangerous to ignore and, in a rare instance of cooperation, a coalition of nations under Miolnor IV of Mourne undertook to cleanse it. Two hundred years ago that shining horde, mounted on everything from killer-tanks from the First World to the great draft horses of Svald, marched into the valley. With lance, bow, cannon and flamethrower to cauterize the Vale, a hundred thousand men roared into the canyon and were met by a million of the damned. Only a company of two thousand emerged at the other end.

So the Vale had been cleaned, although not quite as thoroughly as Miolnor would have liked. In the following two centuries the few creatures that had escaped the battle crept back into the light of day. But now the Vale was a harsh and hellish place of scorched dirt and starving herbage, bearing little resemblance to the green hothouse it had once been. Fortunately, the survivors lacked the power to ever break out of it into friendlier lands, and in the Vale they remained, secluded, hostile, and still dangerous.

Rome thought of all these things as he sat staring at the barren river banks. The ruins of the great battle could still be seen here and there: a rusting helmet, a burnt-out tank, the rib cage of its long dead gunner still struggling to escape the turret. Here a dark movement of mud suggested something a bit more deadly than the normal shiftings of the earth; dark things flickered among the shadows of the bordering cliffs. Sun glinted off the wind-polished remains of a great battle machine or, perhaps, off a primitive heliograph.

The convoy was about a league upstream from Bloody Ford; Rome tried to stay out of the way of the river men as they prepared the craft for a possible engagement. A muzzle-loading cannon of dubious workmanship was mounted on a wooden pose at the bow and loaded with cannister. A brand-new machine gun, handled with a reverence that was completely at odds with its slapdash construction, was set upon its tripod atop the fighting castle. While the fearsome aspect of these rare contrivances inspired some confidence in his heart, Rome was too well acquainted with contemporary standards of design and execution to be really at ease. He felt a little better when several of the crew went below and emerged with Pythian crossbows and metal-tipped arrows.

Gradually the Tyne widened until it was almost a mile across and little more than three feet deep. The line of yellow buoys placed by the preceding expedition ended abruptly just as they were approaching the Ford. The River-master, sitting in the fighting castle, scanned the area with a crude telescope. Rome was on the second boat in line and he heard an indistinct cry from the lead ship. The Master swung his glass around, stared for a moment and then called to the Captain, "Wreckage to the south, sir."

The men stiffened at their stations; hide bow strings were tested, the seating of shot in the cannon adjusted, and the machine gun was briefly checked by the Master. Rome stopped a man running aft to ask him exactly what was the matter. Instead of answering, he handed Rome a second-rate shirt of mail, a leather helmet, and a sword that must have journeyed into the Vale with Miolnor—and had not been polished since. Rome immediately protested about the quality of his weapon. "Gives the bastards blood pisinin', sah," rumbled the man as he continued aft.

They were now getting close to the Ford itself and Rome could easily make out the gutted hulks of two small river galleys some distance beyond it.

The Ford was essentially a ridge of crushed rock stretching the width of the river. Some say that it is all that remains of a gigantic dam that once provided the entire region for a thousand miles around with power; the Berota Wall was to have been its name, and it might have been built by the same race that had built the Yards.

Rome put on his rusty mail and helmet. He turned up to the Rivermaster, who was adjusting the sight on his gun; it broke off in his hand. "What do they have?" asked Rome, becoming aware that his voice had taken on the texture of broken glass.

"They?" said the Master.

"The half-men."

The Master shrugged and tried to refit the sight. "The usual lot: clubs, spears, bows . . . that sort." The man eyed the surrounding cliffs uneasily; a bird-like object was riding the thermals just to the west of the convoy. "And themselves, of course, sir. They've fangs and teeth and bleeding venom pouches. Think of any weapon had by any animal in the World and you can be fairly sure that one of them'll have it."

"Anything else?" Rome's voice had grown even rougher.

The Master leaned over the top of the fighting castle and whispered conspiratorially, "There's the bleeding mind muties, sir, the ones that directs the others. My Dad said that they have the Dark Powers on their side."

"The Powers? Sorcery? Surely you can't expect me . . ."

"I don't expect you to do a thing, sir. You asked me a question and I answered it straight as I could. Maybe in other times they would call some of their acts science or something like that, but now . . . My great, great grandsire was a drummer boy and one of the two thousand that made it out of this hellhole with Miolnor, and by my hand, sir, the tales that he left to the family were unholy, that's the only word you could use—unholy."

Rome was about to question the man about the possible insanity of his ancestors but was cut short by a sharp rattling from the lead boat.

They were almost directly over the Ford now, the rocky bottom sometimes visible when the mud swirled the right way. Rome jumped from the cabin top and crouched low on the starboard deck; he had never heard a machine gun before. The lead boat, which had two automatic weapons, the extra one being mounted on its bow in place of a cannon, was blazing away at something above them. Rome looked up and saw that the flier he had noticed earlier had moved closer and had been joined by several companions.

Shielding his eyes from the afternoon sun, the engineer tried to see what manner of bird it was. The most readily apparent feature was its sheer size: its body was about five feet long but the membranous wings must have stretched almost twenty-five feet across. The sun shone through them, outlining the thin bone structure and lending a ghastly yellow tinge to their surface. There were no feathers or any other sort of covering on the wings so Rome surmised that it must be some form of bat, grown to monstrous proportions with the help of a gene-radiation bomb; with a shock he noticed that the head was that of a human, twisted, drawn out into an almost reptilian cast, with horribly prominent fangs. The parody was furthered by the dull corselet of mail that the creature was wearing; the sun glinted on a double-edged battle-ax clutched in a spindly claw at the joint of the right wing.

Even as Rome watched, terrified and sickened, the thing descended with an ear-splitting scream. Above him the Rivermaster opened up with the machine gun. Other boats joined in and soon the sky was richly embroidered with thermite tracers. The animal evaded the shells for a moment and then a fine network of holes was stitched along one wing; the chain mail buckled and flew into a thousand glittering fragments. The torn body fell into the river not five feet from Rome's boat, its blood mingling with the scum of the river.

"Shrieks, bloody flaming Shrieks," hissed a man at Rome's side. "They fight a battle like a damned ritual. All the time a goddamned ritual: first a sacrifice and then they fight." The man turned away and viciously braced his crossbow against his shoulder.

A shout arose from the afterdeck and all hands looked skyward. Where once not more than five Shrieks had been hovering, there were now well over three hundred. Down they fell, tucking their parchment wings close in.

The Ford began to fill with yelling and the smell of gunpowder. The cannon was touched off, ripping the bodies of two fliers away from their wings. Burning, lidless eyes came driving down from out of the sun. Steel striking out from a yellow cloud descended over Rome, and the man who had damned the Shrieks fell to the deck, his liberated head rolling overboard. Rome struck out, his eyes screwed shut, and drew back his sword dripping with scarlet blood; little bits of yellow skin and mail clung to its pitted surface.

Rome looked hurriedly about him; the boat in front of them had been set afire and was drifting ashore. Halfway back the flagship, engulfed in a swarm of pale bodies, was sending up a continuous stream of signal rockets. The line was breaking up and many ships, not knowing the way through the Ford, were drifting aground.

The bow cannon fired again, shoreward this time, where a force of rafts drawn by half-men was putting out. They were men, that was horribly apparent, but their bodies were torn and brutalized into shapes more nightmarish than the Shrieks. Claws, talon and fang; armored torso and faceted eye; hands arranged along three planes instead of merely one. The water glistened on their weapons and grotesque bodies, the two often indistinguishable.

The boats were now bunching up in a pack, apparently with the idea that their best defense would lie in a concentration of firepower.

On the rafts, Rome could make out small groups of men that actually looked like men. Cloaked and hooded, they were like mourners at a warlock's funeral. One of the figures raised a gnarled staff and pointed it at a straggling ship about two hundred yards off; a ball of blue light bulleted from the staff and struck the ship in the bow. A yell from above Rome: "Did I not tell you, sir? Did I not?" The rest of the Master's speech was cut off as he swung his weapon around and started peppering the waters around the raft. Another flash and the already burning craft exploded. There were four other rafts, each with its own small band of mind mutants, and soon the Ford was a cauldron of fire. Swords flashed and sliced through the heavy air to the accompaniment of machine gun and cannon shot.

More half-men waded in from the shore. Wild curses in a score of different languages and dialects damned the enemies' souls to a thousand different hells. Dark flags and banners of nations whose only heritage was one of hate were unfurled by reptilian hands to rise over the black and silver of the Caroline. Ancestors and gods were called upon; bullets tipped with maldreque from distant Telth roared off into the smoky haze to topple the fire-wizards. Hell was raging in the Vale and its sulfurous fumes rose to hide it from the sight of Heaven.

Rome had lapsed into a state of near insanity; a quiet man whose last battle was in a school's play yard, he alternately hewed arms and necks and then fell, retching into puddles of blood and shredded organs.

Gradually the gunfire ceased; quietly when the actions jammed or with a crash when they misfired. The Rivermaster above Rome had been pointing and training his gun for a full minute before he realized that its mechanism had disintegrated. The Master hit the gun in his fury, hit it again, and then wrenched it from its mount. He grasped the glowing barrel in his hands and leaped down to the deck, the war cry of a mountain clan of Enom rising from his foaming mouth. Swinging the broken gun over his head, the Master jumped into the boiling water. A dragon-man fell to the Tyne's bottom, his helm driven into his brain. The man moved further into the struggle, shattered armor and torn flesh flying from him; black feathered arrows sank through his quilted shirt and buried themselves in a body that refused to acknowledge their presence. A flaming sphere streamed in from one of the rafts and turned the man into a burning wraith; he collapsed into the filthy water, the gun barrel steaming.

Rome fell again, utterly exhausted. He lay immobile while the battle surged about him; blood and water flowed around his mouth and he began choking. He lurched to his feet, trying to clear his throat, the insane fury of a moment ago replaced by a void; he could feel nothing but weariness. Then a voice bellowed in his ear, "Dropped your blade, lad." His sword was thrust back into his hand and he turned to see the aged giant who had done it. The fellow was enormous, dressed in a short corselet of golden mail and leather breeches studded with silver. His tan hobnailed boots were tipped with vicious shards of steel; his meat-hook hands were wrapped in gray leather gauntlets banded with polished metal; he held a colossal broadsword in his right hand, its shining blade and hilt inscribed with many strange words and devices; a crest with a winged horse and armored fist was engraved on the guard and surrounded with brilliants.

"You all right, lad?" The man asked, his voice curiously distinct over the din. Rome looked into his deep-set eyes and scarred face and could do nothing but nod, yes.

Rome tottered down the deck a few paces and then heard a groan rise from the half-men. He saw the old man moving like a scythe-wielder through the half-men, their dismembered parts literally sailing off through the air. The giant turned into a dervish, a whirling Death, his sword everywhere; and through it all he said not a word, uttered not a cry of fury. The Shrieks seemed to simply fall apart while the blade was still thirty feet below them. The man started to move toward the rafts, casually murdering the half-men that stood in his way.

The cloaked figures stirred nervously and pointed their staffs at him. Fires ten times more brilliant than those directed at the ships screamed at the man. Rome gaped in astonishment as the spheres hit the giant and then burst like soap bubbles. An unusually bright and large flame-sphere flew at the man, its yellow-white core burning with a fire so hot it appeared, in its center, to be black. The man halted and then raised his sword before him. He caught the ball as it burst around him, the fire attaching itself to his weapon. He regarded it for a second and then hurled the burning shaft at the largest raft.

The cloaked mutants saw the missile coming and gestured frantically to the half-men pulling them. The sword hit the barge squarely in the middle, and a flash of light erupted, it seemed, from the river bottom. Temporarily blinded, Rome buried his eyes in his hands; titanic explosions assaulted his ears and five successive shock waves battered his tired body.

Fragments of wood and torn robes floated down, burning, from the smoke filled sky. The whole battle was frozen with amazement and awe; then the man turned, his broadsword suddenly returned to his hand. "For the Ship, my lad! Kill the bloody bastards! For the Caroline and the *Victory!*" And he rushed back through the steaming water to the renewed battle.

Rome grasped the hilt of his sword and felt power flowing through him. Then he felt as if he had fallen into a kind of grim ecstasy; he knew exactly what was to be done and he saw that the other men had the same look in their eyes as did the sword-hurler. He found a stooped half-man scuttling along the deck; he brought his boot down heavily upon its neck and plunged his blade deep into the cancerous hide. Rome sensed a maniacal grin distorting his face.

Then he enjoyed killing the half-men; he liked shoving his sword deep into their corrupted bodies; the soft squishing crunch as a mace pushed a lizard head into an insect body became an almost musical sound. Cut, slash, rip, tear their bodies to pieces, mates! See the flow of the rich blood, how beautiful its color, how rich its feel and lovely its taste. Death to the bastards, mates, death to them all so that the Ship may live.

Rome kept on swinging his ragged sword until a man tapped him on the shoulder. "You can stop now, sir." Completely drained, Rome fell heavily to the beslimed deck. He tried to retch again, but all that came up was a little green bile.

The gray haired man was nowhere to be seen. Who had he been, then? Rome was later told that the Caroline, in its infinite wisdom, had seen fit to send men versed in certain rare arts along with the expedition. The man had been the ghost of Miolnor IV, raised from the dead to once again defeat the Vale's ghastly hordes. True enough, thought Rome, for in this land all the preconceptions one had about what should, or should not be, must be discarded. Miolnor IV! And indeed it must have been he, for had not Rome seen with his own eyes the ancient crest of the great house of Mourne on the spirit's sword hilt?

*   *   *

The Government made a great play of the expedition. Although the initial mission of reaching the Yards had been a failure, they had defeated a great and ominous force that would have threatened future travelers. No official mention was made of Miolnor; the immortal grapevine took care of that. The man in golden mail was soon interpreted not as being a lowly ghost, but a truly divine power—the Caroline had God on her side.

All mutant strength, as later expeditions were to discover, had been wiped out along with the dark beings who had stood upon the rafts. The Vale was still a hell, but at least it was one devoid of devils.

A huge pylon of polished steel and iron was erected on the south shore of bloody Ford, amid the battle wreckage. At the bottom of the tower were inscribed over five hundred names of those who had fallen; admittedly, some of the names were changed to provide a glorious death for the bounder sons of some of the better families, or a cover story for certain political undesirables who had vanished from their homes late at night, but on the whole, those who fulfilled Toriman's scheme were given full honors.

XI

Edmund Moresly and his men had left Caltroon as soon as the General had issued their orders. Toriman had given them a cargo of long, thin packing cases and a strange black banner, inscribed with the ancient crest of Mourne's leaders and with many of the indecipherable runes that the natives of the Imperial Vale used for script. Moresly had only a vague idea of what the flag stood for, but this belief was strengthened by the effect it had on the Vale's inhabitants: one moment they were screaming like the hounds of hell and the next all fawning attention and mumbled courtesies.

They had been conveyed to a large cave from which the mind mutants exercised their dominion over the Vale. He could not understand a word of their insane babbling, but that was hardly necessary. The flag was presented to the rulers, amid intense whisperings, and then a scroll, engraved in a similar manner. Moresly correctly guessed that the scroll contained information to the effect that mankind was plotting an expedition against the Vale; Moresly also made other correct guesses about his superior's plans as things logically fitted into place.

Next, still following the explicit instructions, Moresly's men brought up the thirty cases from the boat and removed their contents. They looked like staves, but from the expressions on the faces of the mutant rulers, Moresly supposed them to be weapons of some sort.

Moresly's admiration for Toriman reached something of a zenith as he perceived the grand sweep of history that he had become part of.

Upon his return to the Caroline, he found that the General had died, leaving him another, more complex set of orders and a transfer to the Office of Reconstruction.

He was ushered into Limpkin's office and asked to sit down. "Moresly," Limpkin began, "you realize, of course, that you are here through the late General's recommendations. He held you in high esteem." Moresly bowed his head slightly and said nothing. "You have heard of the ship?"

"Yes, sir. I've heard what your Office wanted the people to hear, and the General told me the rest."

"Then you are fully aware of the details of this, ah, plot."

"Fully. And the particular detail which at the moment concerns myself is the leadership of the agency that is to redirect the *Victory*'s enthusiasm and efforts back into the main body of the Caroline. Since what this office is supposed to do would be viewed by the public as sabotage, at the moment at least, it will be a covert operation; the Office of Procurement—the General thought we should call it that, nice, pedestrian, not very illuminating. Am I correct, sir?" Moresly asked a trifle solicitously.

Taken aback by the man's knowledge of highly secret information, Limpkin slowly answered, "Yes, quite correct. You seem to know more about the project than I do."

"I do, sir; that's why I'm here." Limpkin felt a flash of irritation at the man's confidence, but then he remembered that, as Moresly had just said, *was* why he was here.

"Then you should not mind if I voice one or two objections I have of my own." Moresly nodded assent, and Limpkin went on. "I frankly do not like this idea of creating a whole new caste of people who know of the real mission of the ship, to direct the actions of the rest of the people. These men and women, the saboteurs as you put it, under your office, and the technicians under my ultimate command who will supervise the ship's construction, constitute a virtual priesthood. And all these almost childish devices which you and Toriman have provided to set the elite apart from the rabble: badges, black suits, segregated living conditions, separate schools, and that sort of nonsense. Is it all really necessary? I always pictured the ship as inspiring one huge unified effort by the nation, with only the very highest echelons knowing what was really going on. It almost seems that the General was attempting to set up some sort of tension or conflict whose eventual purpose I cannot fathom but which could, I think, someday explode into class warfare."

Moresly shifted around in his chair and for the first time looked a little distressed. "Yes, well, these fears are perfectly logical. I might say that they occurred to me at one time or another. But I think that the General was correct in setting up this ruling class. First off, notice that when you envision this unified effort to build the ship, you are presupposing a society of total equals. We have an extremely stratified society in the Caroline as it is now. In effect all we are doing is consolidating the social, intellectual, and economic classes into two great emotional classes. The tension is unavoidable, the General said to me once, for thousands must know what it is about, how to falsify reports and test readings so that the machinery that could never really function will at least give the appearance of success.

"I honestly believe that at the worst we will end up with an enlightened, albeit temporarily embattled, oligarchy.

"Also, we must have paragons to which the people can look to be suitably inspired," Limpkin did not look very satisfied. "Of course," Moresly went on, "I can't expect you to accept so rough an explanation; the General's communications and directives . . . "

"They comment only upon the actual mechanics of establishing the classes."

"Well, I fear then, we must trust in the wisdom of the General. He was an extraordinary man, sir, and, if nothing else, he will be remembered for what has happened in the past months: the feeling of purpose and mission—the unity! Why, even in the great legends there is no record of such a feeling, so totally galvanizing the World. The atmosphere surrounding the tales of Miolnor's first march into the Imperial Vale and the vague accounts of the wars against the Dark Powers a thousand years ago are the only things that compare with it."

Limpkin sighed as he remembered Toriman; indeed, he was an extraordinary, a great man, and perhaps it was the way things were if such as he saw fault or purposelessness in the General's ideas. "But I have a more concrete and immediate point I should like explained. The General had picked the Armories as the site for the Office of Procurement. Now why should Toriman picked a half demolished system of old caves so near to the nation that its purpose might be easily discovered."

Moresly interrupted. "But the blast at the Armories occurred after the General's death; he could know nothing of it."

"Then why not just move to a more convenient place?"

"But, sir, surely you realize that it was the General's *expressed wish* that my office be located . . . "

"I am perfectly aware of the General's expressed wishes, but I cannot see why we should endanger this project in the slightest detail. I should think that, say, Gun Hill or the Grayfields, wherever they might be, would be much better suited to your purposes: they're secluded, protected by superstition, and closer to your work."

Moresly suddenly rose from his chair and made as to leave. His tone was that of ice. "Sir Henry, if this is to be my Office, run by myself in the manner that the General prescribed, then I must demand that this issue be settled according to the original plans. In my view the best possible location for the Office of Procurement is still the Armories and if you feel so strongly about it you can hire someone else whose methods are less exacting than mine."

Limpkin stared at the man, not knowing what to do. Then it seemed to him that they were quibbling over a trivial point; Moresly was obviously a good, competent man, as was everything connected with the late General's plans and operations. To lose him over a detail would be stupid, Limpkin told himself, but beneath it lay a fear that the lightest interference with Toriman's divinely inspired scheme might botch everything, as Moresly said. "Hardly any need to do that, Moresly," he said in as conciliatory a tone as his professional dignity would permit. "If the Armories mean that much to you and if you honestly think that the efficiency of your new Office will suffer if it is not there, then the Armories are yours."

Moresly continued to look like outraged Justice. "My thanks, Sir Henry. I'm sure the General would approve of your decision."

Limpkin rose, trying to look as miffed as his new subordinate, but not bringing it off as well. He handed Moresly a letter of authority from George XXVIII authorizing the establishment of his Office, its immunity from normal Governmental procedures, and a blanket requisition for anything that might be needed to put the Armories into proper condition. The two men shook hands and Moresly departed.

XII

The riverboat *Kestral* tied up at the wharf and Limpkin stepped off into the Yards.

They had passed Gun Hill yesterday and the civil servant had thought that its monumental dimensions would have insulated him against the impact of the Yards. The Hill was a vast mound a mile in diameter at the base, rising gradually to a height of just over two hundred feet. He had viewed it through a heavy telescope; it was now overgrown with vegetation, but the trees and grasses failed to conceal the two structures at the top. Placed a quarter of a mile apart, they nevertheless crowded the Hill with their incredible bulk. One of the crew had told him that they had, indeed, once mounted great siege guns and that they had been instrumental in the defeat of the Dark Powers.

Vast hydraulic cylinders, ten feet in diameter by Limpkin's reckoning, studded the machines; pipes and fittings of every conceivable shape and size ran along the bases of the mounts, climbed up their sides and ended, twisted, in empty air. Shell carriages, big as First World trucks, stood scattered all over the Hill, their chrome steel bodies rusting into dust.

The Hill had been the first of the great First World relics that Limpkin had ever seen. They had drifted past the Hill as the sun was falling behind the western mountains and it seemed as if the guns' fire were still scourging the evil darkness there. Limpkin had moved into a near dream and found himself listening for the thunder of the guns' report and watching for the yellow-white flash from their muzzles; all the tales of his rural youth flooded back to him. He was moving through a land which did not exist for most of the World; the Dark Powers, the Builders of the Yards, the whole lot of it belonged to another creation.

As they had passed from under the Hill's shadow, a grassy plain reaching all the way to the distant mountains unrolled itself on the western bank. Limpkin had felt a sadness descend upon him, and he noticed it in the wrinkled expressions and staring eyes of the *Kestral*'s crew.

When the Powers had finally been defeated a millennium ago and thrown back past the western peaks, a final stand had been taken by their most powerful elements. The Battle of the Westwatch was supposed to have finally ended the First World and marked the almost-triumph of the World. The plain that ran for fifty miles from the Tyne to the foothills of the mountains was now said to be a graveyard for the battle's First World victims; the dead lay shoulder to shoulder, head to foot, for virtually the entire expanse of the field. Limpkin tended to view any account of so huge a battle as being more myth than anything else, yet the stupendous fortifications of Gun Hill and the Fortress were quite real, as was the sorrow that he and his men then felt.

They had moored several miles upstream from the delta, for the river had not yet been safely charted for night travel. At dawn they had cast off again and had tied up at the Yards shortly afterward.

Immediately any sadness that Limpkin had carried with him from Gun Hill was swept away by the scope of the Yards, by the height of Westwatch and by the sinister immensity of the Fortress. He walked away from the ancient pier, his mind spinning, for before him, all the way to the ring of small mountains that surrounded the eastern bank of the delta—or so it seemed—lay stretched a field of concrete. Here and there the first small cranes that the first work crews had begun reconditioning stood like candles in the middle of an enormous birthday cake; they only served to accentuate the sense of vastness, of unbelievable space. Limpkin turned to the southeast and saw the ways that were to eventually cradle the *Victory*. Even though its slope into the Sea was most gradual, the near end was still almost fifty feet in the air before the colossal support ribs began.

A year ago Limpkin had sweated over the construction of a ten mile drainage ditch in the Randau Basin and now he had inherited from a vanished race an enterprise so vast that, as one of his reports had told him, the ways must arch slightly to compensate for the curvature of the Earth. Limpkin could not help laughing to himself.

As he walked, not having any idea of exactly where he was going, he noticed that the field was not as featureless as he had supposed. Sharply outlined platforms of rusted metal were set flush with the concrete at random intervals, varying in size from four foot squares to rectangles a hundred feet long and fifty wide; Limpkin supposed them to be freight elevators. Steel tracks were recessed into the surface and wandered, again without obvious purpose, across the official's path. Wondering at the excellent condition of the metal, Limpkin bent over to find the grooves, some of them a yard across, were filled with a clear plastic material.

Limpkin rose and headed toward the land end of the ways where a cluster of cranes indicated some activity; he had, of course, forgotten that the ways were more than a mile distant.

He had been walking for about five minutes when a two-horse surrey approached him. Limpkin shaded his eyes and as the coach drew near he saw that it was driven by Damon Trebbly, the engineer in charge.

One could hardly have found a person better suited to supervise the resurrection of a lost technology; Trebbly, despite his gaunt, perpetually stooped body and perpetually complaining mind, had been a good enough engineer to have been branded a warlock in four nations and a high sorcerer in two others. He had never attended any of the proper academies, had never read the current masters of science and had never been able to accept contemporary standards of craftsmanship, design, or ambition. He had been a child in one of the nomadic tribes that wander the northeastern rim of the Black Barrens; instead of learning to tend his father's griffins and hippogrifs, however, he had wormed his way into every First World ruin and Black Library he found and had memorized every legend that every blind wanderer had sung.

When he had adjudged himself to be adequately steeped in the witchcraft of the First World, he had presented himself to the government of New Svald, offering to tame the Shirka River. He was immediately convicted of insanity, demonic possession, and of being an agent for the Dark Powers. A similar reception was given him when he tried to interest the House of Raud in a plan to rebuild the great bridges of their mountain kingdom.

Eventually news of the *Victory* project attracted him to the Caroline Office of Reconstruction. Seeing at once that here was a man tailored for the job at hand, Limpkin enlisted him as the head of the technical elite which would rule in the Yards—and which would build the ship.

But in the short time that Limpkin had known the man—and the association had been a close one, for much had to be learned and exchanged in that brief space—he had not once seen him smile or show the slightest indication that life was anything more than tolerable. His religion was the technical greatness of the First World; he had grown up amid the memories of men and machines that had conquered creation (but not, as the hack phrase inevitably runs, themselves) and now he was forced to exist in a society which presupposed the failure of its every endeavor. The store of pent-up frustration that he had developed had bent his body and, Limpkin sometimes thought, his mind.

But now the bean-pole figure that sat in the surrey was actually grinning. Limpkin stared in pleasant disbelief and searched for the cracks in the man's skull that the smile must produce. The low, cynical voice had been replaced by a tone that quavered with expectation and hope.

Limpkin greeted the man and asked him how the work was progressing. Apparently making a monumental effort to suppress himself, Trebbly asked Limpkin to accompany him on a little trip.

They set out in a cutter through the maze of small islands that composed the delta and within half an hour of rowing they had reached the artificial island upon which the Westwatch was built. Trebbly mumbled something about "the big picture, sir," and then climbed from the cutter onto the island. The island was about five hundred feet in length and was situated a mile and a half from the Yards, three miles from the Sea, and two miles from the western shore. Six miles to the west sat the Fortress.

Limpkin followed the engineer. He gazed up at the fantastic height of the tower and was at once terrified and intrigued. From its diameter of less than two hundred feet the tower grew upward until its needle top ended over a thousand feet from the waters of the Tyne. It did not climb as an ordinary building might, but really did seem to grow like the trunk of a blasted, blackened tree. It appeared to be hewn out of a single piece of rough gray rock; indeed, except for its height, it was nearly identical to the lonely rock spires that Limpkin had seen as they had sailed past the Black Barrens.

Yet the building was undeniably of intelligent conception. Limpkin entered the small door to his left and saw that the inside was dimly lighted by torches. The two men crossed a vaulted chamber, perhaps thirty feet high and partially covered with crumbling mosaics, and passed into a small booth opposite. They got into a cage-like affair; as it swayed in the shaft, Limpkin noted with a shock that a single stout cord was all that supported the platform. Two of the boat's crew had gone over to a low stone cabinet that projected from the wall beside the shaft entrance and had inserted an iron crank. The cage rose jerkily into the darkness above. "Strongest single piece of hemp in the World west of the Armories," said Trebbly proudly. Limpkin didn't answer.

After several minutes of noisy climbing, the platform drew even with a small oval door. Trebbly stepped out and then helped Limpkin over the combing. Fighting down a wild desire to either cry or run back to the platform and its soft darkness, Limpkin stepped out onto the deck that ringed the top of the Westwatch; it was roughly circular, extending outward from the tower for about ten feet, and was bordered by an exceedingly flimsy looking railing. Above them the tower rose for another fifty feet. Bracing himself against the wind and summoning up his courage, Limpkin moved out to the railing where Trebbly was standing.

Below them were the Yards. Trebbly leaned closer and yelled into Limpkin's ear. "I wanted to bring you up here, sir, so you could get an idea of how really grand this whole complex is." Trebbly was grinning like a fool. Limpkin thought that the boy finally had a toy to suit his gigantic talents. "Look at it, sir! Did you ever see anything more bloody marvelous in your life? Nine miles! And see there, the ways, a hundred feet across and it looks like a ribbon from up here.

"Now, aside from the fact of the Yards existing at all, I've been poking around a bit and, if I may say so, our beloved and mysterious General Toriman didn't do much real investigation when he was here. It's utterly beyond belief, sir. Below the surface of the Yards are storerooms that go down for almost two miles! Goddamn, sir, we don't have to build the *Victory*; all we need to do is assemble her. I'd estimate that almost sixty percent of the structural fittings necessary to build the ship are already down there."

"But the age, Trebbly, metal fatigue and that sort of thing?"

"All sealed up in the plastic that covers the rails down at the Yards; a hundred, a thousand years wouldn't matter a bit.

"And not only parts, but machines to build what we don't have. Cranes, generators, tools, lifts, lorries, everything." An air of disgust invaded his voice. "And all of it good solid craftsmanship. Goddamn, at last actual engines and fuels that don't have to have a torch thrown into them before they'll burn. Sir, I tell you it's a bleeding wonderland down there."

"Then you would say that we have really stumbled onto something," said Limpkin with feigned gravity. Trebbly hardly noticed but went right on in a near fit of joy.

"And the land around here! I don't believe it. I don't see how anyone could believe it. Below the sands out there are the foundations for roads which, I'll wager, lead to some of the richest mines in the World. And foundations for a whole city! Why, some of my men even report that there are whole factories, rolling mills, and foundries under the Yards just waiting to be put together again and set to work. It's bloody unbelievable, sir, too bloody good to be true."

Limpkin swallowed the lump in his throat that had arisen when he had looked down, and grinned as broadly as possible. "Sounds as if we really could build a ship."

Trebbly looked a little embarrassed. "I know that isn't the point of it, sir, but"—he stared at the Yards, looking like a happy idiot—"but as a child, I had heard stories of a race known as the Builders, but none of them can match all this. Damn, but they were a conscientious lot! All that material, all those plans, all that power, neatly packed away and sealed up just so the imperial Caroline could build, your pardon, start to build a myth."

Limpkin was finally beginning to rid himself of his acrophobia and began to stroll around the deck. Trebbly followed behind him. On the other side of the platform, Limpkin looked out upon the gray western mountains and upon the grassy, featureless plain that lay between them and the Westwatch. Clouds were more numerous to the west and the silence and far-off darkness served to dampen his mood a bit. Even Trebbly let his face sag back into its normal cast; he moved to Limpkin's side and pointed down and to the south. "The Fortress, sir," and yet a third Trebbly presented itself to Limpkin: one of cold awe, tinged with something very close to, but not quite, fear.

"Will it hinder you in any way, Trebbly?"

"Not in any way that I know of. In fact, somehow I find myself glad it's there."

"How so?"

"Well, the Powers, you know . . ." Trebbly trailed off weakly.

"Really, man, that was supposed to be over a thousand years ago—if it existed at all."

"I know that, but the Fortress is still there. It's shaped like a hexagon, a mile long on each face; her ferro-concrete walls are sixty feet thick and topped with three feet of stainless steel or some such metal. I figure that about half of that facing has been worn away by now, but when the sun hits it right, it's like a flaming jewel.

"It's open in the middle and the man I've had looking at it tells me that the court is filled with huge, incomprehensible machines, tubes, antennae, and so on. But I do know that it's still quite alive. We at the Yards can hear it stirring every once in a while; jets of steam can occasionally be spotted escaping from the inside, and, well, it seems to be repairing itself. Look over there, just where one of the western walls angles out of sight; it's almost parallel to our line of sight. Now you can't see from here without a glass, but with one you can see that the metal facing that wall is smooth and up to what I suppose is its proper thickness." Trebbly pointed up to the top of the tower. "And if you'll look up there, sir, you can see some holes and bracings; we've found some detection equipment, antennae and the like, under the Yards. They might fit those sockets."

"Detection equipment?"

"Well, sir, it is called the Westwatch. The tower itself is older than anything around here but has been used by many nations. Why not those who defeated the Powers? If, as Kirghiz once told me, the Fortress was built to keep the Powers behind their mountains, then it would need eyes. The Fortress is apparently blind but, like I said, alive; why not its enemies, too?"

Limpkin tried to sound bored. "Then maybe it is best it is there, if it can't hurt us."

Both men stood looking at the Fortress for a moment, Trebbly thinking of his legends and Limpkin wondering what they might be. Limpkin thanked Trebbly then, for the observation was obviously ended and besides, it was almost lunchtime; both turned to go. Then a faint, high-pitched whine penetrated the howling of the wind. Trebbly instinctively looked to the Fortress and then tapped Limpkin on the shoulder.

A plume of smoke was jetting out of the Fort's hollow center. It was not steam for it did not disperse quickly, but collected and climbed over the walls to be caught by the breezes. A small branch of flame appeared at the base of the smoke column. The roaring grew louder until it was quite distinct to both men. Gradually the flame increased in intensity and began to rise. Slowly at first, and then faster, it climbed out of the cloud; Limpkin saw that the fire was issuing from and supporting a dark cylinder. Gathering speed and altitude it began to curve off to the west and was soon lost in the clouds over that land.

Limpkin glanced at Trebbly with the intention of asking him about this curious thing, but he saw that the engineer had the same expression of worshipful awe that he had when he first started talking of the Fortress and the legends that had grown up around it.

❖   ❖   ❖

Instead of mentioning the missile, therefore, Limpkin pointed out that it looked like they would be in for a storm and perhaps they had better retire to the Yards. Neither man said another word on the ride down the tower and back to the Yards.

A storm did indeed hit the Yards that afternoon, forcing Limpkin to cancel any further touring that day. That evening, Trebbly dropped by his quarters for a short talk, requesting, among other things, to eventually try to fit up the detection apparatus that looked as if it belonged on top of the Westwatch.

On the five days that followed, Limpkin was led like an amused child through the new toy store that his friend had just discovered. Trebbly's ecstasies multiplied as he guided Limpkin down into the storage vaults under the Yards and showed him the disassembled factories, vehicles, and the titanic sections that would soon be the *Victory*. Limpkin began to share Trebbly's euphoria for, even though he didn't have the slightest idea of what most of the machines actually did (he was even more confused after Trebbly attempted to explain), he knew that with the death of Toriman, *he* was the ultimate commander of this enterprise.

Finally, Limpkin's six days were up and it was time to return to the Caroline, Lady Limpkin, and work of a more tedious nature.

He bid goodbye to Trebbly and told him to hurry along his work; the first of the People, those who knew only the Myth of the Ship and nothing else, would arrive to help with the physical labor. Also, more men and women who knew the full story would be heading for the Yards as soon as they could be found and indoctrinated; if either man could have had his way, he would have shifted the entire population of the Caroline bodily to the Yards in one move. But such things must be executed with discretion.

XIII

Limpkin took with him a folder from Trebbly: recommendations, requisitions, plans, blueprints, and duplicates of plans being sent for deciphering.

When he arrived home, three weeks later, Limpkin found that the Office of Reconstruction had been renamed the Admiralty; George XXVIII thought it had a rather appropriate air, but Limpkin suspected that the slow-witted monarch had just not grasped the idea that the ship was to fly instead of float. He saw that Moresly was moving along nicely at the Armories and was already beginning to turn out plans for dummy transformers and real power lines that could be set up at the rate of a mile a night.

The first large convoy of common people was preparing to shove off within the month; a contingent of engineers and scientists had already left with enough personnel to more than double Trebbly's force.

Within six months of Limpkin's return, two remarkable events took place. A small dam, not more than fifty feet across, was actually completed; equally amazing, its miniature hydroelectric plant worked. Then, with some secret help from Moresly's rapidly expanding force, a telegraph line was strung from the capital to Kelph on the Tyne, the main jumping-off spot for the Yards.

The day after the line was finished, a ball was held on the grass at Palace Park—the weather being exceedingly mild for that time of year—the first one so staged in over a century. Limpkin with his inherited collection of psychological studies made the most of the affair: speeches by all the great men involved in the project, fireworks, dancing. At midnight George, with his Council in attendance, mounted a pavilion and slowly tapped out the word "begin" over and over on an ancient telegraph key. A crude electric light displayed the dots and dashes to the watching crowd until it burned out halfway through the sixth "begin." Miles away, at a dock at Kelph, a fast galley saw another light blink out the word; it shoved off for the Yards, its captain carrying the order to Trebbly.

Almost exactly a week later the order reached the Yards and the first section of the *Victory*'s keel was lifted into place. Four years after that, the entire keel was finished.

A grand ceremony was held in the Yards and in the Caroline Empire (for so it was now named) to celebrate the completion of the keel. But the whole thing was turned into a rather dismal affair when George XXVIII, who had been lapsing in and out of insanity for the past couple of years, died. And to compound the genuine sorrow that the nation felt for the kindly half-wit, Sir Henry Limpkin, O.O.C., D.S.C., K.O.S., followed the monarch soon afterward. The Council assumed rule of the Empire until George's son Clement came of age and as its first official act made Limpkin the Viscount of Westwatch; his widow said that she was overcome with the sympathy that the nation and the Government had displayed, and promptly ran off to New Svald with a cavalry officer twenty years her junior.

According to Limpkin's will, he desired that a young man named Trensing should become head of the Admiralty. This nettled Moresly quite a bit, for he had expected Limpkin to follow the General's instructions and leave the appointment of Office of Reconstruction heads to the Office of Procurement. But considering the essentially covert nature of his Office and the then-rampant sympathy for Limpkin, his vehement objections were not heard outside of the higher government circles.

Although Trensing's lens-like spectacles and artificial arm (the real one had been lost, along with his family, in the Fairmont Massacre twelve years before) repelled most people, no one could deny his administrative competence. Trensing won even Moresly's grudging admiration when he took over the funeral duties and combined them with those of George; he ended up managing the resulting carnival and drained every last ounce of emotional value from it.

Trensing fully approved of the symbolic way station of Bloody Ford, but it seemed to him that a terminus was needed at the Yards themselves. The ship was still too alien to most people and battles were out of the question in that deserted land. In lieu of the triumphant sorrow with which victors always regard the scenes of their victories, he placed sorrow alone.

So, on a bright day in the middle of spring, when the trees and flowers were beginning their annual struggle against the poisons of the World's air and soil, George XXVIII, Sovereign of the Caroline, Commander of the Armies, Patron of the Arts and Sciences, and Rebuilder of the World, was carried to Kelph upon a huge flatbed trailer. Behind him, on a bier about three feet lower, rode the coffin of the Viscount Limpkin of Westwatch. The trailer was pulled by the ancient truck that Limpkin had sent running about the countryside before the Myth of the Ship was generally known.

At Kelph the coffins were unloaded and placed on board one of the five galleys that had made it back from Bloody Ford. A thirty gun salute was fired from a battery of nine newly cast, rifled cannon; the assembled masses were heartened when only one of the guns blew up during the ceremony. A mausoleum had been built for George just within the northern edge of the Yards. It was made from the steel that had lain beneath the Yards for thousands of years; engraved upon its three foot thick outer door were George's accomplishments, or rather most of the noteworthy things that happened during his pleasantly muddled rule and that sympathy demanded be attributed to George. A little to the east a smaller tomb was built, this of stone from the Yards themselves, and here Limpkin was laid to rest, at the right hand of his king. It was all most effective for the mob of People who had even then come to live by the Yards. A city was growing for the People—as they were now called by the Technos—a thousand little prefabricated houses, each with its own neat, sterile plot. Over to the north and east, among the foothills of the mountains that ringed the Yards and separated them from the Barrens, the houses of the Technos—as the technical elite were now called by the People—were being built, looking down from their rugged heights upon the vast ship that was taking shape under their direction. All classes came to weep, some more for show than others, and bid farewell to the Great Men. Trebbly, observing the rites from his home on Mount Dethmet, smiled approvingly; now he could tell the People to work for the ship *and* for the memory of George *and* for the memory of the Viscount Limpkin. But, as he peered through a telescope, he could not help but feel a perplexing kind of fear, for the People thronged the larger of the two death buildings almost without exception, while his Technos had congregated in a solemn mass of black around Limpkin's grave, their silver insignia flashing in the dark universe of their uniforms. Of course, the explanation was that not many of the People knew anything about the role of Limpkin in the building of the ship. Trebbly turned from the window, for his maid had just finished preparing lunch; he wondered who had mourned over poor Toriman's resting place.

XIV

There had been a great flotilla of boats to follow the funeral barge down the Tyne; the capital, as a result, was comparatively deserted. Perhaps the only man of any public stature left in the city was Philip Rome, now Sir Philip. Both Rome and the People had heartily accepted the engineered meaning of Bloody Ford, and instead of returning to his original profession, he had become what is known as a Leader of the Masses. With subtle Government assistance, and quite without his consent, he found himself recruiting people to work at the Yards. For several years he had done this happily, his stature growing with the legends about the Ford Battle. But the Government, Trensing especially, had decided that he was becoming a trifle too legendary and had ordered him to the Yards to join his People. The day after the Government directive arrived, a silent messenger, dressed in military attire, delivered a handwritten note summoning him to Caltroon; at that moment, George and Limpkin were being buried more than a thousand miles away.

Rome had never really heard of General Tenn, who had invited him to that mysterious stone pile, but he seemed to vaguely recall someone of that name in the war news from Yuma. Anyway, the stationery was of the finest vellum and the coat of arms at its head, a mailed fist and pegasus, was most impressive.

At about eleven an open landau arrived at his house. As the elegant coach trotted through the warm night air, Rome leaned back and gazed at the welkin, trying to guess which star Home orbited about. The town walls were soon passed with little trouble, municipal security being much slackened in those days, then down along the River Road, and up to the northwest where Mount Royal hid half the night sky with its bulk. Rome looked up intently and soon he could make out the denser blackness that must be the Castle. They drew nearer and he could see that the only lights in the place were in the Great Keep.

The landau let Rome off at the main gate, and he walked through the opened gate unchallenged. Up on the deserted battlements the flags of the Caroline, of some military unit, and a personal ensign, probably the General's, hung limp in the tranquil night air.

He moved through the outer courtyards, through the inner wall and neglected gardens, his way guided by smoking torches. A liveried servant was waiting for him at the door of the Great Keep; Rome was most flattered by the treatment he was getting. Not only that, but it appeared that Caltroon had been opened up just for him; obviously, this General thought a great deal of him.

The servant led Rome through many rooms and halls until he was finally ushered into the General's study. Rome had heard of this vast, cathedral-like room from his friends in high places, and it was said that in this room George XXVIII had proposed the idea of the Ship to the Viscount Limpkin and some obscure general named Toriman. Great things had been transacted in front of its fireplace and Rome felt that he was about to be let in on one of them.

As he approached the roaring fire and the opulent desk that was placed before it, he noticed the empty shelves and map trays that lined both sides of the room; yes, here the Ship and all that she would become had been born.

General Tenn was seated in front of the fire and rose to greet Rome. The engineer was immediately struck by the intensely military bearing of the man, the aura of command and authority that surrounded him. His gaunt frame towered some five inches over Rome, the battered face patterned with a network of scars and wrinkles. There was a gray patch over his left eye, but it failed to cover a hideous scar that crept down the General's cheek. A shaved skull and bull neck completed the splendidly martial appearance of the man. Rome was properly awed.

The General introduced himself pleasantly, offered Rome some wine and then a chair; the General wasted little time on preliminaries, however, and soon broached the point of the audience.

"Sir Philip, I hope that you will forgive the appearance of Caltroon, but my duties seldom allow me to be home. I will only be here for another day or two, and that is why I found it necessary to call you here, even though you were scheduled to leave for the Yards. I hope you are not inconvenienced."

The idea of such a man asking him if he was inconvenienced took Rome by surprise, but he hid it as best he could. "No trouble, sir. Your summons sounded urgent, so I thought it best to come. The Yards will not move and I guess that our late Sovereign will still be there to receive my homage when I arrive."

Tenn smiled thinly and nodded. "Well put, Rome. Now it is quite evident, even to the most obtuse eye, that you have become something of a leader among the people."

"I hope that I'm not flattering myself if I say . . ."

"No, of course you're not. You are every bit the leader you think yourself to be; if not you would not be here." Tenn looked at Rome, the firelight glinting off a large signet ring. "Tell me, what do you think of the Government and the Technos?"

Rome mulled it around for a while. "The Government has been most kind to me, sir, and has followed a very wise and daring course in their building of the Ship. As for the Technos, I cannot say; they seem to be competent enough in their direction of the building. But never having been to the Yards, I would rather not pass judgment."

Tenn flicked open a folder that was sitting beside the decanter. "Did you know that the Technos come almost exclusively from the top social and economic tenth of the nation, with ability counting for almost nothing?"

Disturbed by this, Rome asked Tenn if he were sure of his figures. "They are correct," said the General. "They must be, for you, yourself are living proof; if ability and leadership meant more than family fortunes, then why have you not been absorbed into the Techno class?"

Confronted with such irrefutable evidence, Rome asked the General to continue. "You say that you have never been to the Yards, Rome. I have." Tenn looked as if he were somehow wrestling with himself over just what he should tell Rome; he spoke slowly, choosing his words with great care. "My duties in the Army have taken me to the farthest outposts of our civilization. I've visited the Yards several times, twice before George and the Viscount Limpkin even conceived of the Ship, and a few more times since. Frankly, Rome, what I have seen disturbs me."

"The Ship?"

"Oh no, hardly. The Ship is coming along beautifully. A trifle more beautifully than some would like." Tenn gestured earnestly to Rome. "You see, my loyalty is to the Army, not to the Government or the immortal masses or any synthetic class divisions that anyone has dreamed up. I am really at a loss to explain the purpose behind the Technos and the People being split apart for any reason other than that of dominion by the former.

"At any rate, my uncommitted status has allowed me access to information and freedom from restriction that . . . " Rome thought that the General looked like a man who was about to betray somebody. "Rome, it appears to me that the Technos, or whatever you care to call our new rulers, have taken over the idea of the Ship and perverted it. They mean never to complete the Ship."

Rome was astounded. "The Government would never permit such a thing!"

"I know. I said the same thing when the possibility first presented itself and was then confirmed by my studies."

"But what could they hope to accomplish with this trickery?"

"I can speak only from personal observation and conjecture, but it seems that the Technos are using the Ship as a part in a deception. They plan to use it like a carrot, dangling the prospect of escape from this godawful planet to stimulate the masses into productive action—give them a great Cause to work for and all that. But while all of us out there are breaking our collective backs just so our sons may see a better world, the Technos divert a portion of the products and rechannel it back into the country itself. The theory is that as this World grows finer and finer through the work we inadvertently put into it, we will grow less interested in the Ship. Ultimately, we will forget her entirely, turn around, and find that we have built another Home without even knowing it."

Rome did not know how to evaluate the plan. Admittedly, it sounded fine at first. "But, I must say that if it works, it would be a good deal more practical than flying the Ship on a dangerous voyage to another world, no matter how grand," observed Rome, hoping his opinion would not be too far from Tenn's.

Tenn smiled in his spectral manner. "Yes, but don't you see that it wouldn't work? This plan would probably succeed wonderfully in a normal world, in a First World. But this isn't the First World, it is the World, the bastardized parody World, where logical rules seldom hold. Of course we are inspired by the Ship and are now engaged in new works of undreamed of magnitude. But it is only a matter of time until the World swallows them like it has every other effort that we have made in the last three thousand years.

"Another thing. Who or what is to guarantee that our respected Technos will adhere to their own magnanimous scheme? What is to keep them from channeling all this effort into their own houses, as indeed many are already doing, instead of into the country as a whole? They now control all our knowledge, and eventually, whether we get to Home or not, they will control all physical power and wealth.

"Thirdly, there is the fact that the Ship is awakening many of the old, sleeping terrors of the World. The Imperial Vale is a perfect case. We were living adequately and were reasonably happy, but then the Ship necessitated our stumbling into that cursed valley and awakening all the menaces that had lain there harmlessly for several centuries. I admit that this had to be done to reach the Yards and start the Ship. If we complete the Ship without disturbing the countryside any more than we have to, especially the western lands, and leave, then we run a minimal risk. But if we allow our power to be rooted to the substance and being of the World, the Technos will inevitably try to expand. And just as inevitably, their wielding of our power will eventually disturb a force which will wipe them, and in all probability, the rest of the World, out.

"The futility of it all is manifest. If you need any more proof, you need only refer to the Builders of the Yards themselves. Their technological abilities and industrial capacities were so great that now, even though we are actually using their relics, we still feel that we are moving in a myth-world. But even those creatures, with their unlimited power to conquer and pacify, bent all their will, not to tame the hostile land, but just to escape it!" Tenn drank some more wine and sighed heavily. "And the Technos presume to conquer what the Builders knew to be invincible."

Rome sat quietly, alternately staring at the General and the fire. Shocked and puzzled as he was, his primary concern was still that his words should not cause the General to lose some of the obvious respect he held for him. "Haven't the Technos thought of the dangers that you have just told me of?"

"I should think so; most of them are certainly not fools. But I think that they have been carried away by the magnitude of their undertaking—or by the magnitude of the profits they hope to reap from it. They are taking a calculated risk, but they have underestimated the odds; you and I and our future are the stakes they are gambling with."

"I'm overwhelmed by this, sir. I don't know what to say, if anything at all. However, I must admit that what you have told me does seem to—uh—coincide with some suspicions that I myself have long had." Rome immediately set about modifying any thoughts he might have had on the Ship or the Technos, and making them cast doubt on the intentions of the latter; it suddenly seemed to him that great minds do run on parallel tracks. "Yes, now that you mention it, and back it up with an amazingly obvious but previously ignored . . . "

"Or censored," added the General.

Rome smiled knowingly—the machinations of power were becoming very clear to him. "Or censored, it does look as if the Caroline might be cheated out of her liberty and her escape to Home. How does all this involve me?"

"You are involved as a leader of those whose lives and heritages are in danger. You have the ear of the People and, more importantly, you are one of them. They believe in the Government now, but certain unforeseen events may shake their confidence; then the inescapable fact of rigid class lines will come to the fore. When you speak and act at that time, it will be with their own voice and with their own hands."

"And what is it that I must say?" asked Rome, heady with the power that so great a man as Tenn had accredited him with.

"You will tell them nothing, now. You will wait and carry this secret inside of you, as I have done. For all I know, the whole affair might come off even better than planned. But watch! Watch for the Technos to become more authoritarian, to attempt to slow the construction of the Ship, to channel the fruits of our labor into their own treasuries. And when you start to see this, Rome, tell the People that the Ship has been betrayed. If this time does not come in our lifetimes, as it well might not, then we must also be prepared.

"Find men you can trust and share this knowledge with them; if anything it will ease the burden of carrying the suspicions alone. Organize, prepare and wait.

"I know of some men that would be of use to you. Here." Tenn handed the engineer a small piece of paper. "If I can get word to them in time, they will contact you as soon as they are able." Tenn relaxed a little; Rome noticed that the white burn-scar had become a brilliant red in the firelight. "And then, my good man, I have every confidence that the People, once they are in possession of all the facts and led by you or your successors, will act in the proper manner."

"What do you mean, 'in time?' " asked Rome unsurely.

"One of the reasons I've told you all this is because I fear that the Government is aware of my beliefs. As an officer I am powerless to do anything overt, but they must know that I can tell others; if they ever find out about this meeting, my military record and value to the nation will count for little. Of course, if they are as honest as they would have us believe and are working for the betterment of us all, then I have nothing to worry about; but if I have correctly guessed their evil intentions, then they will stop at nothing to silence me."

Rome was about to question Tenn further when the General abruptly stood up and thanked him for his presence. Rome was soon walking beside the General as a servant lighted the way to the main gate.

Rome spent the trip home trying to decide whether to be delighted that happenings of such vast import should pivot on his shoulders, or to be terrified at the consequences that would follow any failure. He assumed the sad look of Great Men who are both aware of their own limitless abilities and of the responsibilities that they incur; he thought it made him look much more dignified.

A week later, Rome finally left for the Yards, looking even more dignified than he would have liked. Every night since he had met Tenn, he had taken a ride out to the foot of Mount Royal to see if the lights of Caltroon were still burning. On the third night of his observations he got the distinct feeling that he was being followed. He quickly turned and headed for the city; but before he was within sight of the North Gate a pack of horsemen, dressed in the dull green uniforms of the Household Cavalry, galloped past him and took the River Road to Caltroon. Rome rode along behind them cautiously; he was relieved to see that the lights in the Great Keep were still lighted. But the relief turned to fear as some of the lights suddenly went out and the night wind carried indistinct fragments of screams and what might have been the rattle of automatic weapons. As the last light went out, Rome was already running through North Gate.

Inquiries at the War Office netted Rome an outright denial that any General Tenn had ever been carried on their lists. The Admiralty had never heard, or said that they had never heard, of anyone named Tenn, but perhaps the Office of Procurement might know. Rome knew nothing of any such Office, but since they had an office in the basement of the Admiralty, he tried anyway. There an emaciated-looking matron with steel dentures said that the only Tenn she knew of was working with the Admiralty and that he had just been sent on a diplomatic mission to Mourne. This Tenn should be back in ten years. Would Sir Philip care to wait?

XV

Vennerian was a fat little man about whom the reek of sweat hung like the fog on top of Mount Atli. He was eternally irritable and perpetually hostile to his situation in life, or to life itself for that matter. But he was a Techno, and immensely proud of the fact.

He was slouched in his office, a wooden shack near the southwestern corner of the Yards, when another even more minor Techno came in. Mad at being taken away from the report that he was already mad at having to read in the first place, Vennerian asked the man, one Kort by name, what he wanted. Kort replied in his slowest drawl that he had finally gotten around to checking out the antennae and detection gear that old Limpkin had ordered put on top of the Westwatch. They had been mounted by Trebbly a month after Limpkin had given him permission, but he still did not have any notion of just what the equipment did; Trebbly had just followed the wiring diagrams and attached the leads to more mysterious machinery underneath the Yards.

And those machines had sat in their little compartments emitting sound and displaying lights that no one had the ability or the desire to interpret. Finally, in an especially ambitious moment, Trebbly had ordered a study of the whole apparatus. Since the antennae at least resembled First World assemblies, it was deemed that an "intensive analysis" would reveal some useful facts. But once the initial command was given, the process ran something like this: "Benman, I want you to find out exactly what those damn things are supposed to be watching." "Right, Chief!" "Fuller, find out what those antennae mean." "Right." "Beam, check out those things up there, will you?" "Yeah." "Vennerian, look after it." "(grunt)." "Kort, looka those flyswatters up there." That was seven months ago.

"Bloody well about time, Kort." Vennerian grumbled. "Find out anything particularly earth shattering?"

Kort drew heavily on his cigar, filling the room with choking fog. "Well, my honored superior"—he crushed the cigar slowly on the bare desk, gazed out into the depths of Eternity, and then continued with much agonized twisting of the face muscles—"yes—yes, I have discovered something."

"Oh?" Vennerian was taken off balance.

"They're all antennae, all right."

"Look, Kort, if this is your bloody . . . "

"Uh-huh, all antennae. Wadda they call it—radar? sonor? Real First World junk. Pity none of us can understand what most of them are trying to tell us."

Vennerian lifted an eyebrow. "But not all of them?"

"Ah, no. That report you gave me said that Trebbly set up seven antennae; and seven are, you know, receivers: infra red, that sort. But it looked to me like there were eight pieces of metal on top of the 'Watch and one of that eight is a transmitting antenna." Kort leaned forward and hissed, "Terrifying, ain't it?"

"Is this crud on the level?"

"Superior, would I lie to you?"

Vennerian decided to get really mad; he colored to a deep red, uttered some oaths worthy of the Dark Powers themselves, and tossed an empty liquor bottle after the retreating Kort.

❖   ❖   ❖

A week after this interview, the maintenance staff was debating whether or not it was worthwhile trying to remove the large splash of blood and gore that a minor Techno named Vennerian had left when he fell from the top of the Westwatch. The clumsy fool. There were always people like him leaving a mess behind for someone else to clean up.

On the same day that a brigade marched out to the delta with buckets and a shovel, a crane operator noticed a curious smell coming from underneath a big transporter rig. Much to his surprise, he discovered the remains of one Gordon Kort intertwined about the forward loading lift machinery. More steel wool for the maintenance staff. Trebbly issued an order requesting that Technos be a bit more careful of where they step in the future.

XVI

Trensing had done a magnificent job of administering the project. But of all the many papers that crossed his desk, he could hardly be criticized for reading only a fraction, such were the pressures of resurrecting a world. As time went on, his personal signature was replaced by a rubber stamp, and then by a staff, all wielding rubber stamps. One particularly interesting request which Trensing never saw was from Moresly in the Armories.

Because of the secret nature of the Office of Procurement's work, it was left pretty much alone by the few people who did know what it was about. Hence, commendations of Trensing were really irrelevant because, even if he had seen the request, he would have felt himself duty bound to approve. The paper merely asked approval to refurbish some of the lower levels of the Armories for the production of modern weapons. The reason given was that the mission of the O.P., as far as most of the nation was concerned, was of a treasonable nature. Obviously, the Office had to offer its men some measure of safety in their work. The Army could not openly support the O.P.'s operations, so they would have to protect themselves from the Caroline citizenry and from the hostile nations or uncivilized tribes that lived in the areas that they were active in.

A committee debated this request and others—material, men, money, etc.—for the Armories. They were completely unaware of the nature of the Office, but since Trensing's latest development report had praised its work—without saying what it was—and its value to the nation—in an unmentioned capacity—they approved it with a top priority.

XVII

There is one more minor incident which might be interesting to the reader. It occurred a full twenty-five years after Trensing resigned in favor of Sir Miller Curragh. Clement had long since died and Edward VI was then on the throne; the head of the Admiralty was Justin Blyn. The Techno director of the Yards was Ord Syers, perhaps one of the worst men ever to have held that post.

The set of engines which Toriman had spoken of so many years ago had been brought up from underneath the Yards. They presented something of a problem in that they were only about seventy-five percent complete and the principles upon which they were supposed to have run were totally beyond the grasp of Carolinian science. There were plenty of plans around, all in the odd script of the Builders, of course, and many of the more advanced theoretical works from the Black Libraries seemed to jibe with these blueprints.

So, after some twenty years of slipshod interpolation and simple guessing, the Admiralty produced a set of instructions for completing the engines. But since it was irrelevant whether or not the engines actually worked, the Admiralty and Syers spent much of their time on making the engines look as if they should work and in designing instruments that would confirm the sham.

The possible blast and radiation effects of the engines and their phony adjuncts had prompted Syers to locate them in as isolated a region as possible; but the Admiralty insisted that they be located within sight of the Yards and of the city that had grown up around them. They were finally located about seven miles down the coast. Their bulk combining with the testing shacks to produce an appropriately impressive and mysterious complex.

Syers had watched the test with his wife and a man from the Admiralty and all had been gratified by the show; the Sea steamed, the earth even up in the Techno-dominated hills shook, nearby glass was shattered, multiple blue-white flames cut through billowing smoke clouds. It was exactly what one would expect to see at the end of a seven mile long starship.

The Techno in charge of the engines and their testing was an intelligent young fellow named Marlet. Although motor vehicles were now quite common in and about the Yards, Marlet and many other Technos still preferred the horse-drawn carriages that Trebbly and his contemporaries had used. Marlet arrived early the next evening with his report. Syers, feeling somewhat self-satisfied after yesterday's success and a fine dinner, accepted the report with many belches and congratulations. Marlet did not seem to share the older man's delight.

"What's wrong, Marlet, old man? Been thinking about the possibility of more tests, fooling the People again and thinking they might find out? Forget it. My boy, I was very impressed by the display you and your men put on yesterday. I think that the People are convinced their precious ship has the power to get off the ground." Marlet stood silently, fidgeting. "Well, then, what's the trouble?"

"As you said, sir, the special effects went beautifully, really tremendous. I have enough tapes and records to satisfy the most intelligent and suspicious members of the People that the engines are fully operational. You see, I set up this parallel rig too, just to let us know what the engines were really doing. Sir, it looks like they really do work."

Both men looked quietly at each other for a moment; Syers tried desperately to figure out an appropriate reaction. "So is that something to be ashamed of, Marlet? So they work, all the better; now they can never accuse us of deception—on this count at least. Why should it bother you?"

"I suppose that you're right, sir." Marlet raised his head and peered directly into Syers' eyes. "But, by Heaven, sir, it just doesn't seem right. That we should do such a slapdash job of putting those monsters together, and that we should just fake what we either didn't understand or have, and then that the whole package should work like the Builders did it themselves."

Marlet cast about for the words. "Sir, it's just too damn *right* to be true. Things shouldn't be working out like this."

"Never question fortune, my boy," said Syers in his most paternal tone.

Marlet settled down a bit. "Again, sir, I suppose that it's the unexpected real success. After all, we're in the business of deception . . ."

"The business of progress, son."

"Of course, but I am upset that Fortune, a lady who has shown us little favor in the past, should suddenly join our side."

Syers turned to a nearby window. Below them, more than eight miles to the southwest, lay the Yards; the barren concrete field that Limpkin had known was now aswarm with the People; cranes moved with stately grace about a growing tangle of steel. The ship was growing and even now, only fifteen percent complete, the eye thrilled to its grandeur and its incredible size; looking more closely, the eye soon found itself rocketing off on tangents of speculation, tracing the unbuilt wings and tail. "The *Victory*, my boy, as you can well see, has grown much bigger than any of us; she is clearly reaching into a realm that may lie far beyond our meager sensibilities, so who are we to question if Fate or Fortune or God Himself chooses to work in His or its own strange ways in our favor?" Syers assumed a look of mindless euphoria, such as the devout assume when repeating Scripture.

"Of course," said Marlet coldly, for he knew that the older man had lifted the passage word for word from one of Blyn's speeches to the People; Blyn had not believed it, Syers did. The Myth of the Ship had taken over his mind almost as completely as it had the minds of the People. Marlet knew that the Admiralty would call it treason, and indeed it would be, but Syers controlled all official communication with the capital; and even if Marlet did get word through, the powerful friends who had gotten Syers installed as director of the Yards in the first place would immediately quash any criticism.

Syers ordered the engines installed without modification and dismissed Marlet. Marlet left in a smoldering fury.

The young Techno felt that he was sitting on something fantastic, but exactly what he could not say. His colleagues chided him for being so suspicious of good luck; but it was the arrogant, second-handed prophetic attitude with which Syers treated his constant pleas for some sort of investigation into the engines and into the origins of the Yards that really inflamed him; Marlet was just as fanatically dedicated to the original mission of the ship as Syers had become to the Myth. Thus it is understandable that in an unusually dark and brooding drunken rage one night, Marlet took a thermite flare from a special effects shack and tossed it into Syers' house.

Syers' post was soon filled by Orwell Cadin, a thoroughly competent man whose abilities and frame of mind more than served to quiet any guilt feelings Marlet might have had. A perfunctory investigation of the fire was carried out, but since many others had also taken a dim view of Syers' position on the Ship, it never came anywhere near Marlet.

In fact, Marlet became almost proud of his service to the nation, and secretly shared the credit that Cadin received for restoring a business-like atmosphere to the Yards. So it was only natural that his growing self-esteem should readily accept a transfer to the highly secret Armories. The order arrived two months after the murder; it was signed by Dennis Hale, head of the Armories, and Marlet half-hoped that this powerful official had heard of his patriotic deed and appreciated its import. However, one can learn nothing of any successes that Marlet might have encountered at the Armories, for when he left the Techno riverboat at Kelph and boarded a coach for his new post, he vanished from human chronicles entirely.

XVIII

Aside from the engines, the most puzzling thing that emerges is the fact that Marlet could disappear so completely into an arm of his own Government. It turned out that the Armories and the front organization, the Office of Procurement, were operating virtually without any supervision whatsoever.

In the eighty years or so in which the Armories operated as a separate agency, it would appear that the Office had simply been created and then immediately submerged from the sight of men. Toriman had given Limpkin comparatively little to go on in the creation of the rechanneling arm of the Admiralty; in fact, the General's instructions on this point were not only limited but also rather confusing in their omission of certain broad points of policy which anyone else would have considered absolutely necessary, while dwelling at great length on apparently minute details (such as the location of its base, the modification of which so upset Moresly).

In the absence of direct instructions, Limpkin had no choice but to turn over all management to Moresly; the only communications with the Government being a bimonthly progress report and the annual "Budget, Capability, & Necessity Report." The public at large, regardless of class, knew nothing of its existence let alone its function.

Left alone, the Armories formed a tight, closed society long before the Technos at the Yards even began to approach such an end. Leadership was centralized within the physical limits of the caves; the Admiralty saw a total of seven different signatures affixed to the reports and budget requests, and it saw four of these men appear in its offices on official missions. Of course, no one outside of the Armories had any way of knowing that all seven of the names and all four of the faces belonged to Moresly, Toriman's man.

The caves that actually made up the Armories had originally been part of a nation called the Aberdeen; its caves, tunnel, and vaults not only occupied the cliffs bordering the Tyne, but honeycombed the plains above the river for a distance of nearly ten miles inland. Formed in an era when nuclear warfare was enjoying particular popularity, its ambitious founders had proposed to construct an entire country below the ground. The Armories were as far as they got before internal strife and newly developed radiations made the tunnels useless: but this was many ages ago, when the weapons and concepts of the First World were still very much in evidence.

As weaponry and diplomacy reverted to more primitive forms, the Armories acquired enormous value as one of the outstanding fortresses of the age. It has been estimated that over a score of major wars had been fought with possession of the Armories as their sole object. The caverns had lately been occupied by the old Garilock Empire; Yuma, sensing the progressive senility of that nation, acquired the complex through the judicious use of Plague carriers. They in turn were followed by the Caroline and Moresly.

Under the successive hands of these many conquerors, the Armories had been expanded and strengthened in the best manner that the age would allow, into a construction that could have rivaled even the Yards. In its seemingly endless corridors could be found rolling mills, warehouses, machine shops, barracks; in short, all the ugly machinery required to give the caverns the name they went by.

Before the war with Yuma, most of the First World vintage glories of the Armories had passed into legend; many of the tunnels were by then either sealed off and forgotten, or the stresses of heavy-handed statesmanship and time had caved them in. While the Armories still retained enough of their former volume and appointments to make an impression on contemporary eyes, most of the caverns' riches lay walled up and protected behind tons of rock. It is easy to see, then, why Limpkin thought he was turning over a devastated shell to Moresly, the war having wiped out the only readily accessible portion.

Not only did the Admiralty grant or rather forfeit complete freedom to the Armories, but it allowed the front agency to operate in a similar manner. The Office of Procurement did maintain an office in the capital, but it was located in a run-down mansion in the secluded Knightsbridge section outside the city walls.

The behavior of the O.P. is quite enlightening when considered in conjunction with future events. While on the one hand it went to great lengths to isolate itself from the Government, it was constantly trying to integrate elements of the People into its ranks; these initiates were not told about the reality of the *Victory*, but they were drawn into what the Government often criticized as "overly frank relationships with members of the Techno class, thus defeating the aim of instillation of a sense of veneration in the People for members of the aforementioned class."

Organizing his People from the Yards, Rome also felt the need to keep in touch with the masses in the capital. A dispatch was sent back to his newly-appointed lieutenant, a man named Crownin who said that Tenn had sent him; at Rome's request, Crownin established his Palace of the People across from the Admiralty on George Street. Two years later, this Crownin was appointed as a "liaison officer" between the Office of Procurement and the People; again, it is strange that no one in the Government was puzzled by this curious arrangement or by the sudden move of the Palace of the People from its George Street storefront to an old mansion in Knightsbridge, right next door to the O.P. office. The conclusions to be drawn should have been painfully obvious, but if anyone had arrived at them they either kept them to themselves or met the same fate as Vennerian and Kort.

XIX

The night was one of singular beauty; the season was mid-spring and the gentle winds had polished the stars to a crystal finish. The man and woman stood upon a small hill to the east of the Yards; below them was another universe of light, for the *Victory* was glimmering quietly in the starlight. The city that had risen around the Yards, the only one in the World to be electrified, spread its carpet of light from the Tyne almost to the encircling mountains; the city's first name had been Georgetown in honor of the late monarch, but Trensing had renamed it Gateway.

It was the sixty-seventh spring of the Ship.

The two young people were both Technos, and sterling examples of the breed too. Both clearly reflected the slender grace and aristocratic bearing that had come to characterize that class in those days. At times, if you looked at them for very long, the black of their uniforms seemed to blend with the night sky and the silver trim gleamed in the starlight like far-off universes, leaving only their pale faces and hands to indicate mere mortal presence. The boy's face was of fine sharp features with deep-set eyes that reflected the complex glitterings of the Yards in their depths. The girl was also fine and fair, but her bearing was of a less earthly character than the man; while the man dreamed of the great ship below, the opal glow of her eyes appeared to drink in the limitless mystery of the welkin. And at times the warm breezes stirred her golden hair and entwined the strands about the galaxies and stars above.

She was beautiful, in the ethereal manner of the queens of the ancient empires; he was quite handsome in the cast of the old knights. It was as if the blood of vanished kings had suddenly sprung up in the new aristocracy of the Caroline.

The stage was set for a predictable chain of events, and much of the conversation was quite in keeping with the time and relationships of that sort, but something was clearly off-key. To begin with, examine their eyes again, for there was too much steel in them. The man saw only the *Victory*, twenty miles to the west but still overpowering in its growing immensity; and even the regal gaze of the girl was barbed with iron, whether from the Yards or from some hidden spot in the sky it was impossible to tell.

Their actions were equally disturbing, for while they stood close together, they never touched; while they talked, they never looked at each other. The girl looked to the stars above her, and the man to the diamond tangle below him.

The boy talked mostly, at first only of the girl's beauty; but gradually he began to speak more and more of the *Victory*. "Ah, can you see her now, my girl? Seven miles long and three across. Seven by three! By Heaven, what a beauty she'll be, too. Even now you can see the curve of the wings and the prow . . . "

"But the *Victory* will never be finished. Remember?" the girl murmured absently, her eyes tracing the constellations.

The boy sighed and lowered his head. "Quite, of course. But when I look at her and at what we've done in these short years, I just can't help thinking, what

if . . . " The man smiled to himself. "And I start seeing
the places where her cabins will be and where her wings
will cut the clouds. All really against what they told us
about the *Victory* and her purpose. But, like I said, I
really can't help it. And then there is always Home to
think about."

"Home," the girl whispered. "Which one do you think
it is? That one?" She pointed to a star near the northern
horizon. "Or that one, perhaps?"

"Ah, now it is you who is the dreamer."

"Possibly, but"—she searched the sky for the proper
words—"but there is a Home out there. Probably not
like the one we tell the poor People about, but certainly
a new world full of green things and life; quiet, open
spaces where you can watch sunsets or dawns without
fearing for your life or having the ring of jackhammers
in your ears." She looked down at the Yards with a mix-
ture of distaste and fascination.

The man turned to her, for he had heard these words
many times in the past few months. He lifted an eye
slightly and sighed for he knew exactly what it all meant.
His tone was now one of resignation rather than one of
hope or happiness. "Then you, my lovely, to your green
wilderness and silent nightfalls; I know that wrong or
futile as it may be, you have come to believe in them as
surely as I have in the Ship." He touched her hand, but
fearfully, as if he thought he would somehow pollute her
in that simple action. He waved a hand at the Yards. "As
for me, I'm afraid that my dream must be placed before
yours if either are to be attained—in any sort of way.
Ah, the Ship, all bright shining metal burning in a noon-
day sun. Hardly as quiet a creation as yours might be.

Thunder, thunder and fire and a huge shadow darkening half the sky. There'll be my world even if it must remain as much of a fantasy as yours." The girl said nothing. "Goodbye then, my lady." He touched her hand again, as if to raise and kiss it, but he stopped and drew back his hand; he walked down to Gateway and to the sleeping Yards. The girl started to walk up into the mountains where the distant lights of her home resided among those in the constellation of Eringold, a wanderer of the western seas.

On the same night a parallel conversation had taken place inside the Yards. Two of the People, both of the thickly graceful sort that muralists love to paint, had found the heat and noise of Gateway uncomfortable. The encompassing highlands were ignored since for the past fifty years they had been strictly the territory of the Technos. But the Yards, deserted at night, had appealed to them. They stood down at the end of the ways where the slipway ran into the quiet Sea and talked of dreams much like the Technos had: the man spoke of the Ship for he was a pipefitter and exceedingly proud of his work. The woman talked of Home for she very much wanted any children she might bear to walk in a kinder land than hers. To them the dreams were more than simple musings, they were concrete hopes, not "but ifs," but "whens." Their hearts as well as their minds were wholly committed to what they were expressing. This was good for it meant that the Myth of the Ship had become part of their lives. The disturbing part of it all was that, despite all the protestations, they were merely speculating: the two Technos and the dead Syers had spoken in identical tones.

XX

To the Admiralty, the *Victory* project was already an unqualified success. All over the Caroline, although its physical appearance had changed very little, one could sense the same spirit that Limpkin had seen rampant in Palace Park. Carefully planted legends took their place beside the quaint native ones that travelers heard at the Yards and then spread, suitably embroidered, throughout the rest of the World; the Admiralty had hired several writers to manufacture synthetic mythology about the Builders and Home; almost anything that they might dream up, if it was about peace, and power, and plenty, was readily accepted and incorporated into the very soul of the People.

But as Amon Macalic, then head of the Yards, sometimes felt the legends and myths were joining the People to the Ship in a tie much more binding and absolute than that of simple hope. Over the whole of the Caroline, not just in the Yards, one could see this tie growing and solidifying, drawing the *Victory* and the People closer and closer together—and farther away from the benevolent rule of the Techno class and the Admiralty. Even in the lands beyond the Caroline, peoples were reorienting limited thinking capacity to include stories of this new creation.

The People of the Yards, however, were the most passionate in their attachment to the *Victory*. The growing status of the Ship in their minds began to be quietly manifested in a singular manner: under the completed sections of the fuselage, small mausoleums could be found. Even more disturbing, some of these gruesome little constructions had what appeared to be provisions for worship; a hundred recognized religions existed in the Caroline and her territories, venerating everything from ancestors to Great Men (Miolnor IV being a current favorite) to the usual brands of pantheism, but now the Ship had truly acquired a capital "S" and all that went with it.

Even the character of the Yards had changed. By their nature and occupation the Technos felt at home in the Yards' bright new steel. That they knew and loved almost as much as the First World had. But since its first awakening, the Yards had grown into something less orderly; in places, it was a metal forest where stories could grow as easily as they had in the Karback Cyprus marches. Under the enormous darkness of the *Victory,* an incredible tangle of pipes, power lines, and ventilation shafts had grown up. Mobile cranes that could no longer reach a section of the hull stood unused for months; steel fittings from under the Yards sometimes waited years before they were lifted into position. The whole lot of it was much too untidy for the Techno mind to tolerate; the People, on the other hand, were quite taken up with it. But even these jarring discontinuities only served to make the eastern bank of the Tyne delta a place that even the First World might not have been able to outdo.

A traveler cresting the mountains around the Yards would suddenly feel all the wretched hopelessness of the World swept away. His eyes would sweep down the mountains, astounded by the designs of the homes he would see there: large, spacious, open, and clean they were, surrounded by rich gardens. Magnificent carriages and horses moved smoothly along the wandering roads carrying proud men in black and silver.

Further down the traveler would see a great city with tall, close-packed tenements and ringed by factories belching smoke and noise. Color, activity and an atmosphere of purpose that he had never felt in all his travelings would drift up to his high perch; he would see great motor vehicles upon the broad avenues, laden with unrecognizable cargoes.

Then, his eye would reach to the Yards and be blinded by what lay there.

The psychological reaction to such a sight, especially after having spent a lifetime getting used to the World, was quite predictable. One would either flee in disbelief, mentally paralyzed by the scene, or, more likely, one would stumble down the slopes, utterly captivated by the *Victory* and all that it suddenly meant to you.

The Technos were continually delighted that their creation promoted such strong feelings in such a short time, and usually let it go at that. Then some duty-conscious Techno decided to send one of their converts back to the Admiralty as an example of the job they were doing out in that godforsaken wilderness.

The Admiralty people questioned the man, a lordless knight from Enom, and were similarly gratified until someone pointed out that the instant devotion of the *Victory* depended to a great extent on the shock of seeing all that accomplishment in the middle of the World. "Quite," replied the other Admiralty people, "just shows how much we've done." Then the man continued to point out that the knight had first journeyed to the Caroline and then followed the Tyne to Bloody Ford and then by devious routes to the Yards. The smiles faded into worried frowns as the Admiralty people began to realize that the knight had noticed no difference between the Caroline and the rest of the World. Seventy years and the Yards had grown tremendously but it seemed that the land had hardly been touched. An eager cipher clerk immediately began to run off a progress report request to the Office of Procurement in Knightsbridge, but a more suspicious mind suggested that any studies that they make of the Ship and the program that supported it be conducted by the Admiralty alone.

To this end a new and regrettably short-lived agency was established. The Office of Extraterritorial Intelligence was meant to be the coldly determined branch of the Admiralty that was to keep watch on all aspects of a program that suddenly seemed to need watching desperately. But the men who were responsible for its creation were still strictured by a childish belief that all was going well, and by a jealous concern that this new agency would find something wrong with *their* particular aspect of the project.

When the Office of Extraterritorial Intelligence was finally put into operation it had a total complement of fifteen men, six horses and some sub-standard stationery. Ironically, its sole office was established in an old church in the Knightsbridge quarter: 25 Stewart Street, a mere two blocks from the O.P. and the People's Palace. The placement of the office was quite accidental and no one took advantage of it until it was too late.

The only mission of the O.E.I. was launched in the early fall of the seventh decade of the Ship.

As the Admiralty began to look about itself, it realized just how completely it had removed itself from direct contact with the rest of the nation and how utterly it had come to depend on mere reports to keep the whole enterprise moving.

Thus it was decided that for a beginning the O.E.I. should send out two parties. The first was to go to the Yards and make as complete a survey as possible of how, if at all, the purpose and meaning of the *Victory* might have become perverted. Three men were assigned to this task and they left the city for Kelph the day after receiving their orders. They were never heard from again and one can only suppose that they perished in the subsequent disturbances in the Tyne delta.

The second party of four men was to confirm a progress report from the Armories. According to the report, a "modification" had been performed on a power chain leading from a hydroelectric dam on the Denligh River in southern Yuma to the Yards. Three transformer stations had been established on the line before its eight cables reached the Yards. All in all the line ran for several hundred miles through four new protectorate nations of the Caroline and the Badlands. That the lines had reached the Yards at all—all but two being dummies—was a bit of a miracle, for while the southern lands that the line traversed did not carry the legendary stigmata that the far north and west did, they still held the more pedestrian horrors in abundance. It was thus only slightly incredible that the Armories reported that only three men had been lost in its modification; two hundred men in the original crew had died. It had taken the Armories five months to carry out its mission; the

War Office engineers had needed three years to build the real and fake power lines.

The first station was reached, but a repair crew from the Armories was at work there. Only a single line was diverted here, but it was impossible to check out its operation without arousing the curiosity of the Armories' men; the secret line was supposed to lead to a village named Kendreal, fifty miles to the northeast. Since the line covered the distance in almost a hundred miles of serpentine wanderings, the O.E.I. party decided to assume that it was working properly.

The second station was two hundred miles beyond the first; even in those latitudes the coming winds of winter could be felt. The station itself was situated among the worn, low mountains that reached up from the Sea and encircled the southeastern corner of the Black Barrens. It was a depressing, sterile place, but relatively safe because there was not enough food to support large life forms. There the three heaviest lines were diverted, two to garrison towns along the Tyne and one to a provincial capital in one of the new protectorates.

The lines had been set up about two years ago, and although no mention of the new power had reached the Admiralty from the garrisons and the capital, it aroused no concern, for the whole scheme was carried out in secrecy, not even the lower echelons of the War Office being fully aware of what was happening. The object was the introduction of the new power into the selected areas in as subtle a manner as possible. Occasionally the lines had to await the construction of a dummy power plant in some suitably visible spot so that no one would guess that the lines had been robbed from the Ship.

The party quickly set to work, for they wanted to reach the Yards before the end of the month. Preliminary tests indicated that all three of the diversionary lines were dead. Fearing that the transformers involved in the switching of power had succumbed to the fierce sun or to the dust storms that seasonally plagued the area, the crew attempted to discover the difficulty: all seemed fine as far as they could tell.

Then, out of desperation, one of the crew ran a test on all eight of the original lines, and was horrified to discover that all of them carried full power.

Understandably shaken, the four set off for the last station, a hundred and seventy miles southeast of the Yards. It was set on the plain separating the mountains that ringed the Yards and the worst parts of the Barrens; here the final two lines were supposed to have been diverted all the way back to the capital of Yuma; standing on an artificial mound and surrounded by a stone wall, the station presented a forbidding face to an already vicious land.

The party had followed the wooden transmission poles from a cautious distance, fearing nothing in particular but having vague premonitions that they might find another detachment from the Armories heading for the same station.

They reached the little compound just before nightfall and hurriedly shut and barred the door behind them. The sun had almost disappeared behind the mountains to the west, but none of the group could contain their morbid curiosity; testing equipment was applied to the transformers and the lines leading into and away from the station. The line running to Yuma's capital was another inoperative dummy, the eight lines going to the Yards all registered full power, and the diversionary equipment was patently phony.

Their worst expectations confirmed and the unavoidable conclusions being drawn, the four men settled down for the night, resolving to make a dash for the nearest Government garrison on the Tyne, two hundred miles to the northwest.

They posted only a single man on watch, despite their fears, so desolate was the surrounding wilderness; the man was named Annandale. Born and raised on the Great Plains east of the Caroline, he was the best horseman of the lot and much more at home amid the loneliness than the others, He had been trained as a weapons expert, which meant that he was lost with anything bigger than an automatic rifle, and had thus been given one of the O.E.I.'s treasured submachine guns; he was the party's protector, but at the moment he felt much less qualified for that post than the others deemed him.

Around three in the morning his drowsy attention was captured by a strange growling noise to the east. Thinking it to be some loathsome creature that had wandered down from the more fertile lands of the east or north—and consequently a very hungry, loathsome creature—he fearfully retreated to the farthest corner of the fort.

The noise became louder and less natural; there was a vehicle of some sort out there. Reassuring himself that he was, in fact, encountering a humanly-created force, Annandale decided to make a reconnaissance of the situation.

Being careful not to disturb the others—for it might after all be only the wind and his imagination—he saddled his horse, briefly checked his weapon, and moved out through the west-facing secondary gate.

He felt safer now, out beneath a familiar sky, even if the ground under his feet was hardly the soft grasslands of his home. Now he had space; space to run, he thought, but tried to dismiss that. Annandale led his horse directly west for a quarter of a mile, using the bulk of the fort to shield his movements from eastern eyes. He then traveled in a wide circling movement that should bring him up a little behind and to the south of the intruder.

Picking his way carefully through the dead scrub and rock, he reached his destination half an hour later. All he could hear now was a low metallic bubbling and what he supposed to be men talking in muffled tones. But he had miscalculated: the sounds were still to the east of him and the station was closer than he planned it to have been.

The moon had set by now, but the brilliant desert stars gave Annandale enough light to see by. He crouched and saw a black, crab-like object silhouetted against the false dawn. As his eyes became better adjusted to the faint light, he detected the stick-figures of men standing by the shape in groups or at work on its hide.

Annandale found a short length of rope and hobbled his horse. He approached as quietly as possible. It was a tank—that he recognized as soon as he got within fifty yards of it. But the armored vehicles that he knew were either rotting hulks, dead and lonely in the green immensities of the Plains, or pictured in the few First World books he had read. Then, of course, there were the miserable, ox-drawn fighting wagons that had been the tanks of his childhood.

This was neither. It was motor driven—even at low idle the vehicle's engine sounded like a sleeping storm. Annandale thought it might be a patrol from the Yards, a resurrected giant sent to guard the *Victory*; indeed that must have been it, for he knew that only the Yards had the ability to put out such a mechanism. But that would have made it a First World machine, and this was definitely not. Annandale could not say exactly what disqualified it; it was the feeling of wanton, purposeless evil that invested the hulking shadow in front of him. No, even that was wrong, for he had sensed much the same thing when examining the plans for First World tanks; but, dammit, they were different. Cold and cruel they were and their evil was of a rigidly directed character; with them, Death sounded out its victims with a ponderous but jewel-like micrometer. They were lower and sleeker, too, clean and light in their titanic manner.

But in this machine, Death was a drunken, moronic brute, careening about the countryside, his ragged scythe ravaging the land in senseless, ghastly arcs. It was anything but clean: even though he was upwind of the tank he could still smell it. Not the sharp odor of polished steel and fine oil, so beloved by the Technos, but one of metallic and human corruption. The starlight played over the cancerous, cobbled skin and Annandale saw that the smooth curves and faceted turrets of the First Days had been replaced by harsh angles and rough surfaces. Nondescript tubes and pipes crawled over its huge exterior like maggots over a corpse.

It was larger than any First World tank he had ever read about; it was not more dreadful or terrifying, for those were qualities inherent in any tank's function, but it was infinitely more repellent. Annandale had always thought of the tankers of old as skilled technicians, accomplishing a job they detested as quickly and as efficiently as possible. The crew of this tank, Annandale knew, would revel in their killings and slaughter—butchers instead of surgeons.

Annandale strained to identify the vehicle. His attention was attracted by the scraps of metal. Some of the men were working on a panel just in back of the turret. One of the men on the ground picked something up and swung himself aboard on the tank's colossal gun barrel. He walked aft to the men; as he reached them, he switched on a torch.

Annandale saw that the turret was a mass of rust and clumsy welds; green lichens seemed to be growing around the twin hatches, and black blast stains marked the punctures where machine guns were hidden. He also saw a black triangle with a white border encircling a star: the ensign of the O.P. and the Armories. There was a crude device ahead of it, a mailed fist and winged horse, but he did not recognize it and assumed it to be a regimental or personal crest.

The men slammed the panel tight and disappeared into the tank through various openings. The engine was revved up, splitting night and polluting the false dawn with its exhausts.

The tank lurched forward, and Annandale saw just how big the thing really was. It began to move toward the station, and panic seized him. Leaping to his feet,

Annandale ran to his horse and flicked off the fetters; he rode unthinkingly for the station, his insane yelling all but lost in the tank's roarings.

He turned to see a piercing light spring from a mount beside the main gun. Blue-white it was, and it played like a hunting fire over the dead land, the grim walls of the station, and finally the horseman. The light steadied on Annandale. Another sound: his companions had awakened and were firing their useless rifles at the monster. The beam was lost in another, redder brilliance; an incredible hollow thud joined the wavering fire. Annandale crouched, trying to hide in his horse's mane. A roaring, like the winter gales compressed and intensified a hundredfold, swept by, almost tossing him from the saddle.

He looked up, partly to follow the shell and partly to call to his mates. The projectile hit the station near the northern corner, sending stone and metal in all directions.

Annandale wheeled his horse violently away from the station as yet another thud and another blast tore the rest of it to pieces.

The tank halted and followed the fleeing rider with its turret, peppering the ground behind and in front of him with automatic fire, apparently unwilling to waste a heavy shell on so insignificant a target; besides, Annandale was wearing the long fur-lined riding coat of the Plains and the men must have thought him to be nothing more than a lone nomad.

Nearly crazed with fear as he was, Annandale still retained his heritage of fine horsemanship; he fled the burning fort and circled around in back of the tank. He rode for several minutes, stopping on top of a blasted hillock half a mile north of the station. The tank still sat there, its evil hide undulating in the leaping of electrical sparks. It lobbed a third shell into the ruins and then finally moved forward; small geysers of dust spouted where its light batteries raked over the wreckage.

The vehicle plowed into the station, shoving rubble from the hill. Once the hill was cleared, the tank circled and its men began rigging a crane on its rear deck; they started to rebuild the station, even then. The only trace of his companions that Annandale could detect was the severed, maimed head of a horse that one of the Armories' men had thrown from the hill; the dawn, just beginning, caught the bloody object and made it seem to sparkle like an obscene, black baroque pearl.

❋　　❋　　❋

Annandale reached the Tyne garrison after three days of constant riding, killing his beloved stallion. During those days he had apparently spent much time deliberating on the things he had seen; the man that stumbled into the Government compound was definitely not the young horseman who had left the Caroline. His eyes, which once shone with delight at the smell of wind and grass, loving the smallest facet of life, had turned gray and dull. His frame sagged as with a great weight; a sorrow had descended upon him from which he could not escape.

He walked to the commander's office, his Admiralty identification serving to admit him. He told his story simply, almost in a lyric manner, as if the facts that he had discovered had already been cast into a minstrel's song. The commander listened in astonishment, punctuating Annandale's narrative with "you can't be serious," and later on, "Gods save us."

The commander directed that all the information be sent to the capital, but he was abruptly informed that all telegraph communication had been mysteriously cut off early that morning. A fast power boat was then dispatched to the capital while the quickest galley available was sent to the Yards.

Annandale seemed more weary now than ever. "Sir, I fear that the storm has already begun. I request only a good horse and rations from you—and my gun, if you please—that I may escape from it for a little while."

"But if what you say is true, then I should think your Office will need you and your gun. The Caroline has need of men like . . . " The commander looked into Annandale's eyes. "Where will you go?" he asked.

"Home," the horseman said.

XXI

The power boat was taken and burned at Bloody Ford and is, therefore, of little further interest. The galley reached the Yards about a day ahead of time; its courier, a fat little man by the name of Shan, was met at the quay by a worried Techno. The boat put about and started pulling upriver while Shan was taken by carriage to the administration complex on the outskirts of Gateway.

The buildings forming the complex were the tallest to be seen. After mile upon mile of pastel-painted People's houses and shops, gaily ramshackle in construction, it was at once depressing yet refreshing to see the black marble towers; all but the lower stories were windowless, glass still being a rare material. Gold and silver edging ran along the borders of some of the structures; silver-gray marble formed a main court where a fountain stood. But the fountain was dry—refuse had been collecting in it for quite a while.

Shan pulled his army coat closely about him, the winds feeling unnaturally cold even for early fall. He was further chilled by the interior of the central tower where he was taken; while the buildings were of First World design, the insides were lit by smoky pans of oil, giving the windowless floors the appearance of subterranean dungeons. Electric light fixtures stood at every hand, dusty with neglect. The furniture too was a strange blend of this and past ages: stainless steel desks and chairs seated secretaries working with abacuses and inscribing the figures on parchment with quill pens.

Finally Shan was shown into a comparatively sumptuous office where the current director of the Yards, Amon Macalic, was seated behind an ornate steel desk. Macalic was a perfect counterpoint for the chubby Shan; thin, stooped and irritable, he was often compared to old Trebbly both in appearance and in ability.

Macalic had been in direct and personal touch with the Admiralty, and was fully aware of the hurried studies that were shaking its internal ranks. He often wondered how the Admiralty would get rid of him if it decided that he had been responsible for the *Victory*'s growth at the expense of the nation. He knew that the ship had been going up too fast, but he could not have slowed down construction without arousing the anger of the People. Not really his fault, he told himself; he had been told to avoid overt sabotage and merely to use the resources as they arrived. The Admiralty and the Armories were supposed to take care of the rest.

And then there was the matter of the People themselves. Macalic had sent back numberless directives voicing his fears at their increasing solidarity. Instead of individually worshiping the Technos, they had united into a mass and had begun to worship the *Victory*. Just as the Technos had donned the black and silver of the Caroline to dramatize their new apartness and divinity, and to show their basic loyalty to the nation, so the People had taken to wearing inordinate amounts of white clothing. There were those cursed People's Palaces—God, what a name, he thought—hopefully nothing more than workers' canteens or what they thought ought to pass for nightclubs, but again it was just that the People should not be doing that sort of thing.

Because of all this, it was understandable that Macalic was not in the best of humors when Shan entered the room, sat down and proceeded to tell him that there was a good chance the roof was about to cave in on all of them. Macalic offered him a little brandy; they both morosely toasted the *Victory* and the furtherance of their own respective lives.

The brandy was beginning to warm their hearts and hopes when a rather agitated young man entered, dropped a sealed envelope on the director's desk and then left. Macalic waited until the door shut and then broke open the seal and read the handwritten note inside; he read it and looked even more miserable than before. "Anything the matter?" Shan asked, immediately feeling stupid.

Macalic looked around the room vacantly, looking for a thing he knew wasn't there. "Well, Shan, it seems that our darling People have decided they deserve the stewardship of the *Victory* more than we do. They have"—Macalic cleared his throat—"or rather, are now attempting to take over the capital."

"What of the Army?" whined Shan.

Macalic touched the paper lightly with his hand. "The Army, I am told, performed just as I should have expected it to. The officer corps, or that good portion of it that knew of the *Victory*, held their posts and I suppose died as valiantly as circumstances would permit. Of the rest . . . you know as well as I, Shan, that the enlisted ranks are drawn mostly from the People anyway." Macalic glanced stiffly at the paper again. "It says here that the Government has retained control of most of the arsenals."

"Good. Then there's hope for them . . . us," Shan said, brightening slightly.

"No, not even there. Remember that the benefits of our technological revolution have not yet reached the home Government. The reliability of our Army's weaponry should still be up to its traditional, dismal standards." A vein of sarcastic anger crept into his voice." Besides, the People are literally hurling themselves at the guns. God, I'd never expected them to be so shattered, I guess you would say, to find out our secret. Never! You'd expect the wretches to behave with a little more rationality." Macalic sighed and raised his eyebrows. "But then again, if the People had ever been capable of thoughtful behavior without the *Victory*, it would have never been needed in the first place. Would it?"

Shan nodded assent sadly. Then the sadness turned to incipient fear as he realized that he was sitting in the very midst of what the People saw now as a huge conspiracy; he felt very conscious of the black and silver uniform he wore.

Macalic pushed a button on his desk and the aide who had delivered the original communication entered. Macalic issued a set of general orders: all weapons were to be broken out; the Army garrison was to be placed on immediate alert with the officers to pay particular attention to the behavior of the enlisted men; work on the *Victory* was to be halted and the Yards cleared of all People; all Techno women and children were to be removed to the highlands; the three Palaces of the People were to be occupied by Techno forces.

Shan respectfully noted that this last action might prematurely trigger any planned insurrection, but Macalic told him that at the worst they would lose some men—who would probably be lost eventually anyway—and at the best they just might upset the whole timetable, giving them a slight advantage.

The aide, who had been turning progressively paler, wrote all of this on a pad and then ran out of the office. "And what do we do now?" Shan asked, feeling some confidence return now, knowing that something was being done.

"We shall sit here, Shan, and wait, and think of all the things we might have done to prevent this day from ever happening." Macalic stopped and uttered a low curse; he pushed the button again. "Here is something that should have been done." The aide burst in, almost stumbling over the threshold. "Jennings, do you know who the leader of the People is?"

"Yes, sir, he's a bloke named Coral."

"Good. Do you know what he looks like?"

"Yes, a big fellow, well over six feet tall. Graying hair scarred-up face, all very tough and distinguished. Ex-Army, they say, but I'm afraid they don't say in which army he might have served. I think he's known especially by a big gold signet ring that's engraved with a hand and pegasus or something."

"The crest of Mourne, I believe," Shan piped in. "Home of old Miolnor IV and his ghost."

"And that of General Toriman," Macalic reflected. "A strange nation, Shan, very curious. Way to the north of us, right up next to the Dark Powers, and one of the World's staunchest defenders against them . . . when such conflicts were going on, of course," Jennings coughed nervously; Macalic was shaken out of his little reverie. "All right then, detail a party to find this man. Go with them yourself so there is no mistake—and kill him."

Jennings turned dead white. "Sir?" he asked in a bewildered voice.

"Kill him—as quickly as you can! Now get out." Macalic waved the man away and returned to his broodings.

When the aide had gone, Macalic set up a chess board, both men were too nervous to play a very good game. Macalic won the first match and they were halfway into a second when they were interrupted by the thud of a heavy gun. Shan felt a fear-borne smile twisting his features as Macalic pulled three pistols from his desk, two beautiful First World automatics inlaid with pearl and ebony, and a pitted old revolver of colossal dimensions. Shan was surprised when Macalic pushed the automatics and their holster belt to him, keeping the revolver. "Come on, Shan," Macalic said in" a harsh, grating whisper. "Would you care to see our world die?" Shan toyed with the idea of making light comment on Macalic's indomitable optimism, but soon dropped it for he felt the same way.

The building was deserted as they walked down the spiral staircase, the sounds of gunfire and shouting growing louder as they reached the ground level. The two men ran from the tower and across the courtyard to a coach that was about to leave. The driver was going to the highlands, but a firm word from Macalic (and an ostentatious checking of the revolver's cylinder) convinced the man that honor compelled him to run to the Yards.

They rumbled through the People's districts of Gateway; both the streets and the houses were empty. Ominous trails of smoke and the crackle of gunfire were coming from the direction of the Techno highlands and the industrial perimeter of Gateway.

They reached the Yards within five minutes. They crossed the barren strip of ground separating it from the city; they passed the tombs of George and Limpkin. Above them, covering fully half the western sky, was the *Victory*; Shan stared up in absolute amazement. The *Victory* was completed up the point where the hundred foot thickness of its wings was more than half fulfilled. Shan's eye discerned the ugly mortuary temples of the

People on the spider web of scaffolding, and then hundreds of the People themselves, dead. An easy five hundred white-clad bodies hung within sight amid the scaffolding and at least as many more lay scattered on the ground.

The coach stopped and both men jumped out, Macalic full of questions and then full of calm orders, Shan still in a stupor.

Macalic was more assured now, taking grim comfort in the fact that he and his men were already defeated; only a formality remained. From what he could gather from the Technos and loyal Army officers, the People had attempted a sudden withdrawal half an hour ago. They were gathering at some point near the mountains, possibly seeking to sweep inward, wiping out all Techno properties in one move. From the amount of smoke in the sky, Shan surmised that they had already begun on the highlands. There was an emptiness in him; he checked his new weapons to see if there were shells in their chambers.

Macalic conferred with the ranking Army officer and redeployed some of their forces; although their heaviest artillery was machine guns and rifle grenades of recent manufacture, the Technos felt reasonably sure that they could, if not defeat the People, then at least extract so dear a price from them that they would be forced to negotiate.

The director of the Yards stationed himself in a well-barricaded machine gun position on the second level of the scaffolding, about fifty feet from the ground and directly across from the main gate, two miles off. The defensive perimeter had been tightened up to form an almost solid ring of machine gun and rifle positions around the edge of the *Victory*'s shadow; black and tan uniforms scurried back and forth below, carrying . . .

A faint yell split the quiet clank of metal and the murmur of busy voices. Shan saw a movement near the main gate; Macalic handed him a pair of battered binoculars. He saw the People, their white clothes stained with black and red from their first battles. Flashes blossomed along the line of the fence, and a torrent of white began pouring through the smoking breaches. They ran forward a bit and then divided, hurrying north and south along the edge of the Yards. For two hours they came, running through the holes and then up to the mountain end of the Yards or down toward the Sea. Running, running until some dropped and were crushed in the rushing tide. Shan could see that many of them had traveled far to reach here, for certainly Gateway could never have housed so many or embraced so many different types. And despite the wildly different kinds of clothing the mob wore, almost every item was dyed a deathly, morbid white. Guns, also white, broke up the oppressive pallor of the mob with the gaping black of their muzzles. Pikes and halberds waved above the crowd; some held crossbows, while others grasped kitchen knives or convenient pieces of wood.

Then there were no more, and the immense crowd stood, two miles from the *Victory*, resting and waiting; their tired, bestial panting sounded like a distant hurricane to the men aboard the ship.

Quiet. Then a new sound, the one Shan had been dreading: engines. The white mass opened at many points and not one, but many tanks of the type that

Annandale had described moved forward. And behind them came yet larger vehicles; terrifying in their sheer mass, guns, antennae and flags sprouting from every possible spot, they rolled out in front of the People, who then closed ranks behind them. Dark, rust-pitted hulls contrasted oddly with the satanic whiteness of the People. Shan picked out the iron fist and winged horse on their turrets; this Coral then, was at the head of it all, for they were carrying his crest. He prayed that Jennings had found and killed the man. The juggernauts drove to a point fifty feet in front of the white mass, and then they too stopped and waited silently.

Five minutes passed. Macalic subconsciously complimented the sense of drama of whoever had planned this operation. The wind drifted in from the west, whistling softly through the naked bones of the *Victory* and bringing with it some small, indefinable trace of corruption.

Then a yell, increasing into an insane roar. Shan swung his binoculars back to the main gate where the People were again opening a path. A colossal tank, three times the size of anything on the field, moved slowly through the passage and continued onward without pausing. The fighting machine was of purest white, edged with delicate gold striping. Shan was paralyzed with fear; every one of its myriad guns seemed to be pointed directly at him. Even at that great distance, the vehicle's engines were easily heard; they sounded like a continuous, never-ending cannonade.

Shan fiddled with the focus of his binoculars and soon made out a man perched on the main turret, his proportions in keeping with the heroic dimensions of the tank—it must have been Coral. The sun sparkled off some object on his right hand; the ring, Shan guessed, thinking how ironical that a single nation should produce a savior, a redeemer, and then a destroyer. In his left hand the man held a glistening broadsword wreathed with blue-white fire.

The fighting machine drove on until it was clear of the masses. The man, his shirt and trousers as white as the metal he clung to, transferred the sword to his right hand and raised it to the sun. Seeming to catch the cosmic burnings, the sword now glowed with a shattering light, yellow flames rising from its tip. "For the Ship then, my People! Kill the bloody bastards who would keep her from you!" The cry drifted across the rapidly diminishing distance with astonishing clarity. The horde picked up the words. "The Ship, the Ship, the Ship . . . !" The chanting swelled with the sound of gunfire and engines until the roaring of the Sea was lost and the wind was silenced in its awful power. "The Ship, the Ship . . . !" Technos and soldiers hunched over their weapons, counting bullets, calculating ranges and arcs of fire. "The Ship, the Ship . . . !" Shan became dimly aware of the hatred that permeated the chanting. "The Ship, the Ship . . . !" A gun was in his hand; he and the men around him began to fall into the brutal tranquillity that Rome had felt at Bloody Ford. "The Ship, the Ship . . . !"

Now it was so clear—here, around Shan and Macalic, the *Victory*, the Technos, the machinery, the steel and iron magnificently cold and inhuman in the afternoon sun. It was the First World in all its tragic power, standing again upon the hangman's drop, as good as dead yet wanting to go in a ruthless, slashing cloud of jagged metal and cordite. The compounded blubber of Shan's plump body sloughed away as he moved into the same creation that the first Ship might have been conceived in. His right hand gripped the automatic with a mechanical fury; the metal grip cut into his fingers and droplets of red flowed from his hand onto the gun, joining the two.

Across the Yards came the People, wild, raging with a passion that could never know the precise, crystalline exactitude that had fallen over Shan. Warm, panting and sweating they ran on, their eyes glazed, their feet moving in long forgotten patterns, their mouths forming a single oath, "The Ship!" Right now, Shan reflected, not a single one of them knew what he was actually doing, while he and all those around him knew exactly what they were about: they were purpose, determination and knowledge, unhindered by clumsy, mindless emotions. The shambling mass that was rushing at them was the World, and that was the kindest thing one could ever say about it.

The tanks, though, were something of a puzzle, for while they seemed to be related to the *Victory*, there was a sense of infinite corruption about them and their crews; but anything that might cause questions about the masses or the tanks was utterly crushed by the concentrated power of Coral and his machine. Of all the thousands of People running toward Shan, only this one could not strike any sort of fear into him.

The wave was less than a quarter of a mile away when both sides fully opened up. A solid sheet of yellow flashes leaped out from the *Victory*'s defense perimeter; a thousand People fell, and several of the smaller tanks vanished in a torrent of heavy grenades. "The Ship, the Ship . . . !" The cry melted into the crashing of big guns, automatic weapons, and bombs.

The nearest tank, the white one bearing Coral, was now less than a hundred yards off; explosions swept away the black and tan uniforms that stood before it. Flame flowers blossomed on its mountainous flanks, but nothing could seem to damage it or touch the giant atop its main turret, his hair plastered back from the muzzle blast of the tank's main batteries.

In an irregular curving line beginning at the main quay on the Tyne and running across the Yards to the Sea, the two forces joined. Macalic was shot through the head, half his skull and brain splattered upon the clean hull of his wondrous *Victory*.

Shan pushed the body of his late superior down into the tempest below, to get a clear field of fire. He used only one of the guns, holding it steadily in both hands and taking dead aim; ten short cracks, reload, ten more, another magazine, ten more. . . . There were no more clips and Shan felt as if the life had been sucked out of him; he felt starved and sick.

He turned to the machine gun position ten feet to his left. The two attendants were dead amid a clutter of empty ammunition boxes, but the gunner was still alive. Shan stared at him, so amazing was his appearance. The man was screaming like a maniac, his reddened eyes bulging from their sockets but still riveted to the sights; his twisted mouth was dripping foam. Even over the thunder of battle, Shan could hear the man's piercing shrieks, revolting and tinged with madness. But the man's body was as cool and mechanical as Shan had been a moment ago. Calmly his hands sighted the gun, pressed the trigger and cleared the action of faulty slugs, while his torso and legs sat rooted to the floor plating. A bullet whistled by Shan and clipped the man lightly on the arm; he swiveled his raging head and glared at the wound briefly before returning his eyes to their work. His arm had not flinched, his body had betrayed not a single evidence of pain. There was only his possessed head that fought to be with the People and with the warm comfort they found in the Myth of the Ship; from the neck down one might have supposed that the man was an accessory of the gun and of the physical thing that was only the *Victory*.

Shan was gripped by an urgent need to fire a gun, that its strength might be his again. He got up and moved quickly toward the raving man. The maniac saw him coming and swung his weapon around, his eyes an extension of the iron sights. A burst tore past Shan to strike musical notes on the Victory's hull; a bullet ripped his feet from under him and he fell into the battle. The man snapped back into his former position just as a shell from Coral's tank punched him and his gun into the Ship's silver skin.

Shan fell, it seemed to him, with extraordinary slowness, drifting like a fat, bloody feather down into the fire and swords. White, black, silver, tan, and red: he alighted on a pile of bodies and bounced off onto the concrete. There was no noise now, not the slightest sound; the whole battle was being performed in pantomime. The colors swirled around him with quiet ease until the black occupied all of it.

✦   ✦   ✦   ·

Shan awoke some time later. It was dusk and the engagement was over. He was paralyzed, with only his eyes retaining any sort of functional ability. He was propped up against the mound of corpses on which he had landed and could see that his left leg was shattered below the knee; better that he should feel nothing.

All around him lay the wreckage of the battle. Coral's white battle machine stood, still untouched, in the middle of a clutter of burned-out tanks. The dead, arrayed in all manner of uniforms, were scattered over the Yards. The columns of smoke were still spiraling up from the Techno highlands, and some fairly large fires were raging in the factory districts. He could not see the *Victory*—it was behind him—but he was sure that any damage even this force might have done would be lost on her vast flanks. The shadow of the Ship cast the whole area into a premature night.

He could see horsedrawn wagons and motor trucks moving through the Yards, their crews wearily loading white-clad bodies into them and sprinkling shovels of lime on the black and tan ones.

Torn banners stirred sadly in the light evening breezes, their brilliant gold and white stained by smoke or blood. A horde of seagulls circled and dived over the field, trying to beat the graves' details to the eyes of the dead.

Shan wished with all his soul that he could cry, but he had by then almost lost the power to even blink. The heap of cadavers shifted and he fell helplessly on his side.

He now saw a large group of Technos directly ahead of him; several thousand, he guessed, for they seemed to be backed up all the way to the main gate. There were many women and children among the captured, so it seemed that the People had not gone on the rampage in the highlands that they might have. A big man, Coral perhaps, was standing on a wagon with a bullhorn held before him. Although he could not hear a word, Shan could easily guess what was going on. The surviving Technos were being given a choice: they could remain and serve the Ship's new captains and escape with them to Home. Or they could leave.

Shan looked closer, for the darkness was getting thicker, and was shocked at what he saw. Many of the Technos were, predictably, weeping or simply sitting on the ground, stunned with sorrow or pain; but one by one, as the tears dried and the sorrows fell into a numb coldness, they raised their eyes, not to the World or to the evening stars, but to the *Victory*. Almost every member of that crowd, Techno and People alike, was entranced by the Ship and with the reality that Coral and his men had suddenly given it.

The choice of leaving must have just been given, for the prisoners were stirring uneasily. Some managed to tear their eyes away from the Ship and looked to their burning homes in the highlands. Others talked earnestly, not looking at each other.

The man with the horn made an appealing gesture. The crowd shifted again and the dying Techno realized that not a single person had stepped forward. *How?* he asked himself, remembering the iron determination of just a few hours ago. Then he remembered his own exact feelings and saw that the courage was summoned in the name of the *Victory*, not for any noble schemes of World reconstruction. The ownership of the *Victory* had shifted and the Technos followed like trained dogs.

He looked up again to see that a single person had stepped forward—a girl, certainly not old enough to be called a woman. Even though her uniform was torn and dirtied, she was still an exceedingly beautiful creature; fair skin, fine features, long gold-yellow hair, she did not belong in this ruin. Hell, Shan thought, she did not belong in the World at all: a First World princess would have been closer to the mark. But her face did not retain the regal calm that her movements expressed. She was confused, and moved her olive eyes first to the *Victory*, then to Coral, to the highlands, and finally to the night sky; she was crying and tried to cover her face with a bloodied right hand. She stared for a second at a young man in the front rows, but he did not see her, so intently was he regarding the Ship.

Shan tried to call to her, but all he could feel was a thin stream of warm blood forcing its way between his lips.

Coral faced her, a curious smile on his face as if he were happy at her leaving. He gestured and a dark coach and two horses trotted up. She boarded and the coach moved off. It was now virtually night, half the sky being richly strewn with stars.

Shan began to forget the girl and worry about his own impending death. *No need to trouble myself about that,* he thought, *here it comes now.* A short stocky man in white was moving along the line of bodies that marked the defense perimeter; he held a pistol and his chest was strung with clip bandoliers. A lime truck and crew followed at a distance.

At each corpse he bent down and felt about the neck for a pulse. If none was found, he passed on; if he found a living Techno or soldier he put the gun to his head before going on to the next. Shan saw only two of the quiet muzzle flashes as the man approached; Shan wondered if a gun were capable of killing someone if he could only see and not hear its shot.

The man was in front of Shan, but all the Techno could see from his position was a pair of boots, painted a dirty white. A hand reached down, but Shan could not feel it touch his neck; he expected the gun to follow but instead the man's tired face came into view. The face saddened and Shan thought he might be saved. The face and boots disappeared. The man moved Shan around, settled him back against the pile and carefully adjusted his head until he was staring almost straight up.

In front and rising out of sight was the ship, now a pale bronze in the twilight, completely filling the world. The starboard wing root began at his extreme left, more than a thousand feet above the Yards; the constellation of Eringold was dimly reflected on the Ship's polished hull.

Shan waited, trying to decide whether to hate or love the *Victory*. At last the man came back, looking as if he had just granted the Techno some divine favor. The man placed himself squarely in front of Shan, his skin now the same color as the Ship's. With an air of infinite benevolence he swung his gun up until it was within six inches of Shan's face. The next thing the Techno saw was a noiseless flash spreading outward from the gun, hiding the man and his Ship behind its brilliance.

XXII

In the two years that followed the Grand Revolution—as one chronicler so admiringly named it—the *Victory* increased its bulk by a good ten percent. The People worked around the clock and a decade of scheduled work was compressed into those two years.

*   *   *

The sole refugee from the Yards, the girl, had started out not having the slightest idea of where she would go. Transportation was provided as far as the Yuma border, but beyond that no help was offered. She struck out to the north, desiring only to escape the Caroline where black and silver uniforms had acquired an unhealthy reputation.

In the third Spring after the Grand Revolution, she landed at Duncarin, capital of the Dresau Islands.

XXIII

At that moment, Admiral Radlov was probably the most powerful man in the World, west of the Tyne delta. And so had been his predecessors, the Admirals of the Fleet, down through a thousand years of history. Under them the Dresau Islands had become mighty beyond all measuring and had imposed their wise rule over seven hundred miles of eastern coastline and thirty major islands. The Islands were also the last archaic holdout of the First World.

Captain Pendred commanded the most powerful weapon in this most powerful of nations, the cruiser *Havengore*. This ship, along with the frigates *Blackthorne* and *Frostfire*, composed what the World called either in legend or in direct report, The Fleet.

It was a bright morning in early Spring when the Talbight estuary was ridding itself of ice, and the mountain streams on Guthrun, the main island, were flushed from the first thaws. The girl had just been escorted from Radlov's office after an extensive interview.

Pendred was then summoned. Although almost twenty years the Admiral's junior, his counsel was often asked in matters of pressing import.

Pendred left his greatcoat in the foyer and entered the office. Admiral Radlov was seated behind a large oaken desk carved from the transom of the ship of the line *Hell Hawk*, of Blackwoods Bay fame. Radlov was an old man, and he showed it more than he cared to admit. The Sea had been a cruel companion to him and had sapped his strength until he could only stand "like a piece of driftwood" and watch the ships. Most of his hair had been torn out by the northern gales and the salt water had eroded his skin until he looked like an abandoned hulk rotting on the mudflats south of Duncarin.

Pendred was merely Radlov twenty years before.

After the preliminary pleasantries and the compliments on the *Havengore*'s recent expedition against the corsairs of New Svald, the Admiral confronted Pendred with the Ship. The Myth of the Ship, the *Victory* itself, the Grand Revolution, and the state of the western World were all related to Pendred from the written testimony of the girl. Pendred, of course, expressed the predictable amazement and then the rapture that most men

experienced when they were told of the real and/or pro-
fessed aims of the Ship. But the delight was not all that
Toriman would have wished it to be, because Pendred
and the Dresau Islands still lived, albeit tenuously, in the
First World, and they retained that age's fierce confidence in itself; what Toriman had sought to resurrect in
the Caroline had not yet died on Guthrun.

Radlov stopped reading and laid down the report; he
sat back in his chair and silently looked out over
Kingsgate Bay. A trim gray schooner was tacking out-
bound with the afternoon tide. Pendred let all the facts
sink in for a moment and then spoke. "And if all of what
this woman tells us is true, sir, what are we to do? Even
if the People do finish this machine and try to fly it, it
will almost certainly kill them all. It can't be intended as
a weapon—they could build fifty Fleets or a hundred air
forces with the effort that they pour into one decade on
this *Victory*. I just can't see how this could affect us."

"You're right there; if the Ship is just that, a vehicle
to carry the scum of the earth to a more comfortable
garbage heap, then it will not affect us. But the original
purpose of the Ship was a part of a hoax. What if it is
still part of a hoax, a bigger and much more insidious
one than the one the Caroline originally had in mind?"

"Then anything might happen."

"Correct. And to help things along, Pendred, I shall
tell you an old seaman's tale. Some of this you'll know,
but other parts are strictly from legends that the Government does not care to see in textbooks and histories.

"Approximately, say, two thousand years ago, there
arose in the center of the World a nation that was supposed to have rivaled the First World in its power and

technical magnificence. Salasar was its name, Ashdown was its capital. It is said that Salasar was originally responsible for the Grayfields and perhaps the Berota Wall, but of course, none of this is readily confirmable.

"Anyway, in their millennial heyday the people of Salasar became much too enamored with their devices and their raw power, leading to corruption and ultimate ruin. An old story.

"It is told, though, that before her demise as an organized nation Salasar's roads, trucks, and aircraft once kept seventy percent of the whole World under her virtually absolute dominion. Eventually, I suppose, even the dominion decayed into outright tyranny. They turned their machines into gods and their rulers into priests." Pendred stirred uneasily and stared at the testimony of the Admiral's desk. "The glory of the First World was first twisted into the shame of this World and then into something much worse."

"If such a thing were possible!"

Radlov sighed. "Much too possible. So the inevitable insurrections and revolutions broke out. Each one was put down with progressively greater brutality until the fires finally caught hold in what is now Mourne and then in the mountain lands of Enom. Warfare spread all around the heart of Salasar and they resorted to . . . to what the peasants call 'unholy' acts in their efforts to preserve their evil rule.

"The final drive began here, on Guthrun and the rest of the Dresau Islands." The Admiral's eyes sparkled faintly with the memories. "A thousand years ago, it was, when the ships and aircraft that had either remained from the First World or had escaped from Salasar gathered in our bays and on our fields. A thousand years ago. Have you heard of the Armageddon legend, Pendred?"

"Yes," the Captain said quietly, "a very, very old story from the First World."

"That's what they thought it was, Armageddon. Sallying forth to defeat the forces of Evil, the Powers of Darkness, to save their immortal souls and end creation.

"So the Fleets, seven thousand ships and fifteen thousand aircraft, left, in conjunction with land forces driving in from the east and north, they engaged Salasar on the plain west of the Tyne delta.

"They didn't end creation, though they might as well have, but perhaps they did save their souls, for they drove the blackest, most dreadful force to ever see the light of day, back across the western mountains to the barren, blasted wastes that lay beyond. The losses"—Radlov's voice trailed off—"the losses were enough to turn that plain into a graveyard fifty by a hundred miles in size.

"The survivors of this misfired Armageddon built the Tyne Fortress to guard the beaten Powers; Gun Hill had been wrecked in the whirl of battle. They built the Westwatch to serve as the eyes of the Fortress. Of the Yards there is no mention; oblique references are seen in the histories of some men, but it is really a moot question.

"The aircraft returned to the Grayfields to sleep and for their pilots to die; the soldiers went home to found new nations, to compose songs of their exploits, but mostly just to forget. The ships—there were less than four thousand now—and their crews returned to the Dresau Islands, founded the Maritime Republics and established the Fleet. But despite all that these survivors did, The First World had just about died. Because it had used the tools of hated Salasar, it became feared by the World it had freed. Of course, the First World is admired today, but most of this World still thinks that a gun kills only people and a wrench can build only destructive machines. I guess that after Aberdeen went down the drain we were just about the only ones left with the old machines and the old, ah, mentality—for what that's worth. The Caroline now has taken its peasants by the hand and shown them that they are the masters of any machine—that it can do nothing unless they will it."

Pendred asked cautiously, "But what has this to do with the *Victory*?"

"Can't you see it? Can't you feel it?" the Admiral said with unexpected intensity.

"Feel what?"

"The hand of the Powers. Look, this whole thing starts when a general that almost nobody ever heard of suddenly calls this Limpkin up to his castle and lays out a beautiful play to rebuild the World. Involving, I might add, a place that no man can say existed before the Powers were defeated; so maybe the Yards aren't as fabulously ancient as the Caroline thought.

"Look at the leadership that sprung up, unassisted if we are to believe the girl, among the People. There are the Armories which somebody set up and secretly geared to assist in the take-over of the Ship and the Caroline." The Admiral glanced around him in frustration. "Well, dammit, Pendred, I can't offer a single shred of concrete proof, not a single definite fact, but the whole cast of the thing, the whole fabric into which these events seem to be woven reeks of a plot of such colossal malignity that the Powers are the only ones that could possibly be behind it."

Pendred began to reexamine the testimony of the girl; he was about to ask a question, but Radlov started up again. "One more thing, Captain, something I neglected to read you from the report. You remember that Coral offered all the Technos their freedom. She says she had no intention of leaving; I suspect that she loves the *Victory* as much as any of them, and the promise of Home more than most."

"Then why . . . ?"

"One of Coral's men, not one of the People's militia, came up behind her and put a bayonet to her back. She was forced to move out and make it appear that she desired to leave. By this time, I gather, she was quite upset and didn't have the slightest idea of what she should do. But she remembers that Coral had smiled at her in a strange manner, motioned, and then a single coach, with provisions for *one* passenger, took her away before she could collect herself. Further, when she was deposited at the Yuma border, she was told quite pointedly that the central World had become most dangerous for Technos ,. ."

"I *still* don't . . . "

" . . . and that the *only* place where she would find safety would be on Guthrun, in the Dresau Islands. And, as 'luck' would have it, she instantly met an out of work mercenary who offered to convey her hither, asking no other reward than her, ah, favors. Interesting chap, from what she tells: tall, middle-aged but still in the flower of his manhood. A scarred face and real martial bearing.

She said that she might have grown to like him, but it seemed to her that his collections of his due on the journey were performed almost totally without passion, as if the man were on some distasteful mission and this were just part of the job and nothing more. Finally our wandering lass remembered that the man carried a gold signet ring, inscribed with a mailed fist and winged horse."

"The crest of Mourne," Pendred said slowly.

"Quite. Mourne, home of such diverse and illustrious personages as our General Toriman, the 'ghost' of Miolnor IV, and more recently Coral, Liberator of the People. Now can you smell it?" The Admiral's voice shaded off from ridicule into a controlled, simmering anger. "Mourne, once the preserver of the World's freedom, now a puppet of the Powers."

Pendred was at a loss to explain his superior's uncharacteristic display of emotion; the Admiral returned to watching the Bay. As Pendred thought harder about what he had just learned, seemingly unrelated facts, little details in the testimony began to change shape and fit with frightening ease into a design whose overall nature still eluded comprehension. "This girl, it would seem that she was selected and brought here specifically to let us know what was going on. Unusual, I should think, for forces engaged in dark plottings."

"Hardly unusual. It's a trap of course," said Radlov impatiently. "Or rather one should say, an invitation. Pendred, we're the last holdout of the First World, the only place on Earth that would be vaguely recognizable to a man from the First Days. The First World should have died at the Tyne Apocalypse, but it didn't—there were survivors. I know that a prophet with a halo on his head, coming walking to us on top of the Sea would suit our preconceptions better than a simple girl, but I cannot help but feel that this will be a final Armageddon for the First World."

"Just for us?" croaked Pendred.

"The First World and its beliefs still live, I hope, in other men and in other nations, although in so small a quantity as to be almost useless. But they will hear this call—indeed, I propose to tell them—and if there is some of the First World in their souls they will move and commit themselves either for or against the new masters of the Dark Powers. Those who do not move—and this will be most of the World's people—will live on. They will not go to the Tyne Delta."

"And this will end, once and for all, the First World."

"And the World, with all its physical horrors and grotesqueries shall reign unchallenged in the universe. Things will be as they should have been."

Pendred's mind was incapable of cogent thought; he blundered around in a fog of forgotten religious myths, new horrors, and now this: the supernatural reduced to brutally natural terms, the spiritual become physical. "What must we do at the Yards if this is the case?"

"We shall attempt to destroy the Ship, a thing which we both know by now to be impossible, and then we shall die."

"And things will be as they should have been," mumbled Pendred bleakly, looking at the floor.

Radlov smiled like a man who has found some small measure of satisfaction in his own impending death. "Captain, we are dying now, anyway. Kingsgate Bay used to be choked with steel ships and what do we have now?

A collection of small sailing ships and three incredibly overage steamships. Give us another hundred years and we'll have trouble defeating a school of tuna. If we just ignore this thing and allow ourselves and all that we value to just crumble into . . . into the World, then we will be no better than the World, and we will deserve its eventual fate. We must go to the Yards, and even if we can't touch the *Victory*, then at least we will give meaning to ourselves in the attempt."

Pendred nodded accord; his heart accepted all that Radlov had said for he had believed it long before he had heard of the Ship, but his mind still weakly fought it. Pendred got up and headed out of the office; the Admiral swung his chair around to face Kingsgate Bay, now rippling gold and silver in the sunset.

"What, specifically, do you plan to do?" Pendred asked at the door.

"Tell the Cabinet, I suppose." Radlov's voice was like dust in the quiet room. "I'll not tell them all, though, of what I've told you; I suspect that several feel such a thing is imminent. I'll just tell them the Ship is a threat to us that we cannot ignore. Then I will recommend that the Fleet be readied and that word be sent to every nation we can find assistance from. The Grayfields will, if at all possible, be resurrected." He said it so resignedly, Penred thought, so calmly did this man call the half-dead corpse of the First World to arms and battle. Radlov continued: "And on some day, more than eighty years from now—it will take at least that long for the Fleet to be completely refitted and for the World to raise its army and forge its weapons, so very many obstacles and difficulties do I see—then we will converge on the Yards."

Pendred shut the door gently and left Navy House.

XXIV

The sun was almost touching the horizon by the time Pendred reached the harbor; he came here often to think, mostly of the *Havengore*, sometimes about a woman who had drowned when the *Obereon* was wrecked off Cape Hale. Despite the dark thoughts, it was a beautiful place, especially now when the western breezes carried the scent of rich fields and new flowers from Kyandra, second largest island in the Dresau Islands and now just visible to the right of the sun. Gulls wheeled overhead, playing among the high masts of gray and black painted sailing ships. Tar, spruce, oak and ash, varnish and fresh forged steel competed with Kyandra's lovely smells. *Defiance, Windmoor, Jewel, Eringold, Vengeance,* and *Janette*: the old names of the vanished ships of the Fleet now floated over the water on the gilt sterns of wooden craft. They were beautiful in the manner of all sailing ships and some of the spirit of the old Fleet seemed to imbue them; but even more than that, they conjured up visions of what the original bearers of those names might have been like. Then the masts lowered and the hulls shrank and one saw behind them row on row of great steel ships, steaming out of the Kingsgate at twenty knots, the breakwater shivering as their wakes hit it. Pendred imagined the grand battle flags unrolled to the morning winds and men, no different from himself, upon the decks.

Pendred walked around the waterfront thinking of such things and wondering if his son's son might have commanded the *Havengore* on that far day.

He almost ran into the girl before he noticed her. Obviously she was the one who had brought the Admiral word of the Yards; the usual Navy rumors had been circulated about her, but Pendred felt that her beauty surpassed all of them. The women of the Dresau Islands tended to be hardy, weather-beaten types, as were their men—heavy of intellect and of limb was the rule, although certain members of the industrial and naval elite violated it quite delightfully. But she was more delicate than any that Pendred had seen. *The Crystal Queen*, Pendred thought, remembering a story he had not heard since childhood.

The two years of hard traveling and the rough attentions of her supposed guardian had hurt her remarkably little. The skin, once so white, had now taken on a slight tan, accenting her large olive eyes all the more. Her hair, turned a deeper gold by the sun, was combed straight, but its sheer richness curved gently around her face to run down her back like a stream of silken threads. Kyandra's winds stirred it and the evening stars gave her a crown to go with the titles that Pendred was silently conferring.

She was wearing a long white dress with a high neck and long, tight sleeves as was the current fashion on Guthrun; it was embroidered with small navy and turquoise blossoms.

He stood looking at her for a minute before it occurred to him that he might introduce himself. He did and was received with surprising politeness. But after the usual courtesies were exchanged the girl returned to her seaward gazing and the man to his fumbling for words.

"Has your Admiral decided to do anything about the *Victory*?" So she did love it, as Radlov had said.

He answered honestly: "He plans to mount an expedition against it."

Her face saddened noticeably. She murmured something indistinct and looked inland where the stars were getting thicker and more brilliant. "Really for the better, I suppose. Still, it could have been so grand, so wonderfully grand. . . . Must you really do it?"

Pendred told her why and she nodded as if she had secretly guessed it all along, but could not admit it to herself. She smiled, not out of any joy or happiness, but from a tender sorrow that Pendred would have thought impossible to express.

Again quiet. Then Pendred offered to show her the *Havengore*. She said that she had seen enough of killing machines in the past several years, but consented.

Pendred's regular launch was waiting further down the quay. The launch threaded its way through the glut of wind ships until a narrow canal was reached. Cast up on the tidal flats that flanked the channel on either side, there lay the dead remnants of the Fleet: burned and twisted wrecks that had come home to die and give up their steel to rebuild their still-living sisters. There was no moon, but the profusion of stars and the clarity of the air provided just enough light to see by, not enough to show the rust-covered wounds of the rotting hulks.

The canal widened until the boat was sailing in another, larger harbor than the Kingsgate: the Stormgate, the anchorage of the Dresau Fleet. All along the far, hill-ringed shores, Pendred said that only a twentieth of it was operational, the rest serving as a parts depot.

To the starboard, two sleek black forms could be seen sparkling in the crystal light. "The frigates *Blackthorne* and *Frostfire.*" Pendred pointed to them. "If you went by the dates on their launching plaques, they would each be over four hundred years old. But, of course, each has been rebuilt so many times that just about the *only* things left over from their first launching are those plaques." They moved closer to the two ships; the white starlight made them look like pieces of sculpture shaped from ebony and edged with silver. The light winds stirred the surface of the Stormgate and the water too was of dark, beaten silver. The girl was quiet, taken up with it all; she could not help but remark on the quiet, powerful beauty of the sleeping machines.

Hearing this, Pendred remarked, "Some day, if you will consent, I think that I shall take you out on the *Frostfire,* the fastest of the three. Forty knots through the cobalt Sea, white spray flying at every hand and all her silken flags unfurled to the winds. Look at her, my lady, look at both of them and see them running out of the Kingsgate, reviving the old legends, all the old greatness and glories. And the *Havengore* steaming after them like a great castle set afloat, crashing through the waves toward . . ."

"Toward the destruction of the *Victory* and themselves."

Pendred fell silent.

Presently another silhouette detached itself from the darkness of the hills. The *Havengore.* Since it was almost three times as long as the two frigates that they had just passed, Pendred thought that it might have extracted some measure of awe from the girl; then he remembered that she had helped build a ship which could carry a hundred *Havengores* in its hold.

The launch luffed up beside a boarding ladder and the two ratings held it fast. They climbed up onto the deck and Pendred showed the way to the bridge, reciting the history of the cruiser as they went. "She was built more than five hundred years ago from the parts of seven older craft. She's seven hundred feet long and can make more than thirty-five knots should circumstances warrant. She is, probably, outside of the Dresau Islands themselves, the largest single, living relic of the First World." They had reached the bridge by now. "And like the Islands, she is dying.

"Look around you and what do you see? A mighty ship designed to defeat nations and humble nature, all guns and gray steel. But in the sunlight, in the light of the World, you can see the rust, the gun tubs that once housed missiles and now carry muzzle-loading cannon, the main battery of nine eight-inch guns crusted with preservative grease—they haven't been fired in almost half a century—radar display casings that now hold astrolabes and sextants."

"And with this you hope to destroy the *Victory*."

"I think that the only thing that we will really destroy will be ourselves. And why not? What is the fault in dying when your world died a thousand years before your own birth?" Pendred's eyes looked to the stars, but he realized that he had really been staring into the reflected light of the girl's eyes. His brutal, doomed world became warmer and the grim destiny that Radlov had charted for the Fleet had become tinged with her own quiet sorrow. He spoke strangely, for certainly his mind in its proper state would have never dared to say such things. "It has become my wish—since Radlov told me of this adventure—that my grandson should be on board my *Havengore* when she last leaves the Stormgate." He took her hand and led her to the commander's sea cabin.

XXV

Pendred was literally enchanted with the girl and the two sailed to the *Havengore* almost every night for a month. Only the launch's ratings knew of it—Pendred's circle of friends was decidedly limited—and their loyalty and discretion was unquestioned.

The Navy and the demands of his command had forced him to forget the fantasies and dreams of elfin, crystal queens, soft voices speaking of nothing greater than quiet and light. Now they all flooded back on him; Radlov's projected Armageddon faded into comparative insignificance. The girl was everything that he had ever desired; her unworldly cast only helped him forget the reality of the *Havengore*'s guns and travel to places that could only exist in the company of a person like her.

But gradually the feelings changed; while she still talked of her dreams and journeys, Pendred became less and less a part of them. Where once the wild speculation had been made lightly, finding their greatest value simply in their telling, they were now personal monologues from which Pendred was almost entirely excluded. If they happened out on deck, she gazed progressively more fixedly at the stars and at what Pendred knew must be Home;

the promise of the *Victory* could have never been obliterated by his small dreamings and the depressing future of his ship. Sometimes he tried with an embarrassing desperation to recapture her imagination with childish visions of Guthrun's wild mountain lands or of the lush forests on Kyandra; every wonder or delight that the Islands might have held were instantly compared to the impossible assets of Home.

He realized that further effort was worthless. "I fear that any son that might have come of this will never set foot upon my poor old *Havengore*," he said absently one night.

"Ah, no," she replied, staring up at the welkin. "He'll sail upon a much finer ship."

"One without a voyage such as Radlov has planned for her, one with no worries of Armageddons." Pendred wondered if she was even listening.

"I guess, although it's not quite like that."

"An end as opposed to a beginning. That it?"

She smiled at him. "You could come with me, you know."

"I could no more go to your ship than you could stay here, with mine." He ran his hand lightly through her hair. "So I will give up trying to make my Islands another Home . . . even for such a prize.

"There is an armed schooner leaving three days from now for the Maritime Republics. From there you can board a coaster and, at Enador, join a caravan along the Donnigol Trace. That will take you, eventually, to the Caroline and from there to the Tyne delta." The girl moved her lips in thanks; Pendred heard only the sandy growl of the surf around the Stormgate.

XXVI

Five years after the girl left, Pendred married. His wife
was also of a delicate manner, coming from the naval
aristocracy, and at times reminded him too much of the
girl. He loved his second wife and lavished all the care
and attention he could upon her and, later, upon his son
and grandson; but it is understandable that when the
Havengore was out on an extended patrol in foreign
waters, and the bridge was deserted save Pendred and
the helmsmen, and his sea cabin twenty feet behind him,
he thought of his crystal queen, so perfect and fair and
so remote from him and his world.

Ten years after the girl left, Admiral Radlov died and
Pendred moved from the cruiser's bridge to Navy House
in Duncarin.

XXVII

When Pendred assumed the post of Admiral of the Fleet,
he found that he had inherited Radlov's plan for the
mobilization of the First World for its final battle.

The plan comprised seven hundred pages of closely
typed print plus another three hundred pages of supporting graphs, charts, and tables to back it up. As a military
man, Pendred was hypnotized by the incredible scope
of the plan. Radlov had called for the opening of more
than thirty Black Libraries—the fact that this might
involve the Islands in several minor wars was taken for
granted. Embassies were to be sent to the twenty-nine
nations which supposedly still had some of the First

World's essence in them. An expeditionary force was to capture the Grayfields in as inconspicuous a manner as possible; there they would, by cannibalizing wrecked aircraft, attempt to produce the first air fleet since the battle at the Tyne delta. Out of the estimated ten thousand planes that Radlov thought had landed there after the Tyne Battle, a total of twenty heavy and thirty light aircraft might be put into flying condition. Confronted by such an overwhelming collection of raw power, on paper at least, Pendred could not help but feel optimistic in his later years. It was in one of these brighter moods that the Admiral composed an addition to Radlov's end-of-the-First-World hypothesis. The battle would be joined, but from it would spring not only spiritual victory, but total physical victory. Confronted by such a mighty host, Pendred conceived, the Dark Powers would be crushed in the battle for their gigantic toy. With the enormous booty that would follow such a triumph, the true and honest reconstruction of the World might begin. And he would be remembered as the ultimate fountainhead of it all; some credit would be given to Radlov, of course, but he was such a defeatist.

XXVIII

Immediately after the end of the Grand Revolution, or the One Week's War as it was known in the south, Coral was elected Chancellor of the Caroline by acclamation.

Coral's first official act of any note was the suppression of those Technos who had chosen to fight on. There were two groups. The first was centered in the mining lands northwest of the Yards, in the mountains. Using the big trucks and equipment and the crude but serviceable weapons that the Armories had distributed to the People's militia, Coral quickly (and sometimes quite literally) crushed the rebels. Within two weeks of the battle at the Yards, high grade ore was again pouring into the smelters around Gateway.

The second band proved a little more tenacious. When the defensive perimeter around the Ship had broken, a number of the Technos had the presence of mind to gather up what weapons they could and retreat within the *Victory*.

For two and a half months the surviving Technos put up a heroic fight, admittedly totally hopeless, but possessing a quixotic charm so absent in the days of the World. They were led by a short little man named Christof Khallerhand.

While only partially complete, the *Victory*'s hull still contained several cubic miles of complex, hidden, compartmented space. And it was Khallerhand and his group who used this labyrinth to its best advantage. The forests surrounding Blackwood's Bay could not have hidden men better.

Coral ordered work resumed on the Ship as soon as the mess around her had been cleared away. But progress was predictably slow, what with Khallerhand jumping out of hatches or drifting through a maze of scaffolding. The very incompleteness of the Ship made hiding easy and pursuit impossible.

Although it is doubtful that more than a handful remember it, there is a little song that commemorates the high point of the resistance; quite catchy and most stirring—which is why Coral personally ordered its repression—it tells of the surrealistic battle that took place in the forward areas of the Ship. The exact lyrics are forgotten, but one can well imagine the story they depicted: tanks rumbling through corridors sixty feet square, phosphorous grenades doing their terrible work, explosions that left compartments coated with the transparent slime that such actions reduce the human body to. The musical pinging of bullets bouncing off the steel could be heard all over the Yards along with the muffled screams of the dying.

Khallerhand had only two hundred men with him, but their knowledge of the Ship's innards allowed them to momentarily defeat Coral's People and hold the forward third of the *Victory* firmly in their grasp for over a week.

At this time, Coral thought that too many potential workers were being lost in what the People of Gateway were calling "the Meatgrinder"; they were also filling the Ship with what many would call ghosts, and a cursed Ship would just not do.

So the section held by the rebels was simply shut up. Iron plate was welded over all entrances, armed guards set around them, and the rebellion was allowed to consume itself; the bodies of plague victims were sealed in with Khallerhand just to make sure. A year later the plates were knocked off and, after the stench had been cleared out, work resumed on that area.

Besides the crude ballad, the only memories of that brief but gallant stand were the occasional black-robed skeletons or rusted guns that workers turned up in obscure corners or in virtually forgotten passages.

Khallerhand had fought and died, not to preserve any high ideas or grand schemes of universal reawakening, but just to retain possession of the god that he had built; there was no difference between him and those of his colleagues who joined Coral; they had all deified the Ship long before the Grand Revolution. Khallerhand had simply adjudged the Techno class, himself specifically, fitter than this upstart Coral to guide the building of the *Victory*. But the song and the sketchy, embroidered tales eventually filtered out into the rest of the World, and it is one of the minor ironies of the history of the Ship that Khallerhand was feted by many as the first true enemy of the Ship.

XXIX

Relieved of the pretense of conforming to the Admiralty's secret schemes, the full resources of an awakened Caroline were channeled openly and totally into the Yards. Along with the new power came new people, a flood of refugees from the misery of the World. Gateway soon burst its old limits and occupied the highlands; the elegant gardens and houses of the Technos were quickly being replaced by shoddy, crowded tenements and narrow streets. Gateway became the largest, richest city in the World, perhaps greater than any that the First World had built.

The great roads leading north and east to the mines and petroleum wells trembled daily under the weight of monstrous trucks. Lights were strung all over the steel scaffolding around the Ship; around-the-clock shifts were instituted.

XXX

Years after the Grand Revolution, when the spirit of that battle was cooling, Coral began to leak ominous prophecies about the jealous and hostile World. "Border incidents," never of much concern before, were now noted by the Government with increasing gravity. Gateway's one pre-revolutionary newspaper, the *Herald,* was now joined by two more Government organs, *Truth* and *The Home-Word.*

The World was a horrible enough place by itself; one hardly needed the strange, anguished animal howlings that the night winds lifted from the west and from beyond the encircling mountains to know that. Now the normally apathetic and crude international relations began to assume the organized horror that haunted the most remote of the Black Libraries. The People of Gateway and the Caroline Empire began to see a barbed ring of hatred being drawn about them. Nations whose existence had been previously limited to quaint legend were now said to be gathering armies against them. The World envied the Caroline and her Ship with a passion that exceeded their love of the First World, and it was out to steal or destroy both the Ship and the Empire. The World, Raud, Enom, the Dresau Islands, Svald, New Svald, the Maritime Republics, Karindale became the all-inclusive "they"—murderers of children, maddened beasts, enemies of the Ship. When the People looked to the east they saw, along with the liquid glint of dragons' eyes, the harsh shine of steel and mail. Stars became signal lamps; wanderers, penitents and lone hunters were the skirmishers for the numberless hordes of the World.

This atmosphere intensified until, seven years after the Grand Revolution, the People's Government uncovered a plot involving a third of the nations of the World in a suicidal assault on the Yards to destroy the Ship with an atomic bomb, or Black Pill as the World called it.

It was this incident, raising the ultimate specter of the Pill, which Coral used to justify his "Program of Security." The first phase was the rounding up of all suspected traitors; there were more of them than anyone could have suspected!

The purge ended, Coral issued his Spring Decrees, part two of the Program. With these fiats the Caroline Empire embarked on a period of activity and growth unmatched since the end of the First World—others, curiously, used Salasar for the comparison. The Army, whose command structure had been obliterated by the Revolution, was swollen to monstrous proportions. Oddly, the men were armed with the crossbows and swords of the World instead of the weapons from the Armories; those weapons had been recalled by the Government after the defeat of Khallerhand. Only a specially recruited elite force had modern guns; those that were left over were either fed into Gateway's furnaces for the Ship or positioned along the border of the Empire. Coral called this last measure an "iron ring from which the People of the Ship could march forth to defeat the World if we are so challenged, and an invincible bastion to which we may always retreat should that eventuality arise."

The Decrees revealed that a huge collection of plans had been discovered in a neglected corner of the rooms below the Yards. Right on the heels of this announcement, Coral said that three riverboats had just brought to the Yards complete plans for the construction of the Ship. Exactly where these boats might have first sailed from was not asked, since everyone assumed that the evil old Admiralty had had the plans secreted away and they had only now been found.

As a result of this almost exhausting succession of discoveries and new programs, Coral announced that the Ship would be ready for launching within seventy-five years, less than half the time allotted by the Admiralty.

Coral spoke of all these things from the unfinished prow of the Ship, his white-robed body almost lost against its vastness but for the sun spotlighting him through a break in the clouds. It had been during the annual celebration of the beginning of the Ship. Below him flew the white and silver of the Empire, the single star still upon it; nearby were the personal flags of the various dignitaries and the subject nations of the Empire. This had been an especially grand day, for the completion of the Ship had finally been brought within the span of a single lifetime; some said that the beginning of the universe could not have been so grand, and others said that *this* was the beginning.

As Coral descended from the Ship, the sun setting, flags and bands all snapping out their own music, and the crowds howling their acclaim, the Tyne Fortress, unnoticed by most, sent forth another one of its missiles toward the barren west. Coral stopped and stared at it, an odd expression on his face. He waited until the rocket had passed above the clouds, then he looked earthward to the blood red sun. "Say goodbye to our star; we shall not be looking on its cruel face for very much longer!" he said for the benefit of those around him. An aide smiled and would have patted Coral on the back, but he thought the better of it and let his lord pass.

XXXI

Two years after the announcement of the Decrees and the Security Program, the new Army of the Empire—exceptional only in its numbers and spirit—began the decades-long People's Wars that were to swallow more than a third of the World before they were through.

As the regiments marched from Gateway, from the Tyne garrisons, from Caltroon, and from a hundred lesser places, the men of the Armories followed them with their great weapons and rooted Coral's "iron ring" to the sterile soil of the World.

The Empire Army carried none of these terrible machines when they left, but at least they found enormous confidence in having those guns protecting their backs. The incongruity of siege guns that were able to plant half a ton of explosives seventy miles away being guarded by horsemen with crossbows and swords bothered no one; in fact, most thought it rather romantic.

XXXII

The final years which separated the beginning of the People's Wars and the ultimate launching of the Ship go by many names. The one given by the lords of Enom is the best: the Burning Time. The two fires, one in the east and one in the west, grew together with agonizing slowness.

In numbers, the Dresau's allies were somewhat less than the Empire. If Coral boasted that the Empire's forces were unparalleled anywhere in human history, he was conceded to be correct. The East found its distinction in comparing their armies with those of the First World, if not in equipment then at least in temperament.

Where the Empire sent forth a faceless tide of its own ruthless citizens, the East assembled a host as diverse as the nations that had contributed to it. Black, red, silver, gold, blue; eagles, dragons, griffins, stars glittered and shone on their shields and banners. Woodland hunters from Raud, hidden from mortal sight by their green and brown cloaks until the silver of their long swords shimmered in enemy eyes; the mountain lords of Enom, befurred and hung with mail and morning stars, their flags of enameled mail, for the gales of their homeland instantly shredded mere silk; short sea-folk from New Svald and the Maritime Republics, looking woefully lost on solid land; tall, quiet marines and guardsmen from the Dresau Islands' new land army, taking obvious pride in their First World guns and vehicles.

A full three score of nations, a thousand tribes, numberless men, wanderers, outcasts, loners who found a grim comfort under the East's rainbow flags and devices—all stood back from the raging fires of the People's Wars, saving what they could but being careful not to waste their strength; all the time, falling back, waiting, preparing, forging new weapons, reforging the broken ones until forty percent of their lands were in Empire hands.

XXXIII

On a day in early summer the last cloudy block of control material was lifted from the Yards and fitted into its appointed place within the Ship; the People looked around themselves and saw that the Ship was finished.

They crowded unbidden out of Gateway and up into the mountains. The Fortress launched another of its endless rockets. The People could only see the *Victory*, shining more beautifully than God in His youth, filling the Yards and reducing even the Sea to comparative nothingness.

Coral stood among them, prouder than anyone. He had not died, and the People had come to associate his impossibly long life and continuing vitality with the same powers that had helped them build the *Victory*. Even the occasional, whispered hint of Coral's possible divinity was greeted by responsive minds.

They watched throughout the day. At that distance no structural seams were visible; the Ship looked as if it had been cast from a single piece of white gold. Night came and presently the moon rose; still the People of the Ship sat atop the mountains. After a while it happened that the silver reflection of the moon upon the Sea traveled from the horizon to the foot of the Yards, mounting the Ship on a titan's scepter. They returned to their homes and waited.

The thought occurred to some that the only people who might have been able to fly the Ship would have been the grandsons of the Technos. When confronted by this question, Coral smiled benignly and told them to trust in the wisdom of the Builders.

To the east, the Army was encountering new successes; they did not yet know of the Ship's completion. Aside from that the Empire was silent for a week.

In the first hours of some morning a hatch opened on top of the *Victory*, and, at seven second intervals, small, dart-like aircraft emerged and flew off to the east, south, and north. No one had built such machines and nothing like them had been brought up from the Yards; the Ship must have made them and therefore the People knew that it was good.

Ten thousand of these darts left the *Victory* during that day, the night, and the following day. One circled over the Yards and Gateway while others vanished in the bright summer air.

Then peace once again, this time only until the dawn of the third day.

Then a huge, booming voice crashed down upon the whole of the known World; majestic and overpowering it was, filling every corner of creation with its glory and triumph. The voice came from the darts, positioned over all of the World, giving voice to the same words at the same time. Rolling like divine thunder the voice spoke these words: "I am the Ship! Come to Me, you children of sadness and pain! I am the Ship! Come to me, for the green and cool quiet of paradise, of Home awaits you and your sons!"

Many looked to their neighbors, or to their wives, or to their children, and gathering a few precious things, started walking east, drawn by the stories and the voice to the Tyne delta. Others looked about them, and into themselves, and sat down to just cry softly and watch their fellows march away. Still others, appearing sadder than all the rest, looked to their guns; the Burning Time was about to end.

The Caroline Army also heard the voice and joyously sheathed their swords. They had built a road from the Yards and from the Caroline into the heart of the World; now this Empire seemed hardly worth the effort. They struck their camps and withdrew.

Now, finally, the dreaded hosts that Coral had spoken of appeared around the whole of the Empire, doubtlessly bent on destroying it in its finest moment. But the People smiled at each other because it was too late.

XXXIV

Admiral of the Fleet Pendred's grandson had neither the personal brilliance nor the time his ancestor had to ascend to such a high rank. When the silver object appeared over Duncarin with its great voice calling him to the Ship, he was the chief gunnery officer on board the *Havengore*.

Eighty years his Grandfather had said it would take, and almost eighty years it was! Beneath Pendred floated a *Havengore* that had recaptured much of its original power. Her great guns had been restored, her turbines were of new steel, and the rust was gone from her armor. In opposition to the diseased white of the Empire, the cruiser and her two smaller consorts had been repainted a glistening black.

Several hundred yards to starboard, the *Blackthorne* and the *Frostfire* rolled in the gentle swell, low and quick in their new guns and colors. Pendred closed his eyes and saw the Fleet of a thousand years ago in similar battle dress.

The voice. A creaking of chains, sirens, and venting steam. The *Frostfire* was the first to move, and then the *Blackthorne*; the *Havengore* fell in behind the two frigates. Black smoke from poorly refined fuel oil poured from their funnels as they ran the canal to the Kingsgate at fifteen knots.

Their wakes washed against the grounded ships on the mudflats. Six hundred hulks of once grand ships watched the passing Fleet in a silence worthy of the dead's eternal dignity.

The channel was quickly cleared and as it opened into the Kingsgate the *Frostfire* quickened the pace to twenty knots.

The quays and streets of Duncarin were deserted; the Dresau Islands' army had departed a month before to join its allies in the west and north. Only a very few people, pathetically confused, stood at the waterfront to bid the Fleet goodbye.

Pendred and his fellow sailors sadly regarded the empty town, now populated only by ghosts and soulless outcasts; it was an infinitely depressing sight. How could it help being otherwise when Duncarin was the corpse

of the Islands, and the Islands were the last corpse of
the First World to finally lie down and die?

Pendred was shaken from his gray thoughts as the
aged cruiser heeled over to starboard. A fresh wind holding the summer scents from Kyandra hit his face.

They cleared the Kingsgate, and although the wakes
of only three ships instead of thousands beat against the
breakwater, it was undeniably the Fleet that was setting
out, again, for the Tyne delta.

The *Havengore* surged ahead into the light chop as
the frigates assumed positions to port and starboard. The
old silken cruising flags were broken out to trail a hundred feet behind the ship's masts. The dolphin and sea
bird crests of the old naval families flew over the eastern
Sea for the first time in a millennium.

Pendred could still hear the dart singing its malignant
song over Guthrun and knew that, indeed, a final Apocalypse was at hand. He felt the fine old steel around him
and the steady pulsing of the turbines. *This* was the ship,
the only kind that a man should sail upon.

XXXV

Garrik, mountain lord of Enom, selected a golden lance
and automatic pistol from his armorer's hands and called
upon his gods to ride with him and his men.

XXXVI

Martin Varnon, citizen of Svald, shouldered his crossbow and set fire to the Empire outpost; he moved off to rejoin his company, already making light contact with the main body of the retreating Empire Army.

XXXVII

Gunnar Egginhard had left his home on Guthrun fifteen years ago to journey across the southern wastes and to await this day.

In his youth he had been one of the better engineers in the Dresau Navy, with a post on the *Havengore* virtually assured him. Then he had heard of Radlov's plans and ideas about the Grayfields; he had thus come to the vast system of interlocking runways and ancient aircraft.

The Grayfields—which some tribes worshiped as the sleeping ground of angels that were waiting for the trumpet call of Judgment to rise and lay waste to the World. Far above Egginhard the voice of the Ship surpassed the power of any Heavenly assemblage.

Around him stood the ruined buildings, pitted runways, and dust heaps of once great planes. In front of him, though, was the concentrated labor of fifty years: twenty flyable planes with more or less trained crews. To his eye, they made up a picture more graceful and mighty than he had ever dreamed of on Guthrun. Legends from the First World, they were, even more than were the three ships of the Fleet.

Their sides had been pierced for cannon and machine gun, their bays filled with powder and Greek fire. He walked to his flagship and ran his hand along her cool, sleek sides, admired the sweep of her wings and the implied power of her engines. The *Victory*, even if she were as graceful as the stories said, was still a bloated parody of the Grayfields' craft; they were clean and came from the hands of men, and so they sailed under the hands of men. The *Victory* was a being unto herself, mysterious and more than a little corrupted in her heritage.

XXXVIII

The man was clad in the glistening white of the People of the Ship. His hair was of a yellow color rarely seen around Gateway in those days. An effort had been made to absorb the Techno class completely into the People, but the man, as his father before him, had clung to his aristocratic past, loving the Ship and the promise of Home in a way that few of the People could understand. But Coral had apparently understood it, for the great man had watched over him and his father, and had singled them out for special attention. Coral never offered any explanation to the man for his concern.

He stood there, along the trailing edge of the starboard wing, five hundred feet above the surface of the Yards. Below him, thin trails of white interspersed with black or brown ran loosely from Gateway to the Ship. A hundred thousand persons lived under his eyes, waiting to be anesthetized and stacked like cordwood in the honey-comb passenger compartments that filled the Ship. Seven feet by three feet by three feet and they said that millions were going to be jammed into the hull and wings, and no one could say exactly how many—the whole World, perhaps.

XXXIX

Kiril had lived longer than anything mortal had a right to, and every day of his life he prayed for death. He had been born a man but the wars, the bombs, the poisons, radiations, heat, and the wizards of Salasar had turned him into a dark, semi-living shape which spent its time in shadow, fearing the sun as normal men fear the night.

A great many years ago, Kiril had come upon the tomb of a king, older even than the First World, and upon the mountain that had been raised over it. Ten years travel-ing due north from Enom had brought him to this cold refuge. Long ago Kiril had eaten the king's mummy and had wrapped his golden coffin around him for warmth. Now he lay calmly, immovable in the granite sarcopha-gus, his body overflowing its confines.

He silently twirled the little metal prayer wheel that he had made before his hands had changed. In between the prayers for death, Kiril thought and perceived and saw that the World into which he had been born was afire.

He saw a curving arm of territory, an Empire that rivaled even Salasar, running from the Sea into the very heart of the World. He saw a ring of modern armaments emplaced, some in the most curious ways, within this arm, guarding its core.

At the eastern end was a great mass of men, some in white and others in all the colors of kings. The white crown was contracting behind the gun wall and literally running to the west and then south to the Tyne Delta.

For a million turns of his prayer wheel, Kiril watched the World tremble and shake as it had in days past when Salasar was being defeated. He saw the Grayfields come alive again, hearing the lonely thunder of its few machines; and he saw the memory of the seven thousand ships of the Dresau Fleet being borne by three small black craft, hurrying to battle.

For a moment Kiril reveled in it. He thought that, indeed, a new day was at hand; then he stopped and saw that it was only the night, made brighter by the hideous burnings of war.

He cried to himself in the king's tomb; he had guessed that even after it had ended, he and his prayer wheel and the grave would remain.

XL

A messenger had brought Egginhard word that the East had passed easily through Coral's gun ring; the Empire was in fast retreat and not even the men from the Armories stopped to man the great weapons. The campaign had dissolved into a foot race, Empire forces halting and fighting only when the East had completely encircled them.

As the two armies traveled west, the pace quickened; now there were only the empty badlands that separated them from the low mountains around the Yards.

By now, if all had gone well, the East should be atop those mountains, waiting for the two Fleets to arrive. An aide ran breathlessly up to Egginhard, holding a black-wrapped baton. Egginhard took the stick and threw it at the sun, laughing. "Now, mate, now!"

He ran quickly for the flagship, hoping that he would remember how to fly the thing; after all, he had only been aloft once before.

He scrambled up the ladder and eased into the commander's chair. Along the sand colored vastness of the Grayfields, the tiny figures of men were seen running through the wreckage and ruin. Three hundred men boarded the twenty airplanes.

Someone atop the flagship launched an orange flare and then jumped inside.

Slowly and with infinite dignity, the eight-and six-engined giants rolled across the runways. Screaming and raging like hurricanes, the air Fleet rose one by one and flew westward.

The few nomads who lived in those regions and who had refused the Ship and the Fleets looked to the skies; many committed suicide. A mere thousand feet from the ground, the airplanes swept toward the Tyne delta in a huge, flattened V.

Egginhard felt no qualms about the certainty of his never returning alive; such things no longer mattered much. He laid his gloved hands on the controls, letting the vibrations soak through his body. He was the master of it all; under his hand did this mightiest of all the East's devices wheel and turn. He was riding a fire and he would ride to his death against the evil of the West. He thought a bomb might be continuously going off inside of him, filling him with energy and inflexible purpose.

XLI

Pendred swung his glasses to starboard at the call of the lookout. Mountains were just visible to the west and several isolated peaks to the east; he focused more finely and saw a thin spike of metal rising, dagger-like, between the eastern mountains.

The Fleet increased speed to twenty-five knots and then to thirty. Signalmen stood by the battleflags.

XLII

Garrik and his fellow mountain lords stood upon the highest ridge above the Yards, marveling at what they saw there. Gateway seethed with scurrying maggot creatures all running for the *Victory.* He turned in his saddle to hear a strange roaring. There before him, twenty small dots quickly grew into a battle line of shining airships. They climbed the mountains and passed overhead; Garrik felt the hard warmth of their engines beat against his armor.

More thunder, from the Sea this time. Three black ships cushioned on catafalques of white foam. The sun glittered off the ships as yellow flashes spurted from their foredecks.

Garrik glanced quickly up and down the ridge.

Kiril, thousands of miles away, shuddered at the battle cries and screams as he saw the three waves descend upon the Yards.

Garrik's men poured out of the mountains like a spring flood, the colors of their shields and armor cutting into the oppressive drabness of Gateway. Already one of the aircraft had lost control and plowed into the city, sending up enormous columns of smoke.

The mounted knights and light infantry cut smoothly through the city; but the Empire Army had set up its perimeter around the Ship and there, in its shadow, the two armies fully joined. The World erupted beneath them.

Five miles at sea now, the Fleet sheered off to the port and loosed its first full broadsides; seven tons of explosives fell on the *Victory*'s hull.

Egginhard led twelve of his machines on a run along the Empire side of the line; Greek fire flowed from their rounded bellies and set a mile of men on fire.

Few could see the Fortress when it awoke, for the *Victory* blocked the view from the east. All could hear it and feel the ground shake violently under their feet. Egginhard climbed above the Ship and saw a brilliant blue fire stirring in the Fortress's hollow center, rising and streaming upward and to the west. It sounded like an impossible, deep siren roar. Where the bolts were landing in the west, there were flashes visible even against the sun.

Egginhard brought the flagship about for another run, the acrid stench of cordite and black powder filling the cockpit. Then a hand roughly grabbed the plane and shook it. Shocked, the copilot looked around and then pointed upstream.

Gun Hill had joined the battle. Egginhard could see the guns, bigger than any four of his proud airships. First one and then the other fired a second round; the muzzle blast flattened the grass for miles around and battered his craft again like a toy.

The motor howl of the Fortress blended in the general bedlam of the battle around the Ship; the majestic rumblings of the Fleet, less than two miles offshore, became cricket chirpings compared to the two weapons on Gun Hill.

Down in the Yards, Garrik drew near to the milling line, skewering an Empire officer on his blade. He drew his pistol and although it killed efficiently enough, it was not violent enough for the mountain lord: its flash was lost in the swirl of steel and its noise was dead an inch from the muzzle. He dismounted and drew an ancient broadsword. Swinging the blade over his head, he waded deeper into the tangled mass of struggling bodies.

Seeing Garrik, his knights rushed to him with mace, sword, and morning star in their armored hands. All around the group, the white masses were turned to red and literally pounded into the concrete of the Yards. Insanely, Garrik started singing; his men joined as a drum regiment from Svald came up behind to beat its murderous war tunes. The old words came steel-edged from Garrik's mouth as he worked deeper and deeper into the Empire line. He felt more powerful than the huge shape that loomed above him, more powerful than anything that had ever lived on Earth. Sparks shot from his sword as it sank into cheap Empire helms and into the softer bone below. The fire from the airships licked close. The glittering swords and polished maces illuminated the scene with a magician's light. The rail-tracks on which the Yard's cranes traveled became big gutters, carrying the blood and shattered limbs down to the reddening Sea.

XLIII

A mile offshore the Fleet began another turn to bring their guns to bear. Penred stood on the *Havengore*'s maintop, rapidly shifting his glass and shouting out target coordinates.

The ancient guns roared majestically enough, but their hits were like match-fires on the *Victory*'s flanks.

The cruiser's captain, Fyfe, glared at the Ship and then yelled some orders down a speaking tube. Signal flags went up the cruiser's mast.

The Fleet lunged forward to ground itself on the Yards. The three ships broke out every flag and banner in their lockers and ran for the beach at forty knots. The agonized creakings of the old hulls were lost in the rising din of battle and in the crash of their own cannon. Forty knots through the white smoke of their guns, trailing the rainbow clusters of pennants. White water burst from the bows as the two frigates and the aged cruiser bounded shoreward.

A and B turrets called up for target bearings. "Targets?" Pendred screamed back. "Targets, you flaming morons? Fire at will! Iron sights! And a forgotten grave to the first gun crew that misses that bleeding Ship!"

The deck jumped and buckled as the five-inch turrets joined the main batteries, and then the twenty and forty millimeter guns cut into the chorus. All but the aftermost batteries were now shelling the Yards. Pendred had never thought the three ships capable of such incredible power, or of himself lusting so in battle. He reminded himself that this was a very special fight, though, and not one to be judged by the standards of previous engagements.

Pendred ran his glass along the starboard wing of the *Victory*. He saw a white figure running along the edge of the wing, golden hair and fair skin still clean in the battle-clouded air. As Pendred looked at the lone figure, a sudden, unexplainable hatred seized him; the closer he looked, the more the man seemed to be his, Pendred's own, double or brother. Pendred found even the suggestion that his image should be serving the Ship intensely disgusting. He also felt a kinship to the man that went beyond physical appearance. Pendred sensed something that had once been beautiful and free in the man's lineage, as he occasionally felt in his own, but here the beauty and freedom had been bludgeoned and shaped to conform to the vague, detestable purposes of the Ship.

"B turret!" Pendred roared into the speaking tube. "B turret, can you hear me?"

"Aye, sir."

"You're under gunnery control now! Remote linkage, remote fire! And load fast, I want your guns as near to full automatic as you can get them!"

"Aye, sir!" came the reply, drunk with sheer violence. "Linkage and fire, remote it is." Pendred swiveled his sighting glass and saw the huge turret below turn in response. He laid his eyes to the crosshairs and caught the man in them.

Pendred opened his mouth to yell, but no sound came out, only a little croak of rage and hatred. His hand closed around the firing button and it turned dead-white with the pressure. Burnings leaped up all around the man, but he escaped. Pendred regarded his bewildered expression as the second salvo was being loaded; he seemed astounded that the fury of the *Havengore* should be turned against him, he who was leading the World's downtrodden to a new paradise. This time Pendred managed a terrifying scream as he pressed the firing buttons. The hits began in back of the man and walked down upon him with fantastic slowness; the first petrified him with fear, the second blew him off his feet, the last caught him in midair and slammed him brutally to the deck, crushing him with its weight of liquid iron and burning air.

Pendred twisted himself away from the sighting scope, a savage feeling of fulfillment coursing through him. "B turret, yours again!" The iron can immediately swung and trained its cannon on some target to starboard.

The Fleet closed up and charged down the mile long channel that led from the Yards to deep water. Some of the few weapons that had been dragged away from Coral's ring shifted their attention from the Yards to the seaward attack; a battery of four field guns set up near the beach cut loose at the closest ship, the *Frostfire.* The little frigate was straddled but her speed saved her. A single cannonade from the *Havengore* swept that section of the beach clear, silencing the Empire guns.

The cruiser was now in the van and less than half a mile from the concrete apron; she veered to the starboard, aiming to hit just beside the ways. The *Frostfire* swung off harder to the right, seeking to bring herself up obliquely against the beach, more than a mile from the cruiser. The *Blackthorne* headed for the port side of the ways, where the fighting was a bit lighter.

Pendred wrapped himself around the mast as the *Havengore* neared the beach. He estimated that the ship was pounding along at better than forty-five knots, an impossible figure even in the ship's youth. But forty knots it was; the boiler room gang stood awestruck in front of their gauges, beholding an honest miracle.

The *Havengore* hit and ground her way up onto the beach. Her old hull broke under the impact and shredded to pieces. She settled quickly into the shallow water and was peaceful for a second while her men picked themselves off her decks.

Then came the sounds, of two more metallic shrieks as the frigates hit. A turret sent three eight-inch rounds off into the *Victory*'s wing as it curved away overhead. B turret planted her shells into an Empire battery that was firing into the swirl of color where Garrik's pennants could be seen. The smaller guns joined in, the port side firing point-blank into the after-belly of the Ship; the starboard batteries simply pushed a wall of flame away from the cruiser.

The *Havengore* was pouring fire, like water from a hose, into the pale thousands that surrounded her. The *Frostfire* was another fire-font, stamping the white masses into the ground and viciously ripping the skin from the *Victory*.

The *Blackthorne* was also doing her terrible work, but her men could see the Tyne Fortress and Gun Hill alive and at the work they had been built for—and they saw the bursts of light and smoke that marked their targets, far beyond the western mountains.

XLIV

The Tyne Delta quaked to the rhythm of the battle; a million men were marshalled on each side and they turned and blended into a nightmare tangle of combat around the silver Ship.

The East had still not reached the Ship. Above the fight, its great ports closed with their millions inside, and the Ship's men hardened their resolve. They would not sail upon the Ship, but their sons and wives would and that was enough.

Men began to bleed from the ears as the incredible noise of the battle burst their eardrums. They did not notice.

The *Victory* stirred. Somewhere in her labyrinthine hold a block of crystal began to send out the commands that had been engraved inside of it.

At almost the same instant, the men of the *Blackthorne* stared west. Under the light of the Fortress a great low darkness arose from the western shore of the Tyne delta. With a roaring of deep trumpets and battle cries, the cloud, now bristling with thin flashes of steel, swept across the plain and across the Tyne, parting so as not to hinder the Fortress in its work.

And the dead of the First World, vague yet terribly distinct at times, marched onto the Yards. The men of the East, their minds already reeling from the violence of the battle, saw no incongruity in the dead of the first Tyne battle coming to their aid. Many of the People found both armored and skeletal hands at their throats, crushing the life out of them. And Pendred, glancing briefly to the Sea, saw that the old Fleet had returned to assist the last of their race; a fog lay offshore where none had lain before, and thunder and cordite lightning flashed out of it.

Egginhard, delirious with the scope of the conflict, brought the flagship down for yet another run on the Ship. He looked upward and in that second it seemed to him that thousands of gleaming silver craft had suddenly filled the sky and were even now diving down with him, upon the Yards. Egginhard, foam dripping from his mouth, his mind burning with a divine hatred for the Ship, dismissed this vision as an illusion. But as he neared the Ship a great roaring of engines rose until it became so great as to be a silence. Blood spurted from his ears as he pushed the stick hard forward.

Egginhard died, his face and upper torso mangled by shrapnel; the flagship shed its wings and fell vertically onto the *Victory.* It hit, gouging a crater a hundred feet across in the hull of the Ship.

All organization was dissolved, all units were broken. The three armies, the Fleets, the Hill and the Fortress swirled and rumbled about the Ship with mind-shattering fury.

Kiril screamed at his visions and while he did not die, his mind broke into a blood-drenched ruin; the prayer wheel stopped in his hand, its appeals more or less answered.

The dead of the First World lived and strove beside the men of the East, tearing the white bodies apart with their hands and throwing the dripping remains at the uncaring hull of the Ship.

Suddenly, vast supports shot out horizontally from the ways and the towers that supported the wingtips of the *Victory* toppled, crushing hundreds. The *Victory* began to move; a wingtip dipped low, shoving the tiny *Frostfire* into the Sea. Plates and supports rained down from the ways, pounding the *Havengore* into a senseless tangle from which only a few guns still fired.

Like a wall, the hull slid from the Yards, exposing the battle to sudden sunlight. Pushing a tidal wave before her, the Ship settled into the Sea.

She turned with astonishing speed until her tail pointed to the Yards. A burst from her engines sent an unbroken sheet of white fire three miles across sweeping over the Yards and through Gateway. The Ship moved forward as her exhausts incinerated every living thing on the eastern bank of the Tyne. When she was a mile from the beach, great movable slabs of metal slid out from her wings and pivoted into the blast of the engines. The Ship rocked slightly, sending scalding waves ashore as the thrust reversers, originally designed to slow her in the oceans of Home, deliberately turned the fire upon herself.

The white sheet now played over the wings and hull, turning the Ship cherry red. Under this new direction of thrust, the Ship plowed backward to the Yards, a cloud of steam rising before her. The few that had hung back in the mountains and had not yet died saw the actions of the Ship and wondered what had gone wrong. But they guessed that nothing had gone wrong, so deliberately, so precisely did the Ship go about her own immolation and that of the millions who slept within her. The slabs, though white-hot and on the verge of collapse, still functioned and adjusted themselves with disturbing facility so as to bring the maximum of heat back on the Ship; the engines throttled themselves so as not to destroy these plates.

With a noise that was somewhere between a shriek and a detonation, the Ship, glowing red at the nose and white-orange further aft, hit the apron and began blasting her way back up the slipway.

She had only brought the first several feet of her tail ashore when the streams of fire that were still flowing along her hull were suddenly polluted with thin black streaks from which a new, darker, blaze shot. The Ship disappeared behind a billowing mist that escaped from her new wounds, drowning her in her own fire-vomit. Through the cloud could be heard a wailing that was obviously the protest of shattering steel, but as in all dying ships, sounded dreadfully human.

Then came a silence so great that the unabated firing from Gun Hill and the Fortress and the busy steamings of the Sea were only like the crying of a child at night. The quiet passed as Gateway began to burn, its shoddy frame dwellings and factories offering fuel second only to the human wreckage that covered the Yards. The entire eastern bank of the Tyne delta was burning; the flames climbed upward, joined and twisted together, creating a fire-storm; bodies and ruins melted instantly, solid rock and metal began to slag down in spots, the eastern side of the Westwatch blackened and split.

Sensing that the battle had ended, the West finally bestirred itself. A pale orange glow and vast quantities of smoke rose above the distant mountains; two brilliant, noiseless flashes—one directly to the west, the other from the direction of Mourne—cast the shadows of the western mountains over the Yards, even though it was early afternoon.

Arching across the sky, two glowing balls, so hot that their monstrous cores were colored a deep ebony, tore through the smoke and cloud cover above the Yards. They were colossal, indistinct bodies, pulsing with uncontainable energy; their heat set the plains below on fire and crushed the small bits of wandering darkness that were still looking for their old graves. The Sea was boiling from horizon to horizon.

The two bodies descended on an apparent collision course, but their targets were the Fortress and Gun Hill. The western ball roared down and merged with the fire-stream that the Fortress was still pouring out; the one from Mourne simultaneously disappeared into the muzzle blasts of Gun Hill's great cannons.

Again there was no sound, only a light that was first blue and then white and then black. The Tyne delta lived for a second in a night as absolute and as grotesquely perverted as any Hell could have produced.

The darkness slacked off and the shock wave rolled outward from the two impact points, snuffing out the fires that had spawned it and sweeping the delta clean of almost all that had previously existed there. Only a gaunt and twisted skeleton reached a mile and a half out to sea and spread its broken wings over the Yard's concrete beaches. Gateway was marked only by a few isolated foundations and the great roads of the Builders.

A charred stump, fifty feet high and overrun with slag, was all that remained of the Westwatch; it still glowed and bubbled from the heat.

Gun Hill and the low hills on the western bank had been utterly leveled; no trace of the guns was left. There was only a great scattering of tiny metal shards.

Unbelievably, the Fortress had survived in some recognizable condition. It was little more than a huge cinder on a plain of blackened ash now, but one could still make out the shape of its hexagonal walls. The machinery that had lived within the Fortress, and which had been built to contain the Powers, had melted and run out into the center court, filling it and solidifying. The basic shell of the Fortress remained, dead and barren, and its vast dimensions would serve as an appropriately monumental tombstone for the armies that had fought and died on the Yards.

XLV

The wreck of Gateway and the Yards cooled, undisturbed for the better part of three months. The ashen soil of the plain on the west bank of the Tyne was lifted by the winds of summer and early fall, exposing, in spots, the white gleamings of ancient bones; in some places, large chunks of earth had been gouged away to display whole skeletons in the remains of their millennial armor; some of the skeletal hands still held rust-covered swords, newly bloodied.

XLVI

When the dust storms had reburied the remains of the first Tyne Apocalypse and had at least spread a thin coating of dust over the rotting remains of the second, and when all had cooled to a bearable temperature, a small speck appeared on the southwestern horizon of the Sea.

The dot grew larger. It was a raft, large and grim, painted in grays and blacks with occasional highlights of gold. All over the craft ran strange and oddly frightening figures and symbols; the armored fist and flying horse of Mourne were enthroned upon the raft's lofty transom piece. It was pulled by a squadron of aquatic half-men, all of the same, fish-like cast. They were green, though more of simple rot than of the green of life; they pulled the raft by steel cables which had been thoughtfully inserted into their bodies and looped around their artificially reinforced spines, tying them forever to it.

The repellent swimmers drew the raft past the hulk of the *Victory* and threaded the maze of islands until they reached what was left of Gateway's main quay. Finding a convenient spot, they came alongside, and the man who had been called Toriman debarked.

He was dressed in black metal, masterfully trimmed with fine, gold scroll-work. A scabbard made of hand-wrought silver in an open mesh fashion held a magnificent sword; heavy jewels were set into its pommel and many rune engravings could be seen running along its blade. The man who had been called the ghost of Miolnor IV carried his battle gear lightly, as if it had been made of silk instead of the finest steel.

The man Rome had called General Tenn walked from his barge and across the Yards.

The man who had been called Coral stopped to gaze at the still overpowering outlines of the *Victory;* then he looked around the east bank of the Tyne, for evidence was still to be found of the battle, the casings of half-melted guns, the shattered lances. The armored man sighed sadly, for many more had answered his invitation than he had anticipated; he thought briefly of a woman, lost many years ago, but instantly forced her from his mind. Too many men had found fragments of the First World still alive within them and had risen to the challenge. And they had almost won; but that did not matter, for they had but to fight a little—just enough to prove their faith, and then die—for them to win. Ah, but the metaphysical complications of it all were so tedious; the armored man nostalgically remembered the simplicity of life and death in the days of his youth and mortality.

But the victory that the East had won was a very personal one; one which extended no farther than the individual soul of each individual who had fallen at the Yards. Creation had been set aright and it was this man who had made sure that the Powers would be in a position of dominance. He had wiped out the flower of the East's fighting men; before him ran a heavily protected road that led straight into the strategic center of the World where seventy percent of its original population lay, helpless and spiritually naked.

The armored man made sure that all was well, all was dead. Pleased, he strode over to a cracked and blackened stone heap near the northern end of the Yards. To his left were the foundations of George XXVIII's tomb; its size had absorbed too much heat and energy to leave anything more than melted slag and a hole where the sarcophagus had been. The bones of poor old George had long since been blown east.

To the man's right a smaller tomb, that of Sir Henry Limpkin, still stood; its smaller size and the shielding effect of the larger building had saved it.

The armored man drew his sword and delicately peeled the steel door away from its frame. Opening it, he sheathed the weapon and stepped inside. It was dark, but the man had long ago ceased to consider light necessary for routine activity.

He easily lifted the lids off of Limpkin's three traditional coffins of iron, lead and sandalwood. He reached in and found the model of the *Victory* that he had given the civil servant more than one hundred and fifty years ago; it was resting on Limpkin's ribcage, his talons clasping it peacefully.

The armored man cleared away the dirt and finger bones that had stuck to the model and took it out into the sunlight. He admired it, letting the sun play over its silver contours as Limpkin had once done. He removed his right gauntlet and laid it on a nearby pile of rubble and bones that had melted together.

He took the golden ring from his hand and fitted it around the nose of the model. Small panels, suddenly limber despite their age, shifted and the ring slid into the little hull until only the crest, the fist and pegasus, remained visible on the dorsal side. The armored man felt a tremendous sense of completion and satisfaction now. He seated the craft firmly in his hand and drew back; he aimed straight for the sun as if he could hit and sunder it with so small a missile. The man hurled the model skyward.

Instead of slowing, the miniature *Victory* gained speed until it was lost. A mile or so over the Yards the model blew itself apart. It became a black flare, made of the same kind of fire that had destroyed Gun Hill and the Fortress. The black light stained the sky and spread cancerously over the sun.

In answer to the man's signal, similar dark brilliants rose above the western mountains from the Sea all the way to the northern horizon, as the thing that Salasar had become prepared to march east.

Out of the Mouth
of the Dragon

To Kenyan College,
and to the men I knew there.

Out of the Mouth of the Dragon

Because God put His adamantine fate
    Between my sullen heart and its desire,
I swore that I would burst the Iron Gate,
    Rise up, and curse Him on His throne of fire.
Earth shuddered at my crown of blasphemy.
    But Love was as a flame about my feet;
Proud up the Golden Stair I strode; and beat
    Thrice on the Gate, and entered with a cry—

All the great courts were quiet in the sun.
    And full of vacant echoes: moss had grown
Over the glassy pavement, and begun
    To creep within the dusty council-halls.
An idle wind blew round an empty throne
    And stirred the heavy curtains on the walls.

Failure
by Rupert Brooke

"And then I saw three unclean spirits like frogs come out of the mouth of the dragon, and out of the mouth of the beast, and out of the mouth of the false prophet.

"For they are the spirits of devils, working miracles, which go forth unto the kings of the earth of the whole world, to gather them to the battle of that great day of God Almighty.

"And he gathered them together into a place called in the Hebrew tongue, Armageddon."

—Revelations 16: 13, 14, 16

*   *   *

"And I saw the beast and the kings of the earth and their armies, gathered together to make war against him that sat on the horse, and against his army.

"And the beast was taken and with him the false prophet that wrought miracles before him with which he deceived them that had received the mark of the beast, and them that worshiped his image. These both were cast alive into a lake of fire burning with brimstone.

"And the remnant were slain with the sword of him that sat upon the horse, which sword proceeded out of his mouth; and the fowls were filled with their flesh."

—Revelations 19: 19, 20, 21

*   *   *

"And they went up on the breadth of the earth, and compassed the camp of the saints about, and the beloved city: and fire came down from God out of heaven, and devoured them."

—Revelations 20: 9

*   *   *

"And all that was written was accomplished in the fullness of his wisdom and majesty: the captains, their armies, and all of the nations of the earth were encircled with the fire and consumed, even unto ashes and dust.

"But among the ashes and the heaps of dust there lived men that had pledged neither loyalty nor had worshiped him upon the horse or the beast. And in time these men raised upon the land their own nations and appointed their own captains and began to worship, each unto the dictates of his own mind.

"But they were men of ash as were their nations, and little grew upon the land save hatred and frustration. So all lived with the hope of yet another final battle, one where the fire would consume all, and the chasm between the worlds would divide and swallow all, even the ash."

—Survivors 17: 6, 7, 8

     ✿   ✿   ✿

"But again mankind was divided and set upon the plain of Armageddon, although it was called Tynemorgan by the men of Salasar, and again the battle was joined and darkness overthrown by light, and yet again the ashes of battle and the men of ash still lived. And at the sight of them strange wailings were heard beyond the sun; a great sadness swept out of the heart of God and into the soul of the ashen nations. Again, though, the hope of yet another ending helped to turn the ash into flesh and blood."

—Book of Eric 2: 37

     ✿   ✿   ✿

" 'Who are these men?' he asked me, his face twisted with anxiety. 'They come into our towns and homes and our own brothers become like them, like madmen possessed by ideas which I cannot even begin to fathom. Who are they?' he asked again.

" 'I don't know.'

" 'My own brother!' He railed on, 'He takes one look at that beggar and then it seems like he, he . . . And then that fleet, those ships come and he leaves without a word to me or to his family. God! With ships like those one could rule nations, ransom any throne on earth! But no, he and the others who betrayed us just got on and left. Men who I thought I had known all my life, they turned on me and left. Who are they?' 'I don't know.' "

—Dialogues of Moreth, *Chapter IV*

          ✿   ✿   ✿

"The battles continue, the last being in memory of my grandfather, breaking and crushing the land into dust compounded; all the Books are erased and many of man's arts have fled his mind.

"There is a thing, a strange melancholy that grows on this world and makes the efforts of men as barren as the soil they are founded upon. Now even the armies that are raised by men to defeat evil fall apart and disintegrate before the battle plain is reached.

"The cancer seems to have invaded more than earth and the hearts of mere men. The clockworks of creation have shorn their gears; stars do not appear at their appointed times; the seasons fail to conform to their immortal standards; and even the surety of a death of pain and damnation begins to seem favorable to the bleeding perversity of earth."

—*Inscription on a ruined gate at the Black Library at Iriam, chronology unknown*

I

The ship had been badly hurt at the Meadows, and her wounds showed pale yellow and rust in the afternoon sun. Almost a year to the day, she had steamed proudly out of the Goerlin Estuary, eighty of her sisters at either side. There had been battleships afloat on that day, an aircraft carrier, cruisers like herself, and fast destroyers. Now only she remained alive.

All the fading might and wealth and tradition of the Maritime Republics had sailed with that fleet; their flags and the arms of their great houses, all committed to fight on what they judged to be the proper side at the Meadows. By rights, not one should have returned, or even have had a place to return to.

So they had fought, valiantly in many cases, and those empty souls who had chosen to remain behind had seen the night sky burning and felt the ground ripple imperceptibly, even though the Meadows were over two thousand miles away. Surely, if anything could end time and creation, the battle that had erupted upon the Meadows would have done it.

They, the empty people, had found a curious comfort in those days, while the western highlands were edged with red and their china rattled impolitely at teatime. They had even begun to pride themselves in being able to view the situation impartially, free from the passions of those who had embroiled themselves in the struggle. "The plan of creation," wrote Moreth in one of his last Dialogues—how easily he handled such terms, "naturally contains form, content, and a goal at which the first two qualities are aimed. It is further natural that the goal should remain permanently aloof from mortal comprehension; the content is, simply, history; the form, one may safely conclude on the most elementary level, is time. Time is, ultimately, a finite quantity, for if it is divorced from limits, then it ceases to be time and becomes eternity, regardless of how many changes may be contained within it.

"The beginning of time went unrecorded because of the simple absence of observers; but now, at the end, there are observers, men such as myself who feel relief and awe in seeing creation so neatly trimmed off.

"We find relief in that this capstone to time and the universe and all the accompanying phenomena serve finally to illuminate the hand of a true Creator, lying beyond time and mere physical presence. All the brilliant sophistries of dead atheists have fallen before the fulfillment of *Revelations, Survivors,* and the *Book of Eric.*

True, these Books have spoken of other battles that were supposed to have ended time, but one can only ascribe poor judgment to their writers, most probably brought on by a feeling of weariness and a disgust with the state of the world.

"But now, we are sure, the final battle is joined, and I have every confidence that those who have committed themselves to the Creator shall carry the day and thus ensure their and their ancestors' salvation.

"I, myself, have not gone to the Meadows. I have, instead, chosen to await the end in my own house, surrounded by my writings and my thoughts. Strange, though I can apparently view the situation with gratifying coolness and objectivity, I could not bring myself to swear allegiance to either side; it could well be that this apathy (that is the wrong word) will be rewarded with eternal damnation. Or it could be that my eldest son, a turret captain on the battleship *Eringold,* may save me (and what of my other two sons? I suspect that they have joined the enemy, but I must not think of that). I have no idea of what shall become of me or of this thing called my soul, and, in the end, I really do not care. Like the authors of *Survivors* and *Eric,* I am tired; I feel that I have long overstayed my time on earth, just as I feel that earth has itself overstayed its proper time."

When the bleeding ship entered the harbor, Moreth drove his sword hilt into the ground and fell upon the blade.

Forty percent of the city's original population had stayed behind, immobilized by confusion or the hopeful emptiness such as had afflicted Moreth. Most of those who had not taken their own lives by that time slowly made their way down to the harbor to see the ship, not to greet her, for they knew that her survival meant that time was to continue and the grinding agony of previous ages would once again be multiplied.

She was named the *Havengore,* after another cruiser which had fought at a previous false-Armageddon; now she was as tragic as her namesake must once have been for they were both, in their time, the lone surviving great ship of once-powerful fleets.

The first *Havengore* had finally contrived to die an honorable death in a battle which, if it did not accomplish all that it was intended to, at least offered an appropriate death to all who fought there. Yet, so disorganized had the battles become that now there were survivors, men and ships even more confused than those who had never gone to the Meadows; they were the ash-men spoken of in *Survivors* and *Eric.* They had heard voices which had instilled in them an absolutely unshakable conviction that *this,* finally, was to be the last act of mankind. They had seen things after which a man had almost no choice but to die. They had fought alongside angels, against demons and devils; and when the noise and smoke had settled, they found themselves alone on the Meadows. The armies had vanished as one would have thought, leaving only their equipment behind to show the survivors there had indeed been a battle. They also left behind pain and despair and hopelessness that was beyond words.

It had taken eight months for the battered cruiser to sail home, dropping off men along the coast, stopping now and then to jury-rig some particularly desperate repairs. She brought five hundred of the Republics' men with her, men who were still trying to decide if they had in some way failed to act in the manner which had been expected of them, or if they had been deserted by their commanders.

She slid past the breakwater at three knots, her twisted and mutilated hull leaving a multitude of small wakes in the quiet water. "B" turret was gone and the bridge immediately behind it had been caved in. The wing of the aircraft which had rammed the ship at that point jutted out over "A" turret, bent and warped from the fires which had welded it to the decks. Three holes of varying diameter could be seen at the waterline; the crane at the stern was bent down until its tip trailed in the water. She was scorched in many places from fires and most of her secondary armament appeared to be out of commission. Two of the seven Republics' flags hung uncertainly at three-quarters mast.

It was very quiet. Not even the sea gulls called any welcome to her; most of them had left with the fleet, a year before. Only silent people, who looked as if they had not slept for months, stared out at the ship and at men who looked distressingly like themselves. The loudest noise was the falling of water as the *Havengore*'s pumps tried to limit the ship's portside list to five degrees.

They all wondered what they should do now. Cry, suicide, accuse someone, anyone? But men could be seen working aboard the cruiser, caring for her, trying to ease her spin; they brought her through the harbor, heading for the shallow water which flanked the mouth of the Goerlin River. The engines were stopped and the remaining anchor let down. By dusk the *Havengore* had settled into the sand on a roughly even keel, the water about ten feet above the waterline.

By noon of the next day they had taken the dead off the cruiser and most of the living; some of her original crew had elected to stay with her, for a while at least.

The shock over the failure of the Meadow War lingered over the city and its reduced population for more than a year. Then, quoting reassuring verses from Scripture or just swearing, the people began to reorganize, giving the city some semblance of its former life.

Aside from the stunted renewal of trade and farming, two great projects came to occupy the city. The first of these was the building of a great cathedral. The predictable reactions to the War's failure would have hardly seemed to have pointed in such a direction, but, with time, as people became accustomed to the world which they were now forced to live in, as they heard even more clearly the wind howling through empty houses and across the lonely earth, they were thrown back upon their initial faith. Perhaps the War would have ended time if they all had gone to the Meadows? Perhaps there were undetected flaws in those who went which prevented a successful conclusion to time?

Besides, when you could bury your life under a slowly growing mosaic proclaiming the glories of the Creator, the taste of your hopes seemed a little less bitter. Eventually some of the men who had seen things which they were sure would cause madness came to look upon those memories as miracles, divine gifts to be treasured for their splendor. The speculations on a failure on the part of the deity grew progressively weaker as the cathedral became a symbol of continuing heavenly favor.

The church was built on top of a small hill, to the west of the city walls. From its steps a road of marble slabs was laid, through the Artillery Gate, where it met the Avenue of Victories with its columns and monuments to ancient battles; then straight down to the harbor and the Sea past the breakwater.

It was quite a splendid road and found a great deal of favor with what still remained of the commercial and landed aristocracy. It became something of a ritual to take one's family out of the city on summer evenings, up to the cathedral to inspect its glacial progress, to comment on some particularly beautiful piece of stained glass which had just arrived from Ihetah-Incalam or wrought iron from New Svald. They stayed there talking with their friends because it was cool and the smells of the inner city could not reach their nostrils. But mostly, they waited for it to get dark, so on walking home, they could not see the dirty, deserted city and harbor.

They seldom visited the harbor anymore and even the briefly revived sea trade soon began to wither. The city became more insulated from the rest of the world, carrying on its chief business within itself, venturing outside only to secure certain luxuries it could not manufacture domestically. The last steel merchantmen had vanished long before the fleet had sailed to the Meadows, but even then a sizable collection of wooden steam and sailing ships had helped to tie the city with such distant points as the Dresau Islands and the crumbling petrochemical establishments of Cynibal on Blackwoods Bay. Now most of these were gone too, partly because the city's great men no longer saw much reason to journey abroad, and also because the War had effectively removed the old technologies and wealths which had made trade worthwhile. Everywhere in the world, only the merest shadow of what had been remained; and what had been was precious little in the first place.

Aside from the cathedral, the only real activity to be found was at the Old Navy Dock. From there a feeble but steady stream of small boats and rafts sailed the short distance to where the old cruiser was still aground. The reconstruction of the ship was looked upon with a good deal less sympathy than was the cathedral by most of the city. Most of the people who had been to the War remained with the ship as did many of the old sailing men who, although they had not gone to the Meadows, found more comfort in working with armor plate than with glass and ornamental iron. Less than a third of the War's veterans devoted themselves to the new cathedral, but along with them were virtually all of the non-seafaring folk who had stayed home, looking now, perhaps, for a convenient way to prove that they too had found a commitment to the Creator and therefore should not be forgotten when the *real* Armageddon was finally called.

In ten years' time they had laid the foundations and the floor of the nave; the cruiser had also shown much progress and was approaching a marginally seaworthy state, but then only the people directly connected with her really cared. True, there had been a rather ugly confrontation between the aged naval officers who had laid claim to her and the officials of the municipal government who suddenly perceived some advantage in having the only steam-driven, steel warship on the coast (excepting, that is, Enador's two river monitors). The issue was resolved when two five-inch shells landed in front of the cathedral; the only casualty was a draft horse, but the point was made.

The seafarers said they were going back to the Meadows, if they could find them, to join other stragglers and fight against still more stragglers. The city was glad to be rid of the rusting hulk and her crew of fanatics. In the eleven years since the cruiser had returned, and thus alerted the eastern shorelands of the world to the failure of the War, the messianic, all-consuming faith that had first sent them to the Meadows had become less and less fashionable. Even the memories of what some men had seen faded; eventually they passed from the stage of memory to lapse back into the form of Scriptural allegory, back into the turns of phrase they had worn before assuming concrete form, for a little while, on earth.

The cathedral now not only allowed one to feel a bit less pain—working on the cruiser could do that—but also inspired new thoughts of a reassuringly familiar and distant character. The cruiser would, within the foreseeable future, sail back and try to die again; but the cathedral, with its eternal immovability, its artistry, was comfortably removed from the brutal reality that seemed to keep trying to re-impose its rule over the earth.

It was in the early fall when the great ship staggered past the breakwater, heavy black smoke from low-grade fuel oil pouring from her stacks. There were no flags, no crowds to see her off as there had been twelve years ago. Her existence was quickly forgotten; the city continued its policies of conscious and unconscious contraction, encysting itself from its fellow, similarly encysted city-states, with only the cathedral growing.

The cathedral itself was finished within a hundred years of its beginning, two decades ahead of schedule. Of course, its building had virtually ruined an already frail economy; but at least its magnificence could blind the eye to the decaying walls and buildings of the city, the silted-up harbor, so that now it was no longer necessary to wait until night to go home.

There was a compensation of sorts; the building was quite rightly considered to be an engineering and artistic triumph of its age. From all around the edge of the world came pilgrims traveling to the town for all the endless reasons that force men to undertake such perilous journeys.

So, despite its efforts to insulate itself from the rest of the world, the pilgrims kept the city tied to Enom and Iannarrow, and to the Meadows. According to the wanderers, two calls for Wars in the Meadows had been sent out during the century in which the church was being built. Both had apparently served to end creation only for those who went and the city's populace took a certain smug pride in their having avoided these abortive Armageddons.

But the Wars continued, by now apparently an indistinct series of skirmishes, fed by the survivors of the main battles and by those whom the prophets could still convince that the Millennium was at hand. On occasion, the western horizon flickered red-orange and the votive lamps in the cathedral would swing embarrassingly when there was no draft.

II

Amon VanRoark's father had grown up with the cathedral, first as an apprentice mason, journeyman, and then as a sub-deacon; therefore it was not so very surprising that he turned out a great deal like it, solid, comfortable, absolutely secure in the idea of eternal time. He found it quite easy to ignore the ramblings of disreputable pilgrims and the lamps swinging ever so slightly during mass. The passage of survivors or new men hurrying to the Meadows, the smoke stains of ships below the horizon, even the occasional glitter of silver in the sky and the far rumblings of aircraft high above failed to shake his faith in the rightness of the way things were.

Considering that his wife was of virtually the same mold, it was something of a puzzle that the young Van-Roark did not grow up along similar lines. Whether it was the insidious influence of the colony of pilgrims that always surrounded the cathedral, or simply an unusually active imagination, the boy preferred the unknown shadow-lands of the past and its remains. The Old Navy Dock with its ruined factories, the old launches and tugboats awash at their moorings, fascinated him much more than the cool, majestic quiet of the cathedral and its liturgical library. The boy spent too much time on the north side of the harbor and along the banks of the Goerlin River, where still more wrecked shipyards and foundries stood, to be socially acceptable.

The disorganization implicit in the world, with the still-usable remains of advanced technologies existing in the middle of cultures determined to sleepwalk themselves into a standing grave, lent an almost surrealistic air to the world, to VanRoark's eyes at least. It was almost as if time, getting ready to finish its assigned purpose, had somehow gotten fouled up and was now trying desperately to get itself sorted out. When he thought of things like this, a very painful feeling came over him: the feeling of desertion that had first prompted the work on the cruiser and the cathedral.

So usually he just did not think of such matters, content instead to ramble through the ruins, feeling the fine old steel and wondering, always wondering, how it must have been when the night sky still maintained enough regularity by which sailors could navigate.

Spring was late in VanRoark's nineteenth year. As he stood on the cathedral's grand steps and looked down through the Artillery Gate to the harbor, he could see that the ocean was still in its winter mood, heavy chop and spray geysering over the breakwater. He could also see one of the rare trails of smoke rising along the eastern edge of the world.

He stood watching for a while, wondering which way the invisible ship might be heading; but instead of moving off or away the smoke trail grew larger and thicker. By late afternoon a small gray dot could be observed under the column, apparently sailing for the city. VanRoark felt a slight twinge of anticipation, for he had never seen a working steamship. Indeed, his father had said that the last one to visit their harbor had been an armed trawler from New Svald, running from Enador's shore batteries and monitors. Her remains could still be seen, beached on the same flats that the cruiser had briefly rested upon more than a century ago.

He ran into the cathedral to tell his father. When notified of the approaching ship, he could only say, "Ships have called at our port before, and I am sure they will continue to do so for quite some time. No need to get upset, Amon; if there is any danger to be had from her I am sure that the militia can handle it."

The younger man tried to point out that in its present condition the port offered no reason for merchantmen to call there, and the local forces would be fairly ineffectual against the guns that such an ancient ship probably carried. The elder VanRoark dismissed this with a fatherly smile and said that he must prepare for evening service.

Amon began to mention the Meadow Wars but his father froze him with a glance before the second syllable was out. "Not in the cathedral, not here," he said in a most unfatherly manner.

Amon retreated into the daylight, stumbling down the steps toward the Artillery Gate, more from sudden fear that he may have profaned the sacred precincts than from any burning interest in the ship.

She was only about five miles offshore by then, a rough pillar of gray alternately buried in the gunmetal Sea and then leaping free of it, white spray falling from her bow and decks with a strange delicacy.

The ship was approaching more slowly now with the clouds of vapor shrouding progressively less of her superstructure. A single twin turret, five-inch most probably, was set on the center line directly below the wide bridge; rough shapes, which VanRoark supposed were secondary gun mounts, bristled at odd intervals along her sides.

A mile from the harbor the ship turned to the wind and dropped anchor, apparently not wanting to risk entering an unknown channel with only a few more hours of daylight left. VanRoark supposed that in earlier days she would have been a moderately sized cargo ship, but she was the largest thing that had been seen along the eastern coast of the world for almost half a century. He wondered where she might have come from, from the Dresau Islands or perhaps from islands even farther to the east. And she was old, older even than the cathedral, it seemed. Her sides were streaked with rust and ancient oil. There were no lifeboats in the portside davits which now faced shoreward, although there was a rather sizable launch secured on the afterdeck, tied to the only remaining cargo crane. She had never been designed to take any armament, but in addition to the forward twin turret, duplicated aft, at least three large gun tubs could be made out on the facing side, their contents hidden under huge, dirty tarpaulins.

But the lines were still there under the dirt and the crudely welded repair sheets: the graceful curve and flare of the bows, the long waterline leading back to a short, cut-off stern; a low, beautifully terraced superstructure set well aft. VanRoark, quite surprising himself, thought that she was much too fine to still be afloat; she should have died along with the world that built her.

Dinner was an unusually tense affair for both of the elder VanRoarks, along with most of the city's population, who were determined not to acknowledge the ship's presence, even though her lights were clearly visible from every vantage point. The absence of any hostile action from her, in most minds, removed any cause for concern about her existence. However, if the crew wished to purchase any provisions, that was another matter.

The young man became more distressed with himself as the evening went on. Before, he could easily observe and speculate over dead and harmless places like the Old Navy Dock, its tiny, rotting fleet of sunken ships, and the illegible inscriptions on the monuments along the Avenue of Victories. Now these thoughts were intruding dangerously close to a full awareness; true, they could easily be nothing but fragments of truth, blown way out of proportion by his notorious imagination, but the refusal of anyone to discuss them, even on the most superficial level, only served to magnify them once again. His own speculations began to expand and connect themselves with childhood stories and legends told by pilgrims on the cathedral's steps; the ruins which had always been taken as a normal part of the city suddenly began to seem vaguely extraordinary.

His bedroom was on the third story of the VanRoark home (cathedral officials being among the better paid of the city's population). Unfortunately, it overlooked the bay and the ship's lights. The night sky was darkly thick with stars, and such a curious feeling it was to look down and see yet another constellation where the Sea should have been, until the rocking of the ship separated its lights from the welkin's. Electric lights. VanRoark guessed at this just as he was about to drowse off to sleep; electric lights had left the city along with the old cruiser a hundred years before. How cold they burned, so cold and silver . . . not with the nice, red flickering of the animal fur lamps used nowadays.

Around four o'clock the false dawn appeared, restoring the mere physical presence of the ship. As VanRoark finally fell to sleep he began to sense a movement that flowed westward from the Sea and the ship, through the city and, ultimately, to the Meadows. It was a completely insubstantial movement, and as far as the city was concerned a limited and retrogressive one. But the feeling was a tremendously perplexing and upsetting one, for it unavoidably displaced the static security of his education, his society, and the cathedral. Very slowly, VanRoark was beginning to rebuild within himself a sense of time and a sense of history, concepts which like the old ships and the electric lights had long ago departed from the world.

III

The young VanRoark had been apprenticed to one of the cartography firms still left in the city; it was something of a wonder that even these few had any business considering that not many people had use for maps. So, more and more, the chartmakers had turned to fancy and imagination, producing works of great artistic beauty but with only the most superficial claims to accuracy.

It was in his shop, seated before the old desk at the back and gazing continually at the old portfolios, where VanRoark had accumulated much of his latent store of bewilderment with his own home. How fascinating it was to trace the old maps, so yellowed and eaten through with worms, and then compare them with those of more recent vintage. Small wonder that the mapmakers had given up the real world in disgust, for even the ancient, seemingly exact maps showed monstrous discrepancies even within the space of several decades: the magnetic field of the earth had reversed itself at least twice in the past three centuries. VanRoark further came to the conclusion that the night sky over his home bore little resemblance to that which had existed even in the time of his father's youth.

He had chosen a roundabout way of going to the shop so that he could avoid any sight of the roadstead. But his mind was still unaccountably afire and it was useless to try to eat lunch; at noon, VanRoark gave in to himself and walked down Bergman Street to Admiralty Square along the harbor.

The old Square had once been a center of municipal life—a function now fulfilled by the cathedral—when the city still owed allegiance to the Sea. Weeds now poked between the marble paving blocks and even the great monumental column to the city's lost ships and sailors was cracked and tinged with blue-green mosses. Despite the low-tide stench that grew stronger as the harbor gradually turned itself into a swamp, it was still something of a gathering place; many of the poorer classes who did not feel entirely comfortable amidst the ornate splendor of the cathedral gardens, along with the old naval families whose heritage was tied only to the Sea, came to sun themselves and let the living Sea remind them that all was not yet dead or dying in the world.

VanRoark walked into the Square, briefly eyeing the anonymous captain who still looked seaward from atop the column, four seadragons guarding his high pedestal; then his eyes moved to the Sea, where the ship rode at anchor. But his attention was ripped back to the old docks that started at the southern end of the Square and then ran down to the commercial districts. A new craft was moored there and VanRoark guessed that it was the launch he had seen on the ship's afterdeck.

He moved toward it and would have broken into a dead run had he not been afraid it should turn out to be just another one of the infrequent hulks that still called at the port. It had to be the ship's; motor-driven, its lines resembled nothing he had ever seen except along the margins of old maps. She was very sharp, only about seventy feet long and obviously built for speed. VanRoark stared in deeper fascination as he realized the ship was in excellent shape and entirely free of rust; in the few spots where her gray and black colors had been chipped only the fresh silver of untouched metal showed through. There were no guns, not even any mounts or other signs that she had ever carried anything else but power; never had he seen anything so full of latent energy, and he could feel his mind being pulled along in her wake, splitting through the fragile, rotten immovability of the city.

The implied movement of the ship drew him back to the Square; a figure had mounted one of the seadragons. A group of sailors stood at its feet, waiting.

He was a rather tall fellow, probably thin for his height, but the shapeless robes he wore hid most of his build. VanRoark could see his face, even though he was still far away; he could see the eyes burning and glittering like gas torches. Loose brown hair fell from his head and down his back. But his eyes!

VanRoark tumbled forward, quite unaware of what he was doing or that others had joined him. He sensed another feeling growing within him, something far beyond those which the ships had conjured; so fantastically complex and alien it was, that it lost and blurred itself with its twistings and infinite surfaces. All he could really define was a shortness of breath and loss of balance, as if he were walking along the edge of a cliff with nothing but fog below him.

He stopped before the monument. He knew who the man was. Then a name, Timonias, drifted through the mob. Timonias. Vision became indistinct, especially along the outer edges of his sight. The gray-green of steps and seadragons seemed to merge with the brilliant white of Timonias' robes, moving slightly in the breeze. Words and thoughts flickered and turned outside Van-Roark's suddenly narrowed world; only one voice and one idea and one person could now penetrate him. He had anchored his moment to the face and eyes and hands of Timonias; he did not have the slightest idea who Timonias was, but he knew him.

Then the hand, more pale than the robe around it, moved up before the diamond eyes and VanRoark was swept along. Never could he have conceived of a voice such as the one the man on the seadragon had: one that spoke, it seemed, without words or sound. The movement which all speakers seek to propel into the minds of their listeners was now existing as a force alive in itself.

Dust, and then from it, stars and planets; diagrams of creation unrolled in the space between Timonias' eyes and his weaving hand. Then history, a thing which Van-Roark had been gradually resurrecting within himself over his few years, came to his reeling mind, bludgeoning it back and forth against the limits of time.

He heard nothing, he was fairly sure of that; but like the name of the man atop the seadragon, the knowledge came to him, emerging and twisting within a consciousness that was unable to close and permanently grasp it—only to remotely observe it and attempt the frail lashups of memory.

Battles, cities, the conquest of the stars and then a retreat; spinning violence and the cool, grinding tragedy of things which he forgot even as they came to him flowed around the world of Admiralty Square. Rise and fall, bleeding defeat and stupid rebirth: things passed by him, and it came driving home that the wrecks had not always lain along the Goerlin's mud flats, that there had not *always* been ruins upon the earth. This he remembered; and because of this, some small, distant part of him sent up a terrible wailing and a sorrow he thought impossible to surpass.

Timonias was still speaking; the wailings died, the sorrow quickly calloused itself against any feeling. Now the pace rose and became even more fantastic; like the burning of blue diamonds and deep opals the "words" spun and sparkled far beyond the hand and eyes of the prophet, far beyond the tragicomic procession that had just bulleted through VanRoark's mind. Now came the final hope, the promise of peace and an ending, a truly brilliant, truly inspired end to the construct of the universe.

For a second, VanRoark drew back, awed and perversely proud of the neatly finished-off picture, the wonderfully complete aspect which time and history had suddenly attained from the words and gestures of Timonias.

Then the thoughts paled and turned to sand to drift away. Only a few grains were left . . . but they were enough.

IV

VanRoark slowly regained his vision; his mind closed back upon itself to find the small fragments that remained. Timonias had gone, as had the sailors and the motor launch. The ship was still anchored about a mile offshore, but the thick stream of smoke that hung above her showed she would be leaving soon too.

He was standing where he had been, before the sea-dragons and dead captain; but it was almost sunset now and the Square was utterly deserted. Long shadows from deserted buildings and ruins formed a tracery across the stones and around the monument.

Far away the shining towers of the cathedral could be seen, the crosses and stars at their peaks gouging the bloated sun. VanRoark wondered how long he had been standing there; if, indeed, this was the same day or year that he last remembered. There was nothing inside him now that he could articulate; not a single concept had remained in any recognizable form. But the ideas had passed through him brutally, and the small waves from their dying wake stirred inside him, much more in his heart and stomach than in his mind.

So it was with no small wonderment at his own behavior that he wandered through the dead streets, trying to dig down through their tumbling masses and recapture them for rational examination. Back up to Bergman

Street, past the shuttered cartography shop, and under the wooden compasses and globes that marked the other shops along the street; most of them had closed down years ago and the weathered signs, decayed and falling to pieces, described the measurements of the street and its new ruins with their shadows.

VanRoark stopped and tried to restore a hanging basket-work globe to its mount; but the iron thorns that had once held metal continents to the framework, now probably melted down for the cathedral, cut his fingers.

The sun was down; a brilliantly moonless welkin recast the weathered wood and ulcerated paint into a vague parody of steel or silver. VanRoark moved on across the Avenue of Victories; dry fountains spouted stars and hideous new constellations. Then the feelings he had been attempting to grasp began to rise to his mind; he was instantly terrified. Echoes of his wailing and sorrow came piling back upon him, the things Timonias had told following behind. He ran from the Avenue of Victories and the cathedral, leaving the night sky twisting with the quiet agony of a dumb animal.

V

Amon VanRoark found a distant amusement with himself in the day immediately following the appearance of Timonias. Somewhere, still miraculously untouched, a bit of himself which cared nothing for matters of such great import as the end of time hung back to watch the curious activities of the rest of him. It was not, in any way, irritation or resistance to the new course of Van-Roark's life. But as he blundered about his room—absurdly trying to decide just what he should take with him to the Meadows and the presumed presence of God—the small bit asked why the streets were not awash with men desperate to get out of the city and join the armies of their true nature.

Indeed, the city seemed completely normal, perhaps even intensely normal, as if it were trying to ignore the extraordinary happenings of the previous day. The usual apathy of most people seemed to suddenly require more effort than usual. The pack of drifters and derelicts who were always sleeping in the ruins around the Artillery Gate squirmed uneasily, with their eyes screwed shut as if a brilliant light had been thrust in front of them. Everywhere the failure and futility which had served to carry so many of the city's generations safely through life no longer appeared to be so natural a thing.

Clearly the city had been touched, but as VanRoark walked about on the day before he planned to leave for New Svald he heard not a word of the two ships or the prophet or anything being the slightest bit uncommon. *Perhaps,* he thought for a moment, *each man is now fighting his own battle, trying to decide whether to throw his lot in with Good or Evil; in a day or two the city will erupt into activity. Companies will be raised, final alliances formed, the promises fulfilled.*

Because of this, VanRoark delayed his departure for a few more days, then a week. Instead of exploding, the city merely closed itself up tighter, driving whatever thoughts that had briefly stirred it deeper and deeper into its routine until they were finally lost. Two weeks after Timonias had visited the city, VanRoark could almost feel the pressure being released. They had entirely defeated the thing that now so possessed the young man, beaten and smothered it until it became just one more of the small, vague irritations that had come to make up what passed for a heritage in those days.

While the city met and easily dealt with the Word, VanRoark only surrendered to it. He began to fear that the Meadow Wars might somehow begin without him. He had tried to talk to his father about Timonias but was met with such determined inattention that he soon gave up. This bothered him intensely. Hostility, anger: at least they were positive and would mean that the elder Van-Roark, too, was taking sides. But this nothingness: "Did you see him, Father, or have your men told you about him and what he said? Did you see the ships? The small, fast one and the big, tired one anchored offshore?" Somehow the conversation always managed to return to such subjects as the impending Feast of St. Mathiason, or the eternal plans of the City Council to begin deepening the harbor, now little more than a marsh.

A small, cold rage began to build up within VanRoark, which made him want to scream what he had heard to every citizen he could reach. But the rage never grew to be very large, simply because he was much too caught up in his own personal adventure to really care much for the trials or failings of others. Besides, he knew perfectly well that it was impossible for him to ever tell another person what he knew; only Timonias could do that and he had gone.

Although the prophet had never stated such, Van-Roark anticipated a brave, grimly happy air on the day he would leave, for he expected, on that day, to have the rest of the city marching with him. *Lord,* he thought, *this should be a time for grand farewells and beau gestes of impossible charm; flags should be flown; people who were enemies to the very centers of their souls should be making one last wish for luck and good fortune to each other.*

Instead, he stood alone by the Artillery Gate, damp from the early morning mists and uncomfortable from the suspicious stares of a couple of derelicts. Behind him was the great cathedral, soft and shadowy in the fog, small rays of colored light hovering around the stained glass windows; the lamps had not swayed for more than ten years. Ahead of him, the Avenue of Victories, its ruins and civic tombstones gradually vanishing in the mist; he could see nothing of the harbor.

He had thought briefly of saying goodbye to some people, especially a woman he knew in the Thurber District—a place of moldering buildings that had once housed the various legations and embassies to the city, when nations still thought contact with the rest of the world to be, if not necessary, then at least gentlemanly. The quarter was known for its eccentrics and odd characters; certainly she was one of the strangest, and one of the most enchanting, of all who lived there. But he knew if he went, it would only be with the secret hope that he might impress her with his plans, and that she, in turn, would somehow dispel the knowledge that was driving him away. He remembered his absolute inability to communicate what he knew to anyone, even to her; and if she already knew, then she had most probably left anyway.

He had not said goodbye to either his mother or father, St. Mathiason having laid a momentary claim to their attentions, and he cared little for the other people he knew in the city. But the girl, that was a real hurt. Small and distant, like the part of him that was so amazed by his actions, she could not change his course, but he wondered if she might have been at Admiralty Square and if she, too, was going to the Meadows; he wondered which side she would be on.

He stood looking at his city until the mists had burned off, hoping that it might suddenly break out of itself and join him. Nothing happened, nothing unusual stirred the warm, damp air. At least he would be leaving in a proper spring instead of the odd winter that had stayed with the land into the middle of May.

In other times—when the Avenue of Victories had not stopped at the steps of the cathedral but had run straight west for more than a thousand miles, through the Great Plains and to the nation of Timmerion—there had been an exceptionally fertile strip of land which had roughly paralleled the coast from the Republics south to the Talbight Estuary. It had been called the Greenbelt, and upon its soil the Republics had raised their most beautiful flowers, grown their greatest crops, bred their finest horses. But the endless wars and catastrophes had crushed and poisoned the Greenbelt into a near-desert, even more barren now than the land which surrounded it. In winter it was frozen to the hardness of metal; in the summer, if the season chose to ever arrive, it would be dust; nothing but ironbush and saltgrasses could grow there.

Now it was spring and the Greenbelt was muck; it clung and stuck to VanRoark's boots and made him feel filthy. But his only alternative was the endless lands to the west, where it was only a matter of chance if he would be murdered before or after he got lost.

VI

VanRoark's luck improved momentarily; four days out from his city, he fell in with a caravan of adventurers from the lands of Raud. They were going south also, but to the vast Enstrich Marshes to hunt for bird-of-paradise feathers and the hides of the water reptiles that lived there; a curious sort of crystal grew in pockets along the reptiles' bodies that was highly prized among certain rulers and noblemen, especially those of the mountain kingdoms of Mountjoy and ancient Mourne. None of them had ever heard of any Timonias, and it was absolutely impossible to draw them into conversation about anything other than women, feats of drinking, or the vast sums they planned to make from their enterprise.

VanRoark was quite aware that he should be getting more dispirited over the absence of fellow travelers to the Wars; on several occasions, when the dubious security and small comforts of home grew large through comparison to the caravan's meager offerings or, at night, when he thought of the woman he had never said goodbye to, a purely pitiful human crying took hold of him. He felt so very old and tired for his age, and the part of him that remained cynically amused observed that even the possessed must still remain essentially human.

That thought pained him: that he should still feel hunger and loneliness and longing. But most of the time, and always in the daylight, the words of Timonias stayed with him, pushing him on.

Gradually the landscape became flatter and the low hills bordering the western horizon leveled off. At times, when the air was exceptionally clear, a gray-green edging of far highlands could be seen. The coastline remained quite rugged, cliffs dropping vertically a hundred feet or more to the Sea.

The Trextel River, which began among the same lake system as the wilder Shirka, emptied into the Sea through an impressive fjord that ran almost a hundred miles eastward. At its real mouth, far inland, there had once been a great trading city, whose ruins were still something of a marvel to those who visited them. Its name is not remembered, but the fortress town of Charhampton, which had guarded the seaward mouth of the gorge, remained. The city and its attendant forts had been carved into the rock sides of the northern cliffs. It had long been a strong point and its scars, everything from the chips made by steel axes to the shadow-impressions of people caught by a bomb that had once exploded in the gorge, attested to its importance.

The trade that had made the city important had vanished centuries ago, or else shifted to Enador, but a few people still managed to extract a living from the Sea or from selling the scrap metal and armaments from the dead forts. The caravan stopped to rest at Charhampton and to wait for the ferry that would take them to the southern bank of the Trextel. The lizard hunters retired to the bars and single whorehouse of the city for the evening; VanRoark might have joined them, but puritan tinges of his upbringing held him back. Overshadowing that was the prospect of exploring the ruined forts, whose galleries and quays ran for nearly a mile downstream from the city until they curved north along with the coastline as it opened to the Sea.

Most of the smaller structures and miscellaneous junk had been carted away and probably remounted in castles from North Cape to Enom. The forts of Charhampton, though, like the fabled Armories of which little remained except for a few caves and a crater on the Tyne River, had been built by a mighty nation of men who could bend almost anything but their own minds to their will. Thus, great and incomprehensible machines remained, rooted to their concrete bases, still pointing across the river or seaward through slits in the rock.

He had been wandering through some ancient submarine pens about a quarter of a mile east from the city itself, when he met Tapp. Tapp was, of course, fairly drunk, a state which he successfully maintained for almost the whole time VanRoark knew him. The young man was quite startled, lost as he was in the dreams and nightmares that the rusting hulks inevitably conjured.

"Good evening, young sir. In search of your new command?" Tapp's deep voice bellowed through the huge pens. VanRoark quickly picked out the little man sitting atop the conning tower of one of the near boats. Tapp gestured grandly at the ragged patchwork of ribs and hull plating.

"And are you to be my crew?" VanRoark responded after a moment.

"Aye, sir, if it pleases you. But I fear that our ships will need a bit of work before we sail." Tapp burst into sudden, explosive laughter at his own wit. Fascinated, VanRoark drew closer, more than a little amazed at his own fearlessness, for he had long been taught of the creatures that were said to lurk in the remains of the dead world.

"And for where shall we be sailing, crew? For Blackwoods Bay, Duncarin or the Isle of Oromund?" Van-Roark knew perfectly well the place he hoped the man would name.

A pause while the laughing echoed out to Sea through the ruined blast doors and torpedo booms. "Why, to the Meadow Wars, young sir!" Then, even lower and more sadly, "To the Meadows . . . " But again the quiet pens detonated to his laughter; he reached behind him and drew out a short, curved saber that caught moonlight reflected from the water outside and from the shell holes in the roof. "Right, young sir, to the bleeding Meadows, you know. Like my great-grandfather, like my granddad, and my own dad. The other two came back, but old Dad pulled it off and managed to die when he was supposed to." He lowered the saber, bent over and lifted a wine sack from inside of the old conning tower. "Juice?" he asked with momentary politeness; and then back up with the sword and his voice filling the pens. A colony of bats stirred into the air and then nested again in another corner. VanRoark said no, but was this a joke or was he really going to the Meadows?

"Joke indeed! The only bleeding joke around here is . . . is"—he fumbled thickly for the proper words—"is that we are here." Satisfied that his point had been made, he took another pull on the sack and flourished his saber in the wet air. Then his voice fell again. "You know, young sir?" He looked up abruptly. "Your name, if I may be so forward?"

"Amon VanRoark." The youth bowed slightly to the drunk. "And yours?"

"Second Lieutenant Tapp, lately of the kingdom of Cynibal and servant of his Imperial Majesty, Bournmouth the Third, Conqueror of Worlds, Liege of Creations. Also lately running from charges of treason relating to the disappearance of the steam frigate *Toriman* and its subsequent reappearance under the flag of the free city of Enador." He drank again from the leather sack, smacking his lips with delight at the foul brew. "And also, my sir, a wanderer, a man of vast passions and laughter and loneliness." Now his voice was soft and dreamy, as if he fancied himself possessed of a poetic soul. Impressed with his own depth of feeling, he lost the thread of his conversation. "Where was I, sir?" he blurred at VanRoark.

"You were Tapp, man of vast—"

"Ah yes, that Tapp. Indeed I was . . . am. You see, I am a wanderer, I've seen many nations, and none of them, and heard at my mother's side the tale of my father marching to the Meadows with all the lads of great Cynibal beside him. And how he never came back, and how, in some way I *still* cannot understand, I should be happy for him in that."

A curious shade of water-reflected silver and shadow crossed over his rutted face, drawing VanRoark nearer, quite against his better nature. Then the little man sighed again and set his voice into a new, solemn tone. "And then, you see, sir, ten years ago a man came to Cynibal all dressed in fine white. And he spoke to us, to me, and he said there was going to be a war at a place called the Meadows, and how, if we wanted to save our souls, we had to go and fight there. Now, young sir, I remembered perfectly well that three of my forebears had set off on just such a venture, probably even heard the same things and had the same hopes. But I had never *heard* the men who had spoken to them. And though I knew all this, I also knew beyond all doubt that *this* would be our last gesture in time.

"So I ditched my commission, which was getting a little hot anyway from the *Toriman* row, and left my bawling old lady and several other broken hearts, to travel west with some fellow lunatics. It took about a year, overland and by Sea, but at last we made it to a place called the Burn. It's a very old place, you know, and I was told that one of the false-Armageddons had been fought there. Ghastly place, sir, all burned and blasted, and the mountains look like they had been melted once. You think the Belt is dead? It's a flaming paradise compared to the Burn. Lord," he muttered, shaking his head and taking a drink, "a flaming paradise.

"But there were others like me there, a whole bleeding army! All come to do old Evil and Time their last." Then, even more slowly, "And, sir, when we marched from the Burn to the Meadows you could *feel,* sir, you could *feel* God moving with us! Two million men maybe—I don't know just how many—and all around us there were . . . were . . . " He began fumbling again, trying to pull thoughts and memories from places his mind had hidden them in, lest they run wild, raging about and turning the sane parts of him rotten. " . . . lights, moving lights . . . and creases of shadow floating around us, but we could still feel them pressing in on us. God! How powerful we felt, so bleeding full of Right and Good and all the . . . Godddd, sir!" Tapp yelled, low and savage. "They were there! The whole bleeding lot of them, sir! I saw them!" He slammed his fists into his eyes and began moaning, only bothering to make the curses understandable. VanRoark wanted to leave, for he was at once terrified and embarrassed by the man; but he stayed and after a while the man was quiet, put the saber into its scabbard and threw the empty wine skin into the stagnant water. VanRoark rose and helped the little man descend the conning tower; his hands were cut by the rusted metal and the red flowed darkly into the saliva Tapp had drooled onto them. He began mumbling apologies to both VanRoark and God, begging VanRoark to take him away from the pens to a nice dry gutter where he might sleep it off.

Moved by the knowledge that here at last was a man who had been to the Meadows and, more importantly, was journeying back there again, VanRoark dragged him back to the cut-rock streets of Charhampton and dropped him into a room which the inn's landlord had thoughtfully provided for drunken members of the caravan. He left the man snoring peacefully, but later that night, when the house was awakened by screaming, he knew that it was Tapp; VanRoark dared not move from his bed or open his eyes until another drunk had silenced him.

VII

They crossed the Trextel River the next day and continued southward between the Greenbelt and the somewhat less rugged coastline. Tapp had joined them.

It took them two months of traveling to reach Enador,
on the south bank of the Talbight Estuary. The traveling
was relatively pleasant, or as pleasant as their world
would allow it to be. Tapp, being almost continually
drunk, did very little to maintain the company, but from
him streamed an incredible succession of lies and legends, stories ranging from amazingly accurate recitations
from Cynibal's treasure books to equally amazing tales
of virility in her brothels. His grand gestures and inflated
oratory easily caught the ears of the young men from
Raud, with their own dreams of piety and pornography,
so Tapp was never without enough liquor to fuel his
memory. VanRoark did not question him about the Wars
again, much as he would have liked to, for he feared it
would break the mood of their traveling as they followed
the end of summer south.

Besides a growing affection for this man with the deep
olive skin and jaundiced eyes, there arose another feeling
in VanRoark. For so long he had been empty, content
only to gather small bits of a dubious past and to move
through his existence with little real trouble or thought.
Then he had fatally begun to assemble the old fragments
into understandable patterns, patterns which the
"words" of Timonias had blasted into a picture of history.

But this was a scar and did nothing to fill up his merely
earthly existence. Now he began to surround it with con-
ceptions of life such as he had never come to before.

Always to his left was the Sea, bright and glittering and forever restless. To his right, the Greenbelt with its dust and poisons and the gunmetal mountains behind it: always dead, eternal, unmoving, except to crumble into finer dust. The Sea was just as eternal, but its timelessness was one of life, not death. How curious that he had never really noticed the life teeming in the Sea, the flying fish and dolphin that cut through its surface and flew over it, the white of its surf and beaches. He looked to the Greenbelt and saw its diseased ironbushes and saltgrasses, a large wolf spider eating another wolf spider.

Once, when they had camped on the straits that separated the mainland from the Isle of Oromund, he had walked out onto the sterile expanse of the Belt. It was dusk, the only time of day that the land acquired anything faintly resembling beauty, a desolate lunar beauty. He stopped and in the half-light spotted a brilliantly colored bug by his foot; most of the Belt's inhabitants were either a dirty tan or dun color, but this one was garishly marked in turquoise and yellow stripes, its legs booted in white and a hood of the same color running up its many-jointed neck and mantis head. VanRoark bent down to examine the creature, and then walked quickly back to the camp, much sicker than he thought he should have been.

The cannibalism of the wolf spiders was to be expected in such a detestable looking breed. But the wondrously colored bug had twisted its long neck over its body and was calmly, methodically disemboweling itself; the opal wings were easily spread so that its jaws might reach its vitals sooner. It was the careful, infinitely methodical feeling of the self-dissection that bothered VanRoark; trapped on the world, or at least ignorant of the Sea, the insect was committing suicide, an act that either implied intelligence in a very primitive life form, or merely the dictate of instinct. It was this last thought and its implications that drove him back to the Sea and Oromund's shadowed hills.

The Sea, though, was always full with that which lived and moved and functioned and was clean. There, life was not scarred from radiation or dying from birth because of disease or starvation; nowhere else on the earth did such life exist, and as VanRoark walked beside it, saw its storms for the first time beating upon its own washed beaches, instead of silted, filth-clogged harbors, his spirits rose. The Wars faded and cooled in him; he kept traveling only because of the Sea and because there was no reason at all to return home.

VIII

VanRoark did not find out that Tapp was dying until they had reached Enador. The weapons that had been used at the Meadows by some men, while not fatal, had given him radiation poisoning. He had lived through the initial dose as he had through the Wars themselves, but it had left behind a small unpredictable cancer. The only outward manifestation of it, aside from the pain and the vomiting of blood, was a bleeding ulcer on the back of Tapp's neck. It had briefly flared after the Meadows, and then subsided, only seasonal fluctuations and the lightly stained collars reminding him of its presence. Now it had grown, round and angry, dribbling pus and reddened lymph down his neck. Tapp took this to be an indication of his impending end; thus the liquor, and the journeying to the Meadows—again.

VanRoark found a richness in the tangle of Tapp's motives such as he had seldom seen in the world. Why was he going to the Meadows? he would ask again when Tapp was sober. And in time Tapp said that he was going to avenge his father's death, to find glory, or booty, or make his death a bit less painful than the doctors had prophesied, or to fight in a holy war, a jihad that had been declared against a human enemy and not creation. Of course, beyond all of this lay the things he had said and remembered in the submarine pens, things that still managed to creep out of their hiding places for a moment to turn his eyes to the ground and to make his hands pick nervously at the bleeding wound in his neck.

He seemed to like the jihad fiction the best, for he could play up an equally false cynicism against it. "Right, then, 'Roark," he would sometimes command, his saber in his right hand and the other clamped upon VanRoark's shoulder, "off to the Meadows to fight for the Prophets with their glittering eyes, and thousands of the Faithful behind us! Ah, grand it'll be, us sweeping the Infidel before us, circumcising them on the run!"

Van Roark would support him with questions of the spires, harems, and other attendant treasures that would fall to them once the Meadows were crossed and the unknown lands north of them captured. He still feared to let Tapp slide down into his memories, yet half hoping that he would.

IX

They stayed at Enador for a week, waiting for a ship to carry them south; the rather doubtful location of their destination didn't trouble them much. Although when they inquired at chandleries, cartography shops, or along the waterfront, they got either a rough laugh, a glob of spit at their feet (at which Tapp's ulcer would blaze deep scarlet and his hand would start moving for the saber's pommel), or a patronizing smile. At least people had heard of the Meadows.

Enador was still one of the few places left on the eastern coast of the world that could still lay any claim to wealth or power; chiefly, her riches came from the Sea, upon which she still carried a reasonably active commerce, and her slow cannibalization of the remains of the Dresau Islands. The Islands had died soon after they had sent their last fleet to fight at one of the false-Armageddons; but her sailors had left a lot behind and now only Enador had the ships and the desire to pick the bones. The two river monitors which allowed Enador to control the Talbight Estuary all the way to Donnigol were armed with Dresau guns, powered by Dresau engines, and fueled with oil that had lain in storage tanks outside of Duncarin for centuries.

But even so, Enador's stance was as precarious as any in the world, perhaps more so in view of the land and sea areas she aspired to control. Too often were the monitors lobbing shells into the rebellious primitives of Svald or Larine when the lizards and hooded basilisks from the Enstrich Marshes swam or crawled north and their eyes could be seen from the city's walls.

Regardless of all this, Enador was still the trading center of the known world, and as such she almost always had a fair amount of commerce in her roadstead and harbor. VanRoark noted that many of the ships were scavengers, dealing in the remains of worlds long dead, like those that brought the guns and sheet steel from the Dresau Islands, the fortresses of Charhampton and the Armories.

As the world drank more and more blood from the bodies of its predecessors and gnawed more deeply into their putrefied flesh, the scavenger ships were forced to sail farther outward, to the fjords and bays of the anonymous northlands or to the Old Nations to the west and south past Ihetah-Incalam. VanRoark and Tapp left the party of hunters and began looking for ships journeying to such far points.

Inside a week they had paid passage on a barque of two thousand tons, the *Garnet*; her master was going to the Meadows, as were they, because of the calling of the prophet. But he reckoned no further than the concentration of military equipment that would surely be found there. A light-fingered crew of sufficient delicacy would be able to garner a rich harvest of small arms and explosives before the Holy became wise. And, who knows, they were sailing to a place of great tradition and antiquity; even if no army was being gathered there, the place should offer more than enough in salvageable material to make the voyage highly profitable.

So they sailed on board the *Garnet* with her mob of greedy half-wits and two others who were merely half-wits, in Tapp's initial judgment. The first, a tall emaciated man named Yarrow, who spent most of the voyage spitting his rotting lungs over the side, was an undiluted fanatic; he delighted at spouting Scripture from any one of a hundred holy books and prophesying a glorious end for the four of them. VanRoark knew that his words were taken with fair accuracy from the very same books which had been Timonias' silent and neglected forerunners; but to hear the grand words clothed in Yarrow's grandiloquent and affected posturing, his theatrical tone, destroyed for the moment all the grimly wonderful completeness of the Meadows. What was supposed to happen there was reduced to a sordid collection of meaningless gestures. Both Tapp and VanRoark avoided this man and let him vent his righteous furies upon the crew.

The other man, Gerideau Smythe, was also a fanatic, or at least he tried to make one believe he was. But somehow his quiet, calm assertions of faith and belief and ain't-we-gonna-stick-it-to-ole-Satan-pass-the-Lord-and-praise-the-ammunition simply could not come off with the same loud, utterly blind conviction with which Yarrow could fill them. Neither did he have the immovable but strangely shrouded convictions that seemed to be driving VanRoark to the Meadows.

He had been a librarian by profession—which meant that half the nations in the world had laws by which he could be legally murdered—first at the Black Library at Krysale Abbey and then at the more notorious one at Iriam. Thus he had grown up among the works which proved that this world had been preceded by another, and that by another, and so forth, until the old maps VanRoark had wondered at found histories to match their mountains and rivers. Of course, to be a librarian in those days only meant that one had to be reasonably literate; but there must have been a devotion in Smythe that tied him so closely to the books he could read but never fully understand.

At night when Yarrow had preached the dolphins into a sleepy stupor and Tapp had predictably passed out, Smythe would talk to VanRoark of the great, fortress-like libraries and recite fragments and pieces of histories and sciences that had randomly stuck in his mind; virtually all of the names were foreign to VanRoark, so many Republics Of and Unions Of. Not at all like the present, when nations drew their names from their dead founders—or their assassins.

It was not at all hard, when his mind was already awash with Tapp's magnificent blitherings, to listen to Smythe's cracked voice, for he was an old man now, and after a while the pious trappings would slough off and the wonder that the libraries had sheltered began to fearfully poke through. It would only be for a few minutes, a half hour at the most, before the guilt that stood behind the religious and moral slogans drove the glittering shapes back; but for the instant they lived.

In the darkness the dreadful state of the *Garnet* was invisible and, with the sordid mumblings of her crew ended for the day, there existed only VanRoark and the Sea and Smythe's voice. VanRoark learned of air ships from the old man, and how the steel ships were able to propel themselves without sails or paddle-wheels; how the old, vanished cities used to look, and how they died, quickly under the bombs, or slowly at their own hands as gangs of kids stuffed homemade guncotton and broken glass into oatmeal cans and let their parents bleed to death on sidewalks; he learned of asphalt roads that had once covered the world, and of the vehicles that had carried men upon them; ships that dived into the sea, and ships that had carried other men on some few faltering steps toward the stars, before there was no more time for such things.

It was, of course, for these things that the man was truly going to the Meadows; even VanRoark came to see that. But somehow, someone had convinced Smythe that the knowledge he had watched over was the very essence of evil, of the dark, power-ravening evil that man had allowed to grow within himself in his younger years. Now, as Yarrow believed, such things were behind him and all man needed was a clean heart and mind averted exclusively toward Heaven. Poor Smythe tried so desperately to ape Yarrow's florid statements of faith, but he was a bad liar and the libraries at Krysale Abbey and Iriam were still very much with him. He had burned Krysale, or rather had been forced to by a group heading for one of the Meadow's unending Wars.

It was in these conversations with Smythe that Van-Roark first began to question his own motives for going to the Meadows. The time of Timonias still had that beautifully rounded-off character that fairly screamed for completion, his head was still quite full of the things he had sensed at Admiralty Square, but now, as the stars above the horizon appeared as the running lights of great battle fleets, he finally admitted to himself an entirely heretical and apparently irrelevant love of the past in itself: the past, free from all the great Abstractions such as were now supposedly stalking the Meadows, peopled only by men such as himself and the machines they might fashion. A regular world, where one's sanity could always resort to certain fairly rigid standards whenever it was in danger of breaking; standing, as it were, on a good solid plain and not perched on the cliff's edge getting ready to jump.

But then Yarrow would come storming up, a hysterically laughing Tapp following in his wake, spouting damnation and Scripture, or else the crew would make itself known and the magic would be ended. Smythe would retreat back into his little, miserably defended stronghold of holy droppings and disavow any allegiance to Krysale Abbey or Iriam; all he wanted to do then was to go to the Meadows and Die like all those on the side of Right Ought to Do. Yarrow would pound him on the back, hurl some presumably encouraging chapter and verse at him; then Yarrow would always turn and toss some further bit of Scripture at the world. But all that VanRoark could see of the world was the Sea, shining with luminous fish and night creatures, ghost-osprey circling the ship and the stars. Then he was sick of Yarrow and the ship, but not with the terrified sickness he had caught from the insect on the Greenbelt. This was an immature, but still rather righteous sickness; by now VanRoark had begun to see his person becoming cluttered and filled up with vague, half-formed feelings and sensations, things that he had never even conceived of at his home city. Even now, less than three months away from Admiralty Square, he looked back upon himself in those days with the weary, bittersweet cynicism that is the fate of youth when it steps, or thinks it does, beyond its previous limits. A world was growing within him, one composed of bits and pieces of ocean, the fragmented histories of five hundred nations, prophets, dogma, time and dying men.

It was this last thing that prevented him from the nearly inevitable blunder of youth which, once having discovered the outlined world inside itself, wallows in it and mutters to itself, utterly convinced that its situation is unlike any other in all creation. They lose their humility in self-inflated bitterness, the young, and wear their self-inflicted scars like the wounds of real wars and sorrows. But the dying men, his association with their real sorrows and torments, those men who did not bother to examine and parade themselves, kept VanRoark's mind from dwelling too much upon itself and thus shutting out all else. It was hardly a love, nor was it any sort of awe, although both Tapp and Smythe inspired their own particular brands of admiration in VanRoark; it was more as if VanRoark, upon finding the gradually assembling fragments within himself, used this knowledge and feelings as a kind of lens through which he could glimpse, however briefly, the dreadfully complete worlds of the two men.

They were the ends of time, human wrecks crawling to their deaths, but leaving behind them a history, and in this perhaps even one or two works that might be worthy of being called just. It was only through men such as these, who had allowed themselves to sense the meaning of their agony, that the Wars could be fought; it was they who built and now would tear down.

In moments alone, VanRoark would muse upon Tapp and Smythe, considering them coldly and granting them ironic titles, which made them look even more pitiful

and ridiculous than they were already: The Final Culmi-
nation of Human Evolution (when he saw Tapp reeling
about the deck after dinner, his ulcer bleeding bright
and clear in the setting sun), Protector of the Divine
Plan of Creation (when he saw Smythe trying so very
hard to explain Good and Right to their illiterate, malar-
ial cabin boy). But then survivors are always more piti-
able than the dead.

There was Yarrow, but he only had a walk-on in all
this, VanRoark sagely concluded. He touched nothing,
allowed nothing he did not approve of to touch him, and
scarcely cared for anything save the sound of his own
voice. VanRoark imagined a ship similar to their own,
but now sailing north to the Meadows, loaded with men
he would eventually be trying to kill; doubtlessly, on
board there was a Yarrow, distinguishable from their own
only in the name of the Great Abstraction with which he
defined his own faith.

Then, with a dispassion that is also usually alien to
youth, discovering that one had lived and would soon
die, he tried to fit himself into this and found he could
not. At times he was the avenging angel going to serve
his God and his Plan, but despite Timonias, he could
never feel quite as majestic as the phrase demanded;
neither was he of the race of men that had built world
after world and then left when their time had properly
arrived; not yet, at least. This was no good; now he was
nothing, going to a probable death for no reason at all.
The Sea perhaps? That would be his heritage and his
ally, he decided.

He supposed that once there had been those who had
built the great ships and sailed upon them, those of the

wanderer caste. The Meadow Wars again receded in his mind and the voyage virtually supplanted it in his immediate thoughts. He began to take up with the crew, not for any companionship but only to learn their arts.

X

Against the ocean there was usually the coast, always on the starboard side, for few vessels cared to venture out of sight of land if they could help it. The lands south of Enador were quite desolate, high rock cliff faces usually screening inland areas from the Sea most of the time. Gradually, though, the land dipped down to sea level. They were getting into warmer latitudes, where warm currents from the southeast fed the mangrove and cypress forests of the great Enstrich Marshes before they swirled out to Sea again, to touch lush Kyandra and some of the lesser of the Dresau Islands. The gray and sand colors of the coastal territories gave way to a flat line of green that turned to a solid carpet when viewed from the maintop. They sailed past the Marshes for almost a week; by day, VanRoark would borrow the captain's glass and survey the steaming wall, watching the huge snakes and lizards that lived there moving through the trees of the water, their heads awash like rotting logs, and the gold and pink birds that rose at their passing. At night, if the moon was bright enough, he could see the eyes and crystal hides of the reptiles weaving through the breathing darkness.

Tapp became more sober as they bordered the Marshes. VanRoark at first thought that the appearance

of some kind of untarnished fertility still left on the land
had lifted his spirits. But it was only that they were
approaching Cynibal. Tapp grew hopeful and despairing
by turn, knowing that if he actually landed there he
would probably be hanged for treason, Bournmouth III's
Curia having a very long memory; still, it was a home
that he had not seen for quite a few years.

The swampy coastline died out, to be replaced by level
sand beaches that shaded off into rolling hills covered
with pale bayonet grass. Joshua trees and cottonwood
broke up the monotony.

Tapp began drinking again; in his memories, the grass
had been green and fair, like the Greenbelt was supposed
to have been once. There were ruins too, the occasional
hull of a gutted tank, half overgrown in the murderous
grass, lying beside cottonwood groves. Then came the
cities, the small ports that grew larger as they neared the
entrance to Blackwoods Bay, the harbors silted up like
VanRoark's home, the streets deserted and the walls
already beginning to show the impact of the wind.

VanRoark had heard stories of this nation from the
pilgrims who had come to the cathedral, of its power
and beauty, how almost alone it still held itself together
and worked its old sciences and arts. Great ships were
supposed to have called at Blackwoods Bay, where
pumps still brought oil up from the Sea's bed, where the
towers still trickled out fuels and lubricants; then the
ships would go back to their home nations at the edge
of the world.

VanRoark wanted to ask Tapp about all this, and what
had happened, even though he obviously did not know
either; but by the time they sailed into the Bay Tapp

had returned to his usual stupor, trying to keep himself unconscious so that he would never see his dead Cynibal.

So Smythe, when he could get away from Yarrow's undiminished ravings and chokings, fearfully climbed the maintop to VanRoark and offered what small things he still remembered. The northern shore of the Bay had been Cynibal's, the southern one having belonged to Ihetah-Incalam, and it was like a miles-long tangle of thorn bushes, wreckages of wells and refineries, oiling docks. Fires were burning amid the tangle and would keep burning, Smythe said, until the wells went dry, perhaps two hundred years from now.

VanRoark had lived with ruin long enough to be at home with these, but the immense scale of the fires made them something apart, as if they had just been destroyed and had yet to die utterly. The worst ones were the offshore wells, natural gas, according to Smythe; there the flame just burst from the Sea, as if giving birth to something vast and terrible, steam and boiling water ringing its pale blue and yellow base.

Where the fires lived on the land, in the iron shrubbery of fallen, cracking towers and distillation units, their constant heat had melted the steel so that the sharp outlines and angles softened and bowed down grotesquely near the flames.

Ships were there too, perhaps those of which the pilgrims had talked: tankers and merchant ships burned and blackened and melted by the fires, sunk at their docks with the dirty, oil-slicked water painting their sides in sickly rainbow diffractions.

Tapp would just sit on the bow, blind drunk and completely insensitive to the coast or to Yarrow's running commentary on the vanity that had called down such a fate on Cynibal. And then as Yarrow rose to some particularly emotional pitch, his lungs would reassert their presence and he would scuttle to the side, dribbling thin trails of blood and saliva down the side. The crew thought the passengers a most amusing collection of freaks and idiots.

They were bound for the western end of the Bay, to a port called Mount Soril, where they would provision for the uncertain journey south and then west. Predictably, Mount Soril was no less devastated than Cynibal; the city had been one of Ihetah-Incalam's most prosperous ports, but that nation had apparently suffered the same end as its northern sister. It had been the plague and its attendant madnesses at Mount Soril. It was still inhabited, now by maniacs and paranoiacs, people who worshiped the sun because they feared the night.

VanRoark went ashore with some of the crew in search of provisions and water; they were armed and really had little to fear. VanRoark found the place weirdly enchanting. There was very little physical destruction, aside from a complete lack of any maintenance for more than ten years, he estimated. The sight of Soril's poor citizens wandering through the overgrown gardens, the clogged pools and gently crumbling buildings awakened an odd pity in him.

They were utterly alone; the diseases and gases of someone's inspired national policy had robbed them of any recourse, not the mouthings of Yarrow, or Tapp's drink, or even the sorry self-delusions of Smythe. Time had ended for them; they were beyond the reach of anything.

Even the crew could sense this, although their feelings were never articulated past the stage of superstitious fear. They had stolen all they needed, their presence having hardly been acknowledged by Soril's people. The few questions they had asked had been answered in a highly elliptical and confusing manner. There had been a war eight years ago between the two nations in which they had wiped out each other. Now the only difference was that Ihetah's dead were still walking around, whereas Cynibal's were comfortably underground. The former had used conventional explosives hoarded and purchased from traders like the *Garnet*; the latter nation had used gases and synthetic plagues that had been mined up from the seemingly inexhaustible Armories and brought overland at great cost.

Smythe had come ashore that last day, and he had questioned the comparatively clear-headed girl who had told VanRoark about the war. "Why did it begin?" Smythe asked gently.

"It was a good fight, sir, a very good fight, fought with honor and courage and cunning on both sides."

"I'm sure, but how did it begin?"

"You know, for a while there—before the war—it could be very fine, you know, the two of us; all very peaceful and lovely. But if it had to end, we guess the war was a good end for it. It was a good fight, sir."

"But who started it?"

"What?" she asked blankly.

"The war! Your well-fought war!" Smythe exploded and at once felt sorry for it.

"Oh yes." She tugged lightly at a curl of auburn hair; VanRoark began to feel sick with helplessness. She was beyond his touch no matter what he might do, no matter what he might say, "Well, I guess we, they . . . oh yes . . . yes!" Her eyes sparkled briefly and she looked up at the men for the first time; she was smiling. "The war began . . . something so little . . . I think someone wrote a book and old Bournmouth thought he was in it and . . . " Then she lost control and began to shake with close detonations of hysterical laughter. " . . . Book, Christ! a book . . . " She really thought it was funny, by the looks of her. VanRoark glanced at Smythe, wondering whether he should be embarrassed or wait for the end of the joke.

Slowly, the laughings and chucklings grated off into long, partially suppressed sobs and curses. She looked up at them once more, her hair matted and the dirt on her face streaked and stained by tears; then she closed her reddened eyes, which might have been opal or green or gold near the pupil but which were now only dull gray, and wandered away from them.

"Should we do anything . . . anything?" VanRoark asked Smythe, hoping that the old man might have remembered an appropriate cure for the disease from his Libraries.

"Yes, leave. Away from this place, Amon, now." He began walking quickly toward the piers, away from the girl; then he stopped and turned to the younger man. "And look at this place—look at her again, once; that's how all of it will be soon,"

VanRoark was unprepared for this. "But the Meadows," he blurted.

"Not even that, I think. Not even our Meadows will stop it." Smythe's voice was harder than he had ever

heard it before. That was the Bad thing, that there was
no confusion in it, as if he were speaking about ships or
history, things that at the bottom of his heart, he knew.

XI

VanRoark was relieved to notice that once they had
shipped out of Mount Soril and were heading clear of
the Bay, Smythe returned to his normal, pathetically confused character; he was much more comfortable to live
with that way.

They stayed close to the well charted northern shore
as they had on the way in, where the fires by land and
Sea guided them at night. Cape Lane was soon rounded
and they glided down Ihetah-Incalam's gentle seacoast.
The harsh, blasted tangles of Cynibal's cities were
replaced by calm white sand beaches and buildings of
soiled, crumbling stucco. The remnants of flags were still
fluttering from some flagpoles along the seawalls and
esplanades. Figures could be seen wandering along the
beaches or through the dead towns; once in a while one
of the figures would see them and burst into sudden
action, yelling and beating his fellows on the back to
attract their attention. Then he might run down to the
Sea or out along a pier, raise his arms to call to them;
but no call ever came. The figure would stand there a
bit, arms open to the air, saluting. The arms would lower
hesitantly and the retreating figure would shake with
suppressed sobs.

They could tell they had left Incalam behind when the
people came running from the cities with swords in their

hands. The architecture and atmosphere of the ruins were strange and alien to all but Smythe, who would smile at things they could not guess at. Tapp worried long and loud that they might run out of liquor; Yarrow was only loud.

The land was sere and charred, the grasses poisoned, the trees stunted, with nothing but bones and corpsenations to mark the passage of men. VanRoark got progressively sicker of the skeletal coastline, deserts and salt marshes alternating with sterile cliffs of basalt and granite. He withdrew from Smythe, leaving the man to his incomprehensible joy as he recognized some feature of a gutted building or hulk lying awash on a reef. Even Tapp was abandoned for the time, or rather they both got the same idea at once.

Tapp was having to conserve his drink now, no one having any idea how far the Meadows might be, and he was rather reserved, at times even brittle, during the day. VanRoark supposed he slept a lot, as he was seldom on deck.

VanRoark only continued his daily session with the boatswain, a burly man named Prager, whose leprous hands were still proficient in knot-tying and the usual business of sailing. He was going to the Meadows for one thing: "A good little pistol, like the one my dad had before it was lifted. Real nice. Automatic, know? Little pearl around the butt, nice heavy feel to it."

"Is that all?" VanRoark would ask; he did not like talking with Prager, in spite of the man's friendliness.

"Well, mate, see this?" He held up his right hand so VanRoark could see the splotches of dirty white along its back and running up the small finger. "Pretty soon that won't be there; gonna tie a nice knot, pull it tight, take my arm back and there's still gonna be one or two fingers where I was holding it. So all you need for a gun is two fingers to hold it and one to shoot it. Gimme that and I can still keep this lot up and running." He motioned toward a group of men lounging in the shade of the upturned jolly boat. "And when that's gone, sir, I'm gonna have Sawdust over there make up a little sort of wooden hand with my automatic bolted right into it. I saw once, in Enador I think, how this guy had a fake hand, like the one I'm talking about, and he had this cord running up it and around his back so when he moved a muscle somewhere, the hand'd move." Prager smiled, almost in anticipation. "So it won't matter if I lose both of 'em. Little wood, little cord, nice gun from the Meadows and I'll still be the only one who can keep the old *Garnet* afloat and headed in the right direction."

VanRoark was repelled at this image, for he instantly conceived of Prager in the last stages of his illness: a wooden man with open bones and slop bucket head, the whole affair being run through a cobweb tangle of strings operated by the stomach muscles and the genitalia which, if not the most intelligent parts of Prager, were almost certainly the most rugged. Then he found it funny and would spend some of his off hours imagining the sailor with rusty nails already at his elbows and knees, a trapdoor mouth, and eyes that opened and snapped shut like a ventriloquist's dummy.

The high Meadows, he thought, the sacred ground where mankind was to spill the last of its blood. . . . It was growing hot again as they moved farther south. The coastline and Sea were perpetually bounded by an insubstantial haze. The wind was slack and irregular; sometimes, when it died entirely and the Sea went dead and oily smooth, he began to view his quest as unvarnished idiocy, and Timonias as a highly accomplished nut and charlatan, nothing more. Tapp and Smythe gradually lost the quixotic charm and courage with which he had formally endowed them. Yarrow, at times, seemed to be the only honest man on board; at least he did not try to hide the fact that he was an idiot and therefore did not have to be ashamed that he should be so taken by such a preposterous myth.

At that instant, Tapp was just an old, beaten man, one who could find no other refuge than liquor from his own failures and those of his similarly flawed world. The grand language deteriorated each time it was used again; the archaic usages that had seemed so wonderfully gallant in the submarine pens were as affected and boring as Yarrow's. In addition to all of these things, Tapp was a traitor, and the age of the nation state had not so completely vanished as to make this less of a blasphemy to some men. The bleeding sore on the back of his neck became a more appropriate emblem.

And why was he truly going to the Meadows? That was a bit harder for VanRoark. Ideally, this new Tapp he had constructed should be running as fast as possible in the opposite direction. But perhaps he had already been in the other directions and found only the things that had driven him from Cynibal; now there might be no place left for him but the Meadows. He would be dead within two years, that was known beyond any doubt, and it could be, as the little man had pointed out himself in one of his heroic drunks, that his death might be a gallant one. This last possibility momentarily grasped VanRoark's consciousness and he concluded that if Tapp had such a fine time proclaiming how he would die, then perhaps VanRoark might also pass some time in so pleasant a manner; he tried it once, snitching a little of Tapp's closely guarded brew and some of the crew's swill.

Actually it wasn't much, but he was tired and inexperienced, so the liquor worked with satisfactory efficiency. He got violently ill, of course (the worst part about *that* was being physically unable to escape Yarrow and his predictable sermon on the evils of drink), but before that he had almost enjoyed it for a while. He grew very quiet and peaceful, and once again the Sea with all its swarming life enchanted him: starlight glistened on the metallic sides of flying fish and barracuda—deeper down in the clear water the shadow forms of manta-rays, colonies of luminous bacteria clinging along the edges of their wings and barbed tails, glowed milk and turquoise. All was as it should be there, all calm and naturally complete, living in accordance with whatever plan or agency had created it. Where, he wondered, could Tapp's raging energy, anger, and defiant cynicism come from in such a peaceful world?

Then the twisted, agonizing howling of the land would sigh across to him and he tried to tell whether it was a man or an animal, and who was feeding on whom. The coast was nothing more than a black outline, like the manta-rays, but devoid of their cool luminosity.

For five days they had sailed past a salt desert that ran only a few feet above sea level, almost to the horizon, where it met a range of low, iron red cliffs. The concrete and rusted steel foundations of the ruins rising above the flats with jarring abruptness were there, as they were everywhere else; collections of flying boats were occasionally seen gathered together, usually about a mile or two inland, the metal panels and fabric torn from their ribs. They looked like dead sailfish or marlin washed up by some storm, and slowly being picked apart by the sea gulls and salt lizards.

VanRoark thought of Smythe then; firstly, because he had been the one to identify the aircraft and even guess that the faded, black and yellow roundels and tail blazons meant they had once served a nation called the Synod; secondly, he thought of him because Smythe was dead too, although not half so beautifully as the planes. He was like the people in Mount Soril, dead but still walking.

It had been the dead men, he remembered, that he had so sagely concluded would truly fight at the Meadows. Now Smythe and Tapp were dead and nothing more. They had not even enough courage to determine their own motivations for the physical formality of death. VanRoark's drunken stupor heaved itself about, vaguely aiming at an anger with men who had allowed the learning of Krysale Abbey to vanish, or betrayed their own homeland, trading them for the doubtful myth of the Meadows.

Unconsciously, his hand felt along the ship's side, looking for an unused belaying pin to use first on Smythe and then on Tapp; he felt around the back of the board searching for one, when he touched something at once sandy and sponge-like, like an old cigarette someone had dropped. He held it up to the starlight; that was when he got sick, for it was Prager's little finger. The land had produced yet another ingenious variation on the usual afflictions of mankind, and Prager's mutated leprosy had cut straight through the finger, rotting bone and nerve alike. Prager, good-humored and stupidly resigned as ever, had left the finger there on purpose; when he heard about it in the morning he waved the cauterized red and white stump in VanRoark's face and laughed himself silly over the youth's still rebellious stomach.

XII

VanRoark recovered from this episode, though now he pursued his education in sailing as best he could alone; ashamed at the sorry treatment he had given Smythe and Tapp, he retreated even further from the two, seldom thinking very deeply about them or their motives.

They had been at Sea for quite some time now and not even several mildly successful expeditions ashore into some ruined city or rare patch of healthy vegetation for food and water helped much in fending off scurvy and pellagra; not even the *Garnet*'s crew were having a very good time of it and there was brooding talk drifting aft from the forecastle at night. They were in no danger, the captain assured them, for the crew, normally a gutless lot anyway, were now even more cowed by their reduced numbers and the captain's monopoly on water and limes, all of which were kept in his cabin and would be instantly emptied into the Sea should any mutiny begin.

Presently, though, they began rounding more headlands, and weaving through a patchwork of islands and archipelagos. The sun shifted, until it rose astern and then on to starboard, over the land. The wind had also shifted and now spilled off the burning cliffs.

Here the territories were utterly unnamed and not even Smythe had the slightest notion of what flags might have flown over the infrequent ruins, or in the service of what gods those hulks might have sailed. But Tapp knew—some of it, anyway. The little man began to come on deck more often, to pace nervously up and down, his eyes flickering between the land and sky.

Every so often he would see something he thought he remembered from eleven years ago, and would scratch furiously at his wound until it bled; and if he did remember he would run for Smythe or VanRoark and point to it and tell how he had passed this very spot so many years ago. But he never seemed quite as sure as he would have liked to have been. He continued to pick at his neck and then he would have to raise a bucket over the side and wash the pus and blood off his hand. By this time the ruins, the devastated factory or church had been left behind.

VanRoark really began to worry about Tapp for, besides his sudden nervousness, he had once again stopped drinking, before sunset anyway. The pain of his disease, which the liquor had previously hidden, now served to once again increase his agitation and brittleness. But unlike the other times, Tapp continued to abstain. VanRoark would ask him if he was looking for anything in particular, some landmark perhaps. Tapp would murmur something indistinct and then move off, away from the younger man.

He continued to drink fairly regularly at night, though, when the ship would heave to along the unfamiliar coast,

its jagged outline sometimes spotted with strange lumi-
nosities. Then Tapp's voice would come flowing richly
out of the darkness: not with the old, quixotic ravings,
but a doggerel song, over and over again, with the
same words.

"Set amid the thorn trees . . . " The words were
slurred but still recognizable.

" . . . her towers soaring high,
her sullen flags defiant against the cobalt sky,
old Brampton Hall, deserted, wounded, left to die,
by allies who turned and fled at Evil's battle cry.

"Then the lads of Brampton Hall, their rifles in
   their hands,
stood and fought the darken'd hordes that strode
   upon their lands.
So here's a cheer for Brampton Hall! Yet her stone
   walls stand
to strive and hold the fall of night against the fall
   of man!"

The memory of the revelations he'd had about Tapp
during his drunk began to fade in VanRoark; the man
had become more nervous, admittedly, but it was not like
the dread he had shown near Cynibal. It was anticipation,
unconnected with any real fear or despair. It seemed
once again that perhaps a man like Tapp could fight at
the Meadows and fight well.

VanRoark eventually got around to asking Smythe
about this Brampton Hall. The librarian ran his hand

through his thin straw hair and said that the only thing he could recall was legend.

There had been a battle, he said, a great one which had finally annihilated a power named Salasar or something like that, the power which had resisted utter defeat for almost a millennium. In commemoration of this battle a memorial had been established. Understandably, for the war had been fought in very strange ways, the monument soon became a shrine, the object of a great many pilgrims. A town grew up around it, one in which a great soldier, Thomas St. Clair Brampton, eventually settled and founded a dynasty. The land was barren and hostile, but his descendants, living by the talents of their swords and minds, established a powerful nation. The name of their home, Brampton Hall, was given to the whole territory.

Now, from there it was very dubious, Smythe pointed out. Supposedly, at one of the false-Armageddons, Evil had actually routed the forces of mankind and broken out of the Meadows, raging about and threatening to engulf the entire world. It was stopped at Brampton Hall, whose families, ironically, had declined to go to the Meadows in their lordly contempt for the prophets and their attendant promises and plans. By this time, the armies had reformed and were able to drive Evil back to the Meadows, there to fight another agonizing draw. Brampton Hall itself was virtually wiped out in the holding action, her people for the most part dead or dying and the rest scattering in disgust as far away from the Meadows as possible.

VanRoark waited until Tapp was reasonably drunk and as close to his old moods as he had been for weeks, and then he told him of the librarian's tale. "Ah, true, the lot of it." Tapp sighed. "Except of course, it could do with a bit more to it, more substance, you know. I'm telling you this all straight down because I've seen the Hall. It's built on the mountains overlooking the Burn; I guess it was that battle they sang about that made it that way, so bad and all." Tapp took a thoughtful pull on his bottle, and said, more to himself than VanRoark, "Then I wonder what the old Meadows look like." He closed his eyes and took a much longer drink as he began to remember.

He resumed after the liquor had burned itself out in his throat, speaking very quickly so as not to allow himself too much time for thinking of the Meadows. "Oh, you'll love the Burn, Amon; at least you'll see a ruin with real character, real substance: great stone and steel walls, feet thick, and iron hammerbeams where the roof used to be, each one almost as thick as this tub here."

"We're going there? I thought the Meadows . . . ?" VanRoark trailed off weakly.

Tapp grinned and reached back to scratch his sore. "This Burn is where our army is gathering. Can't very well have us show up piecemeal, without any organization or anything. You weren't listening very well to your prophet when he told you that part."

"I guess not," VanRoark answered back, at ease again in Tapp's company. "But now it's my turn to wonder: I wonder where Evil is gathering."

"And then you weren't listening to that part either."

The grin faded a bit from VanRoark. "Which part?"

"The part where he, whoever he was, called Evil. We could hardly have the Meadows without an Opposition, you know."

VanRoark was getting confused; he had not thought very much about Timonias lately and all that he could dredge up was a vague collection of impressions, even more incomplete and fragmentary than when he had first begun to forget, across from the Isle of Oromund. "He *also* called Evil to the Meadows, the same person?"

"Right." Tapp was not in the least upset by this, which only served to further VanRoark's distress. "Look, you must remember your Timonias calling to those other types too." Indistinct shapes, terrifying in their very lack of definition turned and heaved just below VanRoark's comprehension.

"I don't know; I don't remember."

"When I heard my man—Lord, I can't even remember his name! Old, decrepit sort, I think—eleven years ago, I'm almost positive that he appealed to both sides. I can't see how he could have helped but do that because, remember, the thing he told you about was History and how it had to end. Well, the Opposition is as much a part of that ending as we are, so doesn't it seem right that he should just state the facts and let each man take his pick? That is the whole idea behind the thing, you know."

"All right, maybe Timonias did say something to them. I don't know, but if he did, then it must mean that he could have been the chosen of Evil as well as Good. The distinction of what *he* was would have lain in *our* hearts and not his." Why, VanRoark asked himself, did Tapp seem to be getting more relaxed and natural as the progress of the argument led to some conclusions that had him approaching a near-panic?

Tapp calmly nodded that, yes, that seemed right.

"Then maybe, if Timonias was talking to us all—both them and us, I mean—he would have used the same words." VanRoark was talking very slowly now; how strange that he had never asked himself this: "Then it could mean that *we* are Evil, going to its army! Tapp, what if that's true?"

Tapp shrugged and took another drink.

VanRoark was now desperately trying to find ways out of the corner he had argued himself into. "You were there before, Tapp; how did it seem?"

"Seemed good enough for my tastes."

"But you're not sure, you could have been wrong . . . ?" VanRoark had almost said, *You could be betraying me.*

"Amon." Tapp raised his hand to VanRoark's shoulder to calm him, but changed his mind and only touched him lightly. "When I went to the Meadows for the first time it was with the full intention, as far as I could tell, of fighting on the side of Good; that's all. I heard the words, as much as anyone could hear such words, and I left to pledge my soul on the side of Light and God; if the same words are used for the Good as well as the Evil, then it's up to every man to sort out their real meaning, for himself, in his own heart and mind. The army you go to, the men you will die beside, they will be of the same substance as yourself; and if it turns out that you have come to the army of Night, it will be simply because that is what you are and to change that would be impossible. Like I said, though, I believe we are joining the right side."

"But you're still not absolutely sure," VanRoark fairly croaked. "Why are you going back if you're still not sure what you might die in the name of?"

Tapp smiled drunkenly at him. "I will die in the name of what I am, nothing else." He looked at VanRoark for a moment, as if trying to decide whether or not he should keep on speaking. "And what I am now, I think, is neither Good nor Evil. I think, I hope it's Brampton Hall; if I die in the name of that, then this trip and the years spent before it will have been right."

VanRoark waited, expecting some explanation of this remark; when none came and Tapp began drinking again and softly humming his song, the younger man gave a short cry that might have been rage, and ran forward, away from him.

XIII

Now it was VanRoark who spent most of his time below, in his hammock, going topside only during the night or early hours of the morning. He had absorbed so much, found so much that was confusing and frightening in people, been surrounded by the reality of the Great Abstractions brought jarringly to earth, devoid of any certainty as to their true identity. The ordered systems he had constantly tried to construct, first around the Sea and then around the infinitely elusive natures of Smythe and Tapp, were now reeling and crashing down upon each other and on top of the new, hideous uncertainties that Tapp had planted in his mind. His consciousness had been stretched from the empty sterility of the Greenbelt to the larger, more nebulous agony that was the entire world; this consciousness had acquired ruins, haunted ones. Questions he should have asked about himself years ago, or forgotten forever, came flooding in on the wake of his distress.

But strangely, the falling, colliding fragments eventually brought him a numbed peace. As they sailed northward he felt washed out; not clean, but nearer to the ordered, hollow confusion of death, the cleanliness of the shroud. He honestly wondered if he should ever feel anything again, ever experience another emotion to the bottom of his soul.

XIV

As a child, VanRoark had often sat on the breakwater of his home city and watched the tanners' hawks hunting the more sluggish terns and sea gulls which, in turn, hunted the fish that lived near the wreck-littered entrance. They were fairly large birds, molted white on the belly and underside of the wings, and a leathery tan on top. Exceedingly graceful, they would ride the winds for hours at a time, only moving their wings to gain an occasional few feet of height. When one had picked out a target, it would drift above it, all very easily and relaxed, and lift one wing in a languid roll; when the hawk was on its back, with its body pointed down about fifty degrees, the wings would suddenly be snapped in tight and it would fall. The easy, near-sleeping grace would become blurred with speed and violence; the talons would strike just behind the gull's neck, the power sometimes ripping the whole skull from the body.

The day was something like that, he thought later; they had been moving back into temperate latitudes and the old *Garnet* was behaving herself uncommonly well. He had been on deck, absently talking with Smythe, congratulating their good fortune at the progress of Yarrow's illness, for it meant he could only rarely indulge in his impassioned speeches.

It was after the noon meal (weevilly hardtack and salt pork which had the prettiest little beetles living in it; the crew saved them and occasionally ran races). The lookout on the mainmast called down that there was a curious dot on the southern horizon. Then a pause; the dot was above the horizon and seemed to be slowly growing. All eyes swung aft, but everyone's bodies—except for Tapp and Smythe, who sprang for the ratlines and began to climb—were frozen.

VanRoark caught sight of the object, perhaps ten miles astern; then it was a hundred feet aft, abeam, and then forward, diminishing again.

It had been an aircraft, with longer and more graceful lines than the tanners'. VanRoark shut his eyes as soon as it had gone and examined the instant: not more than seventy feet off the water, triangular wings that were bent upward at their tips, a single sharkfin at the tail, dull black on the belly, wandering bands of olive and sand topsides. There were gaping holes in her near the wing roots that rounded into exhausts aft; and when she had been directly abeam of where VanRoark stood, the majestic silence of the craft's passage had been shattered by a rolling thunder that beat against his body, shook the *Garnet*'s sails, and almost knocked Tapp and Smythe into the Sea.

Tapp was yelling hysterically from his perch: "Did you see that? Did you see her? Christ! Did you see her?"

Then his tongue got wrapped up in itself as it tried to get out years of anticipation in five seconds.

Smythe was pleasantly dumbfounded in his thoughtful climb down to the deck. He said nothing then, but at dinner, when he could fit in a word between Tapp's endless and amazingly sober ravings, he said that it had been a bomber, a shade under two hundred feet long, capable of exceeding the speed of sound (VanRoark did not entirely understand that), and the last of her kind were supposed to have crashed and burned five centuries ago. He had had only a glance at her colors, but he could identify parts of at least three different national standards. There were two more he could not place. Smythe stayed up very late that night, something he had never done. Prager later told VanRoark that near dawn Yarrow had come up to the librarian, apparently unable to contain his decaying throat any longer on the subject of the plane. Smythe had beaten the living hell out of him.

VanRoark could feel a quickening, a compression of time about him that did not leave enough room to speculate on the Great Abstractions. He managed to look upon the uncertainties as things that fate had already decided for him. The Wars were still going on, he was sure of that now, and he was going to them. They were near now too, within human reach. The simply human took precedence and he wondered if, when men were trying to kill him, he would be able to stand and, presumably, try to do the same to them. Glory began to infect his mind.

The captain, who listened quietly and calmly with his ferret eyes and quick, nervous gestures to Tapp's uncontainable enthusiasm, was also moved. On the one hand he was rather disappointed to see such a powerful machine going to the Burn and the Meadows (even Tapp naturally assumed that the plane was going to join the same side as they), for it meant that removal of "cargo" from its present owners would be that much more difficult. Ruins were so much easier, no self-appointed patriots or saviors clinging to things which were almost useless to them but could turn a fair profit in the hands of an intelligent man.

However, the fact of the plane's being in operational condition had inflamed the captain's limited imagination. When Tapp had gone spinning off into the darkness and Smythe had followed behind, he dreamily explained to VanRoark the marvelous possibilities this situation presented to the circumspect businessman. If things as large as that aircraft were to be found gathering at the Burn, then why not steel ships powered by steam or even more marvelous things? There were twenty nations gunning for Enador and her monitors and steam frigate, and the man who delivered the proper ship could name his price.

As the evening wore on—VanRoark stayed even though he was both repelled and bored—the idea of piracy predictably arose. VanRoark could see the schemes and plans wiping aside the profit and loss sheets that had recorded the captain's dreary trade in rusting guns and stale explosives: a great battleship, her skeleton crew of fanatics sleeping the night; boats putting out from the *Garnet,* muffled oars, knives and metal wire around the crew's throats; then a new command for the captain, with all the world at his feet.

VanRoark left him to retire; naturally, he was unable to sleep and would have gone on deck, but he figured the deck belonged to Tapp and Smythe that night. Instead, he spent the night dreaming, half-awake, his ears still ringing from the aircraft's howling and the patchwork of insignia disrupting the smooth flow of her camouflage, the sun white on her glass, her exhausts yellow-red.

Once, just as he was dozing off, he heard a thumping and thought the sails were being shaken by the passage of another ship; he asked Prager about it in the morning and was told that it was probably only Yarrow hitting the deck.

XV

Five days after the camouflaged bomber had flown past them, Tapp spotted five glittering beads hanging below the sun, white chalk marks trailing behind them to the horizon. They looked at them now with less fear, and the crew hardly cringed when the dim, rolling report of their engines drifted down through the clear air. The captain brought his glass to bear on the formation, but it was so high above them that even he could see nothing more than a blinding metallic radiance.

The planes were over them for half an hour before they were lost from sight and their trails gently dispersed. Once again, VanRoark felt time shrinking and compressing; even the languid, peaceful passage of the formation reduced tomorrow to the next minute and the end of the world to tomorrow.

The first ship passed them the day after the formation; Tapp was by now beside himself with anticipation, checking and endlessly rechecking his memories of the nations that had made up his army with the now prouder recollections of Smythe. *Lord,* VanRoark thought as she passed less than a quarter of a mile to port, *how lovely she is! How old and proud!* All battle gray in black trim, two twin turrets fore and aft, two stacks, a high bridge like a castle's keep, and a clipper bow plowing up the cyanogen water and turning it white; the pendent numbers 2470 were painted on her bridge and transom. The captain read out her name, *W. Lane. So curious,* Van Roark thought again, *that so beautiful a ship* ("Lord, 'Roark, look at 'er, must be turning thirty knots!") *should carry so dull a name,* especially when the wrecks of his world bore names like *Amethyst* and *Jewel* as they careened about the Sea.

Smythe hypnotically recited his usual list of particulars, armament figures, speeds, the nations she might have sailed for and how the ships of her type had acquitted themselves in storms and battles past. VanRoark saw only the fine, long sweepings of her lines and how cleanly she moved through the water, and the silken pennants that trailed for a hundred feet or more behind her masts.

Then she was gone. The *W. Lane* had given no acknowledgment of the *Garnet's* presence, had not even dipped a flag or displayed a signal lamp. But this bothered no one. Smythe, Tapp, and VanRoark were satisfied with her physical presence and to be reassured, again, that such things still existed. The captain and crew of the *Garnet* were relieved that the destroyer, so Smythe had termed her, had taken no notice of them; they welcomed the anonymity, for it meant that capturing her or one like her would be that much easier. The captain wondered how it would feel to have a steel deck under him and not have to worry which way the corrupted winds might be blowing at the moment. "*W. Lane,*" he rolled the name over in his mouth. Really, he would have to change that straight off. Only Yarrow was in any way irritated. He called it a sin for men to so treat their own creations that they handed ownership of their souls over to them.

VanRoark was rather disappointed when nothing was spotted the next day, nor on the one after that. He wondered if they had not, through some fantastic coincidence, stumbled into an area where the aircraft and ships just happened to be in their endless wandering, or if they had blundered onto one of the Sea's old graveyards, rife with ghosts and flying Dutchmen.

The coast was smooth and regular now, with the cooler water canceling the possibility of coral reefs. The scarcity of rivers or turbulences made sand bars a rarity too. They sailed at night, when the star or moonlight allowed. It was about midnight when Tapp's yelling, a little hoarse from all his fulminations, began shaking the *Garnet*. Men tumbled out of their hammocks and grabbed cutlass and ax, thinking they were under attack.

VanRoark ran on deck to find Tapp halfway up the foremast ratlines, pointing wildly at a rising headland to the northeast. "What is it?" he called up.

"Look, 'Roark, over there, on top of that rise. See it? See it?" Tapp waved in the direction of the coast;

VanRoark squinted but could see nothing. He tried again, this time moving back and forth slightly, to silhouette anything against the stars. He began to make out some skeletal structures, bare beams and irregular walls separating themselves from the larger darkness of the headland. "I see it now. What is it?"

"Brampton Hall, 'Roark!" Tapp fairly screamed.

"You said it overlooked the Burn, where the army'd be." VanRoark was vaguely aware of the delighted hysteria that was creeping into his voice too.

"On the north side of it. Soon as we round those cliffs we'll see them." A pause while Tapp's eyes swept the ruins again. "Brampton Hall!" he exploded.

Smythe came on deck, tucking his shirt into his trousers and wiping the sleep from his eyes. VanRoark pointed out the outline of the building. "Goddamn," he muttered thoughtfully.

Most of the crew was up, leaping about the deck or through the rigging, absently rigging flags of truce and weapons, not one of them really having any idea of what they should do. Yarrow, for once, was dead quiet.

VanRoark recalled the trite novels of his boyhood, what few there had been, and thought that now it would get very quiet, like the flowing peace of the tanners' hawks before they hit. But the night was underlaid with small, distant hummings and roars. As they moved northward, rounding the headlands, the noises grew more emphatic, first absorbing the gentle slap of the Sea against the *Garnet*'s hull, and then intruding upon normal conversation. Vivid, sharp eruptions of sound began to break up the monotone, lacing it through with violence and power.

The headlands where Brampton Hall itself rested rose against the welkin to become a rather sizable line of near-mountains curving away and rounding up into the north, where they dissolved into the horizon. Cradled between these hills and the Sea was the army. Even Tapp was struck silent. It looked as if the *Garnet* were sailing directly into a star cluster, whose brilliance shimmered out to them across the surface of the calm Sea. Lights, more than VanRoark had ever seen, tapestried the dark earth with everything from the cold, unwavering shine of electrical bulbs to the rainbow shades of altars and votary lamps. Shapes and colors, nothing more than moving specks of blackness at this distance, hovered around the lights, occasionally separating themselves as fire shone through silk or upon burnished armor and was then reabsorbed.

A sudden call from the lookout shattered the spell. In their fascination with the glittering Burn, almost no one had noticed that the bay to which they were now sailing was filled with sailing boats and steamships. As they lowered the main and foresails, proceeding only on staysail and jibes, they saw fire-reflected shapes on the water as well as on land. The standard navigation lights of white, orange, and pale blue swept out from the coast to meet them on the hulls of five hundred sailing ships. Most looked to be as miserable as the *Garnet,* but others lay tall and proud, their gilt work fresh-painted, their hulls slick in the water, their brass cannon clean and warm in the lights.

VanRoark caught a low whistle from the captain and an order to edge the *Garnet* over to port. VanRoark looked to his left and saw gray walls rising from the Sea, walls with anchor chains stuck into them and pendent numbers of white and gold. Their superstructures were dull in the army's light and they towered above the *Garnet,* sharply outlining themselves against the stars. Van-Roark thought he spotted the *W. Lane* and was amazed at how much larger were the others moored near her. Specter shapes in white and light tan moved upon the warship's decks: turrets, forest-masts with strange wire tangles wound about them, and flags stirring tiredly in the light air; fine lines and ancient metals passed by him as they moved toward the beach.

The captain recovered his senses after a while and, much as he might have liked to pick out his future command then and there, deemed it wiser to anchor and await daylight before he made any concrete plans. The hook was let down about a half mile offshore, between a four masted schooner from the Isle of Oromund and a destroyer like the *W. Lane*, which still chose to carry the standard of the long-broken North Cape Confederation.

Tapp decided to get drunk and spent most of the night on the quarterdeck, sitting on the wheelhouse, singing "Brampton Hall" and other old songs until he passed out. The crew would have shut him up but when any of them advanced upon him, he would only swing out his saber and sing all the louder. His fingers were wet with liquor and his own blood.

VanRoark and Smythe climbed to the maintop and for hours silently looked about them and through the universe they had entered, the ships and the roarings. They saw, past the gray ships to port, a single, unbroken line of stone that might have been the facing for some quay or causeway of undetermined length. More lights moved up and down this wall, some descending from the night and slowing to a stop, others rolling along it with increasing speed until they bulleted free and screamed off, their flight marked by the deep whistling of Smythe's first sighted lone bomber—and then by the far burble of the second formation.

Around three, when the false dawn was beginning to take hold behind the encircling hills, a fog crept in from the Sea, shrouding and softening the lights, blurring and confusing distances, wrapping the *Garnet* up inside the army's universe. Shapes and shadows of ships and aircraft, their activity now much diminished and the lights reduced in number, moved toward them with liquid delicacy and then receded, dancing about the old *Garnet* and her plotting crew. VanRoark guessed they still had more than an hour to go before dawn, which the mist would obscure for another hour anyway, and decided to turn in along with Smythe. Tapp had been unconscious for quite a while and was peacefully sprawled on the deck, his sword in one hand and an empty liquor tin in the other.

No one saw Yarrow during the night and he was not on board the next morning. The captain figured that the fanatic must have slipped overboard in the fog and made it ashore before any of them were up. Tapp did not entirely discount the possibility that the crew had murdered him for the jeweled holy books he had once said he was carrying with him. VanRoark surprised himself at how little emotion he felt at this thought—and even at the humor—for at least the poor old fool would have died where he wanted to, the absence of an Heroic Struggle Against Evil being but a minor omission in Yarrow's pilgrimage. But then, thought VanRoark, progressively more amused with this line of conjecture, perhaps he had put up a brave fight, and if the captain and crew of the *Garnet* were not as evil as Salasar was supposed to have been, they were not, by the same token, possessed of snow-white souls; and if they were then, in some measure, sworn to the flag of Night, it would mean they had defeated the adherent of Light. So it appeared that yet another Armageddon, one smaller than most, had been bungled. At least Yarrow, whether he was among his fellow believers on this world or the next, was happy.

XVI

VanRoark thought that what he had seen the previous night would have insulated him in some way against what he might see in the light of day. While he was lying in his hammock and later getting dressed, he tried to prepare himself to be disappointed by the reality of the army. In a way he was, for the steel ships numbered only nine and not a thousand, and parked atop the stone wall, now revealed as a causeway that stretched from the beach to the horizon, were not more than twenty-five aircraft of varying sizes.

But in themselves, each of them represented more power than any great nation his home world might be able to muster. As he forgot their numbers and concentrated upon individual examination, VanRoark became aware of just how much the night and then the fog had distorted distances and proportions. The *W. Lane,* the smallest of the nine, now appeared even greater in the crowded anchorage while the largest, a battleship of incalculable destructive power, loomed over the sailing ships clustered near her, and cast her morning shadow far out to Sea.

They were towed ashore in the *Garnet*'s longboat along with one or two members of the crew who had honestly decided to throw their lot in with the army. The captain was still on board, briefing his chosen spies for their preliminary tasks.

Close inshore, they passed by the armed merchant cruiser that had brought Timonias to VanRoark's city. The rust was still scabbed about her plating and the gun tubs still marred the graceful lines. There were four other converted merchant ships moored around Timonias' ship, all in varying states of disrepair. The largest was also in the best shape, a tanker only a little smaller than the battleship farther out in the anchorage. The gloss black hull contrasted sharply with her spotless white topsides. As they rowed past her, VanRoark could see that her broad decks had been cleared of pumps and transfer pipes; a twin line of big field guns began aft of the forecastle, broke around the forward superstructure and then continued aft, their barrels and recoil mechanisms shining with preservative grease.

There was almost no surf and they landed easily. The crew stared at what lay before them and then pushed hurriedly back to the Sea and the *Garnet*. Before Van-Roark, Smythe, Tapp and the two who had deserted the *Garnet* sprawled the army: colors, colors swirling and dancing at every hand. Armored men mounted on horses with silken covers galloped back and forth before them, maces and lances held in their gleaming hands, silk pennons trailing from their crested helmets.

Tents fanned out in a random manner from the beach, redoubling the riot of colors with their gay patterns and designs; before many stood a staff or an ensign of some great family or nation or noble order. VanRoark could pick out at least twenty identifiable standards from where he stood, and Smythe said that of those he could place, at least half were of nations he had thought dead or scattered past recalling: the dolphin and seabird crests of the Dresau Islands naval aristocracy; the star constellations of the lands of the House of Raud; the mailed fist and pegasus of Mourne, ringed with a circlet of black oak leaves in penance for some ancient, forgotten wrong; the horse mane and sun disk devices of Larine's barbarian nobility; enameled, chain mail banners from the mountain kingdoms of Iannarrow, Enom, Howth; lion, unicorn, and hippogriff painted shields before the tents of men from Mountjoy and Kirkland and Kroonstadt; the anchor and osprey flag of Enador could be seen flying among a thousand others. VanRoark turned back to the harbor and picked out the low riding form of one of the city's river monitors. *Goddamn! Even the capitalists are here,* he thought. And for every one he could identify there were a hundred that were beyond even the librarian's knowledge.

They walked slowly up from the beach, swimming through the colors and press of bodies, for the types of men easily outnumbered the crests and colors they had first seen. It was like a city fair, when such things were still being held; never in all the world, not even in Enador's brawling markets and wharves, had he sensed such activity and apparent purpose. Here, a thing was being *done,* men were at work on things and not sitting on their fat asses waiting for something to walk up and club them to death.

Lord! The air itself was as alive and electric as the torrent of colors and people. VanRoark felt his head lighten and his joints partially dissolve as they walked, first down one avenue lined with stalls peddling newly-caught fish and lobster, then down another where large, especially gaily colored tents had rather tough looking women standing beside them, even at this hour of the morning. Tapp considered the tents closely, grunting approval when he caught the eye of someone he liked—and then groaning at his lack of money. VanRoark supposed that even the Army of Justice and Light was still made up of normal men who had to live while they were waiting. Smythe had already disappeared into one of the tents.

They walked south along the seaward edge of the camp, pavilion after bright pavilion passing to their left, great, heavily carved sailing ships riding at anchor on their right or careened up on the beach having their bottoms scraped. Gradually, the camp sites thinned out as they climbed up into the mountains toward Brampton Hall's ruin. It was about noon and they were almost to the summit of the headlands when they stopped for a lunch of black bread and cheese that VanRoark had purchased on one of the market avenues. Prices were much steeper than they had expected. After hassling at several shops and idly pricing items they could never afford no matter what their normal price—things like pistols or chain mail shirts—VanRoark correctly guessed that Enador had sent one of her precious river monitors to guard her merchants, not to die in the name of God or

Creation. When they talked to Smythe later in the week, he confirmed that Enador's commercial ventures, along with some of the other trading nations and cities present, went further than selling inanimate goods. That was why most of the shops and brothel tents were near the shore, for they could be more easily protected by the guns of their guardian ships.

These ideas depressed VanRoark more than he thought they should have. After all, was he not a jaded traveler, a wanderer who had left all this world had to offer him to go and seek his just end? But the organization, the emotionless calculation of it all really upset him for a time. Tapp, on the other hand, was fairly philosophical about the whole thing, arguing that if a fellow wanted to make some honest gold out of the end of the world, then who was to say he was wrong? None of this did much to counter VanRoark's recurring doubt that he had come to the right army.

But now they turned on the mountain's slope and, panting from the climb, stared at the carpet the army spread before them. The flat blurring colors and planes they had seen from sea level were now tilted upward, swirling, turning, colliding like buckets of dye suddenly dumped into a whirlpool. As they looked down to the north and northeast, they could see the nondescript, bland horde of tents and shelters in which men like themselves were forced to exist because of their inability or refusal to submit to Enador & Co.'s gougings.

As the density of the camps grew, so did the colors. First a single stripe of red or orange silk, or perhaps a small family banner sewn to a canvas wall, a hereditary suit of mail, ancient and oiled, gleaming by a doorway.

Then came the close packed heart of the army, its random, directionless avenues with their chromatic floods and harsh flashing metal; men mounted on strange beasts, gryphons and other winged creatures that flew above the bazaars and among the myriad flags. There was life compressed, even as time had become compressed for VanRoark, consuming and rioting with itself as if it had to satiate its last desires, before leaving for the Meadows.

There were no priests dressed as the two thought priests should, black and somber as befitted their mission in all this. Nor was there anything which might be taken for a church or temple. Tapp, however, said he had spotted several private shrines inside various tents.

The colors began to dull and fade out as the army once again began to thin out to the north; but instead of simply dying out, the tents and encampments ended abruptly; there was a stretch of several hundred feet and across that VanRoark could dimly make out the priestly dignity of canvas-shrouded field artillery and armored vehicles. They stood at the foot of the mountains, which curved east, and then straight north in a huge semicircle; the northern edge, instead of looping back and closing with the Sea, was split by a river gorge and then appeared to die away into grasslands. More formidable ranges, olive and dark gray, defined the horizon far past the grass plain.

Drawn up between the river and its delta were the tanks and colorless tents of what the main body of the army called the rim nations, for they lived at the edge of the world and, presumably, at the edge of chaos. Tapp said they were the lads of Brampton Hall, and they were not going to the Meadow Wars—they had merely come home. Then he laughed and VanRoark wondered if it was a joke.

At the eastern edge of the army, where the mountains dipped to allow the river to pass, there were four or five long, olive and tan camouflaged vehicles; they were articulated and made up of many separate cars. Tapp called them land trains and said that the longest of them stretched for more than a thousand feet. Moving westward along the border of the army were massed the artillery of the rim nations and their armored trucks and tanks; even at this great distance from them, hulking, brutal forms were clearly visible, even the red and purple flags flying from their masts and aerials. Small figures in tan and black walked in front of them or crawled over their vast exteriors.

The ranks of guns and vehicles were broken at irregular intervals by command tents and temporary buildings, again spined with radio masts and disk antennas. So strange, VanRoark thought as he looked at them, distance dissolving as it had in the fog last night; they were so quiet and firm beside the main body of the army and its erupting life. Soft, rippling colors blazoned on flags of a hundred different nations, and heritages lived below him, even though they awaited the signal to end Creation. Then north, across the hard crystalline soil that gave the Burn its name, the rim nations, almost sleeping, were strangely touched with the sadness of ruins; it was so quiet over there, no sounds drifting up to them over the blare of the army's shops and whorehouses.

The guns and tents, in loose order like tombstones, ambled westward until they reached a point about a third of a mile from the beach. There the aircraft of the rim nations (he was already beginning to identify them as something apart from the army) waited, one or two moving out of line, briefly catching the sun on their polished hulls and wings; they taxied out onto the horizon-reaching causeway. Tapp said it had been built by Brampton Hall, though for what reason he could not guess.

There was a bridge-like structure piercing the causeway two hundred yards from the beach, most probably to let the ships north to the Meadows. They rolled out over this, and then gained speed as their wing roots or tails burned pale yellow. Finally, the rim nations sent some noise up into the hills.

VanRoark followed the pathetically few aircraft as they tumbled westward and then lifted free, gaining sudden grace once they were rid of the earth. Their sound smothered the sea-roaring of the army and for a moment there was only the ground which he stood upon and the shining, silver bobbins streaming across the sky for some unknown purpose.

The ships he had seen last night and that morning, the five gray warships and three merchant cruisers, the tanker with its decks crammed with artillery, were moored nearest the causeway; flags dipped from ancient masts as the craft took off from the causeway, and the infrequent flashings of signal lights winked under their shadowed superstructures.

VanRoark thought at first that the ships and the encampments of the rim nations were already dead; but the planes and signal lamps showed that that was not yet true. They were only tired, sick with age, and traveling toward a resting place that seemed to be forever receding from them; thus the sadness. They had been running so very long.

A week after they had climbed up the mountain to Brampton Hall, he had chanced to wander across the dividing strip between the main force of the army and the rim nations. There had been very few persons around, at least compared to the eternal bustling of the army. He had walked up and down the rows of tanks and big guns, and when he counted them there did not seem to be so many.

There had been a man leaning up against the tires of a howitzer's split trail carriage, the watchworks of its sighting mechanism disassembled on a white sheet in front of him. He was naked to the waist, lean and deeply tanned, but that could have been his natural body color; either way, the contrast to his blue eyes was most striking. There was a tattoo of an armored Death, mounted on a pegasus, on his left forearm, and under it the words, *656th Airborne—the Devil's Own.*

They talked of inconsequentialities for a while, the price of women and swordfish steak, the lack of any life on board Timonias' old cruiser.

VanRoark mentioned the man's tattoo and asked where his planes were.

"Crashed on the way here. Probably still there in the, uh, North Cape Confederation's old lands; it's cold up there. We didn't think we were going to make it down in one piece, 'cause see, we got into these fjords. Walker set us down all right, though. We lost him a while back in the Barrens." His voice was slow, he was paying much more attention to rebuilding the sight than talking.

"How long ago was that?"

"Around ten, eleven years," he answered absently.

VanRoark was taken back a bit by this; he may have heard the call for the same Armageddon that Tapp had. "And you've been traveling since then to get here?"

"Around that, a little less, though, 'cause we got here about four months ago. And even then, we didn't spend that much time moving. The worst part was fishing all we could out of the water and then finding enough fuel for our tractors. We even rigged one up with a steam engine." He laughed a little at that.

VanRoark waited but apparently the man had nothing more to say on that particular subject; he kept working on the sight, carefully recoiling a small spring back into its gauge casing. "Don't you have anything else besides guns?" VanRoark mumbled more to himself than to the man as he glanced down the ranked barrels of howitzers and long rifles, steel cables rigged from breech castings to muzzle brakes to correct temperature warping of the bores.

The man heard this, or part of it, and for the first time put down his gears and miniature screwdrivers. "What?" he said, looking at VanRoark.

The younger man was immediately conscious of a slip in courtesy. "Well, I meant that the rest of the army has its weapons, of course, but they've also got other things; they've got their women and their musicians and entertainers. I think some men even brought their whole families, kids and all. And their shops and stalls, like a whole city was just dropped right down here and was setting up to stay forever."

"They could do that," the man said sourly. "We don't have these things. I know that. All we got are guns, and you know why?"

VanRoark shook his head, no, he did not.

"Because that's all they left us, dumb-ass!" he hissed unexpectedly, jabbing a finger in the direction of the army. "All those bleeding bastards left was the guns we could hold. Everything else, every good or beautiful thing we ever tried to set up in this world, they managed to queer or tear down.

"You know where I come from?" He did not wait for an answer. "How the hell could you, it doesn't even have a name any more! All you'd have to know is that it was dying and with all our power we couldn't do a thing about it. Every time we poked our hands outside of our lands because we needed some oil or some ore or even some clean water, they jumped us, from the front if they had the guts, but usually from the back. Sneaking in at night and slashing some dude's parachute and then repacking it all nice and careful, or putting some sort of bomb into one of our ships."

The man sank back against the cracked tires and wiped the sweat from his bald, bronzed skull. "Okay, man, you've heard my genealogy; get back to your army before you really ruin my afternoon."

VanRoark got up and began walking away, but could not resist asking a question: "Why are you here?"

"To die." The other shrugged, bending back over his work.

"This is the army of Right and Good and all. That's what your prophet said, didn't he?"

"I don't remember what the old bastard may have said. I'm here just because I'm sick and tired of all this, that's all."

"Not for Brampton Hall?"

"Never heard of it."

But that was a week after he had seen Brampton Hall for himself and had already begun to guess that this was what would be told him should he ever venture into the rim nations' camp.

They had reached the ruins of Brampton Hall by one in the afternoon, the army having smeared itself into a mass of indistinct rippling movements, edged by the slag-covered mountains and the camouflaged rim nations. In front of them soared the walls and blasted towers of the Hall, remnants of chain mail banners still flying from warped iron flagpoles. It was as huge as Tapp had said and for the first time in all his travelings, except when he had sat alone in the maintop with nothing but the Sea and a shadow ship below him, had he felt such peace. This was doubly strange, for the Hall, a term which included a whole complex of buildings and walls along the spine of the mountains, had obviously been the scene of a great struggle. Bullet holes, nearly eroded smooth but still recognizable, were splattered all over the walls; iron roofing beams of incredible size twisted down from their mountings as if some fantastic heat, like that of Blackwoods Bay, had made them bow before it.

VanRoark walked with Tapp into the main compound, almost a quarter of a mile square. Grass was growing there; not anything green or vaguely suggesting complete health but, still, an enormous change from the scorched sterility of the Burn and the slagged-down mountains. Mosses reached up the chipped and shattered walls along with a stunted form of ivy, trying to heal their wounds.

There were even bits of stained glass remaining in the arched windows of the Hall itself, fragments suggesting family crests or the lives of great men. VanRoark marveled at this especially, until he saw that the glass was almost seven inches thick.

Although there were traces of the ancient battle in the Hall—someone's femur bone was crushed into calcium dust just under the tarn and VanRoark spotted some unwholesome relic, unrecognizable in its centuries of rust and decay—the peace remained. They walked back down to their camp, a third-hand tent they had bartered away from some drunken louts from Howth. The dark, ill-defined shapes VanRoark had sensed when Timonias had spoken to him again arose beneath his consciousness, but they were different, carrying with them more sadness than exultant triumph.

XVII

In all, they were at the Burn for about two weeks. Further tours of the army's main body revealed little other than that the riotous confusion was being constantly multiplied as men straggled in from the Barrens to the east or as more sailing ships dropped anchor in the clogged roadstead. A week after they arrived, a large tender, gray and somber as the fog banks from which she had silently emerged that morning, put into the anchorage, her scurrying brood of torpedo boats dashing around her at forty knots. The seabird and dolphin crests of the dead Dresau Islands were enameled on her bow, but she flew no flags other than the usual signal banners.

However, two things of real importance were discovered. First that Timonias was still on board his cancerously white ship, probably accompanied by whatever priests might have bothered to come to the Meadows. The cruiser was still close inshore, lying neither with the glut of wooden sailing ships nor with the ships from the rim nations clustered along the causeway.

Even compared to the infrequent stirrings of the steel ships, the merchant cruiser was a ghost ship; not once had VanRoark seen a single living person on her decks, a single wisp of steam escape from her funnel, a single flag hoisted in response to some shoreward signal. When he questioned someone on this seeming desertion, they would inevitably just smile and say that Timonias was on board and what more did one need to know?

He wondered if this lack of watchfulness had prompted the *Garnet's* men to make any expeditions for loot. But the barque was no longer at her anchorage and VanRoark quickly ceased to think about her.

The second thing was his rediscovery of Smythe. He had been walking westward along the no-man's-land between the rim nations and the army, toward the foot of the causeway and the parked aircraft. To his right, a wrecker crane had been drawn up alongside a large armored troop carrier; one of its engines had been removed and several men were working on it beside the tank. One of them was Smythe.

VanRoark moved over and watched quietly, remembering his clumsy conversation with the artilleryman just the other day. Eventually plates were secured again and torqued down; the wrecker lifted the engine over the open hatch and then lowered it gently from sight. Smythe turned from the vehicle, wiping oil from his blackened hands, and saw VanRoark.

He was smiling, obviously enjoying himself; VanRoark asked him under whose flag he had found such employment. They talked lightly for a while, walking down to the Sea under the long wings of the aircraft, their distorted reflections flowing on the aluminum and glass.

XVIII

The next two days VanRoark spent with Smythe and the men from a nation of which he had never heard. The things he used to feel and think at Sea when they had passed the ruins, or even back home when he had wandered along the Old Navy Dock, were remembered. The fears about exactly which army he had joined once again receded before the memory-forms of pilings and bollards that used to hold battle cruisers against the dock.

At dusk of the second day they walked along the causeway, over the drawbridge, and then westward almost a mile, so they could feel the rush of warm air as the aircraft landed or departed; the noise and vibration shook VanRoark and his mind. A violence he had never sensed rumbled within and sent him rising off the world with the green, tan and black mottled craft. When they came in very low over the Sea, over the anchored fleets, he could see their shock-waves rippling up from the water, crashing against the causeway, and then beginning again on the northern Sea.

Smythe told him again how ships like those, but infinitely greater, had once journeyed to the stars he now saw above the eastern horizon—but that was legend.

On the third day VanRoark could not find Smythe; none of the men he had been working with knew where he was, but VanRoark spent the day with them, pulling the turret from a tank and cleaning mechanisms whose workings he could not even guess at.

He finished sometime around six in the evening and left for his tent. One of the men suggested he move away from the army and into one of the rim nations' camps. "Hell, he's closer to those lovely tents where he is now," said another.

"Well, yeah," the first man grinned, "but I think the army's lads are getting a little restive, you know?"

VanRoark did not.

"Well, the whole army is just getting a little tense as far as we're concerned. They think our ships and machines are more the Devil's than their God's. And Timonias and his mates out on their ship don't seem to be helping the situation one way or the other. We need some help; those dudes have got us outnumbered at least a hundred to one and almost every night a couple of them come sneaking across the strip. Christ, most of this stuff's at least four hundred years old and shot to pieces with age and things we could never set straight. Now we got them cutting wires and dumping sand into the petrol. Just like the old days, they tell me; a few nights ago some of them tried to jump the crew of one of our destroyers, pirate her, for crissake!"

"What happened to them?"

The joker answered now: "They found out which ship they came from, an old barque from Enador or someplace, and escorted her out to Sea. Our ship came back with a couple of empty shell casings and no more barque." A short laugh, and then much lower and more savage, "Stinking bastards, stinking pirating bastards!"

"That's part of it too, mate. A lot of the camp isn't too happy about friendly little sinkings like that. They're talking too much over there about things they don't understand."

VanRoark thanked them for the warning and walked slowly back to his tent, the army's lights and colors growing more sinister and menacing; now that he looked it did seem that a lot more attention was being paid to weapons than when they had first arrived. Gryfons were conspicuously draped in light mail and shod with steel-clawed slippers. It could not be that the army was moving on the Meadows, because then the rim nations would have known too. Besides, such an occasion would have been one for celebration and last feasts. This was entirely too businesslike. Most likely, though, it was only his imagination.

Tapp did not return that night and VanRoark assumed he was merely off on some particularly elaborate binge. He could not sleep and spent quite some time debating on whether the camp's quiet was normal or extraordinary. Around two in the morning he decided to try to find Tapp and ask him about what the army thought of the rim nations.

The camp did seem unusually quiet, but it was a broken, fractured quiet cut up only by the rough singing of drunken men. Between the songs of battle and love there was nothing, not even the wind from the Barrens. He looked south to the ruins of Brampton Hall, half expecting to see spectral lights and vapors hovering about them. *Working yourself up into a proper frenzy, Van-Roark,* he thought.

When he couldn't find Tapp, VanRoark decided to look for Smythe. He passed through the sleeping army and across the strip to the rim nations. There too, the quiet was almost oppressive, but there was no drunken singing, only the sandy crunch of a patrol's boots.

He headed down to where he thought Smythe had his tent, near to the line of armored troop carriers where he had first spotted him.

The tent was set back toward the riverbank and it stank, for Smythe had been dead for more than a day; his throat had been slit and the blood had collected in the tent's waterproofed bottom, crusty and granular like the Burn's soil. VanRoark lit a small lamp that was hanging from the middle of the tent frame, and stared at the body. Even in his savage, brutal world, with death and the corpses of nations lying all around, he had never really seen a dead man. Most curious, it did look like Smythe, and the more he looked the more fascinated he became with the exposed arteries and collarbones; it had been a sloppy job.

Then he reached down to touch the dried blood and stiffened flesh; the eyes, which had followed the aircraft and sorted out their allegiance, were now gray and clouded. Smythe? He had been alive; now he stank. If any insects still lived in the Burn they would be boring into him, eating him.

VanRoark stared harder, his eyes starting to water and the top of his brain collapsing. New forms arose in his consciousness, indistinct but pulsing with anger and frustration. And wrapped up in the center of them was Yarrow, spitting his corroded lungs into the Sea. Why? No answer, but Yarrow was there with his holy books and a blade smelling of incense and olive oil.

VanRoark crawled out of the tent, his mind reeling and fighting with itself, wanting at once to get to Yarrow and then asking itself, *Why Yarrow? Why not one of the rim nations' men or one from the army itself? Or Tapp? Or suicide?* He had not even looked to see if Smythe had had a knife in his hands.

He was back in the middle of the army, gradually slowing down as the anger moved back from its first wild ravings. Anyway, Yarrow could be on board the cruiser with Timonias and the rest of the holy men. But then again, if he had done it to Smythe, in return for the beating he had got on the *Garnet*, then he still might be around. The beating and Smythe's apparent defection to the rim nations—that would have been enough to send Yarrow off the deep end.

Could he still be ashore, and if he was, how was he to be found among the army's millions? Inexplicably Van-Roark began wondering if he was going through all this because he only thought that one should be properly outraged at the death of some man, or whether he felt any real anger over the death of the man who was Smythe. Why hadn't he alerted others in the camp? At least they might have helped in the search for Yarrow.

Because of the fumings and self-accusations going on within him, it was quite some time before he became aware of the sounds, smooth or sometimes rasping, but always cold and low. There were only a few isolated singers carrying on the drunken roaring of earlier in the evening. He thought he could pick up the words to

"Brampton Hall," slurred and spotted with obscenities when they fit the rhyme.

He recognized the sound: moving metal, metal being drawn across leather or whetting stone or more metal. Almost like the Sea, except for the occasional, musical pingings when someone got clumsy. Rough and pitted metal, grinding like sand or Burn soil; fresh, oiled, and polished, moving like silk against silk, its sound smooth and brocaded in the air. This did not fit in at all. Van-Roark was quite at a loss to find room for this in his preoccupation with Yarrow, so he tried to disregard it.

He walked quickly, ignoring the swelling raspings and his lack of destination. He heard the singing grow louder too and soon spotted a man staggering down the deserted avenue. It was Tapp and he hailed him.

VanRoark ran up to the little man and asked if he had seen Yarrow in the past few days. Tapp was largely insensitive to this, having trouble remembering anyone named Yarrow at all. "Why?" he asked drunkenly, his grinning face less than a foot from VanRoark's.

" 'Cause I think he killed Smythe!" VanRoark was dimly aware of how hysterical he sounded; somehow he was proud of this, for he thought it was the right state in which to be. Tapp looked at him stupidly. Then a smile of forced recognition spread over his dark features. VanRoark got ready for some predictable graveyard humor about Smythe's mother or comparative worth in life. "Oh yeah . . . " Tapp crooned, lifting his right hand.

The middle of Tapp's face disappeared, nose and upper jaw; his lower jaw flopped down against his throat while his yellowed eyes bulged from their untouched sockets.

VanRoark thought the older man's expression unbelievably funny, like an ape trying to mimic human disbelief. The younger man looked back into the eyes and felt himself laughing along with Tapp at his marvelous joke; how wonderful to have a wit that could make a man's death and one's self-appointed vengeance the object of laughter. Lord, how stupid he had made himself look, how utterly brainless, with just a big dark hole gaping between his eyes and trapeze jaw. VanRoark saw that one of Tapp's wisdom teeth was badly impacted.

He vaguely suspected he was thinking all this in the space of less than half a second. It was ended as a faint popping noise reached his ears, and then the razor edge of Tapp's strangled breath cut through his mind, searching for a tongue with which to scream. Blood, dark and oily in the false dawn and torchlight, burst from the wound with astounding force, splattering against Van-Roark's tunic, and then was smeared as Tapp tottered forward and fell against him.

VanRoark stepped back from the writhing creature, with its knife shrieks so low he could hardly hear them over the sliding metal and the bubbling of its blood.

VanRoark's mind was a confused blank now, a vacuum like that found in the center of an explosion, a storming, uncontrollable nothing that could do nothing but try to explode some more. VanRoark began his own yelling, trying to shut out the sound and even the sight of Tapp. He began kicking at the body, stamping on it to make it stop living or at least to have it make some human scream, some evidence of human agony. It only turned and twisted in the ground-glass soil, the sharp, gurgling sounds still creeping into VanRoark's ears.

Around him, the sliding noises were increasing as were the poppings. They took on power and definition, became loud and vicious.

Tapp's body moved away from him, but it could have been VanRoark who was moving, running through the suddenly living army. His vision was clouded and tinged with red, but he could still see the men spilling out of the tents. The sound of metal against metal was that of shells being rammed into breeches, swords being drawn from scabbards, weapons being assembled—now all in the hands of the army—and the thousand torches that burst into flame.

VanRoark slammed into some men, kept running, his direction determined only by which of his random, flailing movements met with the least resistance. He understood none of this.

Booming, inhuman wailings came to him from the anchorage. He thought that Tapp had found a way to scream. Then he broke free of the tents facing the Sea and saw that it was the sirens of the steel ships calling to each other. He blundered out into the Sea, knee-deep, and then ran, fell, and crawled back onto the beach. In front of him the army was burning: the flames, the madmen, with their war axes weaving in and out of the torch-fires until he could not tell them apart, hurled themselves outward from the center of the camp, gathering fury as they spiraled outward. The line of savagery gathered up its southern end as it reached the mountains below Brampton Hall, then turned back and joined the north, crashing into the encampments of the rim nations.

VanRoark staggered down the beach, drawn inward by the suction of the brutal flood. He fell again, the army spinning around him, alternating with the Sea, where the ships were beginning to stir. Steam escaped from their hulls and stacks with more hideous screeching, metallic. Diamond searchlights flared on their towers, sweeping the wooden fleets as maggot crews scurried under their brilliance. A sane part of VanRoark struggled to make itself heard before it was utterly swallowed by madness and the shattering night; the army was destroying itself: it was murdering the rim nations.

He spun around: Brampton Hall was burning in the reflected light of the army. Again, and the northern limits of the Burn were in front of him; aircraft, some on fire or with tiny figures clinging to their skins, trying to plunge javelins through them.

The roaring of the battle now became more jagged as the rim nations finally wakened themselves to what was actually happening. VanRoark could see sheets of red-yellow lifting upward and south from where the great lines of field guns were; then dying down, but still burning, for they had not even had enough time to pull the tarpaulins from their barrels. The wall, again, as they fired fragmentation shells set to burst thirty feet from the muzzles.

Rapid chatterings of automatic cannon and machine guns, great, brutal detonations and shockwaves beat his head into the sand as the ships began firing into the wooden fleets or shoreward at the army.

He could no longer hear himself, and he could not tell whether it was because the noise was too great or the middle of his face had been shot off and his voice lost with it.

Huge, infinitely vicious rhythms shook and kicked him, driving him first into the shallows and then lifting him back toward the rim nations. *Am I still walking or have my legs also been shot away and the concussion hurling me through the air?*

He felt the airplanes struggling up from the causeway and then turning, some so low they set ships afire and the Sea boiling with their fire-wake; he looked up and saw the bombs falling like ripe, clustered fruit from their wings, as from the limbs of trees. The acetylene light of phosphorus and the billowing, morbidly luxurious clouds of Greek fire and jellied gasoline rose from the army's camp.

The massed artillery on the tanker's decks opened together and a quarter square mile of men disappeared where the shells hit. Everything, everywhere his eye was forced, were fires, fires of every color he had ever imagined or seen on the flags of the army: turquoise and deep opal to blue to white to a hell-blackness from burnings so hot they had no time or energy to squander on ordinary light. Things leaping, being blown into the air, moving as their lives splattered out of them, their limbs blasted away from them as they fell; then more fires and detonations to drive them into the Burn, pounding them into it, breaking their shrieking agony like a sledgehammer against a mirror.

He began running; he still had legs, he thought with a mind that had long since been forced outside of its skull by the weight of the chaos crashing down around him.

He stumbled into the camp, avenues faced and walled with fire. The noise compressed around him, suffocating, collapsing his bones and shoving his eyes into flat disks, fish eyes. All around, running shapes, men who should not have been running, carrying parts of themselves in their hands, trophies of their holy struggle; the sand was slick and glittering with fresh blood and the garbage-shreddings of men.

VanRoark lost all orientation; even the thunderous salvos from the rim nations' batteries or from their ships in the roadstead offered no guide, for they seemed to be all around him. Dark, jerking shapes, tanks or even the serpentine forms of the land trains drove though the fires, their howling sirens, guns and engines rising and then falling as they fled.

A pressure, heated far past any temperature, gripped his arm below the shoulder and rested there for a split second; then, when it had burned its way into the bone, pulled.

VanRoark screamed; for a moment he heard himself and nothing else and spun to see his right arm pinwheeling away from him, turning red, then orange, then blue, then white, as it passed in front of and through the fires.

The wound does not seem to hurt, his mind gibbered to itself; *no, but now I am torn open and through this, all the fury of the battle will pour into me; I will be lost.* The violence erupted inside him; he could *see* the explosions and burning silk of his disintegrating organs.

There is nothing left of me, nothing left but a pierced skin separating one segment of the hell from another.

He saw a man moving like a puppet or character in a badly animated film, from the strobe-light effect of the infinite explosions surrounding him. He was dazed, his eyes clouded to the point of appearing as gray blanks; only his mouth held any sign of emotion, and that was bitterness. He was dressed in the remains of an olive uniform and carried a large pack on his back; from it a dragon's spine of machine gun bullets ran over his shoulder and down into the weapon he was holding. The barrel guard had been lost and the metal was glowing cherry red. The steam from his melting hand drifted around the barrel and joined with the cloud of powder smoke spurting from the muzzle. An unbroken line of green phosphorus tracers streamed from the man and the gun, blanketing and momentarily silencing the rest of the battle, like a hose spraying molten metal onto a blaze.

As the man walked by and above VanRoark, he struggled to his feet, possessed by the idea that he must speak to the man: ask him about his numberless self-deceptions for coming to the Meadows; about the artificial arm he must get when the other had turned to slag; about his barques and battle cruiser and the books in his library.

VanRoark made it but not before the man had almost disappeared into the battle-haze. His voice was lost again; he picked up a broken sword hilt, a severed hand still gripping it fanatically, and threw the lot of it at the man to attract his attention.

Slowly, easily, the man turned back to VanRoark, the smoking green line of shells fanning out from him, swinging around without break or interruption, coming closer, becoming a single planet of green that was transformed to a star filling VanRoark's eyes.

VanRoark fell once again. This time it had been the side of his skull, the right side, that had been ripped apart; he thought he could see the eye rolling away from him, the stump of the optic nerve slapping the ground like a piece of wet gristle.

Ludicrously (it must have been so because he could remember laughing aloud at it) part of his sight seemed to remain with the liberated eye ball. He could see himself, the bloody ruin of his face and the stump of his right arm; and the two eyes calmly, coldly, regarded each other and passed judgment on their relative situations.

He thought it even funnier when, through all the smoke of violence, a gull settled down in front of his right eye. The creature, living in the wilderness, had become too hungry to ignore a feast such as the army was serving up.

VanRoark howled with delight as he thought he could feel the bird take the nerve stump in its beak and rise into the air. He saw his own body, matted and mired with blood, and then more bodies as the bird gained height; then men fighting and a vehicle crashing imperiously through their private war for salvation.

An aircraft shot under his eye, loosed its rolling mass of napalm, silhouetting its bat-wings; then it exploded, falling to earth and exploding again.

He could see almost the whole of the Burn and most of the roadstead, split and scarred with the wrecks of ships and the frantic wakes of torpedo boats. Everything grew diffuse and indistinct; colors expanded and drifted suddenly in impossible ways; encrustations of black and white fires, green tracers and fragmentation shells laced through the Burn's glowing darkness and the Sea. He could see the army collapsing in upon itself, dissolving into its own fire and panic.

A random spray of tracer shells, orange this time, moved upward. He sensed the pressure of the gull's beak lessen and then end entirely. His eye hurtled back down into the Burn, the colors rushing away from a black center, their vague forms becoming vicious shards. Then he saw the inside of the lightless fires and watched, as from yet a third eye, as his vision melted and was splattered all through it.

XIX

There was pain, a great deal of it, and blurred streakings of light that were ebon at their centers, white along the bodies and then refracted into rainbow edgings as they drove into the empty eye socket and ricocheted through his skull.

He could recall the background against which the lights moved turning from black to cobalt to silver and then back again; he could recall the sharp soil of the Burn grinding underneath him, how it sparkled in the reflections from the lights. Then it would become damp and hard; small, penitent waves would wash up against him. The salt stung in his wounds but they felt cleaner when they had been washed.

He moved away from the Sea and through the ruins of the camp; the vague and shadowed impressions were now punctuated with single details, unusually sharp against the formations of color; that was mostly gray now. Charred poles and family standards passed above him, their faces and wrought designs torn and brutalized.

He had thought the machines different from the men, with their filth and tattooed arms. But both had apparently died in the same ways: the smooth skins were bitten into by cold or flaming metal, wrenched away from the skeletons, and the guts of plastic or copper or blood or brain would be knocked loose, spilling through the wound like vomit from a drunk's mouth. The debris dried where it caught on the skin or poured upon the ground. He crept past a tank which had excreted its crew through a gaping hole in its forward parts; in turn, the concussion had torn the crew apart, allowing their own interiors to partially escape them.

A piece of silk, embroidered with swords and basilisks, came into his left eye; it was still flying proud and upright, pathetically arrogant to the wreckage that lay all around it.

Slivers of gray rested in the roadstead behind him. All that was left of the wooden fleets was a tangle of splintered masts, burned flags and rigging. A few shapes, silver or dull green, were piled up on the causeway.

Were they all dead? There was no sound, not even the crunch of sand or some victorious cry from the seabirds as they moved from one meal to another. Nothing: only his breathing, sharp and edged like broken glass—like Tapp's had been.

After the background had shifted from light to dark and back again several times, it abruptly became a flat gray that never changed; a noise finally worked back into his mind, a low purring as vague and ill-defined as the shapes that had moved before him.

The gaping hollowness in him, which had allowed the fires and then the charred silence to move freely in his body, was demarcated by a single bright coil of wire. Then a straight line and more coils until they defined the emptiness with their tapestries. They pulled the edges of the wounds together; the humming grayness was not shut out entirely now, but it was split up and filtered through the wires. A strange coldness welled out from the spiders' webs. Colors began reconstructing themselves in the blank spaces between the sound and wires. Cautiously, feeling crept back into the web-works where his eye and arm had been; the colors moved in with it. The pain had almost died by now except for short eruptions that compacted the light into nothing. The cold became comforting to him even when the pain was nearly forgotten.

XX

The trouble with building from the webs was that he always had to begin with them, for there was nothing else; when he opened his eye to the uniform gray of the world he could see wire profiles of men moving in front of him. In time, the profiles became three-dimensional as more wires conformed to the shapes of faces and limbs.

The colors he had seen when he was blind now moved outward and fastened to the external frameworks, set, shifted, and reset.

He was in a room about eight feet square and seven feet high. It was the uniform gray of unpainted metal, featureless except for a washbasin in the near corner, a door set in the wall opposite to where he lay, and a metal cabinet that might have been a desk; neat welds joined the metal panels of the compartment. There was a window, he thought, on the wall next to his bunk; but he could only see a wavering slice of dawnlight playing up and down on the door.

VanRoark looked down with his left eye toward a plaster wrapped right arm; he should have lost that. He could feel bandages covering the space where his right eye should have been. A very slight motor vibration could be felt through the walls and the whole room itself sometimes bounced unexpectedly. Presently a man entered; he was tall and fairly old, probably in his early sixties. He wore a tan blouse and trousers that once might have been the uniform of some nation. He was bald, white hairs growing thinly on the side of his rounded, heavy skull.

He looked at VanRoark briefly; the younger man tried to speak but found that he could not. The man opened the desk cabinet and unrolled two flexible cables; their heads were snapped into sockets on a metal plate set into the plaster cast. For the first time, VanRoark felt warmth in the space where his arm had been; it poured upward, flowing past his shoulder and then outward to fill his whole body.

The madness of the wire frames evaporated. VanRoark fell asleep, a dark, soft burrow in which there were no dreams, no struggling colors, nothing but the warmth and rest.

*   *   *

"You've been out for quite a while; almost three months." The bald man's voice was deep, but not quite as deep as Tapp's had been; VanRoark noticed that his jaw had not moved when he spoke the words. "How do you feel?"

"Fine," a voice croaked; VanRoark supposed it was his.

"You hardly look it, friend. You came very close to dropping off completely, you know." VanRoark nodded that he did.

There was a moment of awkward silence. "Look, my name's Cavandish. I'd shake hands with you and all but I can see you're a little inconvenienced."

"Amon VanRoark, sir."

"Then, Amon, I guess you wonder exactly what is going on here." Cavandish looked embarrassed with himself at this. "Damn, I can't help falling into stupid understatements and clichés. At least I've relieved you of the responsibility of saying 'Where am I?' "

VanRoark tried to smile. "All right, where am I?"

Cavandish chuckled politely. "Right then. You're on a land train heading east. You see, when the army broke up, we had a lot of trouble getting out and . . . "

The thin smile faded from the old man's immobile jaw. "No one knows. It just looked like the army suddenly took it into its head that the rim nations were either defiling the purity of their mission with their ships and tractors, or maybe they even thought that we were the army of Evil and they could save themselves the walk to the Meadows by getting us then and there.

"I really don't know about it, Amon. I've been told of the armies surviving the Meadows, even after being momentarily defeated by whatever showed up under the Opposition's flag; but I've never heard of anything like this—this suicide. The bastards just turned on us." The tone of voice was still fairly calm, but VanRoark noticed that the man was methodically grinding one fist into a meathook palm. "Oh, by the Lord, we gave them a proper fight. No Abstractions, no allegiances to Good or

Evil or any garbage about ending the world, just a good honest round of murdering and finally a chance to face those bastards who'd been slowly sucking the rim nations white. Right in their stinking faces." Cavandish sighed helplessly. "Well, anyway, we were just about the last vehicle out of the Burn. Lord! You should've seen the bodies. I'd never imagined that the army could have attracted so many men until I saw the dead. Thousands! Millions, for all I know. It sounded like someone popping popcorn, with the tires grinding up their bones.

"We were just getting clear of the mountains, trying to keep up with the only other train to make it out and a couple of fast tanks, when something set off the real fuel carts. So while Maus and I tried to get them unhooked and rolling back into the Burn before they really touched off, the rest of our informal group scattered.

"Things got a little dodgy then because the train's power linkages were all fouled up from the battle. We dragged ourselves out along the ridges and set down in back of some ruins."

"Brampton Hall?"

"If that's what it's called. Mainly, we just hid up there, letting go a few discreet rounds once in a while when it looked like something unfriendly might be trying to climb out of that bone heap to get at us. By the third day we had the train fixed up and we also found you. Christ, man! You looked dreadful, like Death himself crawling up to get us. Maus wanted to put you out of it right there, but Kenrick, doctor to the last, loaded you up and patched you together as best he could."

"There are others here?"

"There were five, but Maus took a dart just as we were pulling away from those ruins and the poison got to him. Lyndir and Zaccaharias got the fever about a month ago, from vampire bats, Kenrick said. Corwin died when we ran into a mounted patrol going home to Mountjoy. And poor old Kenrick just went mad one day, started muttering all kinds of stuff about springtime and a girl named Gold or something. I found a note later saying he was going Home—he capitalized it, like it was a country or something—and that was the last I knew of him." Cavandish shook his great head slowly. "Ah, poor old Kenrick, you might have enjoyed him, Amon."

VanRoark felt the silence descend again. "Were we the only ones to make it out of the Burn? Did they get all of the rim nations?"

He waited a second before Cavandish roused himself. "Almost," the old man drawled slowly, sadly. "A lot of the regular army got off, but I suspect they had taken care to leave before the shooting started. But no, they didn't get us all. I was up in that Hall of yours, watching them while Maus and Zaccaharias worked on the train, but—and somehow this makes me feel good—we just scattered." He threw his arms apart, fingers almost touching the walls of the small cabin. "I guess some headed back home; others just ran out of fear, but still more out of disgust. Amon, I could see the faces of those men as they rode out of the Burn; I've never seen such bitterness. Man, all they wanted to do was run! Run so fast that the only thing they could taste would be their own blood when their lungs burst or when their planes had crushed them flat with the acceleration.

"And I could see that others were moving out to the north, to the Meadows. About seven planes made it off the causeway and five of them headed north. Some torpedo boats and even one of the smaller destroyers managed to get under that bridge and they followed the aircraft. I could see dust trails of trucks and tanks and motor artillery moving north, stopping as they forded the river and then starting up again on the other side."

VanRoark looked up to the old man; his face was the color of copper ore. "Are we headed for the Meadows, sir?"

"No." Cavandish stared out the window that VanRoark could not see; he rubbed his hands over his eyes. "No. We're going east now, to Blackwoods Bay."

"But Cynibal's wiped out; there was a war."

"I'm going there to find some fuel, trying to get enough to get me home." Cavandish glanced slowly around the room and then returned his eyes to Van-Roark. "Did any of the men you might have talked to, men from the rim nations, tell you why they were there at the Burn, and why they wanted to die?"

VanRoark remembered Yarrow first because he had offered the loudest and most involved explanations for his conduct; then Smythe and Tapp, moving back and forth uncertainly between God, the Devil, and Brampton Hall. He remembered the artilleryman with the armored Death on his forearm. "They said they were tired."

"And that, Amon, is what I am. I came to the Meadows because, somehow, it promised peace. And a flaming lot of that it gave me! Traveled for five years to get there, and for what? To see my finest friends shot to pieces or catch some godawful disease that let them bleed to death on the inside; to see the last shining bits of metal my nation and others had hoarded away for this single moment destroyed by the same pack of bastards that had been out to get us before any holy missions had ever been proclaimed.

"Christ, Amon, if they want to fight at the Meadows after what was done to them, then I salute them because they've a lot more patience than I do. At this moment I am sick of everything! I just want to move with my train, just move and never really be anyplace." Cavandish thought this over for a second and then decided to be amused with himself. "Ravings of an old man, Amon. We'll see you tomorrow and get you out of bed." Cavandish unplugged the cables from his cast and reeled them back into the cabinet.

The color faded from Cavandish's image and the skin dissolved from his face to reveal the wire framework; the room was reduced to a gray monotone, outlined and supported by single threads of drawn metal. Then even the wires unreeled back into someplace beyond Van-Roark's perception and he guessed that he slept.

❄   ❄   ❄

VanRoark awakened to the same sequence of wire frameworks and growing colors, but now it was quicker and more like simply opening his eyes. He saw that Cavandish had attached two more tubes to his cast; he felt curiously whole and ready to start getting around again.

As he waited for the old man, he thought about his arm in the cast, absolutely sure he had seen it shot off;

strangely, he thought the space where his right eye had been felt filled instead of empty with vaporous blood. Then there was Cavandish himself; VanRoark liked the man already, but why had his jaw not once moved all the while he was speaking to him?

Cavandish came in, disconnected the tubes and told VanRoark to get up; that he was all right for the moment. For a second, as he rose, the colors blurred into the monotone and their wire skeletons reemerged, stark and shining against the gray. Then the wire was overlaid with liquid flowings; he was standing up, Cavandish smiling tiredly at his side.

They moved unsurely through the door and then turned left, walking down a narrow corridor past three similar doors; all were dogged shut. At the end of the corridor was another door, this one on the right, and VanRoark could feel cool evening breezes drifting through it.

"All right, now. There's a ladder right below the combing and from there it's about ten feet to the ground. Watch that cast, and tell me if you think you can make it." VanRoark grasped a railing on the outside of the corridor wall and swung himself outboard until he could find the first rungs. He was quite surprised at the near absence of pain and his strength.

"How long have I been out?" he cried up to Cavandish.

"About four months. It's winter now up north, you know."

VanRoark was not ready for this and almost lost his balance. When he banged his cast into the steel wall of the car he did not feel any real discomfort.

He stepped off the ladder and looked up and down the length of the land train. To his left, to the east he judged from the sun, were three cars like his own, painted a dull sand and olive. They were essentially just boxes, unpierced on this side save for ventilator slits, about forty feet long and perhaps twenty feet thick. Two wheels, each at least twelve feet in diameter, supported each side of the box. Forward of these cars was the control vehicle; this was much larger, twice the size of the passenger cars. A sheet of glass, canted outward about ten degrees, wound around the forward edge of the car. There was a railing bordering the stepped, two-level roof of the car. An artillery piece, draped in heavy canvas, was mounted near the forward edge of the car's roof.

To VanRoark's right was one more of the boxlike cars and then about six slightly bulged cars. The analogy of a huge wheeled serpent was unavoidable.

"Like her?" Cavandish was on the ground next to him.

"And you run all of this, alone?" VanRoark asked in amazement.

"So far. It's been kind enough not to present me with any difficulties that'd require a Zaccaharias or a Maus to fix. About the most troublesome operation has been you, Amon, and Kenrick seems to have fixed that up well enough for me to fumble through. I'm taking off your bandages after dinner."

"No period of recuperation or anything like that?"

Cavandish laughed politely. "Hardly; you've had four months of that. Kenrick figured it'd be easier for me if you did your healing in one spot and quietly. You'll have to be careful for a while, though; some of your muscles might have atrophied despite the doctor's drugs."

It was beginning to get dark. VanRoark could see a star or two appearing over the control car's gun. They moved over to a small fire, where Cavandish had some coffee and a skewered jackeroo heating. They ate in comparative silence, the old man apparently having nothing more to say for the moment and VanRoark suddenly concerned only with getting some solid food into his stomach. He did not realize just how much it had shrunk, and was gorged after only a few bites.

When they finished, Cavandish brought a small leather case out and drew closer to VanRoark. "Now, you know that you're, ah, different than you were before the army broke up," he began cautiously.

"You mean my arm and eye?" VanRoark asked. "I was sure they had been shot off."

"They were, but Kenrick replaced them with mechanical substitutes which I assure you are almost the equals of your original limbs, maybe even superior in some areas. Now, I'm telling you this before I take off the bandages because some people get fairly worked up when they take a first look at a new arm or leg. These aren't just hooks or pegs, Amon; you have an arm that will feel everything your old one could, move in every direction your old one could. You have a small lens setup where your right eye used to be; it'll pipe images directly into the brain just as the first eye did. And even better; you'll be seeing more with this one. You can adjust the range to see into the far ends of the spectrum, far past the limits where light radiation becomes invisible X-rays or simple heat."

Cavandish considered this for a moment and then decided it was not enough. "Look, I think I know how

you'll feel because I felt the same way myself. You see,
my lower jaw and larynx were pretty well torn up by
shell fragments down on the Burn. Kenrick fitted me up
with a whole artificial jaw and all I need to eat and speak.
That's why I don't move my jaw much—because it's riveted to my skull."

"And what did this Kenrick have? Was he all of flesh
and blood?" VanRoark was amazed at the tinges of bitterness which edged into his voice.

"Ah, Kenrick. No; before we left our home he had
this operation and got a mechanical heart; some of the
motor areas of his brain were solid state electronics too.

"Enough talk. Here, give me your arm and we'll show
that it isn't so bad after all." Cavandish cut away his shirt,
almost apologetically it seemed, and then began making
a long incision on the side of the shoulder and arm cast
with a knife that hummed like the grayness. "All right,"
he said when he was through, "here it comes." He gave
a slight tug and the cast fell apart into five pieces.

VanRoark gazed down at where the stump of his shoulder was neatly tucked into a blued steel collar; the skin
was drawn and slightly wrinkled around the collar as if
someone had carefully riveted and then shrunk the ser-
rated ring around the arm—which was probably just
what had been done anyway. From the ring, which
looked like a bracelet, proceeded an arm such as one
could find on the armored dress of the Great Plains
knights. Finally, there was a hand—or rather a gauntlet,
for the fingers were hinged and a flaring skirt of metal
hid the wrist joint.

He held the hand up to his left eye; it was engraved,
even to the palm, and the hunting parties and serpents

ran down from the shoulder ring in a parade such as he
had only seen in the tapestries of his home cathedral.
There was a small sun in the center of his hand, and tiny
planets with continents of gunmetal and seas of silver
spinning around it. Galaxies patterned the metal folds of
the hand, clustering in thick bands that cut in back of
the solar system, random agglomerations filling in the
cobalt spaces between, and then fading out into the wrist
and fingers. There was a rocket, long and barbed with
graceful wings, one side etched in bare silver light from
the silver sun; it was bound outward. There was a serpent, winged with almost as much grace, coiled about
his index finger; a lance whose grip and guard solidified
out of the universe dust ran nearly the length of the
middle finger. Finally, there was a man, a knight in fine-
etched mail, on his fourth finger—and a queen on his
last finger whose hair was wound around the metal like
the body of the dragon.

Cavandish looked a little embarrassed at all this.
"Please don't be honored, Amon; none of that was done
for you," he said, almost laughing. "The arm is as old as
the train, maybe older, and was used by many men
before it came to you. Some of them were artists and
naturally spent some time dressing it up."

"Dead men's arm?" VanRoark asked absently.

"Well, if you want to be morbid about it, I suppose
it is."

VanRoark did not hear this, for his eye was traveling
up the length of the arm, over the lines of rune figures
and numbers and even some formulae, over forests
seeded with all manner of fantastic animals, unicorns,
hippogriffs, hooded basilisks and gryphons—cut by roads

and cities that spiraled upward around mountains, their streets awash in swarming crowds of etched figures, their battlements and gates proud against skies where the galaxies once again appeared. There were ships upon his arm, fine great sailing craft and steel battle cruisers, no less powerful for their microscopic length.

VanRoark moved the arm unsurely, expecting to hear it creak or feel the hideous scrape of metal against bone within him; but none of that happened. He felt only the cool of the evening air upon it, and when he laid the metal palm to the sandy ground he could feel the rough granules—even a slight twinge of pain as he brushed over a piece of dead thornbush.

He touched himself; the metal was as warm as his skin, but its strength and rigidity was indisputably that of steel.

Cavandish saw him smiling too. "Ah, good, now for your eye." He raised his tool and began to work on the cast. "Keep your eye closed."

"Huh?"

"Keep it closed; even the firelight might be something of a shock after so long." VanRoark shrugged and commanded a lid he was sure did not exist to close; he was almost happy when he felt nothing move.

The cast was removed and VanRoark was further reassured when he couldn't see a thing out of where his right eye had been. "Not a thing, sir."

"Of course not, you've got it closed. Open it."

The younger man blinked his left eye and then tried to repeat the muscle sequence on the right side of his face. There were wires before him again, or rather woolen threads whose color was solid only in their centers and then diffused off into the darkness. The color mists shifted and expanded; he could see the campfire in front of him. "It'll take a little time for everything to sort itself out."

"Who owned this before me?"

"No one at all; now is the time to be honored. Honored not only for the eye but for the incredible job Kenrick did of weaving it into the stump of your optic nerve. A really incredible feat for a man in his condition. There's a small metal plate around it where some bone used to be, so don't worry if you feel the skin pulling a little when you smile or scream or something. And try not to touch the lens—it protrudes a little—feel it?—because it's fairly easy to smudge or get dirtied up. And watch your right hand; you could easily forget it's not entirely human and put a scratch onto it." Cavandish settled back and watched VanRoark for a while; he decided not to mention the grotesque effect the lens tube made twisting in and out of the skull plate as VanRoark focused to different distances. "What makes it run?"

"Body enzymes, the natural electrical impulses of your own nervous system. Kenrick could have told you more. He knew all about men."

"And you know nothing by comparison?"

Cavandish answered good-humoredly. "I am but a poor simple navigator carrying out the instructions of a wise and learned man of healing."

"Ah, a navigator." VanRoark's attention was easily diverted, for now he had already ceased to notice any difference between the functioning of his real and artificial limbs. "You've always been with the land train, then?"

Cavandish considered a moment and then chose to follow the drift of the conversation. "No, not always."

"Then what did you do before the train? Where did your family come from?"

"From there." Cavandish pointed to the welkin. "From that part of the sky approximately, though I can no longer name the star, things have changed so much."

VanRoark really had no idea of what to say to this. The old man continued: "Though not originally, of course. The way I was told it, my family had left the world back in the days of the First World, or very soon after its end, when things were still going just about as they should have been. We are supposed to have spread out along the arms of our galaxy, searching around the numberless suns and finding an occasional world that was green and empty."

There were great pauses between each sentence, and longer ones before VanRoark spoke; it was as if the one was trying desperately to remember the proper questions while the other was slowly dredging up the answers from where they had laid for so long. "Why did they, your family, come back?"

Cavandish sighed. "They came back for the Wars; they all came back, all of the families who had left. It took a long time—which I suppose is why some of the rim nations seem so odd and out of touch with the current state of the world—but one by one, on every world where we had settled, the prophets appeared. And they spoke, these prophets, and we both know how they spoke, the words and the hope—how odd to call what they offered, *hope*—and we came back. All the sciences and beliefs that had lived for a bit longer on worlds named after stars and in countries named after gods . . . they came home. Of course, by this time, home was already degenerating into what it is now.

"But they—we tried, Amon, you'll have to give us that. We landed and founded the new nations that were only supposed to last for a few years, and we built our new machines and began, my great-grandfather told me, with such fine and noble purpose to play our part in all of this.

"Then the systems broke down, at times so ludicrously and utterly that even my proud, unbending fathers could not ignore it. We had lost our ships by then and the skill to steer them through the skies. The rim nations became scattered; some met their planned annihilation at the Meadows. Many, I suspect, were overrun by earthly enemies." Then his lips curled slightly upward, which was as close as Cavandish could come to a smile. "The men we had come so far to help in our mutual destiny hunted us out, and one by one they infected, sabotaged, betrayed the rim nations until all that was left was what you saw on the Burn."

The lips relaxed back into a scar line; VanRoark thought he could see wire mesh behind it. "Why?"

"Why did they destroy us?"

"Yes"—now VanRoark could feel himself smiling sadly—"us."

"For as many reasons as they had for coming to the Burn. Though mostly it seemed to us they hated the machines, the building. None of us could ever really figure it out completely. It was almost as if they just gave up being humans; they were more like the mindless, drifting forces that seem to be controlling the universe these days. They shift and flow and anything that is thrown up in their way—no matter if it is there for Good or Evil—anything that the rim nations shaped and built against the darkness, they hated. They hated the trucks and tractors which could have ended their starvation, the ships that could have ended their wandering."

There was silence then except for the fire and an odd, faint cracking that slowly grew louder. The pebbles and rocks of the wastes, heated during the day, were now cooling too quickly with the fall of night and shattering. VanRoark imagined it to be the huge, malicious applause of the world, complimenting Cavandish on the depth of his bewilderment and frustration.

"What did you build?" Why had he asked that? At this a roaring laughter slipped out of Cavandish's knife-slit mouth; he looked like a ventriloquist's doll whose real voice was coming from somewhere else.

"Me? Not me, Amon. Now, my grandfather, he was a builder; he worked in the shipyards repairing aircraft carriers and merchantmen. And my dad built bridges all the hell over the world—every single one of which was cut down or blown up within a year or two of its completion.

"I, on the other hand, am almost as much a child of this world as the army was; maybe even more so. I was a navigator-bombardier." Cavandish was laughing so hard that he had to stop talking and rub his jaws that had never moved. "I sat in the glass noses of our aircraft, like the big ones you saw on the causeway at the Burn.

"It was good for a while, you know. Because I could sit there alone with all the stars and a ribbon of black asphalt captured in the wire frame of the nose. Then, way off behind you, you'd hear the engines and feel the back of your seat pressing against you. Little dabs of white—no, it was more of a pale green in the star-light—moved under me and the plane until they blurred together.

"There were about ten, twenty seconds, just after we lifted off, while the landing gear was stowed, and that was like a tanner's hawk getting ready to fall or rise. The field was built beside a river and we had to fly down this valley for a few minutes; the engines were throttled back so we didn't clout some mountain and it was quite beauti-ful with the lights along the banks and maybe even some powerboats moving against the current.

"Then we were clear, over the Sea, and Pena would shove everything up against the pegs. Man, you should see the sky when we had to break through some clouds. You couldn't hear the engines at all up there; just like you were a little man sitting inside someone else's skull, with all the darkness around you except for the eye and its wire frame.

"I kept wanting to reach through the eye and grab the lights, especially the one my family had come back from—I knew which one it was then. But I remember that once I touched the glass and my skin froze to it, so I could only watch.

"But the watching was fair enough, in that eye. I have to laugh at myself now; I was young then, and I had given those skies to a woman, because I loved her, and in those days I still thought I owned the sky—whether from inheritance or default from the world I could never say." Cavandish closed his eyes and smiled faintly, and laughed as he said he must, very low and gently.

The eyes opened and were hard. "Pena would eventually come back and say that we were nearing the target. We dropped below the clouds and I couldn't see the stars anymore. I saw instead some dusty plain or plateau, or maybe a coastline where the surf was like a white line of pus trying to keep the land from infecting the Sea.

"Our formation, there were usually about four of us, would make one low run to make sure we had the right target; and then one more single line, stepped formation, if they couldn't throw anything up at us; from four different directions, one after the other, if they could."

"What did you bomb?"

"Ruins mostly. You see—I wonder if I will laugh at this too—when the nations came back, they built their cities and then left or were destroyed. Many of the ruins from the first days—when everything was going straight and no one had left for the sky—a lot of those are still half-alive. Like the Black Libraries, they still held invaluable machineries and knowledge."

"And you bombed this?" *This is like a minstrel show,* thought VanRoark, *with me as the straight man and Cavandish cracking the long, wretched jokes, and even the applause of the stupidly delighted audience in the crackling desert.*

"We had to. My fathers built many of them, but the world had grown too large and malignant for my poor rim nations. You see, many of these ruins which we had built or maintained for a while were then beyond our reach. They were in the hands of the world and they could only have hurt us. I know what you're going to cry to me now; about the knowledge in which all those godforsaken slobs might have found some measure of solace. Sure, we knew that, and we also flaming well knew that they would discard or warp or bungle anything that wouldn't suit their own vicious ends. That's what my grandfather found out when they loaded up an ancient ship they found moored in some northern river with equally ancient cordite they'd dug out of the Armories, and sailed it into his precious shipyard. And my father found out when they cut the suspension cables on one of his new bridges while he was still on it.

"All that we had left were the guns and the bombs. We couldn't get to the books or the machines or the art before the world did. So I sat behind the wired eye and looked through another one where there were only two wires, and when the Library or the church was under their intersection, I pressed a button. The bombs fell; sometimes I could see a bit of star or moonlight on their casings and fins.

"Then Pena would take us up and back to the stars and the river with the landing field beside it, the lights, and the hangars cut into the side of the valley walls.

"There were about forty bombers and a couple of dozen lighter craft operating from that field when I was still flying. As things went on, quite a few of them left for the Meadows and others just dropped apart from sheer exhaustion. Others crashed or were shot down or sabotaged, but mostly it was fuel. It came from Blackwoods Bay and every year there was less and less of it. Then they started sinking the tankers or fouling up the oil, even when we sent escort ships along. Finally, there was that nice little war that Ihetah and Cynibal decided to have.

"So gradually there were fewer craft lifting off. And, oh, you should have seen the lads who still kept flying. Lord! How grim and bitter they grew, how quiet and bitter. They thought of themselves as undertakers, cutting off the limbs and crushing a huge corpse into shape so that it would fit a small coffin. I really couldn't bear those people, either because I had been one of them or had at least come dangerously close to becoming one of them. . . ." He shrugged. "I don't know . . . again.

"The nation was breaking up then; no wars or revolution, just a lot of poor, tired bastards who could see no reason for hanging together any longer. Except, of course, for the air crews that still flew. Every night, while they lasted, I could hear them coming down the valley heading for Krysale Abbey, or Iriam or the Armories or the Tyne Fortress, the Yards, Calnarith, the Wastes, the Barrens—ah, Amon! Such names we left behind us; such sad rotten names. They hung on until there was nothing more to fly, until they had bombed all the places with our names and even started in on the rim nations themselves.

"I traveled around for a while, passing myself off as an optical engineer, ship's navigator, and then an electrician until I met up with Zaccaharias and Kenrick and their crew." Cavandish brooded on this for a while, as if he had forgotten some part. "Ah yes," he said at last in mock triumph, "the prophet! One night I thought the lot of them were the biggest pack of idiots I'd seen since I left home. Then, that same day, I heard a man called Marion or something like that. I listened very hard and when my mind had snapped back into something resembling its original shape, I thought it over again, all of it."

"And you were possessed, on fire with what you had heard," VanRoark added sadly.

"You should say, I was on fire at what I heard. I knew then, just as Lyndir and the rest knew, not only what the prophet had meant, but what he had meant in himself. Understand?" VanRoark did not but he was too shy to say so. "He was the world, just as surely as any man of that army; he couldn't help it, we knew that. But we also knew that the only chance for any peace we would ever have—forget the rest of the world and their blithering Abstractions—would be to go to the Meadow and die. We could see, with the appearance of this last little man and his incredible manner of speaking, the last pieces going bad. That's the bleeding thing, Amon; what the prophet said was only part of it; so many of those that listened forgot to consider the man himself and the failure of his predecessors. That's where the whole bleeding thing comes together; *that* is the end of creation they were speaking of!"

His voice had risen—again, it seemed from some other place than his mouth—with the remembered disgust and fury of that day. Now it dropped back again. "So I came to the Burn. And it seems that I must be more of the world than of the rim nations because, like the world, I could not even die; I lived, much against my will and against all the lovely plans and orders. Now I'm going home. I know that there's no home anymore; it's just a label I've given to my wandering to make it seem respectable."

And then VanRoark told Cavandish his story. The younger man spoke, he thought, almost as Cavandish had, with a voice far and removed; there was even the rude audience of the wastes, apparently almost as pleased with his tale as it had been with Cavandish's. But the world must have become bored; as the night grew colder and the stones lost all their heat, the crackling stopped.

When the noise had diminished and his own voice was like a far sea-roaring, VanRoark became momentarily aware of his new eye; the images he saw through it blurred and redefined themselves.

Cavandish looked up when he noticed the eye twisting in and out of VanRoark's skull and the changing color of the lens as different filters dropped into place behind it. He smiled one of his strange non-smiles and explained again that VanRoark's eye was not limited to visible light now. He would develop more control, Cavandish told him, in time; but for the moment he would just have to put up with seeing the world bathed in red light when there was no moon and heavy cloud cover. The sky above him occasionally blazed with sapphire lights, a whole universe far beyond what he could see with his left eye.

VanRoark began to see that just as there were many things he could perceive beyond the simple world of light and darkness, so now could he see the creations multiplying on his arm. The images were vague and ill-formed, as they had been when he had first used the artificial eye; then, his left eye had reconstructed the images on the wire frames as he had come out of the coma: somehow they frightened him.

VanRoark stopped his narrative. Cavandish didn't display any interest in hearing the rest and, at any rate, VanRoark hardly felt like telling any more of it. The older man helped him back into his bunk and plugged the cables back into the arm.

XXI

Cavandish told him he had been out for only five days this time. It was raining heavily and the plain had turned largely to mud. He led him down through the corridor to the other end of the car and then opened a door, reached out and opened another in the car in front. They worked their way forward until they reached the control car. VanRoark could feel the humming of the engines much more clearly here; Cavandish said the bottom deck of the car held four turbines and dynamos. Current from there was carried outward and aft to electric motors buried in each of the twelve foot wheels.

The control room took up the whole forward half of the car; there was a low bench, raised in the center for the driver. In front of this raised section, a panel was fitted with a steering wheel, throttles, gauges and other things at which VanRoark's knowledge of machinery would only allow him to guess. Cavandish mounted the driver's throne and gestured that VanRoark should sit beside him.

He fooled with some of the controls and VanRoark heard the subdued wailing of the turbines rise under the floorboards. *Why?* he asked himself again. *Why does everything sound as if it comes from someplace other than its obvious source?* The sound of the turbines and now the remote jounce of the huge wheels against the desert soil, four hundred miles away. Ever since they had come upon the army, wrapped and shrouded in sea fog, he realized his senses had become more distrustful of what they reported. Perhaps if this Kenrick had given him an ear of copper and brass, then he would hear the sounds of things as they really were; but he was chilled at this thought and tried hard to listen to Cavandish, discoursing upon the history of the indisputable distant mountains (but only, VanRoark despaired, if he did not increase the magnification of his right eye).

He seemed to be right back where he had been on board the *Garnet,* with all reference points and perspectives falling away from him. This was particularly bad, for he had thought that here, in a creation of the old world or at least one of its descendants, he should have felt more secure than ever, with the steel and fiber of the old worlds riveted and welded into his own body.

The hand and eye burned on him. They felt completely normal except, of course, when his eye decided to wander off into some unknown extreme of the spectrum. It was his own mind that terrified him; it seemed to have developed a sudden talent for thinking up the most perverse observations on his new limbs to fill the spaces where the Sea and the promises of Timonias had been: How would a woman enjoy the touch of the hand inside her? Would he corrode from it? Could he rent himself out to carnivals? And when Cavandish's dead friends saw him walking alone with his arm and eye, would they come in their wrecked and rusted bombers to crush him? He asked himself if it was his own blood that lubricated the arm, or if by now his body was fed by machine oil.

Even then, on his first full day awake since he had left the Burn, these thoughts began to prey on him and he knew that he had the makings of a fine insanity. He also knew that this obsessive madness would involve a monumental hatred for Cavandish; but this was one of the things he chose to ignore.

They passed to the east, bending gradually southward, as there they could find one of the numerous fjords of the Talbight River system; they could also avoid any possible contact with Enador's remaining river monitor. Cavandish said that the one which had been anchored off the Burn had been sunk in the first few minutes of action; a cruiser had rammed her at twenty knots and her badly cast and recast armor had parted easily.

Slowly, the pebbled desert changed into rough badlands. There was only the long, rolling stone floor that marked the roots of ancient mountains; the land was split by sharp crevices that seemed to run from horizon to horizon, like the grid lines on a vast chart or spider's web. Eventually, Cavandish pointed out, the lines would become more numerous, intersecting at more points; boulders would be wrenched from the solid rock and the land would be like the desert they had just left. There were not enough small stones yet for applause to an evening's story, rather, individual cracks that sounded like artillery pieces dueling with each other.

Although Cavandish was now letting him take occasional turns at the wheel, the journey was a boring one. The land was one of unremitting sterility; the huge masses of rock did not even allow the wolf-spiders and other subterranean life which contrived to live in the desert to exist. Oddly, the two men had spoken comparatively little since their first few days together. VanRoark asked the old man as courteously as he could, if there was nothing more to talk about, if the substance of his life was so meager as to support no more conversation.

Cavandish said that if VanRoark cared to put it in such a manner, then he supposed it was true; he added that there were many other things he might have talked about once, but now it would be worse than useless. Then Cavandish asked VanRoark why he did not offer more conversation and smiled his thin, machine-smile when VanRoark saw that he had come to view things in the same light. Talk of the prophets, Armageddon, the army, the Burn, the rim nations, his past—everything was fixed in its own meaningless death; the talk only brought pain.

But there was a thing which VanRoark had never really had; thus it could not have been lost and thus it could not truly hurt him. This thing was History; he had known of it, but Cavandish had possessed it, more than Smythe ever had, and when he spoke of the old countries, of the star-nations, and of the rim nations, now all gone or cracking into dust like the badlands around them, it hurt him tremendously. The train had a small library, really nothing more than a jumbled collection of pornography, technical literature, and history that its previous crews had brought with them and left aboard, or simply forgotten in the chemical toilets. The history, perhaps the most incongruous section of the library, was explained by Cavandish in that, before the Burn or the failure of previous Armageddons, the rim nations had naturally had a great interest and pride in their heritage. If one must know the past to know the future, it was reasoned, then perhaps the study of past days could yield the answer to setting the world right again.

VanRoark read the old, disintegrating books, some of them of enormous antiquity, that Cavandish said had been brought back from the stars when some man's family had come home again; others were of the more popular sort, luridly illustrated but still perhaps containing some fragments of truth. He forgot his new arm and the eye that sometimes showed him the page in the reversed, red-tinted shades of infrared, the barren land, the world on which there might be nothing but the train, and submerged himself in the grand deeds and high aspirations of the past. He rediscovered the hope and grandeur that Smythe and the rim nations' planes and ships had hinted at, safely tucked away in the unreachable past, beyond even the world's immense talent for corrupting things. There the nations remained, inviolate, the sketches of their flags and devices seeding his mind for greater meanings; the few ships, the rotting, decaying merchant cruisers and destroyers that should have been sunk out of simple mercy a hundred years ago, became great fleets and navies. From the ruined fragments of the systems he had progressively erected and then seen destroyed grew a new one, more fragile than all the rest but more awesome, for it was composed of the stuff of nightmare and legend; he learned to dream again, a thing that had not been done in his family for generations.

Cavandish saw this happening and warned him against it. "Amon," he said, his lips opened not more than a quarter of an inch, "stop this reading; stop the thinking, like I have. You must keep your mind blank or at least unformed. Let the random glories of my dead nations rattle around; that's fine. But don't let them have too much company, for they'll grow and soon you'll own them as surely as I did."

Again, as in many times in the past weeks, VanRoark did not understand what the old man was talking about and was much too respectful to ask for an elaboration on the obvious. So he read and thought and noticed that, warn as he might, Cavandish could never really bring himself to actually limit the reading.

As they moved to the southeast he could sense more and more the stirrings he had felt at Admiralty Square, with Smythe on board the *Garnet,* at the Burn, becoming the past. And late one night, when Cavandish was below in the control car, in the green instrument light, navigating the train over an ancient road, he stood atop the car gripping the forward railing. It was cold that night; the sky was clear and the half-moon turned the ragged clouds that had sprung up all around the horizon to a luminescent white. It looked as if the world around them was on fire; VanRoark wrapped one hand tighter around the railing and the other around the barrel of the repeating cannon and felt the cold fire-wind sweep around him. He owned that wind, he thought, the wind that blew out of dead, frozen burnings that had once driven men to incredible heights and then made them continue to fight against a creation that had turned on them and their Creator.

Now he owned the wind and the past and the rim nations, and the stars and the suns around which they had been founded; he owned the steel and the old hands which had worked it into such wondrous shapes, just as completely as Cavandish ever had. He breathed deeply and his wind smelled of bitter metal, cordite, papers and printer's ink.

XXII

They found the bomber two days after they had crossed the Talbight River. They were moving through what might have been a sizable forest but which was now nothing more than a collection of blackened and charred stumps. The land train shouldered them away easily but their crunching made VanRoark think of the ground he had walked upon at Brampton Hall with the ancient bones just beneath the surface. The ground was like ash; a long, dirty plume of gray and black trailed behind the train.

VanRoark was steering and it was Cavandish who spotted the line of splintered trees that marked where the plane had landed. They corrected course to the north slightly and then drove down the avenue; soon, there were deep trenches where the landing gear had dug into the soft earth.

VanRoark went into near ecstasies when he first saw the ship; now it was not something foreign, the creature of someone else's imagination, but a thing with which he felt a common heritage. So did Cavandish, even though his artificial jaw and fear of belief contrived to make it almost impossible to spot.

They approached slowly. The plane's camouflage pattern seemed to be of the usual type, molted green and tan topside and flat black on the underbelly, although the black seemed to extend far past the midline in some spots.

It was an uncommonly beautiful craft: a high T-shaped tail set at the end of a gently tapered hull; long, sharply swept wings, now drooping without the air under them, engines buried at the roots. The port gear had partially collapsed and the ship leaned to that side.

As they got closer, VanRoark could see that the ship's underside had originally been painted a light gray; the black was from the fires which had been built under her. Pieces of her crew's mutilated bodies were stuffed into the engines' air intakes and exhausts. "Our world," Cavandish murmured with his ventriloquist's voice, "and our rim nations." They circled the ship and then stopped before the shattered windscreen and nose.

"I think they were at the Burn. Rather less dignified than a death fighting by the sides of archangels and demi-gods." VanRoark looked at Cavandish with his right eye. "My apologies. That wasn't very funny, was it?"

They buried what they could find of the crew and cleaned some of the blood and ash from the ship. Van-Roark thought of the structure he had built in his mind from his Sea musings and the old books; it did not crumble or break as these others had. He could feel it getting stronger and growing thorns; he could feel the acid welling up into his mouth. Once or twice he caught Cavandish glancing up from his work and looking at him.

VanRoark was no longer young, and the dead had none of the evasive cynicism of Smythe or Tapp; the bitterness and hatred was real now and it grew in power as he kicked the bonfire's debris away from the ship's belly.

They picked out some markers, machine guns from the waist and tail turrets, spent rocket casings, an oxygen bottle and mask, and left the next morning.

The train headed southeast again; Cavandish detached one of the empty fuel cars but elected to keep the rest for what he could find in the tanks along Blackwoods

Bay. They spoke to each other hardly at all now; Van-Roark even stopped his readings. Many times, Cavandish looked as if he were about to try to penetrate the screen; but he always stopped, withdrew his hand, put the book back on the shelf he had just taken it from, or simply said that the story he was about to tell was not worth hearing.

Once, though, he kept on looking at VanRoark. "And now you are like me; maybe even a little worse because you have captured your history from the dreams of other men. You really don't know how we could be as miserable and as just as the army . . . and as vengeful." He touched his jaw. "And you can somehow, just as I still do, either reconcile or just ignore the grotesqueness of things like this. We see them as marvelous creations. And so they are, but you've felt the horror of them too, conjuring all sorts of dreadful fantasies around them.

"And none of this is really correct. They're not glorious or ghastly; they are only the sorry creations we were forced to throw up against the world.

"Ah, VanRoark, I could talk for the rest of my life to you, trying to explain, and you'll still drive yourself into the ground hating everything but the memory of the rim nations and what had gone before them. I've been doing that for years." He looked up and VanRoark supposed that the old man was trying to look parental, which was wrong. "You see?" he asked after a second.

"Yes, I think so," VanRoark answered and smiled, for he did at least see that Cavandish was right on one point: VanRoark hated him.

VanRoark would be almost amused at it during the few times he'd step back and listen to the undying bit of cynicism left in him. But there were few times indeed;

the cynicism which had maintained itself free and clear from any real taint was now entrapped in the wires of his bitterness, trussed up like salted meat hung out to be cured and hardened.

He hated the arm this dead Kenrick had given him, and after a while he hated the life which had come with it. Why had they not allowed him to die at the Burn? Then he would have been free of this mess.

But the hatred did fill him with a satisfaction that had only been approached by his feelings of the Sea. The thorn garden made fertile by the rim nations' corpses had armored itself, even against the things which were of themselves like Cavandish and the eye and arm and the train.

XXIII

VanRoark had naturally considered killing the old man; and once again, he was more amused than appalled at himself that he could think of such an alternative as being "natural." But it would have been pointless, beyond the simple fact that he doubted if he could do it. *Ah, then I shall let my arm do it*, he thought, *for that is hardly mine. Idiot!* came his reply. *You are not ready for thoughts like that. Monstrous thoughts like murder, fine—you've seen enough of that—but don't turn to nonsense like that to justify yourself, yet.*

He left. They were only three hundred miles to the western end of Blackwoods Bay, by Cavandish's reckoning, and VanRoark knew that the land was as hospitable as it would ever be. Winter was beginning to break up, although it should have been still immovably entrenched by the calendar.

The burned forests where they had found the bomber had once covered great tracts of the countryside; this stretch of territory, running from the southern shore of the Talbight down into the vague borders of the Old Nations, still had some semblance of normal life. Before the radiations and plagues had stunted it, the wood had been composed of ironwood trees. Their indestructible trunks, bare of limbs, towered above the blighted ash and dwarf-oak which had replaced them. Many had been burned in piebald patterns by the flash from distant bombs, some with the shadows of men or birds on them like the cliff faces outside Charhampton's submarine pens.

The train had easily smashed its way through the small trees and, by nightfall, its forty foot wake traced to the horizon. Cavandish had brought up the vehicle and coiled it around one of the ironwood trunks, this one at least three hundred feet high. VanRoark thought it looked like a huge serpent, like the one on his finger.

Now if there are signs to be fulfilled, they have been. I have seen the rockets, or at least the air ships; I have seen the serpent, the lances and the knights who held them at the Burn. And the queen? Perhaps he had known her in the old diplomatic quarter of his city; or perhaps she was Cavandish's, the one to whom the night sky had been given.

He could just club the old man and take the train; it would net him a fortune in a place like Enador or Howth. He could operate every part of it, including the automatic cannon, even if he had only a basic idea of exactly what made everything go. But it was no good; he wanted to be rid of the train just as much as he wanted to be free of his eye and arm and Cavandish.

He packed a few things the old man had given him, some food and optical tissue for his eye, and an automatic pistol with five loaded clips.

VanRoark left the coiled train several hours before dawn. His cloak was pulled tightly around him against the morning chill; he found it still astounding that his right arm should feel the cold, that the touch of the coarse fabric could warm it.

Mount Soril had come back into his mind by dawn and he moved northward, away from it, with only a vague idea that he should go to Enador. Protected by his new knowledge, he would scornfully enter into the sordid dealings of that city. *I'll become rich,* he thought, when his cynical self had become sick of the argument. And this would allow him—*to wander,* the histories said to him. *To drown yourself in pity for dead things,* the cynicism said, having lost all patience.

          ✤   ✤   ✤

It took him about two more months to reach the lands of the great trading city-state. He had effectively silenced that annoying bit of himself which had been plaguing his beliefs since Admiralty Square; the thorn garden had grown to fill up his empty consciousness instead. There was no more room left for it.

He had never been through the countries of Enador before, but he thought that from the stories of its wealth and power it should have presented a more prosperous

aspect than it did. Not that it differed from the usual
landscapes of the world; on the contrary, only the crests
on the ruins served to distinguish them from those of
previous empires. He passed along the Talbight, seeing
only very few small fishing craft, made of reeds; there
was no indication of the surviving river monitor.

He asked the people he met in the crumbling and
decimated villages if this was indeed a city of mighty
Enador. It was, they would answer absently, transfixed
by the blued gauntlet showing under his cloak and the
swiveling tube where his right eye should have been.
VanRoark then lost all interest in Enador and plunged
into a fine fit of cursing against Kenrick and Cavandish
and their steel and glass. If only they had just saved him,
he might have passed himself off as the victim of an
honorable war, if such things ever existed, or speak truth-
fully: that he had been maimed at the Burn in the service
of God. And those that knew, those who had heard the
prophets or tales of them, would nod knowingly at him,
acknowledging his miserable but still gallant fate.

VanRoark purchased a brown leather eye patch at a
village called Nine, and took to tying his arm against his
body under his shirt.

He reached Enador's walls without discovering why
her lands had come to such a deplorable state; either the
people had not known or he had not gotten so far as to
ask. The walls were deserted, very irregular in a city of
her reputed wealth. When he saw the gates hanging open
on the west wall, he correctly guessed that Enador had
died quite some time ago. It was not war that had killed
her, for the enemies would have been sure to have razed
the city. It was not plague, for there were none of the

usual sacrificial funeral pyres that would have been built outside the walls.

He could smell nothing, but this could mean that whatever had overtaken her had done its work more than a year ago; he could tell that from the condition of the surrounding lands.

It had been the lizards from the Enstrich, he finally learned. The great war between Cynibal and Ihetah-Incalam had eventually reached northward to the great swamp. The gases and explosives and fires of raiding bands, then completely beyond the original causes of the war, fighting simply because they had been fighting for years and saw no reason for stopping, had probably upset some delicate balance. Except for the Sea, the Marshes were the last great ecological system that still functioned on earth. VanRoark and Tapp had seen only the part which was still being kept alive by the Sea; inland, over the horizon, the Marshes had turned to sterile mud and dead greenery. With no more food, stopped on the south by the poisonous still-burning ruins of Cynibal and Blackwoods Bay, on the west by the equally poisonous lands of the Old Nations, most of the huge reptiles had been forced to move northward to find food. Apparently the great city of Enador had provided the reptiles with an adequate meal in the year or so since VanRoark had boarded the *Garnet* here.

There were not even the usual complement of vagrants living here now. Enador was just a depopulated ruin like Mount Soril, only a bit more grand. VanRoark walked through the city, down its few broad avenues whose fountains were now dry and commemorative pylons edged with moss, like those on the Avenue of

Victories in his home city. It had not been an utter rout; a long siege and then infiltration through the sewage systems seemed most likely to VanRoark. And there had been little panic; the looting was obviously methodical and well thought out.

VanRoark sat on the steps of a temple, resting and trying to figure out what his next move should be. He was quite deep in this thought, with the usual overlay of rim world bitterness, and so did not hear the dragon stepping out of the temple and walking slowly down the broad steps toward him. He did not notice in the least until the sun flashed on the crystalline growths of its hide; even then he thought the prismatic diffractions at the limits of his vision were only caused by his right eye's rebelliousness.

It was only when it had fastened into his right arm that he really saw it. His first reaction, aside from the normal reflex of trying to jerk free, was to curse Cavandish for not endowing the arm with superhuman strength; after all, it was a machine, was it not? Why then had not the old bastard at least given him something truly exceptional?

It was no stronger than the original had been, and seemed at the moment to be capable only of conveying pain to his mind. VanRoark swung his free hand at it, but the creature only released the arm, snapped at his fist and then fastened on again.

The left hand did not report pain. VanRoark looked frantically down at it and saw that it was bleeding jewels like those which covered the lizard's hide; not entirely, though, for the priestly robes of its last meal, purple embroidered with jet and gold, were still wrapped around the creature. A *reliquary*! VanRoark thought madly, a reliquary such as those behind the altars at home, where the bones and mummified hands of saints were preserved for the faithful's veneration. It could only be that, so wondrous the creature appeared. He reached out again with his hand, but this time to caress the encrusted body and flat, armored head.

The lizard did not bother to let go this time, but slashed out with its forefeet. Small scars were dragged out along VanRoark's arm, and they too bled rubies and amethysts. More colors than had been possessed by the army ran from the treasury of his left arm and splashed over an even more fantastic array of twisting and shattering hues. Perversely, all the right arm could do was to continue to feel the pain.

But perhaps Cavandish's work had not been entirely useless; if his normal eye could see such enchantment, such incredibly crafted beauty, then his right eye might see infinitely more.

He closed his left eye and concentrated on the right, trying to force the various filters into revolving, one after the other, within the eye, trying to capture the entire spectrum in one instant.

It showed him only a lizard, about four or five feet long, not counting the barbed tail, ludicrously tangled up in some odd colored silk; the colors of its skin were dulled into a smoky, vegetable luminescence.

Angry and near tears with disgust at his artificial parts, VanRoark closed off the eye and looked at the murderous reliquary with his left. And then he thought, *Here is a fine resting place for my bones, where all the lizard-kings may come and worship the tiny, distorted images of my body that will shine in each of the jewels; just as Smythe once told me that an insect sees a thousand images, one for each of its thousand eyes. And I will rest in its belly. . . . No! I will not, because I will rot away and the reliquary will digest even my bones—and then all that will be left will be the arm and eye, and those who come to worship me will begin laughing.*

He thought of the eye, with the frayed wires that had been spliced into his brain, looking back at the world through the thousand jewel-eyes; he imagined the arm, its engravings still clean in the lizard's stomach, with only a little bone around where it had been riveted and welded onto him, making obscene gestures at the lizard-kings.

With a grating, twisted sob, he stood up and, catching the creature off balance, brought its skull down upon the sharp marble steps; and then a second time and a third until its own jewel blood came bursting out. Studded with opal now, its brains spilled out and it began to dry in the hot sun. Then, it was only garbage.

VanRoark was instantly sickened and vomited his lunch into the lizard's twitching, torn-up body. Now the swimming filigree of color was complete for his reliquary.

He turned and ran down the steps, smearing his clothes in his own food, blood and that of the reptile. He was only dimly aware that he was mad, but the awareness grew and he came to a stop before the city's harbor, much like that of his home. The double turret of Enador's remaining river monitor could be seen to the west, her hull awash, and the great batteries trained to the north and west, waiting.

VanRoark collapsed with exhaustion and disgust with himself. Once, he could not keep a single system of values and guides intact within him. Now there was only the barbed and armored construction of the rim nations and the Sea, while the surrounding person had fragmented, his various parts gone screaming off into places he could not name. Pain was still flooding up to him from both arms; the left one no longer bled torrents of gem-sand, but only blood from scars edged with dirt and purple threads. The right arm hurt even more, the pulses surging along its length with the beating of his heart. He held it up and saw that the teeth had not even scratched it. The engravings were still as clean as he had thought they would be in the lizard's belly; the rocket still fled from the stars, and the dragon, so much grander than the one at the temple despite its lack of jewels, was still wrapped around his index finger. It was perfect, untouched, but it hurt, inexplicably, terribly.

"Oh, God!" he cried and clamped his head into his hands; the metallic click when the steel hand hit the steel eye startled him for a moment. In the rages that followed, he was too incoherent to call upon anyone, let alone God.

XXIV

He began his wandering in earnest on that day; before, even from Admiralty Square, there had been things to run from: his home, Prager, the Burn, and then Cavandish and his dead men's arm. Not that there was no longer anything of sufficient malevolence from which to run, but rather that there was no longer anything that could be called "VanRoark" who could do the running. He could run from himself: his grand, spectral set of memories of the rim nations could run from the much too human eye and arm they had left to him; his fading thoughts of life before Admiralty Square could run from the compounded desolation that had settled upon the world.

The failure of the army seemed to have removed the last props of sanity from the world, and this only increased his fragmentation. He had once worried whether he could still tell nightmare from the real world, but had given up considering that a problem since the two were often virtually indistinguishable.

Days varied appreciably in length from one to the next. The sun itself began a slight pulsation, its energy output shifting from hour to hour; his new eye allowed him to see that this pulsing was duplicated in the ultraviolet, infrared, and radio bands. He used to watch these radiations with a filter over the eye, and when he forgot what their changes meant, he thought them beautiful, like lines of smoke, stitched together with insubstantial gauze veils, drawn progressively outward along the lines of magnetic force.

He collapsed utterly around the memory-system of the rim nations, hanging whatever he could save from his ruin on its spiked armor and letting that which no longer fit trail along as best it might. He felt like the smoky trailings of energy, without will and now deprived of predictable purpose, radiating out into space from a breathing sun that appeared black, when his eye was focused so.

The madnesses came upon him more frequently now and more easily; he was not fighting them anymore. Once, he had broken twice in the same week—although normally he could count on two and a half to three months of uninterrupted sanity. An empty snail's shell, its side eroded by the coastal winds to expose its spiral patterns, had set him off; another time he'd seen an ancient road sign, where there was no road, showing the way to Mount Soril.

VanRoark knew of his vulnerability, but cared little for it; anything he might do now, and there was no reason to do anything, would be futile and meaningless. The madness was, in its way, just as safe and productive as his normal, daily life of food grubbing and speculation upon the real nature of his arm and eye. He dropped this last activity, though, after he'd broken, thinking himself to be the arm and the eye speculating on the nature of the body to which they had been chained.

The seven years that he spent blundering around the world were wanderings of the highest order, for he was more or less lost for most of that time. The varying rotational axes of the earth and perverse actions of the sun allowed him to make only the most rudimentary guesses as to his directions of travel; the sky had been useless many years before he had left home. It took him seven years to find the Sea again after he had fled southwest from Enador.

The lands he had walked upon embarrassed him before the Sea, as if the mere thought of them should infect the life that still flourished there. The flying fish and seabirds, the glowing manta-rays, shoals of silversides, and clean sand beaches, the wondrous power had not been diminished in the least by the failure of the army. True, he no longer spotted any smoke trails below the horizon; and he could never be sure if the booming report and white chalk trails which marked aircraft might be subtle products of the madnesses he had allowed himself. But here, at least, the memory of the great ships and the reflection of the planes' underbellies were still clean and uncluttered by their own wreckages. All the world was a graveyard of ruined craft and men, but only the Sea now bothered to bury them. There was a town named Kilbrittin situated at the very end of a peninsula in the fragmented, northern coastline of the world. It had long held the key to the old North Cape Confederation's endless fjords and harbors, and even the few probing fingers of the Sea that worked down into the territories of Raud. Like Charhampton, it was a fortress town, but there was still reason for its guns and walls to be kept in operating order: things were different in these regions, perhaps because they were so infused with the Sea, and despite the colder weather, the land was more productive. Territories of the broken Confederacy and Raud's northernmost Houses were still coherently organized and carried on a limited trade among themselves.

VanRoark thought them closer to the rim nations for this—and for the sadness that pervaded these lands. The ruins were much more orderly here: what no longer could be used was respectfully buried or disassembled; what no longer could be understood was put away to wait. Kilbrittin was fully aware it was dying and made no attempt to hide that fact from itself.

He found a strange peace here, with the storied fortresses looming above the streets everywhere, their harsh and brutal outlines softened by the winter's snow. When a seaplane landed outside the harbor to the west of the city and moored there for several days, he could feel only that peaceful remorse, without any traces of madness. He could walk down along the quays and admire the low sweep of the seaplane's lines and wings with the engines set high atop them away from the sea spray, and not remember the bomber's crew he and Cavandish had buried. He could look at the gutted hulk of an ancient cruiser being dismantled to rearm the fortresses, and not think too much of the *W. Lane* or the capital ship moored off the Burn.

He found work again in a cartography shop. People at Kilbrittin had become used to men with strange things growing on them, and his arm and eye aroused no more than some idle questions across the tavern's bar. Kilbrittin was not fully of the world, but neither was she of the rim nations, and this she also knew. She was Kilbrittin and nothing more; it was enough.

XXV

Spring had always been a very unsure thing in those latitudes and in those times; but when the first floes of broken ice began to drift seaward from the frozen rivers to the west, he left the city and began traveling south along the old coastal roads.

Remarkably, there still was a coast road. It occurred to him that through all the massive upheavals and geographical changes which had twisted the earth, the coastline had remained substantially the same. He began to think about the Sea again, and was amazed that he should now regard its teeming life with the same odd sorrow he had felt for the city of Kilbrittin. His eye allowed him to see several more levels of life in the Sea: the pale green of lichens on the wings of manta-rays; when he switched filters he saw their cold life fade in contrast to the manta-rays, which now glowed a deep maroon. Shoals of fairy-shrimp looked like the night sky: only red instead of sapphire, in a sky of milk rather than jet.

He felt rather proud that none of this should have produced any insanity. It had been a full year since he had given himself any cause to doubt his senses. Van-Roark took all this to mean that he had reached some kind of armistice with the arm and eye. At times he caught himself admiring the arm, as fascinated by its numberless engravings as he had been when Cavandish first removed the cast.

The memory of the rim nations softened within him too: so much that neither the fortresses nor the seaplane at Kilbrittin could awaken the bitter fury which had once insured their survival in his mind. *I am old,* he thought.

* * *

There was a curving headland, like the one which circled the Burn, rising above the city on the north. An arm of these hills had extended into the Sea in earlier days, forming the roadstead to her great harbor. But now most of the rocks had been eaten away and the harbor was a walled garden of cypress trees and rushes; there were a few hulks of sailing ships set in the garden at random intervals like statuary put there to give the place a synthetic charm or novelty.

The city did not appear too far different from when he had left it; even so, VanRoark camped on the head-lands that night, his eye probing the silent houses and the white line of the Avenue of Victories. He could see nothing against the Sea and the surrounding rocky lands, which retained the heat of the day; the city appeared as a blurred monotone, sometimes colored red, at other times white or black.

VanRoark awoke at dawn and ate a breakfast of dried fish he had brought from Kilbrittin. He rechecked his old pistol and made sure he could reach it quickly; there were only three full magazines left.

VanRoark entered through the little Chandlers' Gate on the northern side of the city, very close to where the Goerlin River had emptied into the harbor. Old Navy Dock ran out into the mud and dust now; the rusted hulls of the tugboats and sailing launches were still tied to the dock, covered in dirt and strangler vines.

He did not go to Admiralty Square and similarly avoided the old Thurber District. His house was reason-ably intact, though it had probably been vacated at least two years ago. They had left calmly, with plenty of thought, as was their manner; nothing was left behind which could not have been conceivably taken on a long journey, given horses and a wagon. There was only a smashed windowpane in his room, and the frail skeleton of the gull that had done it rested on the bare floor; its blood had stained the boards a darker shade of mahogany beneath the dust.

VanRoark had hoped he might feel an entirely sane ruefulness at his former home; but although he remem-bered all the things he had done in it, he could feel nothing. A touch of the fits, he mused, would at least have shown some respect for his parents.

It was still early. VanRoark moved about the sections of the city he had known, around the waterfront districts and rows of chandleries that had been given up years before he had left for the Wars. He summoned up enough courage to venture into the Thurber; the fantastic architecture the dead envoys had brought with them was eroded into even more incredible shapes by the Sea and desert winds: spires and leaning minarets, miniature temples and forts that made the southerners feel at home on the North Sea's shore; soaring, towered embassies that had ended in broken stone and mortar, left behind by their excellencies from Iannarrow and Mountjoy.

Again nothing; he could not even remember her face.

By early afternoon VanRoark had toured most of the areas he had wanted to see. Those which had been missed would have failed to stir him anyway, so he began walking along the Avenue of Victories toward the Artillery Gate.

The cathedral was about a quarter of a mile beyond the gate; he wanted to see it again, for it reminded him of Brampton Hall. The old words of Tapp's drunken song drifted back to him for the first time in years.

Mosses had grown up between the stone slabs, bordering them with green and leaving only a little stained white in the middle. Small grasses and shrubs, saltbrush, had further split up the road. Around the steps of the cathedral the vegetation died out. Aside from some shattered panels in the rose window and the windows flanking it, the huge cross-shaped building appeared virtually unchanged.

VanRoark moved slowly up the broad sweep of steps, carefully searching himself for some small swellings of memory or feeling. There was only the old awe and wonder he had always felt for so vast and magnificent a creation, and the words of Tapp's song. The mosaics of colored glass and sea-shell still rose within the entrance arches of the church, their saints and angels and praying men brilliant and glittering in the indirect sunlight. He wondered what might have caused the abandonment of the town and the church. Certainly not war or raiders; the gold leaf was still on the domes of the transept wings and wound around the serpentine columns before him, though a little worn away by the weather. A single statue, he could not identify who it might represent, had shaken loose from the portico roof and lay broken off to his right. Its fellows, the compassionate popes and archangels, looked down upon it with their calm eyes of inlaid alabaster, opal and ebony, their scepters and shepherds' crooks pointed upward, their left hands gently extended downward to the smashed figure.

VanRoark felt something growing within him at last: the sorrow of Kilbrittin and her fortresses and flying boats.

He advanced into the shadowed silences, through the grills of wrought iron and to the great bronze doors, aswarm with saints and the damned. He was reminded of his arm, but there were no ships on the doors, no hunting parties or fair ladies, no dragons or knights.

Then he saw the ships again and wondered if he had suddenly slipped into one of his spells. He looked up to the vast roof of the cathedral and to the great dome, almost an eighth of a mile distant from where he stood;

the whole cycle of birth, death, damnation and salvation, which was the living skin of the cathedral, was repeated, drawn together from its rambling exteriors and hidden chapels and magnified in grandeur a hundred times. All the Twelve Great Books were illustrated, the false-Armageddons from which so many saints had unwillingly walked away. There were horses, wild with the sight of battle and Heaven, running from the sacred fields, their brocaded hangings flying in a wind of amethyst and silver. There were tanks, blasted and destroyed, whose sense of defeat came from the artisans who had shaped them from pictures in old books, thinking them to have been as marvelously alive as the battle-horses, unicorns and gryphons that carried men in a spiraling path around the dome.

Part of the dome had either collapsed or been holed by a dud shell. The sunlight streamed down through it in dust so thick as to make it appear almost liquid. It joined other streams, colored from ruby to turquoise by the windows, and splashed down over the floor and rows of aircraft that sat parked upon it.

VanRoark believed all of it, until his eye got down to floor level where it should have been swept along the empty, geometrically patterned floor by the closing lines of pillars to the main altar. Instead, sitting with a peace and tranquility that was almost jarringly discordant with their appearance were three rows of big fighter aircraft; the dusty, silent torrents of colored light had turned their stained gray and olive battle paint into soft harlequins. Their high-set wings were tucked back against the hulls like sleeping birds. Now the sorrow descended on him without any madness or confusion. Again he saw a discordance, this time in the smooth, flowing contours of the ships, with the colors from the windows—they might have been poured and shaped from their molten substance—and how they contrasted with the baroque swirlings of men and nations racing across the ceiling.

Why? Maybe they had been brought here by worshipers, but that made no sense; these were creations of such as the rim nations and therefore to be despised. Perhaps they had landed out of chance or plan in the stony summer-hard arm of the Greenbelt that passed near the city, and then taxied, their wings reverently folded and their bomb shackles briefly dipped in the holy water font, into the abandoned church for protection. *Until when for what?*

There was nothing to answer any of this. They lifted above him as he walked forward, the first things he had ever seen that the cathedral could not overwhelm with either its size or beauty. He felt along their flanks, which were cool or warm depending upon whether they had been in shadows or colored light; he had not done that for years either.

VanRoark expected that his mind would speed up, awash and near drowning with this mystery; perversely, it slowed down and became frosted and softened with the dust of the ships.

There were no thoughts, not a single grand conception he could grasp here. He knew that a hunt for meanings or a sign would be wrong. The only fragment clear to him was just what he could see and feel.

And as he saw and touched, he could sense the menacing, thorn-armored memories of the rim nations become softened with the funereal dust, and speckled with the endless colors. Suddenly the system was not so brutal and demanding. It lost its triumphant bitterness; it only was.

The aircraft were pointed away from the altar; he was at the top of the ebon steps, his back to the great altar-block of carved crystal. The twin exhausts of each plane gaped back at him, the tops of the vertical stabilizers about level with his eyes.

VanRoark stood there, looking over their dolphin hulls as he had done with the aircraft at the Burn: the flowings of color moved across their wings, across the flattened, rotted rubber of their landing wheels.

Then he moved from the altar, over the crypt where his grandfather had been buried, and down the north aisle, between the planes and chapels. He had played in the dark, isolated chapels when a child. He would sit quietly off to the side, surrounded by cherubim or between the long, stone plaques that proclaimed the virtues of some dead bounder, and stare wonderingly at the people who would come there. They were different in his thought, for they scorned the high altar's magnificence, almost as if they wanted to pray to a lesser god than that which was represented there.

In one of the small chapels he saw the first evidence of looting; a small window had been removed and the gold inlays of the little altar had apparently been pried off.

The chapel had been built to contain a reliquary: THE HAND OF WOLFE, a plaque told him. The thieves must have been after the dust of the mummified hand because the reliquary case had been discarded under a bench.

Appropriately, the case had been shaped like a hand, but in all its other aspects it was quite unlike the ornate, usually overwrought candy boxes they used for the thigh bones and skulls of others. Maybe that was why he was able to touch it, pick it up and hold it up to the milky brown sunlight of the remaining alabaster windows, and think only briefly of the lizard and Enador; that madness had been lost among a hundred similar and a thousand more revolting ones.

The hand was hollow, to contain the saint's; its outer skin was outlined by the endless flowing strands of poured silver. It was as if someone had made a wax mold of a fine hand, strong but still suggestive of sensitivity and gentleness, and then carefully traced the molten silver over it, letting the interstices of strings melt into each other until the whole hand was not covered but defined by the spider's webbing, and the wax would have been melted away.

VanRoark noticed that while he admired it, he held it in his right hand. The reliquary hand was what the steel hand might have created if it was striving to approximate, but not duplicate, its own life—just as a man's hand had once tried to invest the steel arm with the qualities of his own.

He decided to put it into his backpack and examine it later; he walked back to the nave, ducking to miss the javelin noses of the planes.

VanRoark did not know exactly where he was going then, so he began drifting south again, along the coastal road he had traveled years ago. Then, he had been filled with a boiling, reasonably solid purpose. Now, he had only a vague conception of what he might do and where he might go, as if he could not quite reveal it to himself yet.

He left the Sea at Farnbrough Bay. There were few people along the way; a troop from Larine going to extract some tribute from what was left of New Svald was about the largest party he encountered. There were no young men seeking jeweled lizard hides.

Oddly, he found the Belt, or at least the southern portions of it, supporting some life beyond saltbrush and wolf-spiders. Small, stunted fruit trees, scarcely taller than himself, had sprung up at random intervals, where the infrequent rains had washed away enough poison to let them grow. They fed him as he crossed inland across the Belt. The perversity of the world's weather for once helped him, and an early freeze allowed him to cross the Shirka River and enter Svald.

It had taken him six years to find the Sea, but only two to find the train.

He was moving in a southeasterly direction, across the desolated Old Nations' lands, toward Blackwoods; Cavandish had said he was driving in that direction for fuel.

It was a place of wild, deeply scarred highlands and rolling swells of limestone, overlaid by an inch thick layer of spongy mosses and blown soil. Constant winds kept the few trees which had managed to sink roots into the water-rotted stone low, bending along the line of the ground like old men about to die.

The train was stopped at the bottom of a protective depression. He did not notice it at first, for the faded camouflage blended almost perfectly with the valley's spotty vegetation. Cavandish had made his camp there;

a tarpaulin, speckled olive and tan like the train, had been stretched out from the left side of the first passenger car. One or two of the lines had broken from decay, and the sheet flapped roughly in the diminished wind.

A camp chair was set up against one of the car's wheels. Cavandish's corpse still sat in it. The insects and few birds of the region had trimmed most of the flesh from his bones. He sat there, quite unidentifiable as Cavandish, quite indistinguishable from any of the hundreds of corpses and skeletons VanRoark had seen in his wanderings. The skeleton's sole claim to identity was Cavandish's metal larynx and jaw; it was a tulip-shaped affair of a dull copper material, narrow where it had lain along the throat, and then expanding upward to duplicate the shape of the original jaw. There was a small oval grid where the mouth would have been; it was neatly flush-riveted to the skull—a very workmanlike job.

As VanRoark approached the skeleton he could hear it talking. Later, he would discover that the units powering the artificial speaking unit had unaccountably kept on functioning. In the absence of any coherent signals from the brain—the connective wires lay frayed and tangled inside the empty skull—the unit kept up a sporadic chatter of random sounds, sometimes joining them into a coincidental word or even a full sentence. Usually it was gibberish.

VanRoark was amused at this grotesquerie. "Even from your grave you're telling me your sorrows," he said and laughed at the skeleton; he received a garbled eruption whose closest approach to sense was satisfactorily obscene.

Then he drew back, remembering how funny he had thought Tapp's death at the Burn; and he remembered the first and most violent of the madnesses that had followed. Walking backward, afraid to take his eyes off the corpse, he lost the sound of the ventriloquist's voice under the wind and the tarpaulin's flappings.

Nothing happened; he was properly upset, of course, because finding the train meant he would have to articulate at least part of his plan: that he was going back to the Burn and then to the Meadows.

He returned to the camp and examined the body again. "Won't be able to bury you in this stuff, Cavandish," he said, feeling the jagged rock underneath the mossy ground with the toe of his boot. Cavandish said nothing. "Come on now, Cavandish. I can't leave you sitting out here on that chair talking to whoever might blunder past without being formally introduced."

There was a small burst of noise, short syllables which VanRoark's mind perversely interpreted as "Burn."

VanRoark stood up warily, speculating on how much of this he could allow his mind to play with before it would become dangerous. "All right then, if you really want to." The parchment shreds of skin and connective tissue turned to cold sand in his arms. He almost vomited. Pushing this down and being careful not to breathe through his nose, he carried the skeleton up the ladder and into the first crew car. He found Cavandish's cabin and carefully laid him down on the bunk.

A burst of incoherencies followed him beyond the door and he made quite sure it was securely locked.

XXVI

The machine had been carefully prepared for a long wait by Cavandish. The operating manuals were set out beside the driver's throne, and a handwritten list of special quirks not covered by those manuals had been thoughtfully provided.

VanRoark took almost a week familiarizing himself with the machine again, venturing into areas Cavandish had never shown him. He disconnected the two empty fuel cars, removed the preservative grease from critical parts and generally did what he could to put the train back into cruising condition. He uncovered the gun and took aim on a rock prominence on the northern side of the valley; the first shot landed at its base and toppled it. Intending to pick out some other targets, he found he was shaking too badly to take aim; for the first time in almost a year he felt he might go insane. The gun was hurriedly capped and hidden.

The only thing he could not get working was the train's navigational equipment. The magnetic compass was not worth repairing, considering the world's irrationality probably applied to its magnetic field too, and the rest of the equipment was utterly beyond his understanding.

He was a year moving to the west after he pulled the train out of the valley, always verging slightly to the south for fear of blundering into the Meadows without warning. Endlessly—more endlessly than when he had been on board the *Garnet,* for here there was no Sea—the distances moved under the train, the tarn gradually giving way to the blasted forest where they had buried the bomber's crew years before. VanRoark kept the speed down to what he judged a safe rate, considering the terrain. In the grasslands this was as much as twenty miles an hour, but when the forests or palisaded badlands came up he was lucky to cover five miles a day.

He avoided civilization, for he knew very well his appearance would not cause a friendly reception. The machinery of the first world and the rim nations had been despised before he had left his home the first time, and the situation had only grown worse with time.

He also began going mad again. But this was a very subtle sort of thing, which he mistook for a simple hypnosis from nonstop traveling. Then he became dimly conscious, perhaps so dimly that he could understand it only as a feeling, like the slow dropping of small crystals into a pond: very tiny, falling with a sparkling light that reflected off their endless planes, spinning to the water and leaving rings upon which waterbugs climbed as they passed—all in silence, all with infinite patience and subtlety.

Instead of wrenching violently away from the conventional world and finding himself in what had been always recognizable as a nightmare, he would feel nothing more than a giddiness and a swell within him as the wave passed, so gently as to hardly trouble the waterbugs. Then he would see the white-streaked webs of aircraft in the sky again, heading west.

The damnable thing about it was that every once in a while there really was an aircraft aloft; his right eye would always reveal that. But he deemed this trivial and therefore harmless; he found the small fictions enjoyable most of the time, and refrained from shifting his right eye into

the non-visual spectra, lest it destroy the fragile construction with which his mind had sought to amuse him.

During those long days of driving, which stretched
into their fifth month with no indication he was anywhere
nearer the Burn than when he had set out, he began to
bring Cavandish's body up to the control cab for conversation. He knew it to be intensely morbid, but after all,
the thing *did* talk and would thus protect him from his
new insanity. And when it was talking, it seemed a disser-
vice to call it "it." It, or rather he, could still be the old
Cavandish at times, glaring out of hollow sockets at the
storms which occasionally roiled up from the west, or
late at night, again looking up (if VanRoark was disposed
to place him so) at the constellations above and uttering
properly mournful tones. With time, it seemed to Van-
Roark, Cavandish had regained much of his rare eloquence; the coherent sentences appeared with more
frequency, if he listened closely enough.

Somehow none of this affected him very much; he
thought it ultimately rather pleasant, going to die in the
company of the dead. At times he and Cavandish would
have a good laugh speculating on how VanRoark would
have reacted to this on their first meeting.

VanRoark began to admit that Cavandish had not been
such a bad sort after all; he could see that, now that he
had gone through all the things the old man had tried
to help him avoid. He explained this very carefully to
Cavandish on several occasions, sometimes when they
were on the move (for Cavandish spent most of the days
riding in the control cab by the sixth month), or in the
evening outside the train, for he hardly wanted the old
man to harbor any lasting hatred for him.

Eventually VanRoark was satisfied that he had adequately apologized to Cavandish for his behavior and that the old man had forgiven him. He knew they were back on their old terms when, near sunset one evening, Cavandish suddenly started talking. His voice had become much deeper since his death, for the absence of any brain or flesh allowed the skull to resonate with the artificial larynx, like a sounding board. VanRoark looked up at the sky, just in time to see chalk-marks tracing into the western sun. It was not very high and he would see the silver craft, a glittering bit of crystal, fire-wake behind turning to strands of carded wool.

The two of them sat looking out of the control car's windows until the sun had turned the filmy trail deep pink and then red, and then black, to be lost in the night. There was a silence, and VanRoark thought of carrying the corpse back to his cabin for the night and then watching the sky for a bit longer. But Cavandish began to talk—not as clearly as he once might have, and VanRoark had to sort out a lot of extraneous gibberish—and in the end he knew Cavandish was speaking of the rim nations, and the stars that briefly had been their homes, the woman to whom he had given them, and the dreams he had dreamed when sitting in the frigid, thinly webbed eyes of bombers.

XXVII

He knew they were climbing into the highlands surrounding the Burn because, at times, he could smell the Sea and its wet, fecund life blowing over the dead sand.

They camped for the night about two miles from a rise which might have opened down onto the Burn. Van-Roark did not carry on, for he felt small, only partly unexplainable, bits of pain and fear stitching up and down his spine. He placed Cavandish back in the first crew car, and climbed atop the control car. Leaning on the cannon's shrouded barrel, he looked up into the brilliant welkin. It appeared that he might be at a very great distance in the air, looking down upon the infinite lights of the army; by shifting his right eye's spectrum sensitivity he could see the equally infinite colors the army had once possessed. Magnification brought him nebulas, torn, scattering shreds of what had been suns, their dying pennants embroidered with star-gryfons and strands of silver, like the reliquary hand he still kept with him.

He went to his cabin to get the hand, and then returned. The wrist had been trimmed down and fitted with a lock-joint; he could remove his articulated gauntlet and replace it with the hand.

There was no feeling in this limb; the coldness of its silver base reached past the insulated sockets at his wrist. But it was an indisputably beautiful thing. There was no thought of who made it; whether he had come from the stars or from Mountjoy; or of the dead saint's dust it had once protected.

It was a long hand, long and etherealized, like those of the artists who had built the cathedral; so different from the sharp, blunt form of the gauntlet-hand, which was more like ancient engraved rifles and field artillery than paintings and sculpture. He looked at the gauntlet, at its images of ships and stars and coiling dragons, and at the engraved prince, and he thought how much the noble's small hands looked like the one he had just mounted.

There were no engravings on this new hand, nothing but the hollow web-work of drawn silver. When he moved it across the star-glittering sand and mica-studded rocks, they were all within his hand. When he moved it again, he could sweep all the welkin into its interior, its stars and burning dust pennons captured like fragile birds or fireflies in its cool beauty.

More strangely than anything he had ever felt before, sorrow welled up inside him, just as the comets now danced inside the hand. He could not fathom it, not even by charging it off to madness; it remained, slowly bringing his head down into the hands of flesh and woven metal, grinding his back into the gun's breech.

He wept, at times from the sorrow, and at other times from the anger which came from not knowing where it had been born. *The purest, most beautiful thing you have known since that woman you knew in Thurber, and you cry. Idiot!*

VanRoark fell asleep there, with his left eye red and puffed shut from the tears, and the right staring with a tearless, unfocused blankness.

He did not awake until noon, and then he immediately set out for the rise; he was so eager and fearful to see what was on the other side, he forgot to bring Cavandish up to the cab to view the sight.

The wind came to him again, as it had in the valley and badlands where he had found the train; he could hear it sigh through the bullet holes in the car's skin.

Below him was the enormous depression of the Burn; its sandy topsoil was rippled and coursed over by innumerable lines, the graves of men.

The train reached the floor of the Burn, moving forward slowly; he could hear the crunching of old bones and metal under the great wheels, the same way they had snapped under his feet at Brampton Hall. This hurt him; he could feel the sadness of the previous night returning, not as close this time, but still threatening with its inexplicable sense of loss.

VanRoark brought the train across the Burn and parked it under a huge sloping wing of one of the rim nations' aircraft. Ahead of him, across the causeway ramp, was the river, substantially unchanged; beyond that was the featureless plain, only a little less desolate than the Burn, and the gun-metal mountains to the north.

Aside from the wind and the gentle slap of the surf, there was no noise. He moved fearfully, as if one wrong step would suddenly awaken all the army's ghosts and set them to their mindless, brawling life once again.

He spent the day roaming around the Burn's beaches, looking at the rusted, mutilated hulks of destroyers, the battle cruiser and tanker; he could still spot the ordered rows of field artillery secured to the deck of this last one—except along the starboard quarter forward, where the graceful flaring of her bow had been ripped outward and up like the blossom of a huge, cancerous flower.

There were about ten planes left, not counting the giant transport which now sheltered the train; most had been flattened where they were parked. But two had made it to the causeway, past the drawbridge; they sat there on their collapsed gears, still straining to lift their dead crews and cold fires to the Meadows.

VanRoark walked over the area where the army had been encamped, along the charred lines that might have been avenues where the shops and whorehouses had stood. Brampton Hall was still there on the headlands, marking the graves of the army and rim nations. Occasionally he came upon one of the family or regimental standards that had survived the desert's heated wind and the gales that moved in from the Sea. The enameled banners of chain mail were still bright when lifted out to the sun.

Near late afternoon, though, VanRoark became bored and depressed with the Burn; it was as though only a thin cloth had been drawn over the tangled wreckage, and any move he might make would crush a skull or put a broken sword hilt through his boot. On the surface it was a fairly clean place, with just enough ruin poking through to interest one; it only sickened him to know what lay below.

He went back to the train to get some dinner from its inexhaustible stores. He also had a little wine from a keg that had been marked as Zaccaharias'.

Toward evening VanRoark felt relieved of his depression and judged himself to be fully willing to set out for the Meadows the next day. But something was needed, the beau geste he had so desired when he had left his home city. He hit upon the idea of a dinner; many of the old histories he had read on the train had mentioned that this had often been the custom of warriors before a battle. The great halls would be strung with standards captured in past victories; the deeds of dead men would be recited to inspire the still-living; there would be singing of the company's songs with all their fine proud words of triumph edged and polished like a bayonet by the wine.

VanRoark began poking about, all the time keeping a full cup of wine with him, and soon found an irregular piece of aluminum sheeting, about five feet by fifteen. He dragged it back to the train and set it atop seven or eight oil drums he had come across on a beached landing craft. He brought up more drums, smaller ones from the hold of the same craft, and set them around the ragged table.

He sat down at the head of the table, the dried meats and synthetic bread in front of him, the wine keg at his right hand. The sun had only been up for about eight hours and, despite the fact that it should have been early summer, a few stars were already beginning to appear in the east's dark shading.

The wine had been improved by its years of waiting. VanRoark began to feel the old battle-joy of the dead warriors rising from his stomach. He remembered the bustling, professional happiness of the army.

He must have fellows, companions with whom to exchange vast lies and sing the battle songs. He looked about desperately; the only thing living, of course, was the Sea. Amethyst flashings of dolphins and marlin dancing beside the sullen wrecks and the causeway could be seen. One could hardly invite *them* to supper; anyway, aside from the practical considerations, what did they know of the affairs of men? Had they ever been scarred? Had their beautiful, fragile armor ever been torn to pieces by the bolts of archangels or fragmentation bombs?

It seemed to him that the Sea and all the life it had protected from the horror of the land was a thing of bitter mocking. For a moment the vicious humor of the ocean died within him and he looked down to watch the white surf washing against the beach, futilely trying to wash it clean again; every wave carried back a small cargo of rust and rotting bone into the dark, living peace.

Such thoughts were not for him, though. Perhaps years ago when he had sailed on the *Garnet,* or in the future when the bitterness of the rim nations had softened enough to let him feel, but not now.

Ah! Cavandish. He shouldn't be cut out of this. The old bastard was finally getting to the Meadows and any life which might still be clinging to his bones and his mechanical voice would find salvation, or at least silence. Cavandish would know so much better than the fish or their Sea, for he had certainly been scarred. The bronze jaw, eyes of glass and steel, the arm, all of these showed they had tasted their own blood, drank it in huge gouts; it meant they were human. The fish might have been hurt, but not forever; inexorably, the Sea would heal them, set them right. The calloused scars of men seemed to give them a special vision. They had seen the true nature of the world, and that knowledge had deprived them of the delightful fantasies of life forever.

VanRoark went into his own car first and put on his old automatic, a clean shirt and, after a moment of thought, the reliquary hand.

He had a hard time with all this, wrestling the skeleton out of the first crew car. Eventually he got Cavandish onto the oil drum at his right hand; the shaft of a vanished battle standard was driven into the ground and the man's skull set atop it. There was still enough connective tissue on the spine to keep him from collapsing like a child's set of jackstraws.

Cavandish was soon arrayed like the warrior he had wanted to be, or at least as VanRoark conceived him as wanting to be, with a bandolier of cartridge cases and a semi-automatic rifle taken from the control car's small armory.

The table was still relatively barren. Cavandish told VanRoark to sit down, but the wine would not let him. Soon there were eleven more corpses in various stages of decomposition sitting around the crude table. At least, VanRoark reflected delightedly, he had gotten members of the rim nations and the army to sit down together. Ah, the comradeship of battle!

The armories of the train were almost emptied as he dressed the cadavers in anti-fragment vests, bandoliers, pistol belts, rifles with fixed bayonets. How martial they all looked with their heads propped up by metal or wooden poles; how profoundly their gaping wounds reflected the things they had seen.

As it was nearly dark, VanRoark emptied some petrol out of the end fuel car and set blazing tins on the table. His store of synthetic bread and Zaccaharias' wine was almost gone after he had laid sufficient portions before each man.

"But then," a trooper from Kroonstadt said in a cavalier manner, "none of us will be needing food again, will we?" A small lizard briefly appeared in his right eye socket and VanRoark took this for a knowing wink. A hearty roar of approval went up from the men, army and rim nations alike.

He sighed and leaned over to Cavandish. "This is how it always should have been. Just men, together. . . ." He waited for an answer; none came.

It was night; by the third hour of darkness VanRoark was quite drunk, but he assumed that much of the trouble he had in figuring out the words to the songs had more to do with the drinking of the other men than with his own mind. Mostly, he preferred to lean back and enjoy the singing and comradely trading of insults, and perhaps an occasional aside to Cavandish. He felt quite the elder warrior, who knows he has only one last battle to fight before his courage has been justly and honorably run.

By the fourth hour of night, the pageantry of his arm had stirred to life. He almost regretted that the original hand had been left on his bunk, for he sometimes felt that it was from the star on its palm that all the hunting parties and great ships received their light. But apparently the rust-light from the petrol lamps was enough for them: he could see the waters rolling under the quick hulls of frigates and battleships, extreme clippers running before dull silver storms for harbors no bigger than the eyes of a beetle; the mounted men with their attendants on foot, their ladies riding sidesaddle and their falconers at the ready; great castles and mountain fastnesses studded and plumed with flags like knights. All seemed to be somehow marching downward into the delicate wickerwork of his right hand.

And when he moved the hand, it held fire or its own cold, savage reflection on the underside of the plane's wing, the desert patterns of the land train, the clean, liquid peace of the Sea or the stars and galaxies above.

Near the end of this fourth hour he found that his hand held storm clouds along the northern horizon, turned almost white by the brilliant sky. As the clouds moved to the east and south, it began to appear as if they contained lightning. VanRoark looked closer, hardly noticing that the singing and joking had almost died away.

The clouds covered half the northern sky now and he could see they were being illuminated from below.

VanRoark got up from the table and stumbled forward a few feet. As the cloud cover climbed higher above the horizon, the vague illuminations began to play against a larger screen: green, pale blue, red, and orange burnings flared up from over the edge of the world. A particularly violent explosion lifted its roiling head above the northern mountains, turning the plain-lands and the Sea yellow-white. Seconds later, the sound and even a trace of the concussion hit them. "Our Wars," someone whispered in the flickering darkness behind him. "Our Wars," another repeated.

He adjusted both eyes as best he could and found them reporting only garbled, distorted images; he was sure his drink-warped senses were magnifying the whole thing beyond any touch with reality. The noises were soft—he could hear the whisperings of the men over them—but they seemed ready to break his skull open. The battle's lights were plastered over the back of his head; his vision narrowed until all he could see was the burning storm cloud and a thin bordering of stars and clear sky. His mind began to spin uncontrollably. He knew that the light was dim and the noise no more than that of a light breeze—but they crashed through his eyes, turning his brain into a whorled pulp and his limbs to rubber.

"They're still going, Cavandish!" he yelled back to the old man. "The ships I saw, they were really there! The Wars are still on for us." He turned to the group. "Should we leave for them now?"

"For the Wars?" Cavandish asked coolly; the rest were silent. Aside from the pale flashings of red or orange on white bone, there was little evidence they had ever seen the Wars.

"Where else, old man?" VanRoark replied frantically. The wine took hold more firmly; as he whirled back to face the Wars he could see the ground rushing up at him. It was possible to see the individual grains of sand tremble ever so slightly from concussion.

He thudded down on his left side, unable to move his head more than a few degrees and seemingly paralyzed over the rest of his body. Before him the horizon kept increasing its blisterings of fire and cloud-shadowed light. Then he remembered what was supposed to be going on at the base of the explosions, and struggled to regain his feet; he could not.

From behind his back a new voice placed itself against the troopers' silence and the far whisperings of the Wars. VanRoark knew it belonged to none of the men he had seated at the table, but it still sounded familiar. *It is human,* he thought madly, and then asked himself why he should make this observation. *Ah, VanRoark,* he thought, for speech seemed to have temporarily deserted him too. *You must have been expecting an archangel, the guardian of the Burn's dead and Brampton Hall. But they would have no need of angels,* he told himself in answer.

"They are still on," the voice crooned, as if it had just noticed the spectacle. "Our Wars.

"Our Wars!" the voice suddenly shrieked. "Our stinking, bleeding, *bastard wars!"*

Van Roark began to place the voice, mainly in that it was, to a great extent, not a voice. Of course it depended on words now, sounds like those he could fashion in his own throat, but behind them hovered shapes, great and terrible. The play of detonating light on the back of his skull now had the shapes dancing before it, illogically seeming to cast distorted shadows of themselves over the explosions. Again, the shapes seemed to have been known to him, but they were broken and warped from what they had once been.

They had been Timonias'.

He saw the parchment structurings of creations, shredded and charred past recognition, floating inside the words, as he saw an occasional glowing of a rocket's flight in his hollow head.

But all this is impossible. I am much too drunk; soon the voice will go away and then, tomorrow, we can follow it to the Meadows.

The voice did not go away; it spoke to him, now cooler than it had been in the outburst of a moment ago. "You see them, VanRoark? The men are still coming to them; we could still see the vapor trails of aircraft, still might have seen the ships had we traveled up the coast. They're still coming, the men! And you know what that means?" There was some trace of a grating sob behind the voice, like that of the girl at Mount Soril. "It means that this, like all the others which have gone before it, isn't working! All the hopes of finally putting some sort of finish to this filthy world have been betrayed again!

"And when they have ended, and the Meadows are left for a little while before the prophets and the armies come again, some poor bastard who lived through it will have to write another *Book of Eric,* another *Survivors.* Lord, VanRoark, do you have any idea what is going on there, what must be going on . . . Lord, Lord!"

VanRoark tried to wag his head, yes, he did understand.

Now the voice was unaccountably touched with satiric malice. "Ah, you realize? Fine!

"You bleeding bastard! How could you conceive of it, with the ravings of idiots and the possessed, tales out of moldering books, and your own childish imagination? Great ships and great men, that's what you see—even after you saw how men fight and how they die, here at the Burn, even then you still see men, straight and true, neatly disposing of their odious foes.

"And besides them, you *must* see the angels, the supernatural made natural for an instant to battle on the side of Justice and Light. You see them as men, no doubt, men of huge stature, dressed in robes of light or fire and swords made of stars in their hands. You see them both walking untouched, unscarred, through the carnage of their divine purpose."

Wrong, VanRoark thought. *Once I saw them in such purity and grandeur, but then I wandered into the cathedral and saw the sterile angels and saints of the mosaics.* But he drew back from himself and acknowledged that, for a year, he had not given any thought to the Meadows outside of the hint that he was going to die there. In the company of who or what had seemed strangely irrelevant; now the literal reality of Heaven came rolling back down upon him with the concussion winds from the Meadows.

"I think," the voice resumed, "that they are much like the men: poor, beaten clowns, called out once again from what had also been promised to them as an eternal peace and sleep. I wonder if their wings can be broken and if they hang from their bodies at hideous angles; I wonder if they bleed where the jellied gasoline or sword strokes of devils strike them; I wonder if they feel pain and the endless frustration."

The voice was quiet for a second; the clouds covered a bit more than half the visible sky, or about all of Van-Roark's limited field of vision. It began again, holding in it the vicious malice and groaning sorrow of a moment ago, but now touched with a growing awareness as it heard itself say things it had known, yet never admitted for a thousand years.

All through it, the shapes soared and turned, arrayed like tanners' hawks in tunics of blood-rusted barbed wire. "And do you know what all of this progressively more wretched Creation, this endless succession of abortive Meadow Wars means, beyond the fact of one more abortive ending? It means, VanRoark, that the thing which had given life to all of this in the first place and which had conceived of all the plans is a poor, stupid, fumbling idiot just like the rest of us!

"Ah, that is beautiful! Think of it! The final basis for a million years of theology and a thousand years of philosophy—nothing more than a useless pile of shit!

Noble minds striding the earth, putting their ascetic necks on the block in the name of something which didn't exist. Wars, evolutions, inquisitions, pain, pain: because it was part of the plan, the divinely inspired plan—so full of eternal wisdom that it sickens me now—and therefore how could it be bad?

"The marvelous conceit which must have been in it in the beginnings. The pride, the limitless power, the complete knowledge! And then, when the time came to end it, the first uneasy tremors as it became obvious that things had been created which could no longer be controlled. Time—there was a lovely thing for you, ticking like a seven-day clock from beginning to end and then politely making room for eternity—that didn't stop when it should have. It began doing things it shouldn't, just like the seasons, the air, the stars, none of them behaving as they should have!"

The sobbing currents broke through the words, riding over them like waves of polluted surf. "Oh God, Van-Roark! Look at our Wars and the men who are still trying to get there, even after their own army tried to kill them. After these Wars fail, and they will, there will be another, maybe a bit more successful than this, most likely less. And after them . . . after them . . .

"Man, the only way men know they are alive in this world is because they are still bleeding! Soon, I think, even pain will be lost to us, and then there will be nothing but madness. Ah, to be alive and to have no way of telling it from death! There's a thought to start your mind moving! Carry it a step further and ask how the living will be able to tell when they have at last died! There'll be nothing then, nothing but a darkness filled with gigantic, colliding shapes that will crush men and then tear them apart."

VanRoark lay quietly for a long time looking at the Wars—he dared not close his eyes.

Although now largely with the voice of a man, Timonias still carried with him the power of imagery he'd had at Admiralty Square. VanRoark saw the dark colliding shapes, the torn and mangled skins of men splattering between them, their minds and organs bloody smears on the darkness.

After a while the clouds moved northward again and the detonations all but vanished to thin traces along the horizon.

VanRoark wondered if the prophet was still there or if he had vanished with the burnings. "Timonias? Are you there?"

"Yes." The reply came slowly and in Cavandish's voice.

VanRoark puzzled over this for a moment. "Cavandish, are you there too?"

"I am." The same voice. "I was Timonias."

Oh, Christ-on-a-crutch, aren't the Wars and a dead prophet enough for one evening? VanRoark thought, with a curiously clear and somehow amused fraction of his brain; he had not felt that part of him speak since the first time he had been at the Burn. But it vanished quickly as the harsh light of an unexpected explosion lifted above the earth and buffeted him.

VanRoark tried to think of something to say, but he was utterly at a loss. Instead, after some few more moments of quiet, the voice spoke again. "Amon, Cavandish, the one who had come to the Burn on the train, died along with his friend Zaccaharias two weeks after we left the army."

A fumbling silence; the voice lost the bitter command it had possessed an instant before. "Look, my story, the things I told you about the rim nations and about how I used to fly as a bombardier, all that is true—except that it happened sixty years ago.

"My nation, I told you, simply began to break up. I helped it along in this, for while I was still there and flying out against the world I received . . . received . . . " The voice hesitated and fell, searching within itself to express something but not even the prophet's full voice could have explained. " . . . You know, Amon. I feel the way you must have felt as you walked away from hearing me. . . .

"I was given this voice and the visions to put inside it. I was shown things, oh, such beautiful, magnificent things that it makes me sick to think of them. I was filled up, you know, as if I were an empty jar holding nothing but air, and then I was full of these visions and the knowledge. For thirty years I simply moved through this world with nothing touching me on the inside or out. Then, I was . . . was so full of that lovely power that all I had to do was open my mouth and it would come rumbling and spinning out, wrapping itself around the souls of men just as it should have done, lifting their eyes to look into themselves. And then bringing them to this place.

"So I spoke the words, and I could see the things moving behind men's eyes and all of that only made me more full and more eager to see the final, glorious climax of my mission.

"Ah yes, such a climax my Army of Justice and Light and Good and Purity and Beauty gave me. I had left my ship to walk through the camp. . . ." He stopped talking. VanRoark could hear nothing but a barren, crackling noise, like that which usually came out of the train's radios; it reminded him of the brittle crunching of bones at Brampton Hall and underneath the Burn's dust shroud.

Something had to be remembered; Timonias went on. "I was in the camp. I was dressed in robes so fine and white that I think I could have walked at night by their light alone. I began to hear the noises that leather and metal make when they are being readied for something. It broke loose. My lovely army, turning and tearing itself to pieces, killing men from the rim nations whose families I had known!

"No, that's wrong. It just did not matter to me at that moment—until I saw them being dragged away from their machines and soaked in their own petrol, made to drink it, and having torches rammed down their throats.

"I ran through that camp, Amon, not a soul noticing my presence. I had called them there! I, Timonias! But I found that I could not speak. At the moment when my voice and knowledge were desperately needed, when nothing else but that could have stopped the army's suicide, I could not speak a word!

"I was like the Wars. They're the last place, the final move in the game, but they aren't and the game goes along, making up its own rules while the players can only look on helplessly. So I failed too. The words left me as did the visions, and I have felt only fragments of them since.

"Maybe losing my mouth had something to do with it? I caught a nice piece of phosphorus on the lower jaw and throat near the end. I would've bled to death if Cavandish and his crew hadn't picked me up.

"You really should have known them, Amon. Fantastic men, equal to the best I knew when I was still flying. They knew who I was, they *knew,* and they saw what I had done and what I had failed to do. But they stopped the bleeding and took me away. They found you later and another fellow named Johonner, but he was too badly shot up; they gave him a new heart and even some new motor parts for his brain. He died a week out.

"They gave you your arm and eye and put you to sleep to recover. They gave me a voice again, not my own, of course—I had lost that forever in my, ah, calling—but a voice. I was very angry with them at first because it possessed none of the power and wonder it once had. Before, my curses would have literally driven them insane, knocked their brains loose from their skulls; but then, all I could get out, before I learned how to work the new voice, was static and a few random words." There was a crackling silence and then metallic laughter. "Just as I am talking to you now, Amon; just like I was learning how to talk all over again—for the fourth time in my life too!" Again the quiet. "Ah, yes"—very low—"my life."

VanRoark heard the deep skidding noise of big guns with muzzle brakes, firing somewhere over the horizon. "Are you still coming with me tomorrow?" he called out after some seconds.

"No."

"But why?" VanRoark cried to the voice behind him. "Why are you going, in whose name?"

"In my own name."

"Well, I have none now, neither Cavandish, nor Timonias, nor the first one, Arnold."

"But if only to die . . . "

"VanRoark, I am dead! I was dead the moment the special voice of Creation was given to me—as you were made dead when you heard it, as was this fine company of fighters around us, as was the army, as was Brampton Hall.

"You go to die by yourself, and your own little fragment of creation, complete whatever portion of the great plan might have been designed for you. There are worse things, you know."

VanRoark sighed heavily through his hazed world; the far-off automatic cannons sounded like a person tapping on a windowpane on a rainy morning. "I could live in this world, or even bring children into it. Do you think that would be the sin I suspect it to be, Cavandish?"

"Yes."

VanRoark lay without speaking, random thoughts shuttling through his contorted brain without seeming purpose; gradually a pattern, only fractionally perceptible to him, emerged. "Is there any way to end it, Cavandish?"

"I don't know." The voice was old and very tired.

Frustration and anger compacted inside VanRoark's throat, burning toward his head from all his limbs and eyes. "Then, Timonias! Timonias! You tell me, how can this agony be ended?" VanRoark began struggling to his feet; the ground spun and whirled below him; skeletal shapes, aluminum sheeting and the fire-edged horizon alternated in front of him. *"Timonias, say something! How is it to be ended?"*

The silence swallowed up the three visions, replacing them with a uniform darkness, framed only by intersecting lines of color, each thinner than a human hair.

The voice came crashing into the night, quaking with a power it had thought lost, terrified with itself and even more with what it was saying. But it really said nothing, for there were no words; it was not the same as it had been at Admiralty Square: the purity was sadly, viciously flawed by metallic grindings. The voice struggled briefly above them. Against the vanished colorings of the Wars, the inside of VanRoark's head was filled with an awful shattering of hope. All that he had seen and remembered from Admiralty Square was taken and warped beyond recognition; the plans and shapes cracked, flew apart under the brutal pressure. The brilliant colors of new suns and the golden skin mankind had worn in the beginning of the game turned to the stale, dirty maroon and rust of dried blood, the decaying white of rigorous flesh.

Behind this horror was a greater one, accompanied by a sorrow whose immensity filled his body, drowned the softened memories of the rim nations, of the great ships and the men who had sailed upon them.

A single line of stone, the causeway, was formed when all the few, isolated stringings of color came crashing together, fleeing and detesting the crumbling shapes and the sadness behind them. Even this was compressed into invisibility and VanRoark was left alone with the voice. He sensed fissures opening all along his mind and body, vainly trying to let the voice escape.

At last it did, and rushed out of him, leaving behind it memories of a sort he had never conceived before, far beyond those of Admiralty Square, like the filthy, still-burning ash from a cremation pyre. He collapsed into the diamond earth of the Burn, fleetingly thankful that he was too exhausted to dream.

XXVIII

Around dawn, VanRoark was awake, lying where he had fallen the previous night. Even before he opened his eyes he was aware that his brain had assumed a new, fearful configuration, as if it had retreated to within the ruined fortress the memories of the rim nations had left behind; he sat in the middle of himself, shivering, and looked outward upon the inside of his brain at the things that were arranged there, of which the voice had spoken. They hung like pieces of butchered meat; their bloodied, mutilated forms were made tolerable only by the distance he had put between their knowledge and his actual consciousness.

He peered out at them for almost an hour, until he sensed the roaring upon which the butchered knowledge was hung; it was the sorrow, and the sound of it was that of the Sea. Like clods of dirt thrown upon a field of clear crystal and gem stone, the thoughts were crucified in front of him on meathooks of marlin-bills and the unicorn horns of narwhales. The Sea was the sorrow. Just as the voice had told him, they were the same, for it was in the Sea that all lived as it should have. From the Sea, the last and strongest redoubt of God, did all the life and energy of Creation flow; the waters sparkled clean and free as he opened his eyes. The surf was still as white as it had always been; and again, as it had always done, it washed the beach clean of the poisons of the land. As one moved further from the Sea, though, the diseases would become too strong; the same chaos which had gripped the stars and the land would prevent the Sea from touching anything, from healing it or sending it to some final peace.

He had always known this about the Sea, but had never suspected it to be so literally true before the voice had told him; that was where the sadness of the ships had come from. In each contact with the land, the ships would grow older and more corrupted; the Sea could never heal them completely, and eventually they would dissolve in harbors or come to the Meadows.

VanRoark heaved himself to his feet and turned around slowly. He saw the great, wrecked aircraft and immediately the sorrow compressed around him, forcing the dreadful bits of knowledge closer to his consciousness; he knew that if he ever allowed them to truly enter his mind, he would die. They were too strong and too deep for him to tolerate without destroying himself.

The thoughts were forced away, but the sea-roaring still surrounded him. The table was still there by the control car with the skeletal warriors sitting at their places; maggots were already devouring the synthetic bread he had set before them. Sea gull defecations spotted their decaying uniforms. Cavandish was not there, though. VanRoark moved around the area until late morning and found the skeleton half submerged in the surf near the causeway. He bent down to lift the corpse up and take it back to the train, but he heard the artificial larynx still talking and bubbling underneath the small waves. That part of him within the fortress called it a whimsical gesture to leave Cavandish there, conversing with the Sea. VanRoark wondered if Cavandish was trying to talk the Sea into giving him back his voice. He also saw that a part of him which hung outside, on the meathooks, was too terrified to touch the body.

He edged back to the train and hurriedly started up the engines. The serpentine vehicle rolled out from under the aircraft's wing and moved west along the causeway. He knew he should be heading north, across the shallow river and up into the Meadows, but that was impossible now with his knowledge.

The road was about two hundred feet wide and, once the great drawbridge had been passed, rose about fifty feet from the water's surface. It was constructed of giant blocks of stone, gray to dull olive; the wheels rolled easily over the ancient roadway.

Once, before he had ever seen the Burn, the causeway might have proved fascinating to him with its immense proportions and obvious skill of execution; now it was just there. It had always been there, just as the Sea had always been around it, giving it the power to resist the horror of the land and the air. The water sparkled bright turquoise and crystal; sailfish and marlin leaped beside the passing train with the gaiety of dying children.

The highland cliffs and Brampton Hall disappeared after an hour or two; he stared out at the limitless ribbon and the Sea, ultimately forced to become insensitive to it Time stopped; the sun hung alongside the knowledge for endless revolutions of the train's wheels until the meaning of both was blurred and lost.

VanRoark fell further into his own isolated well; he drowsed in the summer heat, further alienating himself from any landmarks or reference points. He glanced briefly at the ruined navigation panel and concluded that it would have been of no use even if he could have understood and repaired it. Only his eye and arm of metal and copper wire remained fully awake to take the rest of him and the train westward. He had always been on the bridge, always; seconds shrank into days while the sun stayed nailed at the zenith. Only the Sea with its leaping, playful life moved at the edges of his vision.

It might have been noon when he saw the horizon, the green grasslands atop the Sea. He drove down upon them and crossed their surface. In front of him rolled a prairie much like the Greenbelt might have been when it had been alive; crab apple and dogwood orchards were spotted before him. The road continued to travel directly east (how could one tell the direction when the sun was directly overhead? VanRoark wondered).

The city came upon him gradually, beginning with some infrequent, formal gardens along the side of the road and then progressing to villas and small houses.

The battered train seemed to him ludicrously out of place driving upon the broad avenue. VanRoark looked at the magnificent houses and gardens; their images had been suspended in his mind since last night. He knew what they had been intended for and that made it doubly tragic. For the second time—the first had been when he had looked at the aircraft—a knowledge struck much too close to him. Only with great effort was it suppressed, shoved away and hung back for detached observation.

The tree-lined street widened into a boulevard with alabaster pylons and fountains marching down its center, much like the Avenue of Victories at his home. The villas gave way to soaring buildings of gold and glass; VanRoark recognized banners and crests that he would never see upon the towers. Jade, ebony, silver, ruby, and opal met his eyes at their every turning; every precious gem or metal VanRoark had ever imagined called to his vision.

He saw other things outside himself, reflections of the images which were already within him. The twists and convolutions of the road made driving needlessly difficult. The beautiful buildings seemed to be out of plumb in the smallest, most irritating manner; cracks and imperfections in the masonry and in the mountings of the jeweled crests kept his eyes searching for the perfect surfaces he knew must be there.

Small flaws lay over all of the city like a thin, all-pervading coating of dust, infinitely maddening in that their presence was quantitatively so minor in the face of such an overpowering plan. If only he could stop the train and run out with a mortar board and file, things could be righted. The road passed through the city and again narrowed to a tree-bordered street, flanked by pleasant villas and estates. Around noon he reached the end, a wide sweep of shallow steps flowing down to a landscaped plain, green grass and slightly stunted crab apple. Eight or ten miles from the foot of the steps Van-Roark could see a line of white surf. It should have been an exceptionally fine park, even for this land of flawed perfection, but it was not. The imperfections that had warped the city were still present, the color of the grass was too pale and the crab apple blossoms looked as if they had been made from cheap china.

None of the inadequacies that marred the city and the grasslands on either side of it were present in the Sea. As it had everywhere, it fairly screamed of perfection and life. Its colors, the white of the surf, and the turquoise that turned to blue diamond and cobalt as it got farther from the beach, were vital enough to make him laugh joyfully, and then scream when he remembered the senile, soiled creation that lay to the east of it.

He had not seen a single living thing since he had left the causeway; here, gulls and osprey soared over the coast; dolphins, marlin, and tarpon came close inshore to play, the sun shining on their clean, glistening bodies as they cleared the water and arched through the air.

VanRoark took the train past the steps and across the park to the Sea. There was a thin beach, no more than thirty feet, separating the grass from the water and he halted the vehicle in front of it.

Now the sadness was all but unbearable; it circled close about his mind, threatening to strangle it, shoving the hideous, tragic words of Timonias flat against his sanity. But these words also demanded that he not die yet, that he get up from the driver's seat and move to the arsenal at the back of the cab.

He opened the cabinet and took out a long, bolt action rifle; it was of the classic design with which men had murdered each other for several thousand years. This was not important, though; he held it balanced in the silver web-work of his right hand, feeling its cool weight, despite his knowing that the hand should have been incapable of feeling.

VanRoark fixed the bayonet, silver and lightly oiled like his hand, felt the small, solid shock as the mounting catches locked into place. The world was clouded to him now; nothing but the brilliant hues of the Sea and the shining spike of the bayonet in front of him remained in their proper place and order.

Carefully, he descended the ladder; his left eye was puffed shut from the tears, but the right continued to function, unblurred, unshut, performing as it had been intended.

He could sense a great many things flickering by his mind, behind even the overwhelming sorrow. His boots were so heavy in the sand, his left arm and eye so utterly useless. He reached the waterline, but hesitated to touch the water. Instead, he took the unloaded rifle and the bayonet, whose metallic substance owed nothing to the earth or the other things of the Sea's creation except the basic atoms of their substance.

VanRoark waited until a wave had passed and the water drawn back. *From me?* He thrust the bayonet deeply into the wet sand and retreated.

A wave slid in from the Sea and cut itself upon the metal blade.

VanRoark watched as a darkness spread outward from where the water had touched the bayonet; the surf gradually died and the surface of the ocean became as a sheet of obsidian. The turquoise shifted to cobalt and then to dull black; the fish and birds were suddenly gone from the water; the wind stopped entirely and all the world around him became silent.

The sadness dissolved around VanRoark's consciousness, releasing the knowledge of Timonias and letting it fall away with an odd grace. The Wars were over now. He knew that, for it was one of the last bits of Timonias that still hung before his mind.

The uttermost, last thought continued in front of him, and it was a mirror. It showed him that Creation was at last truly dying; by night it would be dead.

But he still lived and thought and functioned in front of the glass Sea. He looked up to notice that the sun had already dimmed perceptibly in its radiance. It was a huge thing, though, and would probably burn on for several more days.

And when it had gone, his right eye would let him see by the light of the stars. When they had vanished, when the last flickering of light had traveled its billion years to his eye, an infrared filter would let him move about.

The heat from all things would be gone too, eventually. But then perhaps some sort of echo-ranging apparatus might be rigged up by his eye and arm. . . .

The Siege of Wonder

'I desire no other monument than the laughter of the madmen I have caused to be set loose upon the universe . . .'

From the testament of Ahman al-Akhmoriahd, fifth century of the Holy City, written in anticipation of the battle at Quetez (Heartbreak Ridge)

I

The man was young and thought: they have named this war too grandly, as they have named this place, the Holy City. He reconsidered: but it should at least be denominated as "holy" with a small h, for it is choked with tombs and cathedrals, mosques, shrines, places of adoration and prayer, sacred groves, enchanted grottoes and temples of nameless ritual. Priests were as common here as he remembered soldiers and technicians to have been in his own home cities before he left. Their silken and sackcloth robes bracketed the dull tans and greens of the common folk. Some were indistinguishable from princes in the richness of their garments; pearls and diamonds were sewn in swirling patterns to the hems of their cloaks, their saddles inlaid with mother-of-pearl and silver, and their escorts often rode gryphons or lithe pegasuses, as suited the varied tones and nuances they wished to lend to their powers.

The Holy City had named it the Wizards' War, as if it had already been won and enshrined in its history. It had been going on for almost seven hundred years when Aden left his home, and was known there only as "the war," as were all the wars of his people's history during their prosecution.

He stepped from the road and balanced on the edge of a marble fountain while some exalted personage thundered by with his retainers; they were all dead men, which showed their leader to be powerful indeed. Flashes of ivoried bone glinted through seams in their golden armor. The dust their horses kicked up became gold too.

Aden held himself against the fountain's rim and easily hid his disgust with the funereal cavalry; he had seen much worse. Outwardly, he mirrored the awe and reverence of the other people on the narrow street. Certain mages, it was widely known, often allowed the dust of their passage to remain gold and diamond chips, instead of transmuting back into dirt, as a reward to the people for their acclaim. Many were that extravagant. Of course, there were others who loathed such obsequiousness, so one had to be careful not to overplay the role.

Aden watched the party with his left eye. An adept mage could have detected millimetric variations between the pupil dilation of that eye and his other, just as he could have discovered the coldness and conductivity that underlay the left side of his skull. But in three years, Aden had been careful never to give such persons any reason to look.

The crowd solidified behind the party. Trading and haggling resumed. The noise, if anything, was worse than it had been before, as each person sought to compliment the magnificence of the magician's dress and his house's livery to his neighbor. The men of power in that part of the world often kept spies in their pay, some human and some otherwise, and there remained the hope of washing one's clothes that evening and finding the gold still gold at the bottom of the tub. At worst, it assured one that the magician's disfavor would not be incurred. Aden brushed some of the dulling gold dust from his coarse tunic and, as if pondering the magician's greatness, put his smudged left index finger up alongside his nose. His eye watched the dust in the act of its transmutation, sucked dry its spectrums, counted and weighed the opaque interchanges of electrons and subatomic particles, and caught traces of the fading resonances that tied it to the wizard's mind.

The information was transmitted through the wires implanted in his skull, neck and torso, and was transcribed onto spheres of frozen helium, suspended by undetectable magnetic fields in titanium cylinders inside his ribs. The natural conductance of his skin also carried quick and subtle messages as his eye spoke directly to the spheres and to the other augmenting devices that were scattered about his body.

Aden ran his hand idly along his neck and chest; this concourse between eye and mind and torso itched. Presumably, his scratching had not distorted or confused the messages.

Aden had been in the Holy City for a month watching, and he felt the weight of his observations pressing against the interior limits of his comprehension. The balls of helium, frigid, unitary, utterly pure, rotated as miniature universes inside of him, informed by the eye, consoled and spoken to by the hybrid creature of his nervous system. The living dead, the dying life, the constant shiftings and transmutations of substance and reality, the extraordinary *inwardness* of this world, all taken from the minds and imaginations of its men of power, re-compressed by the devices of the Special Office, and then jammed into the cramped spaces of his brain, to wait for the monthly block transmissions, when the Office's satellites fearfully skirted the western horizon and he could rid himself of its terrible density. Aden cowered before the knowledges accumulating inside of him, and, therefore, before the wizards. In this fear, he joined the rest of the people who had allied themselves with this and the other Holy Cities. It was so vastly different from . . .

He had trouble remembering.

. . . from the precise night of his own world.

The itching stopped, Aden imagined he could tell when the electrical currents had finished inscribing the new paragraphs on the gaseous spheres.

He pulled his jacket tightly about his shoulders. He had been standing by the fountain for half an hour since the magician had passed by. A few merchants in sedan chairs of satinwood and horn passed along the street. While he thought about his interior circuitries, the eye stirred casually and discerned what it could of their wealth and what they reflected of the economic strength of the Holy City. Such considerations meant nothing to the men of power, and Aden's world knew it, but they still insisted on looking, as if they wanted to find a common ground of normality in the way the wizards fought their war.

These were exercises that might have been carried out by any spy, trivial compared to the recordation of the passing magician and his retinue: transmutation, his personal triumph over death flouted before the people, his unarticulated powers outlined by a perceptible nimbus surrounding his head and chest. These were proper challenges for the capabilities of Aden's eye.

He had to think that, he realized during the first month of his mission, in order to remain functional. Anything less and he would succumb to the same spell that half of the world had already fallen under. Either that, or he would unconsciously betray the curious arrogance that characterized the proponents of each side in the face of the other, the defensive contempt each cultivated toward the other's conception of the universe. He would dwell constantly upon any conceit or belief that would help hold in his delicate and poorly defined equipoise between half-knowing and half-believing.

His mission had been conceived after the philosophers and scientists of his home had, after centuries of war, hit upon the difference between science and magic. Before their realization, the ritual of two worlds shadow-boxing across mutually contradictory and invisible frontiers had exerted a certain fascination on both sides. Neither side understood the manners or methods of the other, and so the commonly perceptible forms of sheer movement often obscured the strategic realities of power and death.

Inevitably, through all the badly aimed attempts at attack and occupation, the two incompatible universes overlapped. The massacre at Thorn River had been the last such meeting. Before that had been the battles of The Corridor, Morgan's Hill, Kells, the Third Perimeter,

Heartbreak Ridge, the Lesser Bennington Isles, Black Cat Road . . . endlessly fractured dreams through which each world sought to preserve its visions of divinity against those held by the enemy.

Those strange times, before the understanding by Aden's world, gave rise to stranger nations and personalities. Science was often confused with magic, as it had been during the latter's first death and the former's birth. Thus arose successions of intentionally equivocal and elusive intelligence and counterintelligence organizations in each world, such as the one Aden worked for, some maintaining so precarious a balance between the universe that they tried to protect and the one they attacked that they spent their whole existences fighting themselves, awarding their own agents decorations when they killed their comrades and erecting monuments to the failure of gallant, purposely suicidal missions. Thus also, the weird romance of the war itself and of the literatures it spawned.

But no one in Aden's home could find anything in the war sufficiently romantic or fascinating enough to dull their grief and sorrow. Instead of composing heroic romances, illuminated by artists (who, it was reported, were often driven selectively insane by their patron magicians in the hopes their talents would reach peaks not otherwise attainable), the men of Aden's home thought more and more deeply upon the nature of their enemy. At last they conceived that their own dreams, those which they retained, were, in the very texture of their construction, tied to objective understanding. Magic and science alike, when they strove against each other, hypothesized similar accomplishments and ends. It was in the methods that they differed.

Science could be understood and therefore controlled. The mechanisms and the sources of its power would be subject to a final switch, accessible to any man, or to any trained ape or dolphin for that matter.

Magic, as it gradually defined itself in the funereal hazes over the Burn, Devils' Slide, Cameron and two hundred other disasters, could never be understood. By its very definition, it had to remain no more objective than art. Its practice must always be intuitive, given only to persons chosen by unknowable entities according to secret elections.

From this proceeded the comparative dullness of Aden's world, and also its tired grace, its acknowledgment of universal things, universal weariness, universal frustration, universal defiance. Contrawise, it also explained the awesome personalities the enemy's world had thrown up, with their barely pronounceable names and tangled genealogies, interwoven with beings of questionable humanity. Their world blazed with baroque, liquid fires, while the men of Aden's world concerned themselves with blackout curtains and light beams so perfectly coherent as to be invisible unless one was their target. The magicians paraded in raiments stitched with gold and silver thread, studded with precious stones, costuming themselves more gorgeously than the inhabitants of myths, for they conceived themselves to be made of the same stuff. It was easy to become lost in their world, when one's own offered so little to stand against it. There was a damp warmth about the magicians' kingdoms that hung about their places and works like the intoxicating sweat of lovers.

Aden's world dressed in white: starched, spotless, undistinguished except for cut and tailoring, which sometimes showed obsessive attention to detail. Almost by way of petulant counterposition, Aden's world became progressively colder and abstracted. Everything must be understood, and they found it an unexpectedly easy step; they had always secretly believed that everything could be reduced to component parts of the utmost simplicity, if sufficient energies were devoted to their study.

The men of power wrapped the world in silks and incense, which hid the poverty of their feudal society and cushioned the jarring discordancies of pleasure and horror that it contained. That, too, formed part of their world's charm.

Three hundred years before Aden's birth, the nations of his world had begun to replace their guns and missiles with antennas of increasing subtlety and precision. The computers grew to process the accelerating influx of information that they stole away from the hidden kingdoms. New inquiries and postulates proposed themselves and more antennas, satellites and robot reconnaissance ships were built to confirm or deny them. Most were destroyed; their lubricants were turned to powdered diamonds, air suddenly ceased to flow faster over the tops of their airfoils than it did underneath, finite masses were subjected to infinite stresses.

But enough of the devices survived to feed the computers and the persons who habitually dressed in white. These people sat before the readout consoles and blackboards in underground bunkers, refining their inhumanity, drawing further away from the wild vitality that had murdered so many of their fellows; their hands were the color of pale marble, veined with red porphyry.

They learned. Within the aching sterility of their silences, the content of magic was reduced to philosophical syllogisms, then to historical commentaries, then to equations.

The first breakthrough, after the initial realization of the difference between science and magic, was in the discovery of multiple spectrums, paralleling the electromagnetic along which all forces and presences had been previously thought to manifest themselves. The electromagnetic spectrum, it was discovered, did not extend indefinitely. At one end, it stopped with the attainment of absolute zero; at the other, it consumed itself in the high-energy situations that comprised the non-dimensional cores of black holes.

By accident and tradition, the wizards had intruded into the parallel spectrums and manipulated them through the sheer force of their possibly divine personalities. Thoughts of a particular nature that coincided with certain gestures and tones of voice granted them access into the parallel spectrums, even though they had not the slightest idea that that was what they were doing.

Propelled by the inertia that the idea of absolute understanding carried with it, the enemies of magic also entered upon the parallel spectrums, not merely blundering across their lines by a gesture and remembered set of mental attitudes preserved and taught for centuries, but quite deliberately invading them, coursing up and down their twisting limits on forces of inflexible constancy. They found they could turn the gold back into dust at will.

The horror that lurked in this was ignored during the first grand decades, when men found that they could strive against and sometimes defeat the nightmares and beauties that the magicians hurled against them. Then it was revealed that Heisner and his staff had found that love was explainable through the application of simple equations to specific portions of the electromagnetic spectrum and the next two that paralleled it. The equations were the thing that people really felt. It was not a simulation. It was an explanation of a given phenomenon in objective terms adaptable to any time and place.

Heisner was elected to the Royal Academy for his achievement, but committed suicide before his formal installation.

The Discovery, as the histories generically referred to Heisner's finding and those that followed, cast an unexpectedly ominous tone onto the new way the war was being waged and, many said, won. The men of Aden's home began to wonder what the universe might look like when they had understood all of magic and all the forces and emotions it had controlled. Magic was art; it lived and died within each individual who practiced it. When a young person sought to know its manipulation, he started with the same fundamentals and elementary skills that his teachers had. In the understanding of numbers, stored and locked inside computers, engraved inside spheres of helium, time meant less; each man stood on the shoulders of his predecessors, gifted and condemned to a more complete span of vision.

They looked, and the ones that came after them looked. Deeper mysteries solidified into geometric masses, the gesturing sweeps of the wizards' arms were quantified into series of parabolas and their radii plotted on spacetime graphs of infallible precision.

The tangle of grid antennas and tropospheric scatter units outgrew the walls of barbed wire upon which the skeletons of hooded basilisks and minotaurs had bleached for centuries. But the suspicions that Heisner had confirmed grew also. The war cooled. Magic, half in fear and half in self-fascination, turned in upon itself, cultivating stranger and more bizarre talents. Its lands were stalked by impossibly shaped beasts; death and life were toyed with by the men of power as if they were flower arrangements, to be composed according to their personal aesthetics.

Aden had known this history when he had begun to work for the Special Office at fourteen. By the time he was sixteen he knew part of what it meant.

When he was eighteen, he was trained, modified, his abilities at analytic thought surgically blunted, and he was sent against the enemy.

He stepped into a side street paved with glazed turquoise bricks. The houses leaned high above him; some had beautiful rugs hung from their upper balconies, out of thieves' reach. His left eye searched the glowing patterns as they shifted heavily in the late sun, his natural eye keeping pace, covering; the eyes of the Holy City were numerous and often as perceptive as his own. He searched through conjunctions of arabesques, twisted vines, heroic battle scenes and erotic myths until he found one with a triskelion of three armored legs, bent as though running. From a distance of thirty meters his eye could see that each foot had a spur tipped with a six-pointed star.

His chest itched underneath the lice in his shirt. He adjusted his clothes to seem presentable and walked into the shop below the rug. The man inside had been waiting for him for seven years.

The air inside was thick with fragrances and the hushed, careful idiom the City's men of commerce often affected. Everyone except for Aden and the serving boy was well dressed. From the cut of their robes, several might have been high civil officials or apprenticed mages. Some turned to him when he entered, but then looked away with cultivated disinterest. The serving boy refrained from bringing him the customary glass of mint tea.

Aden wandered about the shop, examining the less expensive rugs and making what he hoped were appropriately respectful noises as he passed by those of better quality. The very finest, he knew, would not be on display for they had some intrinsic magic woven into their patterns.

At length, the shop emptied. With the evening, the greater wizards of this City and the other towns that thought themselves Holy would be abroad on their chosen work and not on parade for the adoration of the rabble.

The owner sent his attendants home and then turned to Aden. He was fat and rather older than Aden had expected. Half his face had been burned away by some kind of fire. A flap of skin skirted the edge of his right eye, crossed a scar line and then angled downward over part of his mouth. His words were partly masked by it, as if he were speaking from behind a confessional screen.

Aden bowed in respect to the man's rank and deformities, but then raised himself and looked directly into the other's face. The Office's eye evaluated the man's retinal pattern and found a grid of synthetic sapphire implanted there; nothing obtrusive or complex, but useful for vision in the far infrared and ultraviolet ranges. There was, therefore, no need for the password he had been taught.

Aden smiled as lightly as he could at the remains of the man's face. "I imagine . . . "

The other let the right side of his mouth drop and abruptly held up his hand; it, like his face, was scarred and half obliterated. "I cannot help you."

Aden hesitated a bit. "You are Donchak?"

"I am."

"And the rug, the one with the running legs, that's yours too? Is it not?"

The other man nodded politely, but his right eye stayed directed toward the floor. "It is the Office's, as is the eye that recognized it." He said this in the consciously ornate merchant's speech. He had, Aden reminded himself, been sent in over seven years ago to wait for the training of a person such as himself to be completed, the undesigned equipment tested, and the cover established by his own years of wandering through the kingdoms of magic. Still, he had hoped for a guarded wink, or something like "Thank God you've come, Carruthers."

"I imagine . . . " Aden began again.

"I understand," Donchak countered, "and I understand too much besides that. That is why I cannot help you." His half-face was arranged in planes of sadness. "You are too late for my help. Please go."

"With the eye?" Aden suppressed a twinge of confusion. For all its wonders, the eye was feeling more and more like a detonator, threatening to ignite unstable elements both in the City and within his own mind. "I can't stay here with it grafted onto me. You must know that even the small amounts of energy it leaks and the block transmissions can't go unnoticed forever."

"Then leave."

"It's shielded here." Aden heard himself getting impatient. "The mass of energies and spells. The air's so thick with them that it's a wonder anyone can breathe. The only way I got it this far is because it didn't start working and sending until I was through the borderlands and into the middle of this lunatic nation . . . "

"If you feel that way, you must correct the problem yourself." Donchak brought his left hand up and covered the erased portions of his face, further softening the sound of his words.

"Were you betrayed?" In desperation Aden shifted the conversation back against the man.

"Only by myself."

"But this shop? You must be fairly well off."

"The building is mine only so long as I remain the private joke of some men of power. They view it in the nature of a game to occasionally pit their arts against my desire for understanding them." Donchak looked around him. "My rugs are also reputed to have some abilities of their own, which one properly trained could use."

Gone native, thought Aden, and more than a little crazy too. "But you mean the rugs that you sell. The weavers . . . "

" . . . are blind, as tradition specifies. That is correct, as am I." Donchak smiled at Aden for the first time. "That is my one secret from them. My eye is blind, but the last apparatus the Special Office gave me that I kept still lets me see into areas few of them care exist."

"Your patterns, then . . . " Aden's words trailed off as he thought that Donchak must be seeing him as a dancing glow of cobalt, saffron and orange.

Donchak's fractional smile continued. "Simple understanding of the interrelation of the chromatic, spatial and auditory spectra and the responses that can be coaxed from their various combinations." The man could still talk, at least, in the language of the Office. The abstractions of Heisner's successors sounded out of place among the rugs and gilt work of the shop's interior.

Outside, muezzins sang warnings to the City and to their masters' enemies. They vied with each other in the lyric intricacy of their threats, each seeking to exceed the one before him in describing the horrors that waited those who opposed his master's designs. The civil government abandoned the City at dusk and retired to its barracks and offices.

"Are you watched?"

"Tomorrow I shall be. If you are still here tomorrow, I shall be questioned too." Donchak began walking away. "There are spy entities here, and there and there." He pointed with his flabby arms at points in the air as he walked. "I have masked their sensitivities. At any rate, I presume that they will not be looking in the areas where your eye's power drain could be detected. But they see you are here and probably discern that I am talking to you, though they cannot understand the words. Please go."

"But the war. The Office cannot . . . " Aden had spotted insubstantial stains of light hovering in the places that Donchak had gestured toward. He felt his throat and stomach tighten.

"I cannot afford to concern myself with either."

"Myself, then?"

"I know nothing of you. You were a child when I was modified and sent in." Donchak paused, resting his hand on the silver tea service. "You can stay if you choose, if you judge you can hide from my companions"—he waved again to the spy entities. "Wait until the effects of the Office's surgeries wear off and use your understanding to make a place for yourself. It's more than you'll be allowed to do if you reach home again." Donchak continued to stare at him, his eye moving in minute arcs across his body as it gauged the temperature differentials between veins and arteries, and perhaps deciphered the electric crown of wires buried in Aden's skull, reading his fear.

"Then I'll betray you." Intending to be coolly threatening, Aden over-controlled and the words came out brittle and hinting at irrationality.

"I have told you that the men of power know . . . "

"They do not know of your eye, only your mind."

"They have not thought it worthwhile to look beyond my mind."

"But wouldn't they be disturbed to know that some of the powers they've bought, however slight, came from graphs that you learned in a secret police school, or that the patterns that so please their women . . . ?"

"They probably already know."

"If they did, you wouldn't be here. They'd permit your training and your former allegiance, but not that grid. That would be too much. They'd take it from you before they found themselves asking you what you saw with it, as if you were some kind of mirror they couldn't resist looking into. And if they take it from you . . . " Aden shrugged theatrically, only later thinking that Donchak saw his fear and not the gesture. "If you consider yourself a joke now, Donchak, think how their powers of illusion will eat at your understanding when you're left in the dark." Aden felt almost proud that he should have thought of such a tack to use on the other man; it was fortunate he had studied the man's psychological profile before he had been sent in. "Anyway, they cannot be ignorant to what has, or has not been going on. They're edgy and nervous with the way the war has been going."

"But we aren't?" Donchak whispered icily.

Aden ignored him. "That's why they've been going at each other even more than usual lately. All that dammed-up ability and power. They don't dare use it, because that would give the Office and the Border Command and Lake Gilbert a chance for more study."

"Study their power? Had they not studied it enough at Thorn River?"

"That was important. It added a great deal . . . "

"But didn't they see enough?" Donchak drifted on in the same remotely irritated tone. "I was there, you know. The thing that the Office had put into this eye"—he gestured toward the scarred side of his face—"was like what yours must be now. I was caught there and, unlike the others, I could see the magicians coming through the sky and striding across the plains to crush us."

Aden let the advantage of his argument slip away as he listened. Thorn River had been among the last great engagements between science and magic, and the largest to have occurred in his lifetime. He remembered, for an instant, the streams of starved and brutalized refugees that had passed his home for days, heading for the sanctuaries of the Taritan Valley, and thought he found Donchak's face among them.

"And I could see the Border Command ships circling it during the first three days. I could see the masses of attack planes and bombers that waited behind them, waited for three more days, three more hours, three seconds while another variation of the magicians' power was expended on someone, picked apart and catalogued. I saw the face of the wizard that burned me, and I saw the face of the man who examined it and hoped for my death because that would tell him even more about the magic. I even remember their names, though I cannot say the wizard's with the way my mouth is now. The man's name was Etridge." Donchak paused for a moment. "Do you truly want your eye to serve people such as that, people who could watch such things as if they were lessons drawn on blackboards?" Donchak seemed to be genuinely amazed with his own question, as if its articulation had preceded his thoughts and accidentally proposed something that he would not have otherwise considered possible.

"Of course. They're not monsters."

"They watched, cold and bloodless. They did nothing when they might have stopped it, or at least drawn their enemy away. Is that not something worse than simple monsters?"

"Not at all. They were pursuing a"—Aden found the words coming with more difficulty than he would have wished—"a duty. That was the only thing they could do if we were to get anywhere."

Donchak fixed him suddenly with his functioning eye. "There were other ways! A hundred other ways. Mine, the Office's, the regular services', the Academy's."

"It worked. It's working now. Look at what happened to them at Foxblind."

Donchak softened his voice; his eye returned to looking at the floor. "The price was excessive, wouldn't you say? Thousands and hundreds of thousands at Thorn River, myself, the killing of this." He swept his hand toward the door.

"This? The City?" Aden forced outrage back into his voice; Donchak was playing on treasonous grounds again, Aden's.

"There is not enough beauty here for you?"

"Beauty destroying itself."

"If it tried to understand itself thoroughly enough to defeat us, to fight us according to our own rules, it would no longer be beauty. It would just be numbers and knowledge, circling round its own grave. Do you want that?" he asked again.

"I must," Aden said at once, but did not know where the words had come from for he had not felt his tongue move.

Donchak waited for a moment and then nodded, either to the younger man's threat or to the logic of his position. The muezzins finished their arias. Aden glanced through the door-grill and his eye picked up auroral waverings in the gaps between the houses. He saw the distorted reflections of other lights on the glazed paving stones. The mages often said they were practicing their arts for their own perfection and in preparation against the other half of the planet. The fact that they practiced so often and so enthusiastically on each other spoke for itself.

"Where am I to leave this?" Aden pointed to his left eye. "The Office must have a place that is mobile, if at all possible, and protected."

"I am aware of the Office's wants and needs." Donchak muttered and walked toward the back of the shop. A barred door led out to an alleyway.

They left the perfumed rug shop and the stench of the City closed over Aden again. The paving stones were fired turquoise, even in the alley, but the piles of filth and garbage behind each building dulled the reflected light of the magicians' practice.

They passed three brave, or particularly hungry figures digging into the trash heaps. The spectrographic abilities of Aden's eye informed him that at least one of them was a leper.

The City had been named Cape St. Vincent before the war. Then the wizards had come to it and brought their reborn powers and mysteries with them. Within a decade after they had consolidated their rule over the area, they had grown powerful enough to send away the ocean that had faced the city, because it displeased them. The old city's marble quays and granite boulder jetties still surfaced from under newer buildings only a century or two old. With either marvelous whimsy, or, more likely, invincible blindness, the wizards had often built on and around these structures. Aden saw one house that was partially supported by a corroding rolling derrick that one of the first engagements for the city had welded solid; his eye traced the crane's outlines in the facing wall and he thought it to be more of a superimposition of distinct worlds, rather than a single structure.

The geometric grid of the original city had dissolved into a tangle of wandering streets and alleys. This, the men of power often declared, more aptly expressed the subtlety and complexity of their personalities. The men of power regarded it as a great humanizing process, an affair of the spirit as much as anything else. Aden's world watched the process in aerial photographs and regarded it as retrogressive, chaotic, medieval.

Aden speculated how the leper would have regarded the matter. He, personally, had not noticed any great disparity in the number or character of the garbage piles in the cities of either world.

Donchak's eye led them easily through the night streets. Ironically, Aden's more versatile unit was often confused and blinded by the reflected energies that the City's wizards were playing off the ionosphere.

The avenues broadened and straightened themselves. The closely packed houses and shops gave way to the barred entrances of substantial mansions, government buildings and the great halls of the City's guilds. Many were left over from the ages when there was but one reality on the planet, and they were defined by straight lines and euclidean masses. The structures of magic had overgrown and smothered them, like the crane, with intricate masonry and marble traceries. Eccentric balconies, turrets, minarets, arches, colonnades and porticoes softened the old, harsh outlines; mosaic overlays glittered in the wizards' lights.

He was aware of the City's splendor in spite of the darkness. In Aden's home, when men chose to care, they concentrated on the definition of whole, integrated units. Their processes of understanding allowed for little else but the finishing of broad sweeps of brushed steel or oiled hardwood. Straight lines always ended cleanly or merged into precisely defined arcs and parabolas, always so complete that a building, and sometimes an entire block or town might be seen, weighed and comprehended with a single glance. This aesthetic had been pursued with such single-minded devotion that Aden had come to believe that it was as much an expression of his world's hatred for magic's passion as it was an affirmation of its own beliefs.

Aden shook his head as he walked to free himself of these thoughts. In everything he saw and remembered, there was such perfect counterposition. The devastated middle ground had narrowed, allowing each kingdom to press more closely against the other, compacting their energies until each was immobilized by its own fury. The worlds orbited each other, duplicating the death-cycles of stars, until they might become the equivalents of black holes, self-sustaining fields of annihilation.

After years in the enemy's land, he could still be shocked by this. Working for the Special Office meant that he had to keep himself suspended between the two worlds. Too much understanding and he would give himself away to the men of power or their spies; too much belief and he would come under the spell of the world. It was a difficult balancing act, no matter how much insulation the Office's surgeons and psychologists had provided. Donchak had apparently failed in this balancing, though Aden could not say upon which side he had fallen; perhaps on both, and he was being gradually pulled apart like a rope of potter's clay, becoming thinner and thinner until he broke.

Donchak slowed and pointed the way across an immense plaza. Aden's eye read the other man's skin conductance, temperature, pulse rate and blood pressure. He was tense and very agitated, but that was understandable considering their exposed position.

There was a large building across from them, set apart from the others that bordered the square and topped with onion-shaped domes. Mages' light burst across the sky from the left and the strange wavelengths of its luminescence struck against them. The eye mapped alternating serpentines of gold and silver leaf, their twistings separated and defined by raised borders of rock crystal.

Minarets, taller than anything else he had seen in the City, were posted at the building's corners; their upper portions were made of pierced stonework and both of his eyes could see the mage-light through them. There were subtler fires glowing inside them, too, near their peaks; some his right eye could pick up, while others were visible only to his left.

Aden nearly stepped out into the plaza, but Donchak threw out his arm and drew him back into a recessed gate. A quiet gray structure four stories high loomed behind the wrought iron gate. It was covered in half-hearted mosaics and heroic friezes that did little to enliven its studied dullness; another remnant of the old days, probably inhabited then, as now, by the local government.

Aden looked back to the plaza. His left eye immediately became entangled in a ragged interference pattern of the sort he had not seen since it had been calibrated by the Office's scientists and theologians. He wondered if the trouble might be with his own circuits, but his vision remained clear along its peripheral limits. The eye, the spheres of helium and the wire net buried in him conversed among themselves, exchanging small, professional tricks they had picked up during the past years. Eventually his vision resolved itself upon a unicorn.

Donchak whispered the name of a man of power. "That is his cavalry," he breathed.

"Only one?" Aden found his voice strained.

"No need for more."

It moved with such deliberate smoothness and grace that Aden speculated if that might not be the only way the creature could contain its own power. Sudden movements, unnecessary gestures, unguarded turnings of its limbs might accidentally release the energies penned up inside.

The unicorn had a short caparison of electric blue on which were sewn intricate devices, fleur-de-lis, coronets, crossed arms and banners. Illuminations like those held captive in the minarets blazed in its eye sockets with an unexplainably inverted light that sucked the mages' brilliance from the sky and concentrated it into the embroidery of its coverings.

The man walking beside the unicorn appeared to be armored, though Aden thought that he was, instead, naked and the polished metal surface only his skin. Baroque swirlings of men and improbable creatures covered him. As the unicorn and the man walked across the plaza, drawing their light from the air around them, the interaction between the figures on their dress became apparent. Ships and dragons set out from the mountain-bound harbors upon flame-colored seas and ventured from the man's greaves, upward along his thigh and torso, and then leapt onto the swarming heraldry of the unicorn's caparison, instantly compressed into two dimensions and idealized into gold and silver monotones on the blue field. Barbaric hunting parties descended along the man's cuirass, pursuing chimeras with diamonds for each of their twenty eyes, onto the unicorn's saddle and then, with sudden dignity and abstraction, along its crinet and chanfron like engravings in the metal, until they all disappeared with the mages' light into the creature's eyes.

The day's parade of wizards was comprehensible within the meaning of the City, but the unicorn and its attendant occupied another order of perception. Aden thought them to be among the most beautiful things he had ever seen. The sight of them drained his fear away for a moment, as they had the sky's light; perhaps this was why Donchak had fallen as he had. "Where is it going?"

Donchak pointed to the domed building.

"On its master's business?" Although the unicorn was moving diagonally across the square, and therefore away from them, Aden found it increasingly difficult to speak.

"To pray."

Aden's eye glanced at the other man and found that Donchak was inexplicably growing calmer. Blood pressure and heart rates dropping, skin conductance dropping, muscle tension relaxing. "To whom?" he asked, somewhat bewildered, for is not a servant to render allegiance to his master alone?

"To god."

"Which one?"

Donchak smiled with the functional part of his mouth. "Why, to its own, of course." He faced Aden with the sky illuminating the left half of his face, making him look almost normal. "Neither magic nor science has any real claim to theology, yet. Only the Office really concerned itself with that. I would have thought you knew that." Then, moving his head away from Aden to face the unicorn, showing his rutted, slagged right side: "But I have been away from the world for years now and have no idea how far our efforts at understanding have taken us." Blood pressure and heart rate increased a bit. "No. Not in that direction or else there would have been tanks in this square months ago and the jets would have shot down all the gryphons. Wouldn't they?"

Aden thought the man was speaking mostly to himself and so divided his attention between Donchak's unconscious physiological signs and the unicorn. The truth of the immediate situation, he felt sure, lay somewhere between the two.

"We will leave your modification with the unicorn." Pulse and heart continuing to accelerate, Donchak crouched low and then pushed off into the square.

The fountain in the plaza's center commemorated some proto-battle whose specific identity changed as the brass plaques at its base were changed. Again, the counter-positions: in Aden's world the thing would stand for what it was originally built for. When the commemorated victors later became the remembered defeated, it would be torn down amid the shouts of the populace, and a new one erected. Its figures would have the features of actual men, not blank idealizations to serve as the templates for the identities of the mob. Faces, names, dates, crests and arms would have been set and locked solidly within historical experience.

Here the fountain was purely allegory, infinitely flexible and adaptive to a world shared by more than one dominant race.

The unicorn and its attendant passed behind the fountain. Donchak, an indefinite shaft of red and yellow in the infrared, shifted and dodged, keeping the fountain between him and the two creatures. He did not move so badly for one of his age and weight; still, he nearly fell once or twice. Aden felt the beauty of the unicorn being edged aside by his own returning fear and distrust of the City's world.

He waited until Donchak reached the fountain and then followed, running carefully, avoiding the random spells and anomalies that Donchak's eye had not been able to pick up. His own eye showed him how exposed they were. With the magicians practicing their abilities, the only things absent were the limited wavelengths of visible daylight. Great floodings of every other form of radiant energy showered down from the sky or from the towers and minarets of the City's palaces and temples. Strange shadows radiated outward from him as he half ran toward the fountain, each one outlining a different presence.

He was breathing heavily when he joined Donchak. "All right, just keep behind me and get ready to make the transfer when I tell you." Donchak's voice was nearly normal again, but somehow regretful.

"Here?"

"No. In the cathedral." The selective blindness of his eye understood Aden's expression. "It is the only possibility, when it is in prayer, in communion."

"Just who do they serve?" Aden cut in, frightened by something that evaporated before he could capture it.

"A man of great power. I told you. We have to make the transfer then if you want it at all."

"Will we have another chance?"

"Not with the unicorn. There are many other places, static things like reliquaries, memorials, perhaps those heroic figures there"—pointing up to the battling mermen and dolphins. "But none of them would be as close to the men of power as that one. None of them would be mobile or able to report on so many, an infinity . . . " Donchak became momentarily lost in his own words and their meanings.

"Nor would any of them be so easily detected." Aden rushed to keep the talk going. "If we're going to put this on, *in* that servant, how can it avoid knowing what's going on? It's not just going to prance around here, looking over its master's shoulder and turn all his secrets over to us."

"It will not understand, so it will not know," Donchak answered hazily. "Some pain, disorientation, especially when the block transmission signals go out, but to its conception of things, very little else will seem amiss. Anyway, it is continually under attack from its master's current enemies and being reinforced by its master's momentary allies. The suppression of its natural eye and the addition of your own will be lost in the usual input to its senses and emotions." Donchak raised his hand again, this time past the fountain and up to the zenith. "You see those jagged streaks of long-wave radiation?" Aden obediently shifted the filters within his eye; the waves were deep lavender, edged with ruby, though they might have been close to blue for Donchak's less sophisticated eye. "An attack from outside the City. That bar, transiting the waves above the northern skyline, there, is a defense set up by friendly princes. It is aware of all this, but cannot, by its nature, understand as we do."

While Donchak spoke, elaborating on the strategies deployed through the air above them, Aden stripped a piece of soiled embroidery from his shirt and kneaded it between his fingers. The threads softened and twined together in a putty-like ball.

Donchak finished speaking, but kept watching the sky. After some moments, the multiple spectrums detectable to Aden calmed. Saying nothing, Donchak stepped away from the fountain and began running in a curving line toward the domed building. The unicorn and its attendant were gone.

He judged the time and pressed the putty against his left eye. The hydrophilic plastic absorbed the anesthetic quickly. Within a minute his vision dimmed away from the most remote spectrums, then from those nearer to the electromagnetic until only visible light remained; then nothing. Sensory and analytic input ended at the same time. Cued by molecular keys, microscopic transmission links shut themselves off and withdrew into protected sockets.

He felt instantly crippled. Though he had practiced this many times, he had not thought the loss would be so absolute and that the suddenly limited world should press upon him so closely. It was as if the air had thickened around him, compressing him into the two dimensions his loss of depth perception left to him, blinding, gagging, muffling and blunting his mind. This was approximately what was truly happening, but the Office's surgeries and psychological training prevented him from fully understanding it; the Office had determined that irrational terror was preferable to the effects of complete understanding in circumstances such as these.

He started running, staying low to the pavement as he had before. But this time his steps were clumsy and he continually misjudged the distance he had to move his feet. Lines and ridges of magic, now hidden to him, brushed against his legs like insect wings, repulsive in their lush, invisible softness.

There was a huge echoing in his mind, which he thought to be like carrier-wave static, interrupted by the thudding of his heart and the sound of his breath. This was not what he wanted. It could not be what he and the Special Office had worked for.

The frozen balls of helium inside his ribs came to a stop. Their magnetic fields cut out and the motion of his running smashed them against the walls of their cylinders, turning them to colorless dust. The wire net buried in his skull and the lines grafted into his neck and torso went dead too, leaving cold tracks that he thought he could feel.

He had no idea how far it was to the cathedral's steps. He climbed them and stumbled into the shadows of the columned portico. Donchak whispered to him from the dark, and Aden's fear almost overwhelmed him. "This should be simple. You have prepared?" Aden nodded and pointed to his eye; if its circuits had shut down, the only traces Donchak would be picking up would be from the retention links holding it in place. "Good. Then you are, yourself, useless now. Follow me and keep as quiet as you can. Just follow. If you become lost in the dark, stay where you are and wait for me to find you."

Aden grunted affirmatively, not trusting his voice. He was used to examining those around him, knowing their precise reactions to specific words, tones and gestures. Such information had benefited him greatly in the taverns and brothels of the enemy's land; it had also saved him from the inquiries of the civil government and the mages' spies on numerous occasions. Now Donchak was closed to him, as the creatures inside would be.

But the man seemed to be functioning properly. He had obviously planned and anticipated Aden's arrival and the most effective way to expedite his mission. That was why the Office had sent him in years ago, long before it had any idea that a man like Aden would be sent later, or perhaps even what his task might be.

Donchak's actual loyalties, however, were becoming academic. As he had pointed out to him, the wizards knew they were being picked apart, deciphered, understood, their arts reduced to formulae easily duplicated and subverted by ordinary men and machines. They were getting scared, underneath their silk and velvet trappings, and some people at Lake Gilbert had seen panic infecting their habitual illogic. The risk of carrying the eye, even with its nearly undetectable energy leaks, therefore increased daily, and became almost suicidal during the monthly block transmissions of compressed data. Soon, the wizards must begin looking carefully at their world and they would see him as clearly as the eye had seen them. It had to be discarded and the orders were to leave it in a place where it could continue gathering information.

Possibly, Donchak had had similar instructions for whatever might have been placed in his right eye socket before Thorn River and the Border Command snatched it away from him.

The main doors were made of brass, engraved with the same complex designs that were set in the alabaster windows above them. Donchak nudged Aden away from the columns and led him through a small door to their left.

Aden blinked his right eye to adjust to the interior. Spheres of were-light hovered distantly in the nave, turning the marble floors to dusted silver but failing to give any indication of where the building's roof might be. Aden found himself straining to define the building's distances and colors; all his remaining eye allowed him were gray lights and pools of impenetrable shadow.

Most churches are built with many subtle distortions and trompe l'oeils concealed within the alignments of their masses. The idea is to deceive the worshiper's sense of perspective and to make the building as much a part of his devotions as the words of the liturgy—or at least to make him feel as if he is in a grander place than he really is. Assuming such tricks were present here and that the building was not under the spell of one or another of the men of power, the unicorn and its attendant were about one hundred meters away, in the center of the nave, twenty meters before the main altar.

Donchak led him down the northern aisle, the nave's supporting columns screening them from the unicorn. To his left Aden noticed various recessed chapels and crypts. Occasionally the drifting were-light illuminated one, but the contents remained closed to his comprehension.

The attendant was kneeling, his head resting against his chest, hands hanging straight down along his sides. The unicorn stood patiently behind him. Neither showed any sign of life. The figures on the unicorn's caparison had melted into a spider web pattern that hid its contours like fog. The figures on the mancreature's skin remained distinct but were frozen in attitudes suggestive of prayer.

Everywhere, everything was silver-gray with only the ivory and cinnamon of the high lancet windows to relieve it. They stepped through this hazed atmosphere like swimmers, moving with great care so as not to cause eddies in the air around them, vortices that might brush against the unicorn and its attendant, intrude upon its devotions and alert it.

Donchak stopped behind a column and watched. Aden knew it was possible that Donchak was seeing the physical reality of what held the creatures so transfixed. He might also have come here to pray.

He pressed his thumb and little finger against each end of his left eye socket, and brought them together gently. The optic nerve and the muscles that manipulated the eye were already severed. It compressed noticeably and he felt the last retention links breaking under the pressure.

The eye fell out into his other hand. He thought: There I am, my third and twentieth dimensions, my ability to see and understand, reduce, particularize, analyze. For a moment he expected the rest of his limbs to begin dropping onto the floor until he was nothing but a heap of individual components. That was how the computers at his home knew him; was it not, therefore, reasonable to think that that was how he truly was?

But there was a feeling of relief that he did not fully admit to himself. He was unsure if he wanted to see what the eye could show him in this most powerful and disturbing of places. He could turn his own eye away from the chapels, but, if the Office's eye thought it necessary, he knew that it could see through his closed eyelid.

Aden touched Donchak on the shoulder and held the eye out to him. Donchak took it, weighing it in his hand and doing little to conceal his distaste.

Donchak edged around the column and out into the nave. He grew smaller to Aden's remaining eye, but seemed to get no further away.

Aden again felt the designed terror and grandeur of the cathedral. Deprived of the eye, he could no longer reduce light or motion to their component parts or analyze the transmutation of physical substances into etherealizations by covert spectrometry. For a moment, Aden thought himself to be sinking to one knee, but found he was still standing, pressed against damp limestone. Balls of were-light dipped and wandered about him, patrolling the length of the nave. Infrequently, one would venture between the columns, illuminate one of the chapels and then return.

With great effort, he focused his attention on Donchak. The latter was walking obliquely toward the unicorn. Aden hoped the other man's sandals made no sound, but the rush of his own, unmonitored blood made hearing tricky and deceptive. He imagined groups of the lights to be clustering above Donchak, following him across the nave, spotlighting him for whoever else might be worshiping or was worshiped in the chapels.

But these were surely random gatherings. As soon as he had one formation clarified, it would slowly shift and scatter. Anyway, if Donchak was being watched, the patterns of the lights' watching would be those of high magic and not rationally perceptible. They could only be suspected and felt, never diagramed.

Donchak was alongside the unicorn now. The top of its jeweled saddle was level with his head. Donchak seemed to be moving his lips and speaking inaudibly to the creature. If it heard, it gave no sign.

The man-creature remained immobile, his posture frozen into an expression of remote listening. Aden's mind roared within itself for more information, more lines, more colors, more movement, more known factors and dimensions. He had not even been able to see the attendant's face. He did not know if the attendant had one. Nor did he know whether man and unicorn were slave and master, equals or perhaps the component parts of a single being. All he could perceive in the metallic light was the robed fat man moving as carefully as a mountaineer along the flanks of the unicorn, his hands suspended over its caparison and chanfron.

So suddenly as to make Aden nearly gasp from surprise, Donchak spun upon his right foot and stepped squarely in front of the unicorn. Its horn appeared to be made of twisted strands of gold and ebony and was over a meter long. Donchak stared up at it for a moment, as if he were examining the design on one of his blind weavers' looms. His back was to the attendant, but he did not seem to care. His lips kept moving, and Aden heard certain unidentifiable words.

Donchak twitched and shifted with a multitude of small, painfully circumscribed gestures and muttered phrases. Bloated and maimed as Aden found him, he managed to imply that some feat of enormous physical and spiritual strength was being performed, as if he had made himself some kind of fulcrum for the balancing of violently opposed forces. Aden knew that if he was right in this feeling, that he and the unicorn, its attendant, the cathedral itself, the two eyes of the Office and uncountable other forces were part of the balancing. He could not immediately decide whether he was more frightened by the fact that Donchak might be able to do such a thing, or by what the consequences might be if he failed.

His right hand describing intricate traceries, Donchak carefully reached inside the shield that protected the unicorn's right eye. He held himself like that, perched on his toes, his legs visibly shaking from the effort.

Then he brought his hand down and walked backward alongside the animal. He followed his original path across the nave, reentering the aisle several meters from Aden. He did not wait there, but continued to the door.

Aden watched the unicorn and the attendant. They were precisely as they had found them, frozen, perfect, lost in the contemplation of their own terrible infinity. Then he imagined that Donchak had left him there and rushed after the man as quickly as his fear and blindness would permit. The alternating avenues of silver light between the columns played across his eye, distorting and confusing his sense of distance so that he almost tripped and fell over non-existent obstacles several times.

There were noises behind him. Scrapes and shufflings that could have been the unicorn and the attendant rousing themselves, or the echo of his own breathing trapped by irrational forces in the chapels and crypts on his right.

Donchak was waiting for him at the door. He shoved Aden through with startling strength, but then checked himself long enough to close it with no sound louder than that of the tumblers in its lock.

He was cradling his right hand in his left, and his blasted features flowed without interruption into his functioning half, poisoning it by its pain alone. Aden dug into his pocket and offered him the remainder of the anesthetic. Donchak accepted it and rubbed the substance into the palm of his right hand, and then outward on his fingers.

When he had finished, he walked down from the portico. Instead of directly crossing the square, he turned south and entered the first side street. The road narrowed quickly. The houses became more dilapidated and the smell worsened in proportion to the distance they traveled.

Aden nearly walked on the other man's heels out of fear of becoming lost. Inside his new blindness he knew that his threats of exposure had been a terrible thing, but if Donchak had meant to dispose of him and thereby protect himself, he would have done it on the way to the cathedral, not after he had left the eye with the unicorn. But that, he reconsidered, might have been the whole point of it, to trick him into giving up the eye . . . The Office could have foreseen these variables, made allowance for them, given him reliable contacts and firm alternatives for action. But that was not the Office's way.

The mage-fires glistened over them. Now that Aden could see only within a narrow range of the electromagnetic spectrum, he thought that they had dimmed somewhat. Paradoxically, he felt more awed by them; he could not see and isolate the heavy particle bombardments that were directly affecting the workings of his cortex, producing the feeling.

"Are they still there?" he finally whispered, after the streets had begun to twist toward where the City's docks had been.

Donchak shrugged and looked to the sky. "Possibly. Perhaps there were no wars or assassinations or upheavals desired by their master tonight. Or perhaps he had a particularly terrible act in mind and they are still gathering their courage and powers for it." He spoke more to the paving stones than to Aden. "They are strange things. At times I wish . . . " He broke off as they passed by a party of lepers butchering the inexplicable smoking corpse of a dray horse.

"What did you do? My eye . . . ?"

"The eye is with the unicorn." Donchak turned down another, still filthier street. The houses soared above them, leaning together so closely that in spots their gables and balconies touched, cutting the sky down to irregular slits of auroral brightness. "They go there every night to pray. I do not think even their master knows fully why. They are totally creations of magic, more completely than any other thing in this part of the world, even more than the beings the magicians have created out of pure thoughts. They are weapons, healers, vessels of great power and vulnerability. They are very old. Some say they were alive before the War itself." Donchak's voice grew tired and he stopped to rest against a wall.

He resumed walking after a minute, picking up another street. They were probably circling back toward Donchak's shop, but there was no way to be sure. "I simply made sure that they were both oblivious to us and then placed the eye into the socket of the unicorn. I hope I was correct in assuming the Office was still using K-type connectors?"

"N. Very little difference, but much more reliable." Aden felt himself regain some control over his feelings; shop talk does it every time.

"Then the thing will function by itself."

"Yes, fully. But I still can't imagine how you did it. The thing had its own eyes. It just wouldn't stand there with its groom or companion a few meters away and let you mangle it." Aden had meant to say more, but he remembered how easily the eye had lived inside of him for the past few years.

"I understand both of them. Not their purpose, I admit. I have no wish to do that. But I do understand their presence and the way they define themselves to you and me and to their master and to each other." Aden thought that he had heard the refugees coming back from Thorn River using the same tone of voice that Donchak was. It was a sort of chanting, internalized, polished and given to an artificial syntax which only emphasized the speaker's bewilderment with the things he was explaining. "The unicorn and the man are things of purest magic. The eye is a thing of irreducible logic. It exists in the same place as the unicorn's true eye. The two are hardly aware of each other's existence. Each one reports the things that it was designed to see, in the language suited to those perceptions. The creature should feel or detect no more than a remote irritation. It just does not have the capability to understand or guess at what we have done and neither does its companion."

"But we do." A hint of condescension.

Donchak exhaled lightly and it might have been a laugh. "Not entirely, not perfectly. For all I know, we might have made a trade and the essence of the unicorn's eye is now coexistent with mine, and the picture of your face is hovering before some gentlemen of power."

Fear crossed Aden's face. With his grid, Donchak could see the deepening flush and the sparking of loose connectors inside his left eye socket, like a brooch or pendant. "Could the unicorn ever learn to see with it? I mean, apart from whether it works for us or the enemy uncovers it?"

"Impossible." The Thorn River voice again, but more slowly as if the possibility hadn't occurred to him until Aden mentioned it. "No. I think we have the advantage in this. If the eye was like the devices I remember, you could not have scratched its capabilities in less than a decade. It could be addictive, you know. Such a perfect analytic tool as that could come to control you. One keeps looking, forever looking and discovering, peeling back layer after layer of apparent truth until one begins to wonder if the layers are infinite or whether, weighing it all in your hand, you have not felt its mass fractionally diminished, and know that you possess a device that, with patience, will reduce it to nothing."

"Could, will that happen to the unicorn?" Aden was wondering just what the Office had given away, and why.

"No. I told you that. The two, the unicorn and the eye are mutually exclusive. Interaction is impossible." Donchak might have sounded irritated, but Aden could not tell; he had forgotten how to read faces with his own eye. "Anyway, you are rid of the eye and, I presume, the main object of your mission. You should thank me, Aden. I have saved you from some agony."

"The war demands a great deal from all of us," Aden responded, hoping to say the correct thing and guessing that he had not.

Donchak turned the blank side of his face to him, saying nothing more until they reached his house.

II

"Will you stay?"

"You have asked me that. In any event, I doubt that the men of power would let me leave."

"Are you that closely watched? They apparently didn't know what we were doing last night." Aden sipped the tea Donchak had warmed.

"They watch me in the manner of their world, as I elude them in the manner of my own. I only wonder if I can survive myself in all of this."

He could not stop some of the tea from drooling down the right side of his mouth. "I have many things here. Friends, though all secular and powerless, a prosperous trade, the sympathy of some ladies for my face and for my blindness. If I were to go back, I fear that the desire for complete understanding would overtake me again. I understand enough."

"But you refuse to understand any less. You understand so much of this City, Donchak. The unicorn and its attendant. There's nothing back home that can begin to guess at them." Despite what he had just done, Aden found himself becoming irritated with Donchak again. *The fellow speaks as much nonsense as everyone in this place.* The locked doors and shuttered windows allowed Aden enough room to think that way.

"It is a question of perspective. At this moment, I feel up against some kind of limit. I have seen and taken apart all the things I can. I can feel the edge of my abilities here because to go beyond them would require a kind of seeing which I am not capable of.

"But, at our home, I remember things having been different. We were still beginning when I left. We had been looking for only a century or two, but we were aimed for . . . " Donchak's slagged features hardened. "We had only been looking for a century or two before we could see things like Thorn River. See ourselves seeing it, dissecting and analyzing ourselves as much as the magicians.

"They only look at themselves, you know. And did you know how repulsed they are by us? How sickened?"

"It's their fear." Aden replied.

"That as much as their pity and disgust." Donchak's voice was as it had been when he first mentioned his hatred for the Border Command and reluctance to help them. His condescension and unctuous sympathy frightened Aden as much as it had the first time; it seemed to be founded upon an elusive base of contradictory vision that not all the Office's deft equivocations could equal. "They see us as thieves and desperados, intent on destroying everything of any beauty or life."

"What beauty has their war been fought to keep safe? They declared it, fought the first battle at the Burn, murdered their first town there."

"The beauty they are fighting is their own," Donchak said with even malice. "They know it. They will protect and keep it safe from everything."

"From the eye, too?" Aden used his best point and exhaled with the effort of its saying.

It worked with more visible impact than had his threats of exposure. The conversation was fixed on treasons and betrayals, Aden thought, and was it not therefore proper to remind Donchak of his own most recent one? "That was done for you and the Office. The information—if there is any that can be understood by you—must be kept apart and guarded. The unicorn has access . . ." his voice trailed away in its own sudden weakness.

"I'm sure they know, but I'll tell them again when I get back." There was some genuine feeling to Aden's words, and he was surprised by this.

"Then for that alone, and for them"—he gestured to the dimly luminous spy entities—"you should go. In the morning you should go." Donchak started to walk away from him when his expression shifted again. It was so slight that Aden could not be sure if it was not his imagination, which was only now coming back under his control. The eye, he told himself bitterly, the eye would have seen it, and the electrical and fluid currents that had flowed beneath his skin through nerves and vessels torn apart by the enemy at Thorn River and imperfectly repaired by his enemies at home. Or perhaps it could not. Donchak, Aden was becoming more and more aware, while not a total traitor or adherent of magic, was something of an alien, a foreign creature whose lunar features and moods did not function according to the dynamics of his home world.

"You should not, I think, go the way you came."

"What?" Aden could not remember saying anything about his route to the Holy City.

"You should not return the same way. Things, clues, hints of what you were might still be lingering in those places, though they might not have been traceable to you here. They can still read your mind, you know, if they want to badly enough."

The idea struck Aden as amusing: rather like trying to read a book with all its pages torn out. "Then how? Air pickup would be impossible even if there were some way of notifying the Office I needed it."

Donchak's voice shifted as subtly as his expression, with such indefinition that Aden missed some of the words as he tried to confirm or dispel his suspicions. "No need for anything so daring. I would only suggest that a more cautious and relaxed route be used." He walked around the room, idly tracing the designs in his rugs with his burned fingers, sometimes gesturing so that it seemed he was caressing the waverings in the air that Aden guessed were the spy entities. "Go north from here, through the Fishers' Door, to the City at . . . " He spoke a name that escaped Aden, saw the man's ignorance and used its old name: Clairendon. "The ocean is still there, and if it has continued to please the men of power who hold sway there, there will also be a river. Follow it inland." Donchak went on describing landmarks and reference points that Aden only half paid any attention to. He thought the general outlines were clear enough, however, and found that his conception of the route Donchak was suggesting fit his recollection of the central kingdoms. After some time he thought he had matched enough foreign place names with remembered aerial photographs and radar composites to be fairly sure of the way.

He was intensely tired, and that might have been part of his mood too. The trip would take much longer, but the prudence of Donchak's suggestion could not be ignored. Now that the eye was gone he could easily miss traps set by his enemies or by his own inattention. The way it had been, as he reconsidered it when Donchak had left him in a second-floor storeroom, was almost easy; trying it a second time, in reverse and half blind, would probably be much more difficult. He recalled crossing the square to the fountain, and then the part when he had run from there to the cathedral without the eye.

The rugs on which he lay were hard and stiff with newness; the blind weavers' designs framed him in Donchak's darkness, and he wondered if they were ones with magic woven into them. He wondered if they were float-ing in the air; the room was without windows and there was no way to tell if he was not, or if the magic was of another sort.

He studied the dark around him again and found noth-ing. But the Office, whatever its intentions, would surely give him another eye when he returned, and that would permit him to understand.

III

"Wake up! Wake up! They know! You must leave!" Aden bolted awake. His right eye was filled with the bright rectangle of the door and Donchak's face centered in the middle of it. "You must go! Now!" There was nothing in his left eye but the coolness of morning air. He felt that he had awakened inside a narrow pipe. The previous night and the memory of who he was came back with painful slowness while Donchak was holding him and shaking madly.

He tried to read Donchak's face. He saw no tempera-ture or conductance differentials, infrared differences, muscle movements or nerve signals; the man's back was to the lighted door and he could not even simply see his expression.

The panic came without any knowledge. That had not happened for years and he was sickened by his own lack of control. He tried to stand, fell from his new, unarticu-lated fright at the knowledge Donchak's "they" had sto-len from him in his sleep, then rose again.

"Here." Donchak shoved a wadded bundle of clothing into his hand. Another man came into the room, took him by the shoulders and propelled him out into the hallway. It was lit by animal fat lamps and stank as the City's alleys had.

Aden pulled on his shirt as they half ran along it. They turned, entered a stairwell that was lit by a single panel of stained glass that ran the height of the building; the pattern was of a golden serpent and the sun behind it burned into Aden's eye, dispersing the bits of rational thought he had managed to arrange in the hall.

"They know, they know!" Donchak kept repeating with monotonous panic.

They reached the ground floor. Donchak grasped his hand once, and the other, silent man took him out through the same back gate they had used the night before.

The sun was unbearable for a moment, though at that hour in the morning the alley was still screened by the houses on the other side. Aden choked on his own helplessness, and therefore let himself be guided down the reeking alley and out into the turquoise streets. He thought that they were heading in the opposite direction from that the temple had been in, but that was of no consequence.

The streets became wider and more populated. Food sellers' and spice merchants' stalls flashed by along the limit of his vision. Aristocratic ladies escorted by parties of elaborately armored men walked among them, sampling the newest delights in jewelry from the South, carved furniture from the East, the skulls of centuries-dead admirals just recovered from the bottom of the

City's exiled sea and set with gemstones, gold and tourmaline for those among the City's powerful who were
inclined to the unusual and ironic.

The man beside him remained silent, guiding his steps
with a strong and certain hand on his elbow or shoulder
that always seemed to be intended to keep him slightly
off balance. Aden considered trying to escape, but
doubted if he could break the larger man's grasp; if he
was trained, he would sense the tensing of Aden's muscles in preparation for any violent movements. And even
if he did escape, he would be lost and a prisoner of the
City itself instead of Donchak's man.

The City's life swirled around them. Grand houses,
palaces, temples and government buildings rose on
either side of the street. Their gates were guarded by
animated statues that challenged some who came too
close, welcomed others or simply watched with their
enormous gemstone eyes. Aden shrank away whenever
his stare met them. His eye had shown him that some
did emit some kind of rudimentary power, while in others the effect was purely psychological. It was impossible
to tell the difference now and the weight of their presences fell over and against him with disturbing substance.

This is what they see, this is what they feel, every day
of their lives, he thought to himself.

There was shouting ahead and the man drew him from
out of the road and alongside the wall of a garden. They
stopped and waited as the noise grew louder; like his
vision, Aden felt that his sense of hearing had become
flat and two-dimensional, with the depth taken from it.
The difficulty in breathing which he had experienced in

the cathedral came back to him, although the sun was now fully into the sky and ordinary people thronged around him.

The party broke through the crowd to his right. There were two magicians, ten mounted deaths and four dragons without riders. In the cathedral the newness of his blindness had helped dilute the sight of the unicorn and its attendant as much as it had accentuated their unworldly beauty. He had had some hours now to remember how he had been before the eye was implanted and to think and reflect upon how he had become even less.

He could not tell whether they were great men of power returning from their work or if they were of lesser state, going to attend their masters and to learn the lessons of the night's battles, for they both wore masks of beaten silver. So perfectly idealized were the faces on them that Aden was momentarily convinced that his own features had been placed on them. Then he found the courage to blink his eye and the masks returned to gods or demons, depending on how the light struck them.

The crowd's babble grew as the magicians approached, and then stopped abruptly; comparative silence encircled the party at a radius of twenty meters. They came within five meters of where they stood and Aden heard the pounding of his heart explode into the quiet that enveloped their passage.

Dust rose from beneath the hooves of their mounts, but Aden could see it only as gold. The ten deaths, more gorgeously attired than those he had seen the day before, trotted with agonizing slowness behind the magicians, at a speed calculated to allow enough of their stench to reach the crowd and give proof of their immortal decay. Strange and frightening devices, suggestive of the price the magicians had extracted from them for their release from their graves, spangled their tunics.

That was all there was, suggestion, hints, outlines drawn with nighttime darkness in the morning, extending backward through all the perspectives which the loss of the eye had denied to him. Aden felt the mystery of the City as its people did and cowered before it. Yet he could not look away.

The dragons strode behind the deaths, hazed with the golden dust, moving at a half-march with their long, reptilian legs, the natural armor of their chitinous hides indistinguishable from the light camails and segmented breastplates their masters had given them. Their eyes shone with internal light and revealed a murderous intellect.

They paid no attention to him and passed. Evidently they were not privy to the knowledge Donchak was. The noise struck up again, as it had the day before; the ritual of that hour ended.

Beggars rushed away from the wall and into the street, scraping at the chinks between the paving stones where the magicians' dust had settled. Aden looked down and saw their fingers beginning to bleed before they were knocked over by the renewed progress of more sober-minded persons.

The man grunted and resumed walking. Aden felt his fear replaced by shame and then by the morning's confusion. His sense of personal abandonment became impenetrable and he did not notice when Donchak's man had to get him out of the way of another passing man of power as his palanquin was borne across their path by eight cyclopes.

The Fishers' Door had been erected where the canneries had been in the old city of Cape St. Vincent, when there had been such things as oceans, and before there was any need or thought of walls for the City or doors carved from fused bodies of the wizards' vanquished enemies.

Aden passed through the Door and stared dully up at the thousands upon thousands of forms, faces contorted in agonies that might be still continuing; arms, limbs, hands, all intertwined around each other and frozen into the two huge slabs of the Door. Their endless features were blurred and remote, as if a layer of smoked glass held them together instead of the power of the City's wizards, but Aden's remaining eye could still see enough to be sickened. As with the two magicians, though, he could not look away. The brutality of the Door was too monstrous for him to encompass, and even with the eye, he suspected that the motives for it might have escaped him. Again, he was left with the mystery and found it quite enough.

The man abruptly released him into the currents of men and beasts that compressed themselves into the Fishers' Door as they entered the City or left it, spreading out onto the branching, marble-paved roads that led out to all the other kingdoms of magic. He had said nothing, shared none of Aden's confusion or Donchak's apparent panic. Aden wondered if the man even had a face, for he was able to remember only blank, dark skin, outlined with traceries of purple tattoos. He also recalled the attendant of the unicorn, who had also been faceless,

yet as warm with lives and patterns. Perhaps, he hypothesized as the crowds swept him past the Door's thousands
of tormented eyes, it was the function of such blind and
faceless men to guide creatures like unicorns and secret
police spies before the former had gained their eyes and
after the latter had had theirs taken from them.

The City's walls soared above him, their height impossible to estimate with his single eye, covered with murals
and mosaics that raced away from him into blurred, violent luminescence. The Door's traffic carried him away
from the City and pushed him off to the side of the road.
The land around the walls was gently rolling prairie and
the light colored it the same gold and bronze that the
light in Donchak's house had been; Aden saw that it did
not reach into the Fishers' Door and the eyes there shone
with light the magicians had put there, and none other.

"They" knew. Donchak had said so. But the mission
was mostly completed, with rather more success than his
superiors had probably anticipated at its beginning. The
wisdom of Donchak's suggested route still seemed correct, despite the way the man chose to make sure he
took it. Imaginary alarms might have been sounding in
the City. He thought that he could hear the deep tolling
of bells above the roaring of the road's traffic.

IV

He walked for most of that day. Once he learned to
compensate for the false distances his eye conveyed to
him, the miles passed with comparative ease.

There were few magicians abroad, for there was little need for them to resort to mere walking or riding where long distances were concerned. The road was a wearisome place for them, and perhaps evocative of restlessness and questing, and therefore to be left to ordinary folk and commerce. The familiar tiredness of the road and the harmless pageantry of its traffic replaced his fear. The memory of Donchak's faceless servant vanished first, for there seemed so little to the man. Then Donchak fell into some kind of perspective of his own, that of a simple traitor or harmless lunatic.

The unicorn remained, however, dimly attended by the metallic giant, floating alternately through the darkness of the cathedral's nave and then through the new emptiness of his eye socket, waiting in both places for the summons of their master, carrying the Office's treason with it to spy on his designs and plottings.

People spoke to him, reassuring in their trivialities. Strangers remarked upon nothing more sinister than the beauty of the weather or the fields of wildflowers that the road gradually climbed into as it left the City. Drunken centaurs yelled and screeched to themselves as they pulled cargos of women to the City's markets. Despite the obvious poverty of his dress, men still approached him to peddle ornaments and charms of indifferent workmanship. There were also other fellows who cautiously approached him and offered articles that could not be purchased where the magicians were closely watching: prisms, rusted ball bearings, charred printed circuits picked up on centuries-old battlefields. The road was more open than the City, even though he often saw rocs patrolling the skies above it.

V

Following Donchak's directions, largely because he had no others, he continued on the road as it went north. It became less grand as it left the immediate territories of the Holy City, losing its marble paving blocks and turning to cobblestones and then to packed dirt, but the people on it became no less fascinating. If anything, Aden marveled at how easily they had fitted their mortality around the presence of magic. Palaces rose distantly through forests of sapphire-oak and diamond vine, or perched on fairy tale escarpments too eccentric to permit any real menace to flourish. The formations of rocs diminished until only solitary eagles with wings of translucent carnelian watched the road for the magicians. Magic was always in evidence, but usually as ornament or backdrop. Women wore necklaces of were-light and occasional seers had wildly grotesque familiars perched on their shoulders, but there was never the hint or implication that forces of illimitable power were being kept and refined, or that vengeances were being harbored against entire nations and philosophies.

Aden wondered if it had been like this on the roads he had taken on his way to the Holy City. He could remember nothing on them but brutality and oppression by omnipresent powers. Even when the magicians or their retainers or tentacles of power had not been detectable to the eye, he recalled a different spirit in the people. He could not believe that the loss of the eye, great though it may have been, could have changed his perceptions this much. Donchak's suppressed rage at the Border Command or his ostensible panic were different, more complicated things. Here he sought only to know if a person was smiling or walked with his weight on the balls of his feet so that he could move suddenly to this direction or that. Surely he did not need the eye to understand such things.

Perhaps it was simply that the hold of the City or its belligerent sisters was not so strong in these places. Or, he thought again on the next day, perhaps this was just a sign that the war was ending. The reasons became less important as the beauty of the countryside increased.

VI

Clairendon seemed a reversed image of the Holy City, where the constructions of magic underlay those of the old world, rather than the other way around. It had once been a port and it remained one despite the magicians' dislike of the ocean, anciently the highway for his world's battle cruisers and submarines. Its clapboard houses were intact as were its open, wandering lanes, the palaces of the mighty hidden among them as discreetly as they had been in the forest. Its men of power did not seem to have the morbidity of taste that their brothers in the other cities of magic did; they could be seen tacking through the harbors of the city in magnificently carved pinnaces, the visible display of their power limited to the filling of their sails when they moved against the wind.

He spent more time there than he had intended. Its magic, like that of the road, was made of soft, intensely human stuff, even when it was wielded by immortals. Its sky glowed only fitfully at night, and then as much from the auroras as from the battling of the magicians.

But the season was progressing. It was already mid-summer and he guessed there would be at least one stretch of high country to traverse before he could reach his own lines. He took the road that bordered the river flowing into the ocean near the city, as Donchak had suggested, climbing back into the emerald and turquoise forests and their singular peace.

The first attack came one week after he had left the ocean city. The road followed the river in a gently curving arc to the west and southwest.

At first Aden was pleased that his remaining eye was sharp enough to see them approaching up the river valley, utterly silent because of their speed. They seemed like motes of dust, anchored in a gently shifting space that did not quite match up with the one the river and the road occupied.

Their size also grew according to different laws of perspective than the river's. They were small for an overly long time and then their dimensions exploded outward, instantly growing wings and vertical stabilizers, gun pods and iron bombs slung from hard points, aerials, turrets, blisters and canopies, their proportions suddenly gigantic.

Aden thought his heart to be stopped; but he had perceived all of their approach in the space between its beating. They were bombers and the alternating black and red stripes on their wings showed that they were from the fortress at Dance. The span of their wings bridged half the river's width. Their leading edges and noses were glowing yellow from the speed of their flight.

The people on the road looked up calmly, wrenching their shoulders and necks to keep the aircraft in sight, and then looked back to their fellows or to the oxen they were leading. No one but Aden showed any surprise. Fearing discovery, he forced himself to stay on his feet and keep walking.

The sound of the ships and the blast from their weapons hit him simultaneously, knocking him to his knees and compressing all the air from his chest.

Two men dressed in turbans and satin robes grasped him by the shoulders and helped him to his feet. "Are you all right?" the shorter of the two inquired mildly.

Astonished, Aden turned to face the man. His features were long and finely drawn despite his lack of height. A column of thick smoke was rising from the river shore directly behind his head. "Just a surprise. I didn't . . . " Aden wondered dimly if he was using the correct accent.

"Of course. The land around here is so enchanting. It is so easy to forget about the War." His voice was patronizing but Aden detected no suspicion in it. The two men then stepped back, bowed slightly and merged into the crowd. Aden followed in their direction, edging toward the river's shore.

He found a shaded spit of land and walked out onto it. The strain of trying to appear unconcerned made his limbs move in jerks and he felt that all the magicians' spies were now watching while their masters decided whether it would be worth their while to crush him.

Nothing happened. He turned his head downriver. The line of smoke reached up far above the bordering ridge line of the river's valley. But it shifted and bobbed uncertainly as the aircraft had, subtly out of phase with the world around it. Aden saw a large river trireme at its base and guessed that it had been the planes' target. It was untouched, suspended within the smoke like the eyes of the vanquished people in the Fishers' Door, its oars moving with their own slow rhythm. People moved nonchalantly about its decks; the water around the ship was smooth, broken only by its wake.

Aden watched the smoke thin away and disperse. The trireme stayed, moving downstream. Its flags and rigging remained motionless, the crew and passengers showing no more acknowledgment that anything unusual had happened than the people on the road.

On his way to the Holy City, he had seen occasional evidence of his world's assaults on this one, but he knew that these were usually ancient freaks, when the laws of probability had allowed the destructions of his world's weapons to coincide with the constructions of magic's. He had never seen one of the futile attacks before this, and he thought he felt a careless, languid triumph in the people on the road. The ships had come, raging with their geometric fires, and done no more than cast a shadow across the sun.

Aden got up and back onto the road. The feeling of invincibility grew stronger, reaching into him and sparking something that might have been contempt for the futility of the way his world was fighting this war. Midday fireworks, but little else. He found it equally difficult to understand what Donchak had so feared about the implantation of the eye. It had been there for over two months, yet even the ships from Dance could do nothing.

VII

The second attack was an artillery barrage directed at a palace made of malachite. Aden knew that he was still at least six hundred kilometers from contested border areas, so it must have been rocket-boosted shells launched from diminishing caliber Gulrich guns. Aden spoke the words to himself and marveled at how out of place they sounded.

They poured down from the stratosphere into a tight circle around the castle, wrapping its towers and turrets in spheres of gold and scarlet fire. The barrage lasted for half an hour, and Aden watched all of it from a grove of dwarf pines by the side of the road.

Whenever there was a break in the shells, he saw the castle's emerald beauty inside the fires, inviolate, too indifferent for contempt, its flags and pennants rippling lightly in the winds of this world alone. Large hawks and gryphons from the castle occasionally rose through the detonations, containing their explosive ferocity with the simple grace of their flight.

There was the light and the vision of destruction, as there had been on the river, consuming themselves without reference to their intended targets. But this time, there was also a singing inside his mind and wild, incoherent bursts of electric shrieking coming from the places where the Office's annunciators were buried.

Aden thought that it might be evidence of the gunfire reaching out into their target world, touching it with more certainty than the smoke column's shadow. Again, the people on the road reassured him; they turned to observe the attack, or stopped and chatted with their neighbors against the backdrop of the explosions, but then moved on showing no more interest than they had for the attack at the river.

The sounds came in step with the explosions. Aden recalled as much as he could of his own circuitries, tracing their patterns under his skin as if he were reading a map of a newly alien country. If it was not the Office, calling and asking him to range in the distant batteries, then it might be the detonations themselves.

The eye could have seen the lines of electromagnetic force whipping outward from the inviolate castle, prodding sympathetic currents by induction from the wires and dead, metallic masses. He was still of his own world; he could see and hear the violence of its war, however futile the kingdoms of magic rendered it, and he was again surprised at how saddened this made him.

The shelling stopped. Aden got back to his feet and stepped back onto the road. His ideas of balance and accommodation remained consciously intact, but he felt the reasons for them dissolving before the invulnerable beauty of the castle and the countryside. The power of his world was becoming as shrill and panicked as he had imagined the wizards of the Holy City to be.

Emerald light engulfed the people in front of him. He watched as they jerked themselves around to stare directly at and then through him. His heart folded in upon itself and he was momentarily convinced that he had shown his guilt too clearly. But they were looking past him.

He turned also, and found that the southern half of the castle was gone, replaced by a dense cone of green light. He glanced back to the road and saw the teamsters and merchants squinting silently at the new light; their faces were suddenly as unreadable as those in the Holy City had been when he had first lost the eye.

Aden pushed himself into the standing crowd, excusing himself quietly in the deafening silence, moving as carefully as he could around their gaze. "They have found us," a man muttered as he passed; his voice was not upset, but the words were there. Aden thought within himself that he was the man's and the castle's "they," just as the man might have been one of the "they" Donchak had warned him of. He turned involuntarily and found that the man was looking in his general direction and that his face was covered by a mask of woven gold with faceted, obsidian eyes.

"Only this once," a companion said, and Aden thought that the man had raised his voice just enough to permit him to hear it. The second man's face was also covered, this time with a smooth chromium mask whose eyes were closed and whose mouth was locked shut.

Aden slowed and almost replied to the two men. But he found that the only words in his mouth were embarrassed assurances that the explosion had been an accident, just the odds playing that had characterized most of the war's centuries. He said nothing, but the men adjusted their blank and closed eyes to stare pointedly at him.

VIII

Aden knew that it was early fall, but it appeared as if the magicians of this area, however discreet their palaces and ways, favored spring and summer. The road left the river and climbed steeply into highland plateaus; snow-edged mountain ridges could be seen on either horizon, but he found the meadows full of blooming wildflowers. The groves of ghost pine were speckled with their white and turquoise cones; in Aden's world, they produced such cones only once every five springtimes.

The land had been but recently conquered by magic, and many of its cities and villages were still half ruin. Glowing hulks too far away to tell whether they were of rocs or gutted half-tracks spotted the mountainsides at night. Aden found the effect not as sinister as he recalled it to have been in the lands in front of Joust Mountain or around Castle Kent and Everwhen, where such wreckage had been allowed to remain as memorials to what had happened there.

He left the road and climbed up into the alpine meadows to examine one of these memorials, vaguely thinking that, if it proved to be a device of his own world, he should be somehow obligated to discover what he could about it, so that the descendants of its crew would know.

Halfway there, he saw that the light had been reflected by a white pavilion whose fanciful tangle of columns and ornamental beams resembled a roc's skeleton from the road. A garden spread out from the structure, lighting up the mountain with long splashes of brilliant color. Rose vines and morning glory, still in flower though it was afternoon, climbed up and through the structure, ornamenting it as gorgeously as any of the gold-encrusted temples that the lowland kingdoms had erected to their patron deities. Streams of silver water ran down past him, and he crossed over them on footbridges of rock crystal.

Aden recognized the magic in the place, but by now found himself able to enjoy it. The destruction of the castle had been largely forgotten; the small victory of his world had been buried in tens of other futile attacks on the road or upon the cities it linked together. He had watched, first in fear and in shame after the castle's destruction, then with greater calm as the rockets or shells curved down from space, imperfectly guided by satellites which, after twenty years of probing, had still not found an immovably fixed point in the kingdoms of magic on which to fix their ranging lasers. Inevitably, they missed, falling into streams or groves of flame-willows that smothered the violence of their detonations.

The fighter-bombers were always the same. They bobbed and wavered through the air as the first ones he had seen did, their crews probably sick and disoriented with the way the world outside their windscreens or radarscopes refused to conform to what they sensed were the motions of their ships through it.

Aden found a clarity of vision in the fires that they left. As they burned themselves out, seldom touching anything, they acted as a lens for the beauty and strength of his enemy.

Before, the eye had disassembled and explained the world in rigorously comprehensible forms. The fires acted in the same way. He watched the world's beauty, sometimes inverted or split apart in simulation of a prism, its components arranged and recombined, not according to any final scheme of priorities or energy potentials, but according to the way they were formed by the men of power. He watched them growing through the explosions of his own world, saw the individual brush-strokes of their creators expand apart, suggest their gene-sis in the loves and triumphs of other mages. He believed that he could feel a great substance and weight of emo-tion underlaying the creations of magic, entirely separate from the realities that his world assigned to them in the parallel spectrums.

He briefly wished for one of his world's attacks, but then reconsidered that the fragility of the pavilion's grace needed no explanation or analysis.

There was a chair in the center of the pavilion. Aden stopped and turned around, looking for someone who might occupy it. He saw the two men several hundred meters away, in the direction of the road, one with the chrome death mask and the one with the black stone eyes. They stood apart from the traffic of the road, staring in the direction of the garden with their undirected gaze.

They were as they had been when they observed the destruction of the emerald castle. In memory, he also found their opaque faces in the crowds that watched the attack on the river trireme; and after the castle, during a rocket barrage that fell upon an astrological observatory that had spread outward four kilometers on either side of the road, and when squadrons of dive bombers from the fortress at Whitebreak had emerged from the sun and squandered their fury on the ice gardens that some magician had carved from his personal winter.

Donchak's "they"; possibly, but he could read as much serenity and mystery into their masks as he could menace and pursuit. They seemed primarily watchers, as was he.

There was enough, however, to dry his mouth and accelerate his heart perceptibly. He turned away from them. The chair in the center of the pavilion was now occupied by a figure in pale blue robes, with a loose cap of darker material.

He had previously avoided any approach to persons of obvious power, but this one appeared relatively mortal. The person was only seated amongst magical works and not clearly magical herself.

Aden began walking again. If the men from the road were following him, it was unlikely that he could do anything to throw them off now. He also found the presence of the woman in the pavilion resolving itself into terms he could understand. First, he had seen only the beauty, without immediately assigning any gender to it. Then, like the beauty of this world seen through the lens of the other's obsessive destruction, he recognized her as something human and impenetrably mysterious, composed of parts that could be seen, detected, yet never quantified.

The whores of this world had been decipherable to the Office's eye as biological and elementary mental functions; at times the eye had hinted to him that he had seen their souls. The eye of his own world, having been trained and selectively fed and starved on the Office's peculiar diet of perceptions, had seen less clearly, but had nevertheless understood enough. This was different; at last his eye had come upon a new way of seeing on its own.

Her hands were flawless. She was over fifty meters away, and he saw that clearly. The nails were closely trimmed and her fingers were long and had almost no creases between them.

She was holding a book. As she shut it and looked up to him, he saw, first, that its cover was of light tan leather into which many designs and emblems had been patiently worked.

The bone structure of her face was precisely drawn beneath pale skin, but her nose was smaller than most and her eyes correspondingly larger. She might have tended toward the sterile idealization that the mask of the man on the road had, or those of the two magicians who had so terrified him when he was leaving the Holy City; but instead of stepping over this line to inhuman abstraction, her beauty veered slightly before its own mirror. Enough reality remained to reach into his own world; she instantly summarized all the racial perfections he had seen in the kingdoms of magic by being, ultimately, unlike any of them.

"Aden?" she said over the distance that remained between them. He did not think it at all remarkable that she knew his name.

He nodded and smiled up to her, wishing for something to cover the emptiness of his eye socket. He was in rags, his beard was tangled and he smelled.

Her eyes were gold and olive, but shifted into gray and then back into a turquoise as he tried to decipher them. She brushed a strand of auburn hair from her face and he saw a spark of blue light, dancing at the end of one of her fingers like a miniature star freshly picked from the night.

"Is this yours?" he said when he thought himself close enough to be heard; he was delighted that his voice came out with some clarity and strength.

"Yes. This and most of the mountain behind it."

Aden felt the enemy's world rushing away behind him, and he involuntarily looked around to check his own position in it. The road was still below him, choked with riotous pageants, but the two men who had been watching him were gone.

Surprisingly, she was still in the pavilion when he turned back. "You seem to know my name. What's yours?" The war twisted and heaved distantly within his mind; it coursed up and down the limits of his cranial net, trying to prod more echoes from the attacks he had witnessed from the road. Not even Donchak had known his real name; only the Office's eye had known.

"Gedwyn."

"Are you part of the war?" the wires and dead annunciators inside of him asked transparently.

She laughed as if he had said something amusing, and put down her book. "No more than you are. Have you come to take all my secrets from me?"

Aden pointed to his eye. "I'm afraid such things are a little beyond me right now. I . . ."

Her features saddened, and Aden was instantly embarrassed that the suggestion of his blindness should have made her feel that way. The fact that she had known the secret of his name but not of his wound occurred only to his crippled parts, his wires and semiconductors; they strained against the unaccustomed warmth and peace that they sensed around them.

IX

The garden was attacked four days after Aden had arrived. Gedwyn had left him for the morning to watch, she told him brightly, for the different sorts of peace that she could see traveling along the road. Aden nearly pointed out that he had seen very little peace on the strategic maps at Castle Kent. But he did not want to risk her displeasure, and was not sure he had ever seen such maps in the first place.

Surely, she had the power of transmutation. Aden therefore lay on his back, staring up through the ghost pines and wondering if any of the hawks or pegasuses he saw circling above him could be her. He wondered if it had felt this way seven hundred years ago—before the war came and crushed all but some of us. The war, he had often read, had swept away all the dreams, as all wars had the habit of doing. But Heisner had demonstrated that the way this one was being fought would not only prevent their returning with the peace that might be won, but would destroy them along with their enemy.

Instead, he saw the cruise missiles gliding along the ridge lines, dipping and shifting clumsily with the rough mountain updrafts. There were four of them in a diamond formation, holding tightly to one another so their ECM boxes and radars could protect them from the pegasuses.

They banked to the right and drifted down the slopes toward where he was. Aden got up after a moment. The intrusion of his world registered slowly at first. Then their geometricity cut against his mind and he felt enraged that they had presumed to disturb the peace of Gedwyn.

"Aden." She was at the end of a path, terraced on either side with banks of orchids.

He opened his mouth to warn her, but could not define the peril to her.

The first one struck a kilometer behind her, where the pavilion might have been. The shock wave blew the folds of her dress forward in the direction she was walking; her hair was also lifted like a nimbus, diffusing the following light of the explosion around her face and turning the paleness of her skin to gold.

The two flanking missiles struck down on either side of the path. Their concussions pressed her clothes back against her body, dissolving the violent abstraction that the first had given her.

The inside of his head roared to him, but Aden found the noise remote and hardly noticeable. Aden saw the fireballs thin away as they ballooned outward from their impact points, until they were only veils of yellow white when they reached her.

Small bits of litter, individual leaves on trumpet vines burst into sharp flame, like the one that Gedwyn wore on her right hand. They, like the veils of fire from the three explosions, wrapped themselves around her, as the were-light had around the unicorn and its attendant. Aden marveled at how easily the anamorphosis of this world transformed the structured violence of his own into its serenity. He watched with his single eye, seemingly able to detect the individual molecules that chose to give themselves over to the missile's combustions, and those that remained as they were. The abilities of the Office's eye diminished in comparison to the perceptions of his own, and he briefly wondered if the Office's wires and antennas were listening and watching what he now saw. The fourth missile struck against a waterfall in the grove behind him. His cranial net screeched as the outer currents of its explosion reached him. He was not Gedwyn nor was he made of the garden's magic. More flowers ignited on the ground as he fell toward it, his personal blackness obscuring her, but allowing him to see the look of concern that crossed her features. Aden, in turn, felt ashamed that his death should in any way cause her displeasure.

X

The missiles had been hunting their enemies in dimensions other than those which Aden or Gedwyn or her garden occupied. Aside from some burns on his back and a persistent ringing that hovered about his cranial net, Aden suffered no serious damage.

The star on Gedwyn's hand, however, was gone. She said nothing about it, but he associated its extinguishment with a dark shading to her voice. He found her awake at night beside him, holding her hand up against the night sky, the orbits of the Office's imagined satellites tracing across the sky behind it. His eye could see a thin line of scar tissue running along the finger that the star had been on; its texture was rough, but it reflected the silver of the sky and the glowing cones of the ghost pines with a gentle parody of what had been there. His one eye saw that even her wounds were made of enchantment.

She did not. With the passage of days, the uncertainty that he had discovered in her voice grew deeper. She spoke, instead of his own secrets, of her concern for the safety of the garden.

She was an immortal and had planted the garden during the first, great flowering of magic, before the triumph of rationalism and the discovery of light and empiricism. She and the garden, like many of the creatures of power, had gone into hiding in those centuries that followed.

She had emerged when the alignments of the universes shifted to summon them back. Before the cruise missiles had found the garden, she had held bitterness and unbelief only for the fact that a war had attended their return.

Her references to the first, ancient retreat of magic increased. Aden noticed that she spent less time in the contemplation of her book, and more staring at the road or up to the sky. She fell into the habit of rubbing the scar that the four cruise missiles had inflicted upon her against her lips, perhaps talking to it and asking it where the star had gone.

Aden wondered if the star had been the intended target of the missiles. He asked Gedwyn this once, as they sat on the rim of a fountain, watching butter-colored hollicks building their miniature caves in the boles of ghost pines. She only shrugged in reply and looked again down the meadows to where the road twisted away from them, toward the border.

In contrast to what he perceived of her changing mood, he felt his enchantment for her growing to such an extent that he wondered if she might not be using her powers to do more than simply pry an occasional secret from his mind. But this seemed both unlikely and presumptuous. He was, he constantly reminded himself, but a fraction of her real age and an agent of the nations that had sent the missiles against her.

The second attack came when winter had closed in around all of the mountains but the garden. The snow line reached down to the road and the people on it were dressed in fabulously dyed furs that gave them the appearance of hollicks from the distance of the pavilion.

The garden kept its summer. The water from its streams and fountains ran freely and then froze into crystal glass mounds where it crossed out into the countryside. The tracks of hollicks and chamois led to and from the garden through the surrounding perimeter of snow and ice. The nighttime air had the same clarity and sharpness that he remembered it to have had in his home. But he could lie naked in the garden's evening beside Gedwyn, seeing her hand sweep across the galaxies, and wonder what he might possibly have brought to the garden, aside from the missiles and his own dead circuitries, that could have caused her to let him stay. He had never had the occasion of asking such questions at his home.

No warning this time. The sky simply turned white, as if a light had been turned on in a small room.

The wave fronts reached his cranial net and shouted a warning before the light was fully perceptible. Still, he almost opened his eye, as if he thought he could see what was happening and tell Gedwyn that a fusion bomb had been set off at the top of the atmosphere, and that by the time he had finished telling this one thing to her the snow would have been melted from the valley and the travelers on the road for a hundred kilometers would be charred husks within their furs.

But she placed her hand over his eye, protecting it, he imagined, with the finger and its scar; he thought there was a sense to this, the wounds of his own world protecting them both from later, more terrible ones.

He felt warmth beating against his body, casting web-patterns of shadow along the shallow ridges of buried wires, revealing the few trivial secrets that he had managed to keep from Gedwyn. This lasted for a minute, and then ended.

She took her hand away. There was a lavender blur of light centered in his field of vision, but that was all. The garden was intact; the hollicks picked up their quiet night conversations with the nesting rocs and pegasuses.

"That was ours," he said unnecessarily; the wizards' combat had never been so quick or monochromatic.

"Do you know what it was?"

He told her, and then: "But, like the missiles, it doesn't seem to have been meant for us. Not even a near miss this time." Aden stretched himself on the summer grass, feeling its contrast to the sharpness of the stars.

Gedwyn sat up and then rose to her feet; like someone whom intruders had wakened from a half-sleep. "That was the garden, I'm afraid"—addressed as much to the hollicks as to Aden. The animal sounds fell and then stopped.

She put on a cloak and padded carefully away from him. Aden got to his feet and followed, again embarrassed at the clumsy barbarities of his world and at his own uneasiness with being left alone in the quiet.

Low flower beds opened onto the meadows, now clear of snow. The length of the road seemed to be on fire and its thin guttering line was suspended in a featureless, smoking dark. The quiet of the world outside the garden was absolute, and Aden's cranial net reminded him of the "dead rooms" the regular services kept at Lake Gilbert, where every sound and echo was absorbed by fiber cones and the men who were being tested in them were suspended in chicken wire cages in their centers.

Gedwyn drew her breath in sharply, and continued like that, as if she were breathing through a gag of coarse fabric. She held her left hand out before her; the scar on her finger picked up the light of the burning road as it had the winter stars. Aden could sense her trembling. He wanted desperately to comfort her, but he felt all her endless centuries of grace and power beside him, facing his blind eye socket, visible only in two dimensions, and that only if he turned his face away from the valley.

The road kept burning. In areas that he thought might have been those she was pointing at, the fire seemed to flatten out and verge toward cooler, more metallic colors. But it flared back to its original intensity as soon as she moved.

He thought that he could hear snatches of foreign languages between her sharp inhalations. For the first time in months he was reminded of the nighttime streets of the Holy City and the pathetically majestic battles that were always being fought over them.

Gedwyn stepped away from him, seating herself on the pavilion's throne and continuing her mumblings and gestures. Shoals of winter air drifted past his skin. Processional instabilities could be felt at the edges of the garden's interface with the new, burning winter that his world had brought.

It, they had "known" of this part of the world, Aden slowly realized, his heart shriveling with sickness and shame. Information that had not been available before had become known; they had deciphered it and explained it to the bombs they sent out. This one had understood, more completely than the fighters on the river, or the artillery shells or the cruise missiles.

He wished for the eye. Gedwyn's mystery was enough, so long as it was her own; now the bomb had posed one that surrounded it. While it could not touch her, it destroyed everything that surrounded her wonder, isolated it and left it spinning in its own dark patch of existence. Its knowledge placed Gedwyn into a crushingly reduced perspective, and, with it, Aden's feelings for her.

He had last felt this exposed when he had fled the Holy City; after that the road had hidden him from everyone but the two men. Now he stepped away from Gedwyn, conceiving against his will that whatever he felt for her had been treacherously lured out from behind the Office's defenses. The two men did not need to watch him any more for his presence would be easily perceptible to any magician who cared to look, even if Gedwyn did not.

The bomb had seen him, the satellites must have, the side-looking radars of the planes that constantly traced the borders between science and magic had seen. He was part of their war again. Gedwyn's withdrawal, if such it was, meant nothing. She was still tied in all her beauty and gentleness to the war, as much as the eye and the cruise missiles were.

Aden felt his nakedness and how the burning winter dark brushed against it. He turned and walked into the garden. Gedwyn was still standing in the pavilion, moving her hands in disconnected arcs. Aden wondered whether she was trying to reassert the authority of magic over the valley, or simply trying to keep the garden's summer intact.

Aden walked toward the center of the garden, seeking whatever warmth magic's laws of thermodynamics had concentrated there. He became aware that he was being propelled as much by his own confusions as by any desire for immediate safety or revulsion with the bomb's casual incineration of the valley.

The war was back inside of him. Unconfirmable lines of force tying the bomb's spent power to that of Gedwyn, and Gedwyn to Donchak and the Holy City, and Aden to all of them proposed themselves. The wires inside his skull stayed silent, but their matrices provided convenient frameworks for his speculations to attach themselves to and replicate.

Heisner's mythologized fear stood beside his shame, both watching his mind begin to shake itself apart. Gedwyn was becoming lost in her own bewilderment and in the brutal shroud of perception that the remembrance of the war infected Aden with.

He was running. His clothes were piled under some laurel trees, a hundred meters from the pavilion. Aden scooped them up and pulled them on clumsily, without losing much speed except when he got his boots on and laced. More hypotheses came to him, unbidden. The possibility that what he felt for Gedwyn was love was more disturbing than if she had simply enchanted him as she so obviously could; the spells would be her own and, like her other mysteries, unknown to him. But Heisner had dissected love and found only two pages of calculations. Aden was no mathematician, but imagined scraps of equations intruded into his mind, coolly chipping away at Gedwyn's image, invalidating and falsifying what he felt for her.

All the fragile, humanly scaled relationships that he had discovered since leaving the Holy City frayed and came apart. The forces and threats that they had held in equipoise strained abruptly at the limitations that they imposed; they spun wildly at the ends of the tethers of Gedwyn's beauty, the garden, the gentle chaos of the road and of Clairendon.

Against this and his own self-disgust, the overpowering logic and perception of the bomb was comforting. It, in contrast to everything he had touched since he had reached the Holy City, met Donchak and yielded up his eye, was made of immovable things. It had spoken in a single voice whose one meaning carried across every part of the parallel spectrums that it chose to address.

The valley's winter instantly stripped away the artificial warmth of the garden. He fell on the ice that edged it and hit solidly on his right side. His hands skidded across the rough surfaces as he levered himself up and plunged into the snow. That also was only a border. The ground beyond it was still warm from the bomb.

He continued running downhill. The cold air stank of burning flesh and all the cargoes that had been traveling the road twenty minutes before. His feet moved erratically in the mud. The guttering line of the road grew before him, deadening his night vision so that, even when he did look back, he could not see where the pavilion was. He ran along its edge, an uninterrupted tangle of intertwined caravans, wagons, corpses, blurring into long smears of color on his left. Eventually he was able to generate enough pain so that he did not think about Gedwyn or try to decide whether the dreams to which she was so irrevocably tied were worth that much sorrow, or, if they were, whether it was because he had nearly made them his own.

XI

The bomb's summer deceived the flowers and trees that the magicians had scattered along the length of the road, triggering profusions of stunted blossoms that contrasted uneasily with the black and brown wreckage.

That lasted for five days. Then the bomb's presence faded and the valley's winter came back in a single night, freezing all their colors and snapping off new stems like glass. Aden emerged from the blasted caravan in which he had spent the night and saw the borders of the road marked by trees that were half in bloom and half in winter, like cheap china figurines. The wind was enough to break them, and all day, as he walked, he heard this sound like a fire, inhabiting the frozen mud and tangled corpses.

The weather did, however, reduce the smell.

The road ended ten days after he left the garden at a walled city whose minarets were all jagged, broken stumps. From there, other roads led back to the east, or to the south or north, but they all curved away from the west, where the alpine plain sloped downward toward a pink-and-salmon-colored wilderness.

Aden searched through the city for a day and concluded only that it had been deserted for some time. There was fresh water and he managed to trap a roebuck who had broken a leg trying to escape from a complex of empty alchemic laboratories.

The altitude dropped quickly. The patches of frostbite on his feet and hands healed and scarred over as the weather improved. The country, also, became scarred and barren. It was crisscrossed with rills and dry riverbeds that slowed his progress. But the land protected him from thinking of Gedwyn; its clean brutality drew lines of distance and memory between her and his mind.

The comings and goings of aircraft increased. Their contrails served the same function as the riverbeds, drawing lines all around the world, quantifying it according to their inflexible wisdom. Gedwyn became lost inside of their limitations. She was again the enemy sorceress and he, again, the escaping spy.

The first evidence of his own world was a mound of slagged and rusted metal. Sections of gears and I beams protruded from it. Aden could not guess what it had been. Aden guessed it to have been left over from the very first engagements that magic had fought with science. From here, the wreckage should get progressively more recent, like the geologic ages of the fossils pressed into the stratified sandstone cliffs that he passed under.

Instead, one hundred meters from the wreck, Aden found a sentry tripod. It consisted of three braced legs, a central column which housed its perceptors and a laser ring; two blue and orange beacons were stacked on top. The whole mechanism was made out of machined stainless steel.

The sand had blown up around the base plates on its legs so it must have been there for some time. Magic had not moved against the tripod but allowed it to stay and watch, serving as a base point for the triangulations drawn by the surveillance planes and cruise missiles.

XII

The man was dressed in a khaki walking suit with a wide-brimmed hat against the world's sun. He was sitting on a shooting stick and looked quite at ease, despite the two wrecked bombers on the lake bed behind him. "They've been like that for about eight years now. Experimental stores, you know. Pity they hadn't been dropped on our friends over there." He got up and pointed at the hulks with his stick. "Havinga." The man went up to Aden and shook his hand; his skin was rough and cool and tanned a shade darker than his clothes.

"Are you from Dance?" It was the first Border fortress that came to mind; his lips were cracked and it hurt to talk.

"Only the Office. We've seen you coming for some time. We, ah, picked up a trace when you left the eye and Donchak turned you in, and then later . . ."

"Donchak?" Aden found the man's memory distant enough to question who he had been.

"Ah, yes. Really nothing we could do about that. You were just too far in and the only thing we still had planted on the old fellow were perceptors in that eye. I don't think he has any idea he's still a little wired to us." Havinga had a large, open face and the sort of coarse features that a tan looked good on. Aden liked the man immediately, despite what he was telling him. Donchak was another age and place. His profession had been treason and betrayal and he could not find any reason to reproach him for it. "Of course we got a clear fix on you in that garden, but the Border Command had other ideas by then. I really can't tell you how sorry we are about that." The Office knew of Gedwyn, as it had of Donchak, and he quickly changed the subject. "But, you know, the war's been going rather well lately—that eye of yours has helped us enormously—and it may be that we're finally getting ourselves out of a job. Have to recall even old Donchak and pension him off."

Aden felt himself suppressing laughter at the absurdity of the conversation. Havinga must have seen this, for he smiled more broadly and clapped him on the back. Aden almost collapsed but kept on chuckling, louder and louder. "My eye?"

"You can't believe how friendly the Border people have been to us since we let them have some of it. But don't worry, only enough to let them win their war, nothing much else."

Enough to find the garden and the valley? Aden was laughing too hard to ask.

"Certainly wish we could plant one of those eyes on the appropriation committee at Castle Kent, though."

Havinga took him by the elbow and led him away from the burning airplanes, toward an open car parked beside a grove of blood-colored thorn trees. The dry lake bed dropped away behind it to the horizon, where Aden thought he could make out green hills, topped with the magic whiteness of his world's Border fortresses.

XIII

Etridge was nearly old, and he thought: They are dying. The scopes and visual readout arrays in front of him reflected the idea on three-dimensional graphs. Above him, the aerials interrogated the mages' world. At regular intervals, silence engulfed the world and they listened to it in bunkers a hundred meters below the nickel-steel roofs. Then the active ranging units would cut in and their energies blasted across the land, probing at the shrinking frontiers of magic, raining down tropospheric and stratospheric scatterings, or battering horizontally against them, streaming through the passes and valleys of the Cameron Hills.

For months the reflected energies had shown them less and less. The static and carrier waves had come back to Joust Mountain unmarked for twenty-one consecutive days. The recordings were restudied and reanalyzed, because the traces were undoubtedly there; the skies above the sacred cities had to be glowing, the secrets of the wizards could not have been completely unraveled.

After seven hundred years there was quiet. The people at Joust Mountain, and at the other Border fortresses of Dance, Whitebreak and First Valley hypothesized progressively more subtle stratagems and deceits of the vanished enemy. Perhaps, instead of leaving, the enemy had only set them back to where they had started through one stupendous feat of magic, so enormous and pervasive as to have its limits drawn beyond the range of their instruments. Perhaps, then, all the green-and-yellow-bound notebooks of computer and special group analysis were now invalid, the universe upon which they were premised and toward whose understanding they had pointed discarded and irrelevant to the future centuries of the war.

Because of this and his age, Etridge also felt anger and frustration. They could not be permitted so easy and conclusive a victory; they chose this universe as their battleground and they had no *right* to move to another. Neither could they die, he raged inside his tightly locked heart; we have worked too hard to understand everything about them.

"Well, where are they? Where?" He was aware of how clearly his irritation showed.

"That, I should think, is your job." The man from Lake Gilbert was the same age as Etridge, but since he had not spent his years at places like Joust Mountain, his voice contained only bewilderment and a shading of relief. The enemy had vanished. That was enough. If it continued that way for a thousand more years without a single new fact being uncovered about them, he would be satisfied.

"Are you sure the regular services haven't taken any offensive actions—commando raids, plagues, new sorts of bombs, missiles, anything we might not know about that might have thrown a scare into them?"

"Your rating is higher than mine. The services have left that part of the war to the Border Command. We only move against the enemy when he appears inside our lines. And then we always give you people a chance to look them over before we try to cancel them."

Eighty-three thousand people had died under the mages' basilisks or been turned into blocks of fire, while reconnaissance drones instead of attack ships overflew the slaughter at Thorn River. Etridge had helped supervise that observation. He had watched his scopes as he did now, and seen the thousands of deaths individually translated into quanta of light, energy, plasma, and magnetic disassociations. He remained convinced of the correctness of what he had ordered there and was bitterly defensive at any hint of its being questioned.

"If there had been anything like that, you would have known."

Etridge was glaring at him, pale olive eyes clear for his age, focused on a point within the other's skull. The man from Lake Gilbert self-consciously edged away; he felt as uncomfortable with Etridge as he did with everything else at Joust Mountain. He told himself that this was wrong. Etridge had often proved himself a fine and courageous man, and the fortress itself had been the place of his world's first blind victory against the men of power. The lake that had separated it from the Cameron Hills had been destroyed in that battle, drained and evaporated by the forces that had contended above its surface. Its bed was a featureless plain, seeded with the wreckages of hovercraft and dragons. After five hundred years fragments of the dragons' animating power remained, turning their skeletons from ivory to obsidian to shell, twitching and shifting, gradually working themselves down into the dust.

Etridge had ordered a study of their disintegration as contrasted to that of the aircraft and tank hulls. They found the decay was more orderly in the latter case; the steel and aluminum proceeded through various forms of oxidation, or else their radioactive fuels decayed through their half-lives, pacing through the periodic table with planetary certainty, their paths described by straight and predictable paths that always ended in known, stable elements.

The variables which controlled the dragons' rot took much longer to understand. Before that had been achieved, Etridge liked to think that the servants of each culture retained their masters' perspectives of the universe after death. The decay of machines was mechanical; the decay of the dragons was, like their life, pure mystery. But in the act of discovering the mechanisms of the dragons, he came to believe that he had converted them to his conception of the world, that he had reached across the lines to grasp their peculiar and individual deaths and summarize each one in the notebooks held prisoner in the fortress. Ultimately, he discovered an allegiance of their deaths to the life of his world.

He could do this because Joust Mountain was also where the first inquisitory antennas and computer banks had been installed, one hundred and ten years before Heisner's suicide. As the world's mania for understanding deepened, it became surrounded by whirling dish antennas, and the walls and revetments protecting its guns were buried under latticed towers.

It covered a ridge five kilometers long. To the east the grass and cottonwood trees grew up against its walls. On the eastern side, where the land sloped down to where the lake had been, all obstructions had been removed to provide open fields of fire. This land was charred and crystallized into rough glass where the antennas' energies had burned and ended every living thing in front of them.

The use of such high energy levels was unavoidable. It was often the only way the enemy's secrets could be penetrated. On evenings when the passive aerials were shut down and the active ranging systems monopolized the parallel spectrums, the sky over Joust Mountain flared as it did over the Holy City when the men of power were sharpening their skills.

Now, at Etridge's recommendation, all of Joust Mountain's facilities were on line. Passive and active systems operated together by occupying alternating sections of each spectrum.

Etridge stalked along the oddly formal terraces where the turrets of siege guns had been replaced by side-looking radars. The man from Lake Gilbert, several inches shorter and more adequately fleshed, walked behind him, then dropping back and nearly becoming lost in crowds of uniformed fanatics clutching the colored notebooks that seemed to be the fortress' main currency.

The facing walls on their left were blank and slanted upward to shoulder away the concussion blasts that the magicians had never thought to use. The ceramic armor had been perfect when it had been installed, four hundred and fifty years ago, and aside from a light brown defining the seams between the plates, it remained untouched for all the thousands of meters of the eastern galleries. Except where someone had managed to scribe the words "reductio ad imperium," in careful script. The words would not have been noticeable to the man from Lake Gilbert except for the same tan discoloration, an indication of the motto's age.

"Where?"

"I said, there have been no offensive actions of any sort."

"Then they've gone. Do your people have any theories?"

"The continuum is infini . . ."

"Goddamn it is."

"Infinite, and the possibility always exists that they have opened up new areas of it." The man shrugged. "First there was one spectrum, then the parallels were discovered. Possibly there are divergent areas of existence."

"There hasn't been any action on their part for years. No appearances, no creatures of light in the streets, nothing freezing the air inside jet engines." The man from Lake Gilbert realized Etridge was hardly aware of his presence. "I wonder if we've acquired something like a critical mass of understanding. Nothing sudden, but just gradual accretions, year after year. Half the old magazines here are filled with reference books and tape summaries, all piled up, cross-indexed, cross-referenced, constantly revised and brought up to date by newer findings. Our computers talk to at least a dozen other Border installations on a regular basis. They can tap into nearly every unit of any consequence in the world if they feel they're running into a particular problem. Could be. Just enough."

"But our knowledge alone could hardly make them vanish. Retreat and re-entrench maybe, but not just vanish." The man wished he was back at Lake Gilbert, walking with his morning coffee along its quiet hallways, confronted by nothing more disturbing than the portrait busts of dead heroes.

"They listen to us, you know," Etridge mentioned offhandedly. "Not in the way we examine them, disassemble them, and do the same to the pieces that are left.

They just listen now and then in their own ways." The contempt and condescension in Etridge's voice was unmistakable; the man from Lake Gilbert thought it inappropriate. "We only began to understand how they did it about eight or nine years ago. They use a number of means, but the non-corporeal ones all operate on the same final principles. Of course, there was no real reason to interdict them." The man from Lake Gilbert paled at this. "Joust Mountain isn't an offensive base, just a forward observation post that happens to be impregnable. All their listening and watching could tell them about was themselves." Etridge began smiling to the east. "Joust Mountain: the Wizards' Mirror. We just kept at them, about how they did what they were doing."

"That can't be what happened. You seem to be speaking entirely in metaphors, not hard facts."

"Metaphor was the only way we could talk about the magicians' world until the strategic shift from offense to understanding. There was no common reference or standard in their actions. Now, maybe, we've offered them one."

"And if they've taken it?"

"Then they've done one of three things. They have become like us. They have found another place and time which can better protect their goddamned mysteries, or they have turned their last mysteries on themselves and died." Etridge was grinning broadly now; the prices other people had paid at Thorn River and at scores of other places might have been worth something after all. We've pushed them to the edge, he thought, shown them the short end of the pier and the fools walked off it rather than admit it ended.

"We know it's not the first, because if they became like us they'd be tossing atomics at us before we caught on and did the same to them. I also imagine they'd be pissed as hell at us for having broken up their little game."

Little game. The man from Lake Gilbert shuddered to himself. Seven hundred years of the little game where millions had been ground to pulp between two opposing forces that could not understand each other well enough to carry on the well-ordered killing of normal wars. Seven hundred years of the little game where men marveled speechlessly at the non-exclusivity of their world and the thought that other gods might stand against their own.

He must report this man to Lake Gilbert, or to the government at Castle Kent. Etridge was proposing a single, unthinkable triumph. If what he was saying was true, he should not be in a position of responsibility, not at such a critical strategic and historical juncture. The victory he hinted at smelled of Heisner's achievement.

If only there were more armed people here. He was a soldier and did not like the paradox of a frontline post like Joust Mountain being staffed with people who clung to computer readouts more passionately than the regiments at Lake Gilbert did to their automatic weapons. But then, it seemed that the people at Joust Mountain did everything more passionately than those at Lake Gilbert, Everwhen, The Corridor, Castle Kent, or in any of the cities of the world. The guns there implied respectful fear and caution; one had to be ready because one did not *know*. Know what the enemy was thinking, know how he performed his feats of wondrous violence, know when and where he might leave his preposterous castles and strike against them.

Here, they were blinded by looking into the night, against whose visitation Lake Gilbert and its divisions waited.

The man must be reported. This is not the way the services should protect their world.

"It could be that we've shown the bastards the edge," Etridge repeated. "A few more weeks, a month or two at the most, and we may have to go and look around for ourselves."

"I'll pass your evaluation of the situation along to Lake Gilbert."

XIV

The doctor, who was a machine, found Aden sitting in a wicker lounge chair. Graceful oaks and maples framed the hospital behind him. It had been the home of an immensely wealthy family before the war, and the Special Office had taken great care to preserve its Georgian tranquility. It was free of the baroque pretensions of the magic's architecture; neither did it have the sullen massiveness that their own world had necessarily adopted in the times when the enemy might appear anywhere. The Special Office had found that it greatly comforted its people.

At the far end of the lawn, where the dogwood groves started, the doctor could see the long knitting needle barrel of a Bofors gun weaving back and forth across the sky, waiting as it had for decades for the enemy, not even sure if its ammunition could harm the particular avatar he might choose. Its splayed base was overgrown with ivy that the groundskeepers had trimmed and weeded; the paint had been polished off its controls so it looked like one of the ceremonial guns that were fired to celebrate Republic Day at Castle Kent.

The Special Office thought that people were more at ease with machines that looked like machines, rather than like people. Thus the doctor, while manlike in his general form, had no face. His oval skull was brushed aluminum and it reflected the sunlight in frequencies which the Office had discovered to be comforting to its people.

The doctor walked over to Aden and introduced himself. The man looked rather older than his service record listed him to be, but that was to be expected. He sat down in another chair, slouching easily on his spring steel spine, and folded his hands in front of him.

"We think you'll be well enough to leave us in a month or two." The voice, like the reflective abilities of the doctor's skin, reassured Aden. "I must say, though, that not many of us thought you'd come along so well when they brought you in."

Aden smiled to the doctor and nodded. The device was easier to talk to than an actual person at this moment. "Yes. I lost track of things . . . How long was I . . . ?"

"Less than six months after you emplaced the eye."

Aden was embarrassed by his vagueness. "So short?"

The doctor had no face but Aden had the impression that he was smiling. "Not really. You've been here for almost four more. And all of them have been rather important months, what with the war winding down and all." The doctor stretched his polished arms and looked around himself. The hospital was a beautiful place and he liked it more than any other he had been assigned to.

"I know. Donchak said that was happening in the City, and, ah . . . "

"Havinga," the doctor put in helpfully.

"Yes. He said the same thing. I wonder what it will be like, not having the war around."

"They're practicing for our new world in some of the southern districts and in the Taritan Valley. Getting wonderfully eccentric and irrelevant. Some jewelry making, art, quite a bit of music playing, storytelling and people back in bright colors. The reports are really a delight to read."

"The government's not afraid they're being subverted by magic?"

The doctor inclined his featureless head in a way that indicated amusement to Aden. "Not at all. The Border Command, of course, has its usual dark opinion of the matter, but the people at Castle Kent just feel that they're turning away from understanding and Dr. Heisner's numbers, not towards magic."

"Then it might be over."

The doctor nearly said that, yes, they'd won, but he knew the kind of victory Aden felt it would have to be. "It might." The gun was still emplaced at the bottom of the lawn and the communication aerials were still strung between the hospital's ancient chimney pots; but it might be over.

"Will we be going back if it is?"

"Not immediately. No, not for some time. Those people in the Taritan, I think, are going to set the style for the moment. People will just want to rest and get all this damned purity of oppositions out of their systems. We don't all want to end up like old Heisner, even if the Border Command thinks we should."

"And the other half of the world?"

"We'll just let it heal for a while, I suspect."

Aden looked into the soft penumbra of the doctor's face. "Heal?" he whispered, but did not know why he found the word so disturbing.

The doctor knew and he ached for the young man. "Yes. We've been hurting each other for so long. We need the time as much as the land over there will for the enchantments to die down."

"Will she be there?"

"She?"

The word came into his mind slowly and for a second he continued to look at the doctor without saying anything. "Gedwyn"—he was not sure he pronounced it right. "What about her magic? Will that be gone too?"

"The magic of her garden will go. That's where we first picked you up. You really had us concerned after you left the eye . . . "

"Then it was magic, all of it."

"Not what held you. That was, ah, love. That's why we really weren't too concerned with you and it was relatively easy to stop any treason charges from being brought by the services. They understand those things at Castle Kent more than they used to." The doctor forced himself into postures and tones of reassurance. His work with Aden had come along so beautifully, and he felt some of it eroding.

"But that is just magic too. Heisner explained that, didn't he?" Aden's voice was shaking.

"You are not a very strong man, Aden." The doctor felt it necessary to release the pressure. "Brave and honorable, but not strong."

"No. I guess not," Aden said softer than dust. The charred ribbon of the road recoiled against his heart, winding all the way from Clairendon to the sentry tripod, bringing with it the first clear memory of Gedwyn he had had since he was brought to the hospital. He wrapped his arms around his chest despite the warmth of the air.

"But, you must see, Aden, that the Office never wanted strong men. The Border Command takes all it can get and the regular services only want enough to get by. But we, you and I, cannot afford such strength. We work with too many fragile things that break so easily. But we have to use them. That's been our job through these centuries."

"Who sent the bomb?"

"The device was due to be sent in anyway from First Valley. The Office just modified it a bit so that you and she would not be hurt."

"This is not hurt?"

"It's minor compared to what you both would have felt had you stayed any longer. The lives on the road were going to be lost no matter what we did. We only changed so much of it so that two of them could be prolonged a bit more." The doctor sensed Aden's acceptance of what he was saying. "Your Office continued to watch after you and after its own enemy. We only covered your treason with one of our own."

"And I could not have seen any of that by myself, without the eye?"

"You were half blind, you know. We had to provide you with enough light to get you moving again."

"I still am half blind." He touched the bandages covering his left socket.

"Yes."

"Could I have another?"

"A normal . . . ?"

"No. Like the first one the Office gave me."

There was some uneasiness in the doctor's voice, but with no facial expression to match it with Aden could not be sure. "But you know that one was a one-off project. Incredibly complex and expensive. You know it would just lead you back to where you started, back on Heisner's track. Magic is gone or at least withering. Without its mysteries to look at, you'd turn in on your own life and world.

"Anyway, the, ah, Office is being shut down. Funding has always been difficult. And now that the war is winding down, the services cannot see the need for us. Centralization, that's what they say is necessary. Things that will look at the enemy, or what's left of him, from the outside, that won't have to go there and risk getting caught when their outrage shows, or just, ah, succumbing to the appeals of that place." The machine felt embarrassed again.

Aden had not noticed; instead, he was struck by the thought that the technique of external observation and contact was just what the robot was practicing on him, as if the Office itself was distrustful and afraid of its own people and sought to deal with them from a distance.

"I just want to know why, why all or *any* part of this happened. May still be happening."

"This?"

"The war, the love, the road, Thorn River," Aden suggested for he was not entirely sure himself.

"The eye would not tell you why, only how."

"Didn't it tell the Office why?"

The doctor shifted in his chair again. His smooth oval face remained toward Aden, perceiving him in all medically and psychologically useful spectrums, vaguely comical in its pretensions at humanity. "I don't know." The voice seemed to come from somewhere else, so abrupt was the change in its tone; it was harsh and disjointed, as if it had been synthesized on the spot.

"Is that why the Office is closing?" Aden asked.

"I wouldn't know about that. Even the rumors"—the voice becoming more conspiratorial—"hardly include the eye or what it showed us. Only that it's gone blind lately." The doctor threw his outspread fingers up and away from his hand, attesting to the frailty of mere machines. "Nothing seen from it for months. Just interference patterns and static."

Aden nodded in agreement. Logically, there could be no great identity between the eye and the Office or the war. No matter how important the information received from it could have been, the eye was only a small part of each. But it had been so great a part of him; the memories of its omniscience grew, it seemed, to fill up the emptiness that he now perceived to have been left by Gedwyn.

"But it is still there, in the creature?"

"The unicorn?" The doctor replied ingenuously, "Oh, yes. At least before the carrier waves went dead. We could be fairly sure of that."

Aden thanked him and did not think at all about why a doctor should know such things.

XV

They thanked him for his years when he left the hospital, gave him some money (apologizing that there was not more), new clothes and a service weapon.

He was empty. His left eye remained empty, covered by a leather patch; his body was still heavily woven with dead wires, empty couplings, disconnected links, empty vacuum chambers, power leads branching from his nervous system into cavities that had held the various mechanisms of the Office.

The Office and its war had been taken from him, and he could find nothing in his world to replace them. There had been the short memory of Gedwyn, but he had requested the doctors to blur this, for her remembrance had been very painful.

He therefore continued to dwell upon the Office and the war, as he had done for all the preceding years. True, the Office's war had not offered one much of the terror and exhilaration that it had provided for other people on either side. As soon as action broke out in any area, the Office always withdrew its personnel to quieter places. The battlegrounds were the conceded laboratories of the services. The Special Office preferred to watch its enemy and its powers in repose.

It had been a comparatively gentle sort of espionage, carried out by people who lived most easily in paradox, contradiction and indirection. It was predictable that the Office should have become faintly alien even to itself.

Politicians had regularly questioned which side the Special Office had really been on. The Office, not officially existing, naturally declined to respond to their accusations.

But information had been obtained, and had found its way into the computer pools of Aden's world. Most of the Office's strange, abstracted evaluations wilted under the fanatic empiricism of the services. But enough had proved valuable enough to keep the Office alive for centuries.

Indeed, as Havinga had said, one of the minor breakthroughs of the past decade had been Aden's emplacement of the eye with the unicorn. The monthly block transmissions, five-second bursts of accumulated information and observation, had for a few months provided the services with the first hints as to how the internecine battles of the men of power were fought.

But like most of the information provided by the Office, it smelled too strongly of the other world. Even before the Office was formally closed, the services and the Border Command had stopped listening to it. They had made what was judged adequate studies of the Holy City's internal politics, and reduced those studies to green-bound notebooks filled with Llwyellan Functions.

That had apparently been enough for them. Aden wondered why it had not been enough for him.

He was too old or too young to be doing this. He had not been ordered. All his commanders had been scattered, perhaps like himself, and he had known only a few of his fellow agents.

Get there, he thought. Get there and find out why he had come and then why he had left. At first he was preoccupied with just taking another step or another breath in the high country air, but that lessened in the month since he had left the fortress at Dance. He was following approximately the same route he had taken when he had left the City. The diminishing power of the war had only slightly changed the geography.

The alpine valley was about five kilometers across with a stream traced along its northwestern edge. Sharp granite walls rose two or three hundred meters on either side, featherings of melting snow running from the ridgeline at intervals. The grass and wildflowers seemed particularly brilliant, but that might have been due as much to the clarity of the air as to the plants themselves.

His remaining eye was sharp. Although he had not fully compensated for the loss of depth perception, he could easily pick out mountain sheep grazing along fracture lines in the valley walls, a kilometer or more distant. They fed on patches of grass and scrub plants that surrounded the ruins of hermits' pavilions.

The powers of this world, like those of Aden's, had not been uniformly devoted to the prosecution of the war or in ostensible practice for it. Aden had always found some comfort and interest in the renegade mystics that were attracted to the interface between the enemy worlds. Of necessity, they avoided areas of frequent activity like Joust Mountain or the Holy City, but gravitated to areas like this. He had sometimes thought he would have liked to have done so himself, assuming a new name and holding himself out as a teacher of worldly science or a traitorous magician depending on which side a passing visitor might be fleeing from.

His feelings, he thought, must be like that the robot doctor had toward the new societies in the Taritan Valley: vague envy at the stability they had apparently found and frustration at his inability to come up with a good reason for not joining them.

He had been walking for some time before he realized that the wildflowers and long meadow grass were giving way to a neatly trimmed avenue. The wind did not touch the individual blades of this new grass, nor did it move the brittle china blossoms of rosebushes, chrysanthemums and ground orchids. The stream beds, too, became sculptured as they moved across the valley floor.

Aden slowed. He touched the gun in its shoulder holster for assurance. The pavilions he had come upon before had all been in disarray and ruin. The bodies of their occupants were bone or ash; whether they had fled from his own world or that of magic, they had apparently received a common message or come to a single conclusion. And they had left.

They had also been crazy in the first place. One could never expect too much of them and the Special Office had regarded the information they freely gave to its agents with great caution.

The northern slopes of the valley became a recognizable garden, perfect, immobile, rigidly held by a power Aden recognized as non-rational. Luxuriant creepers with lavender and white blossoms were frozen against carved rock outcroppings, hiding terribly suggestive shapes with wings and talons and crowns of fire. Small rodents were similarly paralyzed between dust-muted flower beds. The skeletons of birds were trapped in the seasonless growth. He could feel the brittle grass snapping under his boots and shattering like glass.

The pavilion was largely open, being little more than an intricate lattice of arches, columns and curling gables, and there was a magician seated on a flower-choked throne near its center.

It looked too fragile to have withstood the mountain weather, but Aden guessed that the structure and the garden around it had been sturdy enough to have stopped time, and, therefore, rain and wind should have been minor concerns.

He was satisfied with his lack of open fear. Logically, he should have stopped when he first saw the grass standing against the wind, drawn the gun, fitted the sight and let the Office's circuitries decipher their meaning. But the Office, unlike the services, had never depended totally on machines nor abdicated to their way of thinking. He told himself that he had recalled his old training, dredged it out from under his ruined heart and protective surgeries, and evaluated the situation correctly. Time was stopped here; one who was moving through time and therefore dying could be trapped only if he stopped too. That must have been what happened to the birds.

The beauty of the pavilion slowed him and invited his senses into its confusing tracery. The magician inside of it was magnificently clothed, seemingly in orchid blossoms, beaten flat, and overlaid on heavy gold foil. A book which he knew would be poetry, although he had never learned more than a few of the hundreds of script languages the wizards had written in, was open on his lap. The eyes were closed, yet the shadowing around them hinted powerfully at awareness. As he tried to steer to the right of the pavilion, he also noticed that its shadow contradicted the position of the sun; they were held in place by the magician's spell as absolutely as the lives of the flowers and the meadow creatures.

The immortality of the garden was that of a single moment. The magician had chosen one instant, when the relationships of all the things around him, from the line he was reading to, possibly, the specific quanta of light that was falling upon him from remote galaxies, conformed to some scheme or balance which he judged to be perfect.

It was not precisely a suicide. The uniqueness and unity of its conception slowed Aden further. He wondered where the boundary layer of the spell might be, how many angstroms above the captive flowers it hovered. The gun could understand all of it; but he found that he could not reach for it; he could only feel the anger of its mechanisms against his chest between the lengthening interval of his heartbeat.

Aden knew what was happening and part of him cursed with the gun at his stupidity and vulnerability. If he had had the eye, he would have understood all of this; the magical beauty would have been quantified and he could have protected himself against it. But it was not so completely terrible. It was like all the enchantments he had known in this world, though only those cast by the vaguely remembered love had touched him so closely.

The association eroded the surgeries and in an instant he grasped her name. Panic spread through him with

the same, measured rate as had the realization of what
was happening to him. He strained his eye back to the
pavilion and searched through the thick, dawn shadows
that covered the magician's face. Despite the hour she
had apparently chosen to capture, she looked much older
than he remembered. That, the doctor had mentioned
to him once in a different context, was how it almost
always was.

He remembered what the Office's hospital had tried
to protect him from, and in the remembering slowed
even more, half wishing to pass into the spell. But he
could not do that. The birds had been trapped in it, but
had not been chosen by Gedwyn to be part of it. So it
and she held them there, transfixed by her beauty to die
of exposure and thirst and starvation.

Aden felt his heart closing in around itself. He continued to look, and although the thickness of her robes
completely disguised her body, he began tracing its contours, remembering its extraordinary softness and
warmth, even in the artificial summer of the garden. He
remembered, for the first time, how little they had spoken; but that only allowed him to believe that he could
remember each of her words and the time and place she
had said them. He found his body more densely inhabited by her than by the scars of the war or by the wire
nets and antennas of the Office, and wished with frightful
intensity that he would slip completely into the spell.

The sound of the approaching ship cut cleanly
between him and Gedwyn; then it reached inside of him
too, and separated him from her memory.

He was far enough to the side of the pavilion to see
the approaching ship without moving his head. It was

flying approximately level with the ridgeline, weaving slightly from side to side to give its cameras a better look at the terrain.

Twin-engined, propeller-driven, cautiously made of wood, though the men of power would have never condescended to look for magnetic anomalies in their routine observations; only Aden's world would have searched for intruders in such a way. Its sound deepened against the quiet of the garden and he could hear the rush of air over its wings. It traveled with a graceful deliberation that was separately visible as it diagramed its own passage through the valley; there was its awareness of itself, that included the minor ionizations and subatomic reactions triggered by its presence and by the pressures and vacuums its motion induced.

Aden felt himself moving to face it, rotating on one knee so that it seemed he might be kneeling, as he had in the temple before the unicorn. He felt the garden's power eroding in proportion to the aircraft's approach. He imagined he could feel the wide-bank cameras perceiving him, separating his being from the timelessness of the garden and only incidentally from himself.

The cold, camouflaged image of the ship, motion, and wisping oil smoke from its port engine filled his eye. Without depth perception, it came upon him suddenly, as if it moved freely through a space of its own creation; beside this idea Gedwyn's feat of stopping a single instant paled and shrank.

He saw where it had been patched from the wizards striking at it during other nights, where fins had been added or removed to perfect its movement through the air, saw the blankness of its radiation-proofed windscreen and ball turret dome.

It was a Special Office ship. It carried time with it because it believed that time could stand against magic and against the final desires of its own world.

Aden moved his head in a quickening arc as the plane flew over him and down into the valley. He found himself walking after it, past the pavilion, still looking at Gedwyn, but no longer held by her.

As he looked, a vaporous dust drifted off the flowers and the framework of the pavilion. At first he thought that it had just been the wind from the aircraft blowing free the summer's accumulated pollen. But the usual mountain wind had dislodged nothing when he approached the garden.

The haze thickened until it appeared the garden was made entirely from damp, smoldering wood.

It was the time the Office ship had brought with it, infecting the garden, gradually and unintentionally reducing its subtleties to known factors, opening up the closed surfaces that kept the air and sunlight out and Gedwyn's own life inside.

There was another sound, muffled like a hand falling on a quilt. The book had fallen from Gedwyn's lap. She in turn, had bent slightly forward, her right hand slipping up from her chin to her mouth, shielding her hurt and sorrow. The time-mist rose from her too. The shadows over her eyes lightened as their captive darkness vaporized.

Aden started running, and his movements were sluggish and painful. Enough of his heartbeat returned to remind him of the necessity for fear. This helped. He ran through low hedges of ground orchids, kicking them into granulated diamonds.

The edge of the garden was fifteen hundred meters from the pavilion. Aden ran on for another hundred meters, feeling the freedom coming back to his legs and arms, feeling the wind again and the rough meadow grass.

He fell down next to a clump of bayonet grass, the product of the valley's first peacetime spring. The cuts it put in his right hand were shallow, and for a moment he enjoyed the certainty of their pain. Then he reached into his tunic and unclipped the gunsight from his holster. He looked back to the garden and found that the haze was gone. Everything appeared to be unitary and whole again, immune to the further progress of time.

The spell had been displaced. The book was still face down at Gedwyn's feet, and she remained bent slightly forward; her eyes were still shut but the shadows around them were qualified by an equivocal light. Every blossom that he could see had lost at least one petal.

Gedwyn still held a moment, but the ship had loosened it enough for Aden to escape. The fact that he knew the Office to have been closed over a year ago did not bother him; he had worked for it for years, firmly convinced that it did not exist in the first place. Surely, if he had lived and worked at addresses that did not exist, called telephone numbers that were not listed in any directory, talked to people whose names had been erased from all the world's records, the presence of one fugitive aircraft was hardly worth puzzling over.

But it was an Office ship. If it had been piloted by any of the services, it would have been pursuing absolute knowledges and the garden would have burst apart as the power of its spell was set free in a hostile vacuum of inflexible understanding.

In its way, this was crueler. Gedwyn persisted, but no longer in a time fully of her own choosing. Aden guessed that if any conscious thought was left to her, she would soon go mad, locked into a prison of her own building, unable to escape and correct it or choose another. The book with which she had chosen to spread her personal eternity, the particular word, faced away from her and the symmetries it had formed with the pavilion and alignments of the stars were now flawed.

He held this thought within his mind, equally with the memory of what he had felt for her. The gunsight and the aircraft stood between the two, mediating, translating, allowing him to exist with their equal truths. Aden knew that they could be removed easily and he could submit himself to the dominion of one or the other, and thus become like the Border Command or like Donchak. Such choices were not the manner of the Office; choice itself was not.

Closely packed columns of figures and symbols lined the gunsight's reticle; internal gyroscopes stabilized it against the trembling of his shoulders and hand. The gun understood the magic that remained, but Aden could not believe that it knew or understood Gedwyn, or if it did, that it could communicate its understanding to him in terms he could grasp. But the doctor had told him that the bomb had known, after the Office told it.

He dropped the gun to his side. She was again remote; her features were blurred at the distance and partially screened by the pavilion's latticework sides. She became as he was, a thing mostly of the Office's creation, and he could no longer be sure whether there was enough of the thing he had loved or of the enemy magician left in the garden to compel her destruction.

He walked away from her as he had the first time, slowly and uncertainly, scarcely daring to breathe lest the noise of the air in his lungs disturb the balance the Office had commanded and plunge him irrevocably into one side of the war or the other.

XVI

Etridge picked up the notebook Stamp had placed before him. "I didn't give you much time."

"Quite enough."

"I forgot how much things have improved now that we have fewer distractions."

"Just simple psychometric monitoring and evaluation. Interpret that with post-Heisner theorems and Llwyellan Functions."

Etridge held up his hand. "What will he do?"

"We're not that far along yet." Stamp permitted himself a smile. "But based upon what we understand about him now, he will report nothing to Lake Gilbert. The man was subjected to too many conflicting allegiances in too short a time for him to evolve a rational course of action."

"Or even an irrational course?"

"No course at all. Given his personality and the way in which he perceived things, he'll abdicate to stasis. That is safe. It's served the world fairly well for years now."

Etridge ignored the implied reference to Thorn River. "He'll abdicate to stasis and to the victory we've given him."

Stamp smiled again, but less surely than before. Now they were talking about something besides the man from Lake Gilbert. That had been a single person, like any other that had lived and like the millions the antennas had listened to, examined and probed. His background had been known and, as he told Etridge, when the understanding of his psychology and history were applied to his current experiences, his future conduct would be accurately predicted. But Etridge had placed the man, and therefore, Stamp could not help but think, those who had watched him, within the context of the ended war.

The war: simple, absolute, present in the sense of distant oceans or winds that seldom intruded into one's immediate life. Stamp often conceived of Joust Mountain as a university and its antennas as laboratory tools vastly removed from the phenomena they studied.

A victory would have to be claimed; positions would have to be consolidated, lingering traces of magic crushed, isolated covens rooted out, understood and ended, the lands divided and scoured clean of legend. Was that not the imperative of victories?

That it could happen this way, so quietly yet so absolutely, terrified him.

"Anything else?"

Stamp guessed that his distraction showed. "As before," he responded, shuffling the other notebooks in his hands. "Incoming bands remain almost uniformly blank. All the systems here and at Kells, Dance and other installations for two thousand kilometers report the same thing. Some traces remain in spots, and we're trying to see if they don't conceal some sort of pattern that we should be picking up on. Aside from that, it seems that organized hostile activity within the enemy's lands has stopped."

"No life?" Etridge questioned with his pale hand. He was dressed in finely tailored gray which emphasized the elegance of his frame.

"Yes. A great deal, but all conventional. There's no power coming out of the kingdoms."

There were aerial holograms of crumbling, deserted cities, squares filled with hungry mobs cowering at the sight and sound of the aircraft, unplanted fields, canals dried up or flooding out into new swamps, the carcasses of pegasuses and leviathans bleaching like those in front of Joust Mountain except that there were no wrecked machines nearby to explain their deaths. Against this, balancing the ruin, was the life that had been suppressed by the reign of magic: trees and flowers and things that lived by themselves, rather than by the whim and fancy of men of power.

"Have you gotten anything from that eye or whatever, in the unicorn?" Etridge asked offhandedly as he organized some files on his desk, almost catching Stamp unguarded.

"I really think they tried to design too many functions into it. Internal power, transmission, analytic functions." Stamp tried to shrug off the overreaching of Special Office technology. "No wonder its signals got screwed up so quickly. Only the Office would waste their time with such gibberish."

"We had to watch it and listen to it through their eyes and ears, not our own."

Stamp shifted his weight, betraying his unease. "But it was still garbled nonsense."

"But are the signals still coming in?"

"We accidentally caught part of one three months ago. As I said, it was static and nonsense." Stamp's voice was sagging against Etridge's pressure. He had not wanted to look closely at what the transmission might have shown. It had come from inside the new silence of the enemy's world and its content had initially been determined by a fabulous beast whose existence persisted in the empty kingdoms, drawing their minds outward from the walled safety of Joust Mountain to meet it. "Why can't we just ask the Office, or whoever's running its operations now, how to listen for the eye if it's so desperately important?"

Etridge laughed behind his nobleman's hand. "That's the simplest question of all. The Office does not exist now. It's never existed. Haven't you ever asked one of its people if it did or didn't?"

Etridge's face snapped into a new alignment, slitting his eyes but failing to mask their madness. "Listen again, Stamp. I want the channels unlocked and I want the information captured and understood. I ordered that done when we discovered that it had not been shut down by the Office. I appreciate the technical difficulties involved, as well as I know how you all must regard those signals. They come from the enemy, just like all his goddamned spells and curses and bolts used to, and you're scared that you're going to get your precious hearts singed by it." Etridge read the man's thought. "Or discover that there's nothing left and it's just the call of a poor, dumb, lonely beast who hasn't been fed because we nailed its masters. I want every available scrap of information for when we go in."

"Sir?" Stamp paled noticeably under the room's fluorescent lights. "Offensive action can only be authorized by Lake Gilbert."

"Lake Gilbert has made no such authorization for one hundred years. They've forgotten how. At any rate, this will only be a reconnaissance."

XVII

Stamp had evaluated the man from Lake Gilbert correctly, for he reported nothing more than what he had been told. That alone was sufficient to freeze his superiors into a similar paralysis.

The regular services had withdrawn from the frontiers, as if they feared the silence of the enemy more than the threat of his power. Various reasons were used to justify the retreat: money was needed to rebuild the battlefields within the world (there was a circle at Thorn River where nothing had grown through the crystallized soil since the battle); policy decisions had been made to shift from active ranging to more subtle, passive methods; the battle was over, but the enemy had spitefully devastated and booby-trapped his own land so that nothing but time could make it safe again.

Aside from the budget cuts, which were real, Etridge and the other frontier commanders were delighted with this course. One spent less time looking over one's shoulder for spies from Lake Gilbert, Castle Kent or the General Accounting Office. Long-range offensive vehicles and ships were more easily requisitioned and it was simpler to keep their discoveries secret. Etridge felt that he had more room now, in back as well as in front of him.

At first, Stamp hardly noticed the hangars of Joust Mountain filling up again with hovercraft, heavy-lift helicopters and ground support ships. But some days it did seem that the worst days of the Third Perimeter and Thorn River were back.

The mood was difficult to place. He sensed none of the exhilaration that Etridge showed on progressively more frequent occasions. It was something apart from what the fortress had known before, more alive than any of its years of watching, more anxious and fearful than any of the times it had sent its garrison back to their own homes to strive against the creatures that had materialized there. Perhaps it was Etridge's madness, lying like anodized pigment over the fortress' perfect surfaces, blurring the clarity of the images that had been reflected on them for centuries.

On the upper galleries, the antennas and aerials maintained a twenty-four-hour watch, though the order for it had been rescinded by Lake Gilbert five months before. The strain Joust Mountain was placing on the world's eastern power grids should have signaled its unauthorized activity. But then, Stamp knew, that could be ignored unless the drain was bleeding the cities white.

The evening air glowed fiercely above Joust Mountain, and there were similar fires over the opposite horizons, where Whitebreak and Dance were. Stamp enjoyed that part of it, even if it was the old man's insanity. He felt it tugging at his heart, gradually taking him from the world, away from Lake Gilbert, Castle Kent and the cities where he believed he had left so much, and turning it obsessively to the east, beyond the lands the enemy had occupied with his false religions and transparent heresies, out to where the antennas had really been looking from the very first.

XVIII

Aden squatted beside the beggar. The man's limbs were covered with ulcerous sores. A cataract floated in one eye, giving the illusion of mist and hidden circuitries.

"I imagine," Aden began quietly, the journey down from the mountains having wearied him, "that the men of power have left."

"Not left, sir. They are simply gone. I perceived their going though I permitted myself to understand only part of it."

"How did they go?" Flies circled around the man's open lesions. Out in the wasted fields, figures scraped and dug along irregular furrows of corn and stunted wheat.

"They fought among themselves."

"They had been doing that before."

"This time there was desperation in their acts. They sought to extract or prove"—the ancient man faltered—"some understanding beyond the understanding shown to them during the testing of their mysteries."

"Did they find any?"

"No. None at all. What can lie beneath the truth but itself?" Like Aden, the man was very tired. "And not even they could make it otherwise. Some of them turned their powers on themselves, others upon their retainers and familiars." The man touched himself when he said this, the expressive blind man's touch implying betrayal. "And upon their enemies. Others, upon the people." He held his withered arm out to the houses around the square and reached out to include the entire village and its surrounding field. "It was a terrible time, sir. Endless plagues, marauding creatures which had been harbored especially for the enemy were turned loose upon our lands."

"Those were probably the only places they would still work." Aden rubbed his single eye; the other was covered by a leather patch with an eye engraved on its surface.

The man nodded. "I had a form of power once myself, you know. But I kept getting it confused with what I understood, and that was not power at all but something else."

"Something more?"

"Less. It could be more than power only if you did not have it inside of yourself. You—I could not live with it that close. It was too much to be carried inside." He turned in the dust to face south. "Out there, do you see? It was the most beautiful palace where princes of one family had lived for four hundred years. Waterfalls, gardens, game forests that reached up to our walls, wise men and poets singing . . ."

"The epics of Thorn River and Heartbreak Ridge." He knew that the remark was uncalled for.

Though Aden had used his own world's names for the battles, the man seemed saddened by their mention and turned his eye downward. "I understand that those songs were sung everywhere." He roused himself, as if the frailty of his body could not withstand Aden's remarks. "To your question: no, some must remain, I imagine. Fugitive, probably as mad as I." He permitted himself a laugh to show that no harm had been done. "And some of their works too."

"In the Holy City?"

"If not there, then not at all. Were you ever there?"

"You don't remember much of that, do you, Donchak?"

"Donchak?" shaking his head. "Ah, yes, yes. No, I do not, but I am very old, sir."

XIX

Joust Mountain's antenna arrays moved with an imaginary wind. The vague humming of their radiant energies had diminished noticeably, and the air did not smell so strongly of ozone as it usually did, though the wind was from the east.

Bridge walked before its walls with conscious dignity. A double line of hovercraft and tracked vehicles waited between him and Joust Mountain, men standing by their sides, shifting against the unaccustomed weight of sidearms.

Stamp was too caught up in the sight to realize that Etridge was speaking to him: " . . . complete mapping of the areas?"

Stamp walked quickly over to him and held up a note-book. "Yes. The traces turned out to be a little more numerous than I discussed with you, but nothing which substantially alters the picture we had last week. This readout is an hour old, and the strongest concentration is still here." Stamp opened the notebook, selected a small-scale map and pointed to where a great number of shaded radii intersected. "Area Twelve, the Holy City."

"Holy, I'm sure, only in comparison to the rest of the other kingdoms." Etridge was amused. Behind him, a loose formation of wind ships rode the thermals over the dead lake, engines out, spiraling lazily up into the morning.

XX

Aden watched the imagist for an hour before he slipped him a coin. "A beauty," he said. In response the man shut his eyes and then plucked up the thought that Aden held at the edge of his mind.

He moved his hands, and the air between them shimmered and condensed into the shape of a woman. She was very well shaped, and this was clear despite the loose robes she had been dressed in. A good imagist knew the touches that compliment memory, and those which blatantly exaggerate it and thereby offend. She was tall, which was also correct, and with fine delicate features overlain by pale skin that was nearly translucent. The nose was small, and the eyes hovered between green and slate and blue.

Aden nodded approvingly. The man was very good, much better than the sort the smaller towns usually got by with. But the most common subject of a public imagist was lost loves. They acquired, if only from sheer repetition, some facility in gathering from a man's mind what he chose to remember, rather than any great truth about what the person might have really been like.

When magic was whole, the best imagists were prized by even the mightiest men of power. They could read secrets of startling depth or shape extravagant fantasies from the surfaces of other men's thought and then build them into visions of unbearable intensity. Not surprisingly, most of them succumbed to their own talent, drugging themselves as their visions fed and multiplied on each other.

Aden waved the image away. As he expected, the sight of her touched him, but not deeply. The magic of the imagist functioned like the gunsight's marvelous technology. Both allowed him to see Gedwyn, but only from a distance that existed in addition to those of time and memory. Both reduced and quantified her, both could be dismissed with a gesture.

He felt something like relief when the picture was gone. It was as if her memory, which might otherwise grow out of control, had been removed from his heart. It would grow back again, but each time it would be proportionately weaker.

He was growing, acquiring a manly depth of memories and history, but did not know why there should be a feeling of self-disgust left in the place the imagist had taken the picture of Gedwyn from.

Aden threw the man two more corns and smiled stiffly. The men around them made comic groans that he had not permitted a more explicit insight into his affections.

"Allow us the design of mystery and power." In ordinary times this would have been a joke, for common people could not bear to see such things any more than a street imagist would be able to conjure them.

"You are from the past, my sir," the imagist replied in a professionally respectful voice, scooping up the money. "There are none left."

"I have been away from my home, and did not know that the question is no longer asked."

"Only rarely." Pain crossed the faces of the imagist and his other patrons; some of them rubbed their jaws in their hands and drifted back into the street. Still, the man seemed to feel an obligation to his trade and for monies already received. He became silent again, moving his hands until the outlines of an onion-domed temple formed, stained from the weather, alabaster windows blank and dark. It faded quickly and was replaced by another picture, this one of a slim aircraft, propeller-driven and like the one that had flown over Aden in the mountains. The plane wove and turned like a weaver's shuttle between the man's hands.

Aden attempted to look shocked for it had been heresy to so portray the devices of the enemy. "Apologies, my sir. It was all I could show you." The plane evaporated. Aden saw that only he and the imagist were left in the tiny park. The others had left when the temple had appeared and then started to vanish. "I took it more from my own mind than yours."

The man was staring directly into Aden's good eye. As he did so, his face relaxed into a familiar weariness. Aden said: "Office?" slurring the word so that he hardly recognized it.

"My sir?" with forced astonishment. He whirled his hands again, and the picture of an eye formed between them, suspended in a web of copper wires. It lasted a second before going. "Your money's worth, my sir?"

XXI

The imagist's village was bitterly cold in winter, and the fields and ruined palaces near it were encrusted with ice. But when the wind died and the sun was not hidden by storm clouds, people still found it pleasant to come out into the wide, barren streets to spy on their neighbor's food supply and conduct themselves as they had before, when great enchantments protected them from the weather.

The imagist was out at his usual place, the hood of his sheepskin cloak thrown back for the sun, practicing the same tired round of illusions for the same crowd of idlers and bored farmers. He took care to make a picture different each time the same person requested it, and many in the village remembered his picture better than the actual events on which they had originally been based.

He sometimes thought of himself as not only the shaper of the village's memories but as one who created its present as well. He knew this to be a fantasy and the progressive intensity with which it asserted itself troubled him. He had thought of going home, but that would not have solved the problem of illusion. If anything, it would have only intensified it, because that world, unlike the one he presently inhabited, had not been stripped of all its closest dreams. It still abounded, he guessed, in thought and life enough to bloat his imagination. He decided that he was safer in this world, where almost everything of the heart and mind had been carried off by the magicians when they fled.

On this morning, however, he was thinking of his own world, testing his memory with the picture of severely uniformed men who never smiled and from whom light never shone. His audience had no idea what he was doing and thought it only to be some long, diverting myth about the imaginary time before their War.

Because of his absorption, the imagist was not particularly surprised when the gray man edged his way forward through the crowd and threw him an unfamiliar coin. It merely seemed that one of his pictures had found a mirror in the people around him.

The man was of medium height and the skin lay easily about his mild features: blue eyes, long, artistic hands and fingers unscarred and uncalloused, well-fitting clothes with archaic lapel flashes on the jacket. He smelled oppressively clean.

"You wish to see, my sir?"

The other man inclined his head. "The design of power." He had at least studied some of the local idiom. The imagist decided the man was real, or at least an illusion sustained by someone else.

The picture was an easy one for the young man carried its component parts constantly before him, as if he were afraid they might slip from his grasp if they were not held so tightly.

He began with a line, formed it into a triangle, which thereupon expanded into a square, to a pentagon, hexagon, octagon, a sphere growing tangents that curved off into diminishing radius arcs that, before the image was completed, hinted at Llwyellan Functions.

"I had wished the image to be yours rather than mine."

"I have no images of that sort left to me, nor do the people around you. Yours was the only one I could find." The man looked up the street and the imagist caught the picture of armed men also dressed in gray, reflected on the surfaces of his mind. Beyond them were vehicles painted white and olive, caked with frozen mud and dust and much too large to fit into the village's streets. The imagist noted that all of them carried one or more antennas, mostly dished units or flattened cylinders, and found the one that was examining him.

He felt his hands wavering in their movements, and stopped before the image disappeared into abstraction by itself.

"Anything else, old man?" Another person dressed like the first, but taller and with fiercely ascetic features had come up to him.

The imagist sensed his own fear as strongly as when the men of power had begun to leave or destroy themselves. He instinctively closed his eyes and searched the land around the village. He found other things in the silence but he was now badly shaken and could not identify them. "Yes."

"A picture then," the second man ordered too loudly. "A picture of the powers in this land!" The younger man looked embarrassed.

"Lost the knack so soon? Allow me to assist." A third man joined them and handed the speaker a green notebook. The imagist heard the sound of motors grinding at the still air. A low fog of crystallized ice rose from under the plenum skirt of the hovercraft parked at the end of the street, lending it the appearance of slow burning. The man raised his hand and pointed to the northeast. "You may find some form of power . . . "

"Sir!" the imagist shouted as the picture blasted across his mind.

The bolt hit and leveled the block of houses on the opposite side of the park. There was no sound or shock wave, just an intense heat that drove them back behind the nearest wall.

"No power? Goddamn bastard!" The second man grabbed the imagist by the front of his cloak and nearly lifted him off his feet.

His mouth working through the usual signs of terror, the other man yelled, "I don't understand this. It can't be this! It hasn't for years!"

Etridge smiled back and dropped the other man. "Relieved, Stamp?" he hissed as another block of houses and godowns detonated. Then he stepped back and began trotting along the undamaged side of the street, back to the vehicles. Stamp followed uncertainly.

The imagist and the man who had brought the book to Etridge stayed for a moment. They saw that the fires left by the two bolts were made from extraordinary colors; despite the rush of heat released by their impact, they now danced above the ruins without warmth, as if they had used themselves up all at once and remained only as an after-image in their eyes. One or two people staggered from the houses, seemingly unaware of the gold and scarlet flames that were eating at the backs of their skulls.

The third bolt consumed the burning people, the imagist and the man beside him.

Stamp looked back in time to see this. More bolts hit the village and their fires spiraled upward and joined together. "Firestorm!" he yelled to Etridge as they ran through the village gate.

"Not melodramatic enough. Not enough drama. No fuel for their dreams," Etridge shouted back. The engines of the hovercraft and tanks accelerated in front of them. Light half-tracks scattered at right angles to the road, side-looking radars moving in nervous jerks to stay fixed on the burning village.

They reached the lead hovercraft. It lifted off as they boarded, dipping slightly as its gyroscopes came into phase. Three identical units floated backward, away from the village.

The individual fires kept twisting together until the density of their light cast a shadow against the sun. Branches grew downward from points a hundred meters from the ground, and as they watched, the pillar assumed shape and animation.

"Splendid!" Etridge remarked to the bridge crew when he saw this. "Nearly the same thing they tried at Foxblind. If it really is, it'll have the shape of some wonderful beast, like a minotaur or such. They're incapable of thinking in terms of simple power, always anthropomorphizing this or that so each act has the personal mark of the man behind it. What do you say, Stamp? Two to one it's a minotaur."

"The same device was employed at Thorn River . . . "—trying to appear knowledgeable.

Etridge's face went through a sequence of closed and guarded expressions. "Yes. Except there, they used hundreds of those fire things, and each one had the shape and the face of the last person it killed. We didn't know how to fight them then."

Dust swirled outside the hovercraft's windows as it slid backward. The fiery column danced in the half-light, seeming to grow in rough proportion to the distance they traveled away from it. The planes of Etridge's face matched the lines of the craft's bridge and the flanking turrets on either side of it. "Pointless melodrama. Wasted effort!"

Two men behind him received the input from the circling tanks and from the antennas on the four main ships.

"They never seem to learn or understand," Etridge muttered over the engines. "They always give us enough time."

"Sir, the second unit thinks they have something. They want to experiment."

Etridge nodded, the man spoke into a microphone, and the hovership to their right tentatively opened fire.

All four ships stopped their rearward movement and watched as it continued shooting. Two kilometers away, the fire-beast detached itself from the village and began striding toward them. Etridge's smile came back when the bull's head defined itself.

"Not working very well," Etridge commented absently. "Anyone else read the input differently?" Responding light, chromium against the fire-minotaur's yellow and red, angled out from antennas on the two hoverships on their left. Similar lines were drawn from three tanks racing around the northern side of the creature.

An officer came up behind them. "Rather different from previous stuff. But we're running interference patterns with the scatter antennas too, and I think that might do it."

"All right. Let's get closer."

Stamp placed both his hands on the grab rail and moved his feet apart. He had read and studied the phenomena the men of power had conjured for centuries, but his actual dealings with them had been as remote as most of his contemporaries, those who had grown into the war's world after Thorn River. He had always seen the wizards' might and their own through the reductive prisms of computers.

Now that they were moving forward, diminishing perspective and the beast's own increasing powers made it grow alarmingly in the windscreen's aldiss rings. The glass darkened automatically to compensate for the brilliance.

"Additional presences behind the subject," a man at the console called out.

"Close on them." Etridge's smile widened, breaking his facial planes into patterns of broken glass.

The driver accelerated the ship. Stamp saw more lines of the chrome light emerge from the top of the windscreen and join with the fire from the other craft at a point on the creature's neck. Blocking radiations combined with its own indefinite structure and made it difficult to tell if the beast's raging gestures expressed any problematic agony or were merely part of its slow, dancing attack.

If there was only some sound, Stamp thought, not just the eternally competent murmuring of our own engines and the afternoon light from the armored windows.

Etridge is enjoying this, he also thought, far more than the ship itself was; to it, and to most of its crew, the menace and wonder of the beast was that of an enemy, no more unique or terrible than a rifle squad or a fighter-bomber. Among some old combat units there had been a saying to the effect that "there is only one kind of dead."

They were all older than himself, and had fought this enemy for years before Thorn River. They were absorbed in the ship's dials and scopes; the driver and fire control personnel looked at the minotaur through target and range grids projected onto the windows in front of them. Only he and Etridge had no assigned station and there was nothing in front of them to block or polarize the fire-creature's power. Stamp wondered if the two of them were succumbing to it.

"Cavalry behind it," the man called out again.

"Nothing more?"

"No sir." The man paused to examine the readout. "And these're much simpler. Tanks on the right report they've already eliminated one or two."

"Good. The survivors may be throwing their palace guards against us, Stamp."

Stamp mumbled something he hoped would not show his concern. Two silver dots appeared far above the minotaur. Simultaneously with their sighting, a nimbus of visual anomalies edged the beast's outline.

Every vehicle in the column, except the lightest half-tracks, joined in spinning the cool, sharp lines that wavered and bent only where they passed through the giant.

The hovercraft on their right paused and then resumed gunfire. This time its ammunition was perfectly suited to destruction in the dimension which the creature's life and energy came from. The shells began cratering its body, disrupting the sustaining life that the enemy poured into it, freezing its fire so that it could splinter apart like dense red crystal.

The other main units joined in, replacing their inquisitory lights with gunfire. Stamp felt a release as the reports thudded against the cabin walls and the creature finally bellowed out its pain.

Etridge anticipated his question: "That's not the minotaur, Stamp, but the despair of the man who built it"—turning smoothly to the younger men and then back to the village. "We've shown him something which he'd rather not have seen. Haven't we, Anderton?" The fire control officer accepted the compliment without any sign, keeping his eyes on his ranging scopes. "And now our survivor of power finds that he can't let his little vision go. We've contained his puppet and we've also snared his sustaining powers. Listen to him!"

Etridge crossed over to the right side of the cabin and slid open a window. The cabin was filled with the deafening sound of the batteries and over them, the long pathetic wailing of the fire-minotaur as the chromium lines shackled it, dragging it to its knees and holding it still for their barrage.

The bridge crew clamped their earphones more tightly to their heads and tried to ignore it. Stamp could not, but found it less unnerving than the linear hum of the ship's engines.

The creature lost its form and dissolved back into the low, brilliant fires it had arisen from twelve minutes ago. "Short glory," Etridge said. There was a line of armored deaths, carrying lances made of darkness and mounted on gryphons, behind the flattened village. "Ah! The costume ball!" and clapped his hands together.

The driver edged the throttles forward with what seemed to Stamp to be needless theatricality.

The line stretched for at least two kilometers. They stood utterly, stupidly motionless as the light and the surgical gunfire concentrated on the rider at each end. They refused to move as they were enveloped in Joust Mountain's merciless understanding, refused to show emotion or come to the aid of their fellows when their limbs turned to powder and the gateways their lances defined between their own world and that of their master were brutally slammed shut.

"Are they alive?" Stamp breathed.

"Alive enough for us to murder them. Like I said, Stamp, that is their failing. They must always personify their powers and try to make them the reflection of their own thoughts."

"They're artists. They have to do it that way. It's the only way they understand . . . "

"They understand nothing! That's what they think is the base of their power. Ignorance made into a religion."

The four ships advanced into the village. It had been consumed to feed the creature's minutes of birth and

life, but the ships elevated to three meters to be safe.
The remaining fires played against their sides, impotent
and sucked dry by the ship's light.

"Now . . . " As Etridge spoke to the driver, the hovercraft on their right collided with a thick column of
masonry; it had been wrapped in a fire which Anderton's
instruments quickly analyzed and found to be of the
same composition as the minotaur. Too late; no one had
been looking at the fires around them.

The burning rock cut into the ship's left side, shearing
away the plenum skirt and gouging into its understruc-
ture. The window on that side of Etridge's ship was still
open; the screech of tearing metal and ceramic armor hit
them along with a last, undefined echo of the minotaur.

The wounded hovercraft spun to the right and dug its
nose into the burning ruins. The other ships, although
they had identified the fire, did not shoot for fear of
hitting it. Its metal structure ignited in five of the non-
visual dimensions, turning white and slagging into a glittering lake.

The fire penetrated the engines and fuel cells. The
glass on the right side of Etridge's ship went black except
for the open vent window; the light from it drilled into
Stamp's retina, threatening to dissolve his heart.

"God, kill it!" Etridge screamed to the computers. The
three remaining craft swung their antennas and weapons
downward along their own flanks. The batteries went
automatic, driving shells of unimaginably complex structures into the remaining humps and masses which hinted
at animate power. Gyroscopes rocked violently against
the ships' roll axes to compensate for the hammering
recoil and concussions rising up alongside the hulls.

Stamp dove at the window and slammed it shut against the physical pressure of the exterior light.

The hovercraft bathed each other in radiations and shells they themselves only half understood. That was enough.

The glass cleared. The fires were gone, flattened into common reality. Only the line of cavalry stood before them; the vanished ship was forgotten. All three hoverships leveled their batteries upon the northern end of the line, accidentally crushing the nearest tank, and swept along it.

The noise was similar to that of the minotaur and its dying, but now the windows and ventilators were closed and it had the distance of memory. "His most truly beloved," Etridge observed with forced calm. As the distance closed, they could recognize skull faces and shreds of putrefied flesh hanging from seams in their cuirasses and greaves. "The minotaur was a robot. Our man of power gave nothing to it which was of his own but some life. But look how he must love those things. Look, Stamp! Can you see starlight shining through, no, inside their lances! He's given them power of their own. He must trust them greatly."

"We've hit the fourth unit," the driver shouted over the muffled howling. He pointed to his left and the rest of the crew reflexively followed his hand. The hovercraft farthest from them was drawing away, near side tilted down, escaping air driving it across their path against the rudders in full opposite lock. "She'll ground!"

Speed brakes snapped open on their ship and the one next to them. They dug into the air and slowed them enough for the damaged ship to arc in front of them. Its guns and antennas were all pointed at the line of deaths, at maximum elevation raking them and shattering individuals as if they had been made from ivory glass.

"Look at this." Etridge's voice was flat and unemotional in comparison to when he had spoken of the enemy. Then, he had sounded as if he were about to take a rival's love; but the dying craft presented him with no mystery or challenge. The reasons and causes for its actions had been understood before the Wizards' War began. The ship could have never served as the gateway Etridge sought.

He watched the terror spread before the careening ship. Its windows were solid black, so he could not gauge its crew's reaction.

Its magazines detonated and a long club of fire and hard radiation descended on the southern third of the line. It drowned them, burning them from the inside, cremating their interior blankness and turning their peculiar nights into ash.

The cabin darkened again to protect the men from the other ship's arsenal. Ventilator guards snapped shut and nickel steel shields locked over them. The silence returned, now absolute, and the only light was from red battle lanterns.

Navigation and fire control grids were projected across the closed windows to guide them. The completeness of the schematic diagrams showed how thoroughly these enemies were understood. Energy graphs, spectral analysis, frequency and dimensional readings sped crisply along the borders of the windows.

The computers anticipated Etridge's anger. The other ship appeared as a schematic on the left side windows;

dense columns of information showed that it was destroying the northern end of the line. Etridge's ship concentrated on the middle, and at a range of one hundred meters it broke.

The coherency of the line fragmented. Individual deaths fell apart or burst into saffron flame or ran straight into the guns of the two ships and the flanking vehicles. Others ran to the east. The instruments traced the lines of power that drew them and, one by one, cut them.

They passed the spot where the second ship had touched down. Readings indicated a shallow gouge in the earth, at right angles to their line of travel, and fatally high radiation levels, but little else.

The windows cleared. Eighty-three deaths remained before the hovercraft, most of them charred and shredded. Their mounts were similarly mauled, some running comically on two opposed legs, the stumps of their other legs repeating the movements of running, their balance presumably held by the same power that sustained the lives of their riders.

Stamp could see stars inside their lances, more absence than presence, as they swayed drunkenly against the gun and lightfire. He felt himself sickening, equally from the grotesquery of the spectacle and from an overwhelming sense of pity and sorrow. "They're done," he whispered, and was astonished when Etridge raised his hand and ordered cease fire.

Instead of turning about and attending to their wounded, Etridge added: "Pace them. This distance is fine."

"They're dead."

"Quite. I'd say they were before we attacked. Now they are truly dead. That might be death they hold in their hands." Etridge smiled. "Mr. Anderton, please direct our antennas and those of the other unit entirely to those fellows. I don't think our man of power has anything else for us today. And see if you can get those two wind ships down low enough for some close looking."

The officer behind them spoke into his microphone.

"They've been understood, sir. We know them!" Stamp was aware of how tenuous his ground might be. "The graphs have all placed and fixed them on the spectrums. Why not wipe them out and end it? The others . . . "

"The others should be watching them as closely as we are. As you should be, Stamp." Etridge was parental; he might actually enjoy Stamp's little treason. "We know them and the chemical and atomic reactions that sustain them. See?" He pointed to patterns of luminous dials along the right side of the cabin. "We know how they're dying. We have wounded them sufficiently to give their own form of death enough momentum to proceed on its own. They are heading for that death, real and absolute. But we musn't hurry them. No, no need for that. Just pat them along with a little flash of light or a kiss of the Mountain's choicest amatol, just enough to keep the bastards moving along that path so we can watch them running, watch how their gifts of power run off and try to hide themselves."

At irregular intervals one of the antennas above them or on the other ship went active. Quanta of light drove into the functioning riders who were not dying at an appropriate speed.

They followed them until the smoke from the village and the wreck of the first hovercraft was below the horizon. They fell individually, taking with them whatever plan they might have had to attack the ships and the tank column. Etridge directed the ships to pass over them as they dropped. Articulated arms inside the plenum chambers snatched samples of bone and armor and chitinous skin as they died and transmuted back into the elements and energies from which they had been formed.

The ventilators opened. The screaming of the last deaths entered the cabin, instantly captured on wall-mounted oscilloscopes and written into spinning globes of frozen helium. Later, the computers at Joust Mountain would take this information, their agonies and pain, and relate them to all the mysteries they had accumulated over three hundred years of watching, understanding their meanings as they had been reflected in the carbonization of battlefield flowers and in the blinding faces of distant stars. Their inquiries had to be made on such a scale for the ways of men of power were vast and infinitely devious.

"Bring the planes down and block them," Etridge said.

They maintained the distance, devouring the stragglers as they fell. Stamp saw the aircraft turning into the wind far ahead of them.

After ten minutes of casual pursuit, he could see the two aircraft on the ground. They faced the approaching ships, noses high and resting on their tail wheels, momentarily suggesting foreshortened crucifixes. The featureless plain gave no hint as to their size; Stamp knew the wingspread of each one was over ninety meters. The wings themselves were antennas. Everything that Etridge had chosen to accompany him was devoted to perception.

They played their questioning radiations back and forth against the hoverships, through the knot of ghostly cavalry. Opportunities for such examinations occurred only when magic erupted within the heartlands of its enemy's world, and there had not been such a thing since Foxblind. The tape banks and helium spheres choked on the rush of information that poured into them.

Etridge was pleased. When there was less than seventy meters between them and the aircraft, he said to Anderton, "End them all."

Light, this time in pale, fan-shaped arrays, beat against twenty-two survivors. The planes laid down their own light too, and the deaths faltered and dove into the ground. Some of them melted into the surface ice, hazings of steam rising from under their disintegrating bodies.

The two hovercraft deployed their drag skids and eased to the ground. Etridge waited a moment and stepped outside. Stamp followed and was overwhelmed by the smell. He had not imagined that anything could have so fouled winter air.

The wind ship crews jumped down from the wings and strolled into the wreckage. Every one of them carried hand analyzers of one sort or another, machines that tested the discoveries of the other machines. They chipped at the fairyland armor with geologist's picks, placed samples in glass bottles and watched as the fragments cracked and vaporized the glass. These fragments, in turn, were deposited in successive containers until something was found to hold them.

There was some joking, but most of the conversation was taken up with numbers and code references. Except for Etridge: "Is that death?" He pointed with his boot at one of the black lances the riders carried; its owner was dust and damp rot beside it.

"Will it kill you? Probably. Its form and composition derive from . . . " Anderton's voice, flat and metallic over the hovercraft's loudspeaker.

"No! Is it death? True and actual death. Not just a device that could cause it." Etridge stared down at the tapering shaft; it appeared more of a hole or tear in the ground than something that lay on top of it.

Stamp squatted and found the perspectives the thing reported to his eyes violently contradictory. Starlike objects flickered inside of it, but these were fading.

"No, sir," Anderton answered after a pause. Stamp imagined that he sounded as disappointed as Etridge looked; but that was probably the effect of the scene and the amplifier.

"The lines are gone," Anderton continued. "Our man of power has left."

"Before we told him too much about himself." Etridge addressed the hovercraft.

"That may have happened. The sounds of those things couldn't have been entirely their own. As you said about the minotaur."

Etridge stopped listening and turned to Stamp. "If that has happened, if he has left us now, how can we follow him? How will we know where to look?"

He's really asking me, thought Stamp, and held his ignorance like a precious secret.

XXII

Aden recognized more landmarks as he left the ruins of Clairendon and neared the Holy City. The fields, as with the rest of the enemy's lands, were blasted and sterile, waiting for the rains and the ancient, alien seeds they would bring. The ruins of fabulous palaces and villas sat against charred hillsides or along the drained channels of rivers that the magicians had summoned only for their sound. He remembered how, when he fled the City, the towers of these great houses had risen above the forests, flaunting their gardens and erotic sculptures against the patient watching of Joust Mountain and Dance.

A few of the shells hinted at inhabitation, if not by princes, then possibly by powers which had detached themselves from their makers to become self-sustaining, as the gravitational fields of celestial black holes had been thought to be.

Shadowed lights could be glimpsed behind the stained glass remnants of windows. There were also signal fires on isolated hill forts, and Aden occasionally thought he could see the sky flickering and glowing as it had over the Holy City. But this was not much; these mysteries were not being swallowed up by his world's understanding but by the emptiness around them.

He now walked through a field becoming lush with spring grass and the wildflowers of his world. There was a small herd of pegasuses grazing there, strong and powerful. Their caparisons were slitted to allow free movement to their wings; these rested against their flanks, colored like golden cock pheasants. Their armor was meant for flight, being limited to quilting under the caparisons and a crinet of silver mesh.

All their saddles were empty. Aden guessed they had been the scouts of a man of power, such squadrons usually affecting the most extravagant liveries, as he guessed that all their uniforms and bravado and the power they had served had been explained and unraveled by Joust Mountain. Because their task had been reconnaissance, as his had been, they would have discovered their own reality and that of their master before anyone else.

XXIII

Anderton pointed to a diamond fixed on the moving map grids and reference lines. "I thought we were going to be the only ones out here." He went on with ponderous, Border-bred irony. "And there, and there, and there again."

"But nothing like this," said Etridge, moving closer and pointing to the first diamond.

"No, sir," referring to the rows of dials and linear readouts to his right. "It almost seems to be one of ours. Except . . ."

"Well?"

"Multiple fixtures and nets within the subject's cranial structure. The readings are indefinite, but we can't hope for much more at these distances."

"Active?"

"No, not for some time. Conductance indicates that the nets haven't been used for anything for over two years. It's all very well hidden," Anderton concluded, hoping for approval.

"The Special Office used to wire up people like that." Etridge seemed to be addressing the rows of dials.

"The Office has closed."

"It never existed. Right, Anderton?"

The other man looked to Stamp for assistance; Stamp turned away. "That's supposed to have been the way of outfits like that."

"Like what?"

Anderton fidgeted with his headpiece. "The undercover people, the spies . . . "

"Imagists," Stamp mumbled involuntarily.

"Ah, my aide was watching after all." He returned to Anderton, whose look of relief accordingly vanished. "As you say, that is the way of outfits like that. That one is closed, but that act of organizational death is, itself, an admission of the life they steadfastly denied. Interesting, don't you think?"

Stamp saw Anderton mustering his courage in the set of his facial muscles. "That can't matter much to us. If the thing existed, all its lying couldn't change that fact."

"Our opinion is secondary to what they were thinking of themselves," Stamp cut in, irritated with the way Etridge was playing with the man. The strategy of his world permitted no fascination with paradox and contradiction for its own sake, and Anderton was innocent of such things. "People listen mostly to themselves."

"And eventually one comes to speak and think in a warped shorthand, comprehensible only to one's self or to others who live in the same dream," Etridge finished for him. He smiled his approval to Stamp and this increased the other's anger. "That's what our princes of power did until we accidentally showed them a more captivating dream, the one we're sleeping through right now."

"Sir?" Anderton was honestly puzzled at the equation of his own world with that of the enemy.

"Don't worry. Our dream's the right one. Isn't it, Stamp?"

"It appears to be the only one, sir." Stamp turned on his heel and left the bridge, Etridge looking after him as if it had been some kind of triumph.

"Get on the channels to Lake Gilbert and ask them if there're files open on the person with the readings you've picked up at that first position."

Anderton nodded to a man farther down on the console. Circles of yellow and green light switched on and then off, and the other man pressed his earphones to his head. "The files are closed," he reported after some minutes. Anderton busied himself with his instruments before he could be drawn back into his commander's disturbing way of discussing a target with wires in its head. Range, speed, weight, respiration, molecular composition: the man obviously existed, so what was the use of talk of nonexistence?

XXIV

Aden knew that the wires and grids that remained unplanted in his body were without power sources. They had no way to gather information from around him, nor did they have any place to store signals from the Office, had it, too, been functioning.

Because of this, Aden first suspected that one of the pegasus riders had survived. There was nothing visual, but rather tentative movements and half-formed ideas turning like shadows beneath his conscious mind. He vaguely connected this feeling with those the unicorn and its attendant had inspired in him years ago. But the grazing pegasuses had no intimidating cathedral to help propel his mood from discomfort to terror.

Also, there seemed to be only one concept now, quite different from the spectrum-wide wave fronts of thought that the unicorn had hinted at. It swam out of reach, its texture metallic and sharp for all its lack of definition.

Aden touched his fingers to the sides of his hand. The old patchwork of wires branched out from the inside of his skull through an occipital hole grommeted with a ring of pure gold. His thick, ash-colored hair made the pattern invisible to one who did not already know of its presence.

The wires moved under his fingers. Again, so small and elusive that he might fairly judge it as imagination.

"That's over, gone," he muttered to the pegasuses. Two of them looked at him in momentary agreement.

The sound of his own voice startled him, as if it had suddenly revealed him to covert watchers. But he had been in the open since he had left Dance. Hiding was impossible, particularly when he had entered the abandoned kingdoms of magic. If he had not been seen, it was because no one was looking for him.

Now there was something. The Office, perhaps, attempting to contact him in its appropriately non-existent way, to call him back or to urge him on.

Or the pegasus riders, centering him in cross hairs drawn with fire in the open air, preparing spells and enchantments of terrible finality.

Or his world had come already, and he had only felt the brush of its inquisitory antennas as they reviewed the power and meaning of everything left alive in the enemy's land.

The last of the three was the most logical. It was proper that his world should come and occupy the vacuum left by the defeat of magic, thus preserving symmetry and balance. But he knew the occupation would be total when it came and that it would find no reason to stop with what might soon be understood as a minor victory.

Individual wires pulsed. His conception of his world's victory shrank as he began to suspect the dimensions of the field on which it had been fought.

The pegasuses' gorgeous ornamentation became the rags of refugees too inconsequential for the forces of either side to destroy. When he was a child, he had watched creatures like them struggling along the roads leading from Thorn River. They had been burned and starved and brutalized by forces so alien that their bodies seemed unsure as to what sort of death was called for. The pegasuses, grazing in their rich field, were the same, for their eyes had been turned to cinders by the things they had witnessed. They had been deserted by their commanders and their creation, and there was nothing left for them. But they, unlike the victims of Thorn River, or of the Third Perimeter or Foxblind, were not yet fully aware of this, so they persisted in their wonder and existence.

Aden touched the long-barreled automatic in its holster. The Office had fashioned it so that it could change the nature and composition of its ammunition in the magazine. The Office, however, had purposely made it fragile and needlessly complex. It was machined to tolerances more suited to match competition than field service. He was not even sure he could remember how to work it.

He resumed walking. The wires continued to pulse for some moments and then left him alone but for the thought of the Office, orbiting through its own strange, self-created nighttime, pondering its own existence and never wishing to approach any answer.

Aden smiled tensely. His skin stretched against the eye patch, hiding its edges and making the stylized eye engraved on it appear to be his own: brown cornea, black iris, brown pupil.

XXV

The riverbed was carpeted with sword grass. Scarlet and yellow wildflowers spotted the greenness. Small trees that survived the spring runoff thumped against the plenum skirts of the two hovercraft. Like Joust Mountain, they were flawlessly white, arrogantly perfect despite the dirt and fires that the kingdoms had hurled at them.

The column had waited after the first village, conversing with the computers of their home until they understood what had happened to them. Then they buried what the powers had left of their dead.

Etridge kept asking about the Special Office. Nothing obtrusive, just occasional inquiries as to what this closed Office file or that sealed Office report might have had to say about the way the enemy had moved or what its dark lances might have actually been composed of.

As they had supposed, the animating forces behind the fire-minotaur and the dead cavalries were basically the same as those used for ages, with only minor variations drawn from one or two neglected corners of the parallel spectrums. How they had managed to come upon the column undetected required more study.

When the study group at Saart finally understood it and fabricated machineries to duplicate it, Lake Gilbert broadcast this knowledge to places where the remaining men of power might be listening from. Seven thousand kilometers from the Holy City, the castle of the prince who had carried out the attack and committed his last and most favorite retainers to its success, turned from the sunlight of which his father had built it, to stone and then to rust, and then to slag.

A trio of wind ships hovered above the castle, observing its disintegration. The acuity of their watching nearly took the mystery of the castle's death away from its dying prince and exiled both him and it in the world they could not conceive of fully enough to hate.

Etridge was pleased with the course of the mission. Stamp made an opposing show of his displeasure, hoping to find the point at which Etridge would drop his insane dialogues and simply accuse him of insubordination or treason.

The kingdoms, however, continually provided them diverting nests of lingering magic. Stamp celebrated each irregular assault that hit them. Etridge was similarly prideful when they slowed and then understood each one.

"Reductio ad imperium" had been scrawled around the base of one of the ship's antenna mounts. Each man saw the other staring at it in odd moments, and saw him regarding it as his own. Gradually Stamp came to attach a tremendous weight of bitterness and irony to it. Etridge found it a perfect expression of the soldier's ethos in this war, just triumphant enough to distract that soldier from how far the phrase begged to be taken.

Etridge leaned close to the windscreen, enjoying the torrent of grass passing under the ship. A ranging mast extended twenty meters outward from the leading edge of the ship like a bowsprit, anticipating drops and irregularities in the ground's contours. The smooth, relentless movement put him in mind of his own obsessions. He considered how the appeal of the mysteries and their solving, one by one, acquired their own propulsive force, gradually forming the conviction that the horizon might not prove to be an eternally receding one.

Why, he marveled to his own reflection, did Stamp seem so repelled by such a suggestion? Certainly the searching was the greatest part, not the thought they might someday actually arrive at a complete and literal understanding of the universe. But, he also permitted himself, if such a position could be reached, it might include an understanding of primary creative forces, gods, if you will, and in so understanding them, encompass them and take their measure.

He could not hope to do things like that. He was a soldier, not a theologian or a philosopher. On cue, the jumble of misconnected nerve endings in his right side that the observation of Thorn River had cost him burned lightly. Not badly, but enough to remind him of that place's terror, and that this business of understanding and unraveling had to continue. If men did not continue it, if they allowed the momentum of their victorious strategy to dissipate, then they would have shown themselves to be as careless and blind as the god that created them.

How: that was what they were discovering, but very seldom the *why*. Transmutation, parthenogenesis, animation of the dead, generation of love, psychokinesis, all the dread mechanisms the enemy had used from Heartbreak Ridge to Thorn River. With each understanding, they revealed themselves to be only the operant expressions of deeper and more complex motivations. He recalled an Office memorandum on the subject which he had read years ago, but could not attach any great importance to what it had said.

The only thing one could do, Etridge considered, was to attempt to understand everything. The sum of these understandings might eventually equal and then exceed the understanding of the single motive for all of it.

Etridge laughed as he visualized the personifications of eschatology and existentialism (both comic, lumbering giants, the former dressed in priest's robes and the latter naked) running on convergent arcs, colliding and merging into a single creature whose chief distinction was in the possession of two backsides: the Meaning of the Universe. He forced down his chuckling when he saw that the bridge crew was staring at him.

XXVI

The valley where he had seen the pegasuses widened out into rolling plains of wild wheat and prairie grass. Groves of cottonwood trees marked the turning points of drainages and streams.

The sky above him was immense. It swallowed the clouds and all other presences within and below it, and turned down the edges of the horizon until one felt one's self trying to balance on one foot to avoid falling and rolling down to it forever. It was nothing like he remembered it to have been. Perhaps the men of power, jealous of the sky's presumption, had kept it shrunken and contained. They had exiled the ocean from Cape St. Vincent because it displeased them. Surely the sky could not have posed significantly greater problems. He wondered how it might have been done, and his face tightened when he thought that if it had been accomplished, then there were machines at Lake Gilbert and Castle Kent working at the problem, translating the gestures and alchemies and ancient disciplines into the precise language of the parallel spectrums, which any man could learn to speak in its single dialect.

On the opposite bank of a stream he saw the imprints of tracked vehicles, a meter across. The tracks led in from the west, followed the stream for a short while and then turned to the south, along his intended path.

Diesel fuel and grease stained the grass. For a moment he found its smell pleasant. At least the vacuum left by the men of power was being filled by something.

One of the tracks passed over a crushed dragon's egg in the semicircle of its stone nest. The unhatched embryo had struggled halfway out of the cracked egg. The ants had carried off its eyes and tongue, leaving the chitinous outer skin; the sun had shriveled its filmy wings and turned the emerging diamonds on its breast and tail to dull pebbles. Once, Aden knew, dragons had been as immortal and as invulnerable as any magician.

XXVII

He found the first tank the next day. It was hardly recognizable as such, being a mass of crystallized metal shards and melted slag. The wreckage suggested rapid alternations of freezing and burning, shifting back and forth across the spectral planes too quickly for the vehicle's defenses to lock onto any single manifestation of the enemy's assault.

The ground near the wreck was chewed up and littered with shapes Aden assumed to be bones and weapons. He picked up one such fragment and found a dryad's head carved upon it. Her eyes seemed to move even when he held it perfectly still; the face studied him in this way for a minute and then closed its eyes.

Aden put the fragment in his pocket and looked around. Far away, again to the south, dust and smoke rose below a spindle-shaped chunk of rock, floating above the prairie. There was a castle built atop it, and the distance could not diminish its delicacy or its outrageous fantasy. White marble minarets braced against the wind by buttresses of malachite and onyx marked the borders of the island and rose about the central keep. That, too, was of white stone, underlain with the captured light of the moon so that, although there was darkness under-neath the island, the castle itself held no shadows.

Following the tracks, Aden saw a line of eight large vehicles and several smaller ones strung out along a ridge a kilometer from the air-island. Three of the tanks or halftracks were burning in ruby and contradictory black.

One of the fires suddenly turned to the same distant blue as the sky. The vehicle inside of it disappeared in the flash, seeming to shrink inside of some gateway the fire had opened rather than being consumed by it.

Aden counted the seconds between the detonation and the sound. It matched his estimation of the distance between them. After all, it had been the death of some-thing from his own world.

He followed the ascending pillar of colorless fire back up to the island. The castle's beauty hypnotized him as he walked. Despite the mental defenses he tried to erect against it, for the mountain garden had shown him how vulnerable he remained to such things, he still found himself irresistibly drawn; the significance of the burning tanks below nearly erased by their graceless deaths.

Richly dressed figures moved unconcernedly along its towers and parapets, reminding him of the river trireme, occasionally gesturing or playing musical instruments whose sound reached him instantly or not at all. Aside from the burning units, there was little activity on the ridgeline, just the revolving dish antennas and ship aeri-als nodding to the wind. Two or three men wandered around the damaged tanks.

The sky was growing around them, progressively reducing the castle's enchantment to dimensions that fit inside Llwyellan Functions.

The tanks are only watching, Aden thought, and recalled the galleries of Joust Mountain, Kells and Dance, and how they had held their fire while thousands were incinerated for fear that their own actions might distort or contaminate their readings.

Why was the castle fighting at all? Surely its seigneur knew what had happened and why. But, Aden thought as he kept moving toward the ridgeline, if he had known, then he would have necessarily understood his own art, and the despair which had engulfed the kingdoms would have driven him to self-annihilation. Perhaps that was what he was now attempting.

He was less than a hundred meters away when a tank in the center of the line probed the castle's walls with a burst of rocket fire. There was no immediate effect. The gunner paused, probably changing magazines, and then tried again. This time the color that erupted where the round struck was that of the sky, the same that had consumed the other tank. Despite the angle, Aden could make out cracks and fissures spreading outward from the point of impact along the walls' marble facing.

Responding to this success, four other tanks and two half-tracks joined in with similar fire. The rockets left the faceted turrets cleanly and the vaporous trails of their flight remained taut in the still air, except near the walls, where the blast concussions smudged them.

They chipped patiently at the castle, tearing away fili-grees of marble and sheets of gold leaf. They were not simply rockets. Aden knew that if he had the Office's eye again, he could have seen the projectiles striking the castle in every dimension and plane it existed in, crushing its beauties into formless, undifferentiated molecular pulp.

The people on the walls became more agitated, their gestures wilder and less assured. One shot blasted a bridge of spider glass from under a running figure. She fell but evaporated before reaching the ground.

He was growing sick and did not know why. It was like the sicknesses he had felt each time he left Gedwyn. It grew stronger. If only the tanks and the castle would leave, both of them. Let the tanks go on with their explorations and let the mountain drift on its mage-wind for the few years left to it.

The Office's gun was in his right hand. The grip hummed like a captive insect as its circuitries changed and modified the composition of its ammunition. The wires under his scalp were hurting again, feeding undecipherable impulses into empty connectors around his left eye socket. For the first time he wondered if the secrets the eye had observed were still inscribed on the individual atoms of the melted spheres, garbled, confused but possibly retaining a singular logic.

It was a double-action automatic that could be cocked and fired with one hand. He raised the gun to eye level. One of the men who had been working around a burning tank saw him and shouted. His voice was lost in the rocket fire and crack of splitting masonry.

He started running toward Aden, looking back over his shoulder at the floating castle. Fires were beginning in its courtyards and the island itself tilted strangely on its axis. Fragments of the bolt that crushed the lead tank hit the man as he ran, turning him to the color of the sky and then to white ash.

Aden's gun fired at the same time. The gun barely moved as pistons the diameter of human hair jumped backward along its hexagonal barrel to absorb the recoil. The safety was on, and his right index finger was resting against the outside of the trigger guard.

The weapon had been pointed at a tank that was not firing, but which had been watching with its antenna arrays. He could not see the bullet hit, but one of the vehicle's slab antennas abruptly stopped rotating. As the gun intended, for it adjusted its ammunition to conform to the nature of its target, the communicative chain was broken; Aden saw this in the suddenly erratic rhythms of the other antennas.

This could not be right, he thought wildly. The gun fired again, hitting an identical antenna on the tank immediately behind the first. "This is not my work!" he said aloud to the tanks. "My ideas aren't that . . . " The gun fired a third time, and the untouched antennas jumped and spun as if they were frightened birds. Some twisted around to regard him with nervous intensity while others wavered between him, the castle and targets he could not see.

Light came arching down from the keep, striking a tank and turning it to ice. The other units responded with ferocious bursts of rocket fire, but only half of the shells hit and a third of those detonated. Trumpets and drums sang out from the castle, at once strident and fearful; they were pitched too high and often broke and faltered in the middle of calls that needed piercing clarity. Flags ran up and down the towers without apparent purpose.

Aden holstered the gun, his hands shaking with fear and uncertainty as if he expected it to forcibly resist. It hummed against his chest in the same frequency as the wires of his cranial net. He backed away, first cautiously and then at a run, running as the soldier had, looking back frantically at the continuing exchange of fire.

His sense of distance vanished in his panic. The shock of his knees locking too far above the ground drove up through his frame. He was strong and practiced in the uses and limitations of his mutilations, but there was too much surrounding him here. He had never seen the two forces actually joined in combat, reducing each other to powder, each force imprisoned by the ground on which they had to stand to strike across their divergent universes. He had lived all his life in a borderland wide enough for the Office to cultivate its extravagant paradoxes and contradictions. There was nothing but an interface around him, the two realities jammed up against one another, drooling maniacally and blindly into each other's universes with no room left for him at all. There had to be room, he was shouting to himself.

Both sides were desperately squandering their powers when he looked again. The island descended until it almost touched the earth. It tilted and spun with the same irregular rhythm of the antennas. Strangely lighted shafts traced outward from the castle. They ripped into the line of torn and burning vehicles, destroying some but failing to visibly affect others. Some of the shafts struck outward, cutting long, smoking furrows in the thick prairie grass and setting it afire; others lanced upward toward the zenith, trying to wound the sky.

The shooting by the surviving tanks became equally erratic. Some of the projectiles slammed into other vehicles while others missed hitting anything, detonating kilometers away on the prairie or rising upward like star shells, casting shadows down into the castle's interior.

The sounds that reached Aden over the pistoning of his own heart were like the screechings of fatigued metal pulling itself apart under impossible stress.

Aden stopped when he heard this and turned to watch the underside of the island dig into the ground. It tilted forward, digging a trench toward the tanks. He could see into the courtyards and gardens inside the walls. The perspective momentarily disoriented him for it seemed as if he was looking down on the castle from some altitude, rather than standing on the ground. It was the same illusion that the sky and the distant, sloping horizon played upon him when he first saw the island.

The building cracked apart and slid from its foundation; then the island itself dropped down onto the vehicles. There was the blue light again, an oval splash of sky reaching down into the earth, ignoring the boundaries of the horizon, spreading outward to where Aden was, threatening to cut the ground from under him and plunge him into a gulf of metal-colored sunlight, without limit or definition.

The concussion caught him around the hips and in the small of his back and lifted him with scornful gentleness. It carried him upward, through the sky and then toward a growing circle of blackness that he entered. Within it there was no sound or movement but the distant humming of the wires inside his skull and the Office's gun puzzling over this new environment, postulating what sort of enemies might live within it.

XXVIII

Hovercraft were like ships, Etridge was fond of pointing out. They answered their helms slowly and with an imprecision that demanded a practiced hand at the wheel. They had to be sailed over the earth. Their routes of passage had to be carefully planned for inclination, surface integrity and clearance between landmarks. All that, at sixty-five kilometers an hour. A properly handled two hundred tonner could be an impressive sight, racing across a foreign plain, the ground beneath it turning to dust as if it had been ignited, antennas and gun turrets regarding the passing landscape with disconcerting stability.

Stamp was glad at this moment that Etridge had selected him as his aide, if only to have been on the hover-ships and not the tanks. But he still would have felt more comfortable if they were following along with their treads and wheels and jouncing antennas. Etridge had been told by Lake Gilbert that they had been wiped out, and had been asked what the hell they were doing out there in the first place. Etridge replied, as he had before, that in view of sharply decreased enemy activity, a reconnaissance in force was justified. But so far into his lands? Lake Gilbert persisted. Etridge played with the radio spectrums so that it appeared that his position was nine hundred kilometers west of where they actually were.

The lack of solid information as to the column's destruction pleased Stamp, as did Etridge's scarcely concealed anger with it. He noted how the veins and muscles stood out from the old man's neck and how the planes of his face jerked from calm for the benefit of the crew, to repressed fury as he again reviewed the readout tapes and the last communications with the column.

"The men of power still seem to be around in some force."

"And ability." Etridge balled up a sheaf of papers and threw it into a corner. The hoverships were traversing a long canyon floor and they bucked and rocked as the helmsmen braked with their engines and drag skids.

"We may not be so far along as we thought."

"We are. The tanks had that, whatever that fairy-tale contraption was, blocked and halfway understood. It should have been turned into dust."

"It was," Stamp mentioned gratuitously.

"So were our own people, goddamnit! There was no reason for it." Etridge picked up another sheet of print-out. "No, that's not right. There are reasons. They just look like questions right now. Here." He held the sheet under Stamp's chin and then snatched it back. "Multiple readings, 'jokers' we called them before Thorn River, showing up just when the column signaled that they'd figured out the castle's power."

"Another mystery, another manifestation of that magician's way of doing things that they couldn't analyze before it got them. *We* didn't see the power of that fire-beast when it came in. It was even hidden from the wind ships."

Anderton came up to the console and braced himself. "Pardon me, sir, the readings aren't completely unknown. If you'll look along the third and fifth lines you'll see they're identical with the ones we picked up a few weeks ago, when we asked Lake Gilbert about the Special Office files."

Etridge's eyes turned inward. "You're sure?"

"Just about. Not only the same sort of power indications, but maybe the same person or entity."

"All right. That could make sense. Tell Lake Gilbert that . . . "—seeing Anderton's question—"tell them again that we have got to have access to their files."

"If we gave them the reason," Stamp ventured carefully, "wouldn't that indicate just where *we* are and what we are really doing?"

"But we are not here, Stamp. We're just making a border land reconnaissance as standing orders and my rank as director of Joust Mountain both obligate me to do."

"Then it seems we will be playing the game the Office used to."

"The game was never played because that player never existed." Etridge's voice showed he was forcibly suppressing the destruction of the tank columns and the loss of the castle's mysteries. He rubbed his jaw lightly. "But if we are doing that, where do you think it will take us?"

"To victory!" Anderton replied mechanically, though the question had been directed to Stamp.

XXIX

They traveled beyond the range of the wind ships. That was another advantage of the hovercraft. Although they were restricted to relatively flat surfaces and gentle gradients, their tremendous lifting capacity allowed them to carry the shielding necessary for fusion motors.

Large animals of reassuringly non-magical varieties were unexpectedly plentiful with the warming weather, so food was no problem.

Stamp had hoped that the distance they put between themselves and home might have eroded morale and forced Etridge to turn back. Instead the men seemed to draw closer to Etridge. The lack of any other authority from home gave his fanaticism space in which to grow and acquire the appeal that Heisner had found so terrible.

The frequency of enchanted ruins had obligingly increased as they moved farther into the kingdoms. At each one, they stopped and studied until they had understood the details of its construction and the heritage of the man of power it had been built to honor or protect or entomb.

There were small engagements too, but nothing like the fire-minotaur and the dead cavalry they had encountered at the first village. Only forlorn and solitary hydras, poisoned wells, badgering homunculi the size and shape of bats, all hideous little dreams that the ships' computers easily handled.

They lost no more than one or two men to each of these irritations. Stamp perversely speculated as to whether Etridge was not also studying their deaths as well as those of the monsters that had inflicted them.

They were within two days of the Holy City. The land around them was covered by a magnificent forest of oak and ironwood trees. Many of the boles on the trees had been laboriously carved or had naturally grown into semi-human masks. They had to move slowly, while the laser guns of the lead ship cut an avenue for them. Stamp watched the faces drift by as they passed, many of them charred and smoking from the light, and they regarded him with murderously tranquil eyes.

Anderton explained that the trees were endowed with unusual phototropic tendencies. The carvings were also the result of gene mutation and when the sensitized bole-endings picked up side flashes from the lasers, they naturally followed. There really was movement and apparent changes of expression, but it was the mindless reaction of cells to ordinary occurrences.

Against this, Stamp pointed out the extraordinary naturalness of the faces in the way they moved and narrowed their eye-carvings, tightening the bark around the skulls that might have been carved underneath them. Anderton replied, "suggestion," and offered to show him the psychological gradients to prove it.

In any event, the gunner continued, there was no need to worry. Morgan, the life-analysis man, had found evidence of rapid gene deterioration. The power that had forced the trees into their simulation of watching, perhaps as an elaborate mockery of the masses of antennas that surrounded the cities of their own world, was located in the Holy City, and it was failing. Soon the forest would be like any other and Anderton remarked that he might like to come back when he retired from the Border Command and build a house from the fine, sturdy trunks.

The lasers burned away the forest for a radius of seven hundred meters when they set down that night. Etridge ordered that their full power be shunted into the guns once the lift engines were shut down, and they paved the cleared ground with a seamless sheet of green glass five centimeters thick.

Their losses had demanded that the crews spread themselves more thinly than they would have liked. It was therefore easy for Stamp to enter the ship's auxiliary radio cabin unnoticed. He shut and dogged the door behind him and sat down at the console. Why, he asked himself a dozen times before concluding that there was no answer, did he out of all the survivors have the need to cling to the ruins of magic. Certainly Etridge's abilities of command had been sufficiently demonstrated; why then did he further judge the nature of the mission that the man had undertaken.

The man did not even give him the comfort of reprimand or rebuke; there were only his opaque syllogisms, each one of which made Stamp feel like he was being shoved along more and more certainly by the velocity of the man's obsession.

He thought he had felt the air of the forest cutting more deeply into his heart as Etridge guided them along, peeling the stabilities of the regular services from his memories with the same reductivism that he used to shatter the remnants of magic. His family, his ambitions, dead lovers, the peace his home had established against the encircling violence of the war, they had all been eroded by Etridge, their definitions erased by the course and direction he had chosen for the ships.

Stamp shook himself and opened the appropriate channels. He left the "voice" switch off; video readout would be more discreet.

He slowly typed his inquiries and accusations, and when the screen in front of him was filled with luminous green letters, pressed the "transmit" button. The information went out in two block transmissions of a fifth of a second each to Lake Gilbert; identification, location, force, personnel, course, casualties, destination, the code for suspected incompetence of command.

Stamp received no immediate response and repeated the message. On the third try, Lake Gilbert answered by correcting all of his information. They were, Lake Gilbert silently, unctuously informed him, thirteen hundred and seventy kilometers northwest of his reported position; they had sustained only two casualties due to enemy action; one tank and three half-tracks remained with them; their line of travel roughly paralleled the fortress line between Kells, Joust Mountain, Dance and First Valley. The reconnaissance was, Lake Gilbert trusted, going well but it reminded the sender to refrain from aggressive activities against the enemy or any deep penetrations into his territory until the strategic parameters of the war had clarified. Interference with their operation by Special Office was impossible in that no such organization had ever existed.

Finally, reports of incompetence, unless sent from a "recognized combat area" were ineffective if not confirmed by a medical officer. Since both their doctors had been killed, Stamp left this item out of each of his three succeeding attempts at attracting Lake Gilbert's attention. Each time, he encountered the same response. He thought of opening voice channels and arguing with whoever was on the other end of the transmission, but decided against it since it was probably a machine.

The words from the last reply stayed on the screen for a minute and then erased themselves. He could hear only the ventilators. Television monitors on the panels above his head reported the flat gleam of moonlight on the sentry tripods around the ships; their beacon lights shone an alternating blue and orange.

The faces on the trees were gone and lost now. There were just the beacons and the white, silent bulk of the other hovercraft on the aft monitor screens. Even at rest, the ship implied motion, silent and imperial across a night paved with glass made by laser cannons. In his frustration and loneliness, he imagined the faces of all the creatures of magic upturned and staring under the surface of the glass road, acting as its foundation, absorbing the shocks of passage that began with the whispering of the high wind ships, descended through the captive storms of the hovercraft, and led, eventually, to the grinding of tank treads and hobnailed boots. They would scar the surface of the glass road, until those who marched upon it could no longer see down into all the lost myths crushed underneath, and they, in turn, were spared the sight of their enemy's triumph and rightness.

He thought, that is happening now, and I find it progressively more difficult to preserve whatever dreams I might have had about this magic. Since the raising of the fire-minotaur, I have seen nothing to indicate that there is anything more than parlor tricks left, dragons pulled from silk hats, as Etridge put it. They were more real when I looked at them through the radio telescopes at Joust Mountain, or read of their barbarities on commemorative plaques at Thorn River and Heartbreak Ridge.

"You see the logic of it?" Etridge had come into the room behind him. Stamp felt broken and far away enough to mask any surprise.

"I see the necessity of it, even for myself," Stamp answered after a while, with some bitterness staining his words. Etridge did not dispute it.

XXX

From the hills above the Holy City, Aden could see a line of blue gray along the southeastern horizon: the ocean was coming back. Soon the place would be known as Cape St. Vincent again. The ocean would advance and drown the palaces and pavilions the magicians had built on the dry seabed as evidence of their power.

He had watched the City for two days, sitting in the same place, trying to fit the patterns of its overgrown gardens and rubble-choked streets into his memories. Three and a half million people had lived there, ruled and overawed by two hundred and seventy men of power and a horde of lesser magicians, monks, acolytes, apprentice sorcerers.

Now only occasional figures moved across the blasted plazas. Pegasuses in tattered liveries, their wings the color of canvas, wandered out of the City and came close enough for him to identify them. Packs of wild dogs harried those that could no longer fly, easily encircling two or three at a time and destroying them.

As he watched, the line of the ocean thickened at the edge of the world, though that could be an illusion brought on by the setting sun. Dark specks that were probably islands seemed to move and acquired the silhouettes of battle cruisers and aircraft carriers.

The 18x scope sight was fitted into the front of his holster. Aden removed it and locked it onto the barrel, just forward of the action's lug pivot. He reversed the holster and clipped its narrow end to the butt to form a shoulder stock.

The scope perceived the City, as it had Gedwyn, in eight of the parallel spectrums. It reviewed each one in turn, progressing outward from normal, visible light, revealing the completeness of the City's desertion. The gun's magazine vibrated in a different harmonic with each filtering system the scope used.

The core of the City retained hints of beauty and power. Aden recognized the domed temple where he had found the unicorn and its attendant and where his eye had been taken from him. The scope revealed successive dimensions of beauty as it interrogated the temple's minarets and vast mosaics, found its alabaster windows unbroken and its bronze doors locked and awaiting the arrival of men with powers sufficient to open them.

The fountain was there too. There was no water coming from it, but the dolphins and seraphim gushed luminous scarlet and turquoise plasmas that poured over the fountain's rim and across the plaza with the insubstantiality of clouds.

The quarter where Donchak's house had been was a tumble of gutted shells, freestanding walls and piles of masonry. There were also traces of sorcerous power left in that area of the City, but it was mostly of the minor sort, orphaned homunculi, incantations stopped in midcasting, one demon assassin, exhausted by the vengeance locked in his heart, hunting a man who had died by his own choice months before.

The wires woven into his head sang as they had for the past two days. Instead of the intermittent monotone he had grown used to, Aden read another level into their pain. Perhaps it was the unicorn that was reaching out to him; he had not admitted to that possibility before. Perhaps it had used the eye in the way that he could have, had he had the time and the peace, had he not worked in the interests of his world, had he not fallen in love with someone from the other.

He rubbed his hand against the leather patch, testing the emptiness behind it and the carved ridges of the perpetually open eye on its front. It was conceivable that the Office had rigged the patch for perception and transmission without telling him. The doctor-machine had seemed pleased when he had shown it to him, just before he left for the Taritan Valley. But, even if this was true, the motives of a mythic organization embarked on missions consisting principally of self-deception could hardly matter to a man in his situation.

That situation being one of treason. The classical offense against the deities, someone had pointed out to him, was vanity, hubris. But there were no gods left to offend in the world, only nations, and the highest attainable sin was therefore treason. In distracting the tanks and possibly allowing the castle to escape into death, he had committed the first treasonous act in the kingdoms of magic, where emulation of the godhead had formerly been the worst a man, commoner or magician, could aspire to.

I affirm my world, even when I act against it to preserve magic against transmutation into numbers and
equations. Good; that implied that there was still some
room left between the two worlds for him to function in.

The land to the south of the City, between the flattened hills and the ocean, was thick forest. Aden examined it through the scope sight, noting the broken towers
of obsidian and tourmaline that rose through the green
cover. Strangely colored birds the size of men and
dressed in armor soared above the land, darting back
and forth above the forest to catch the thermal currents
rising from its borders with the hills.

There were sourceless flashes of light too, that suddenly illuminated irregular patches of the woods, rushed
through the various spectrums and then faded. The
explosions or signals were rarely accompanied by any
sound, but he could usually pick out wisps of smoke and
plasma rising lazily from their general location. One such
area appeared to be at the end of a dark, twisting avenue
that had been cut through the forest. It had not been
there the night before.

Aden examined it through the scope. The path followed the contours of the land, holding to implied, geometrically precise curves and parabolas as it wound along
the ancient drainage and rills.

There were other blast traces scattered through the
forest. They marked the destruction of isolated pockets
of magic and power and the trees had grown thickly
over where they had been. They had imploded upon
themselves and left nothing behind. The avenue was different; it was rich in heavy particle radiations and the

peculiar resonances which exotic alloys often touched off in adjoining spectrums.

The vehicles were at the end of the road. They were fast and well armed. The army of occupation. Aden imagined the land collapsing in on itself, rushing to surround and smother the last few secrets it held—not quickly enough.

The gun murmured to him, sentient, probing the asylum death offered the men of power and their works from the pursuit of the Border Command. Death remained special and singular, but the war had merged it with love and loyalty and hatred and all other mysteries. Aden could think of nothing which could truly differentiate death from the rest of them, aside from the fact that it had been the first and was now the last. There was nothing which showed it to be beyond the reach of the men in the hovercraft and those that would follow, any more than the other mysteries had been.

Aden dropped the gun onto his crossed legs and found himself shivering despite the warmth of the air. He ran the gun's barrel along his sleeve, absently tracing the veins and scars and lines left from the skin grafts and emplacement of wires.

He should feel differently. This was the end of the war. Instead he felt as deserted as the City, spoken to only by buried scar tissue and memories of unicorns more distant than that of the one woman he had been able to love. Is this not, he asked the gun, how all old men feel? Then, knowing that he had always felt that way, he further considered that the Office had always been old, too.

As the air darkened, crystallized tree stumps reflected the first ship's laser cannons. Around it, the fires of the dying kingdoms incinerated the tombs of mages, fertilizing the land with their transmuting ashes, luring vines and seedlings into the charred clearings to hide their shame and defeat.

XXXI

Aden stayed on the rock outcropping for most of that night. The two ships had settled to the ground just after dusk. Their clearing of a wide security perimeter would have blinded him if the gunsight had not automatically shifted its filters.

Blue and orange monitor light marked sentry guns posted around the encampment. A complete darkness reached more than three kilometers beyond them into the forest. After that border, the forest resumed its decay, exploding quietly and burning away or dumbly stalking enemies who had made themselves invincible.

Dragons sometimes roared out, seeking the bidding of vanished masters. Enormous blocks of stone that had been welded into towers and redoubts by ineffable forces broke apart and fell into moats filled with the glowing skeletons of ichthyosaurs.

The gun could not hear this, it could only see. Aden lay against a rock with cabalistic inscriptions chiseled above his head and drifted from the forest's night to his own, then out to the night that was demarcated by the orange and blue beacons. At some intervals he thought he could hear the ocean, at others Gedwyn's voice.

He was sure the eye was still in the unicorn, though much had changed in the world since he had left the hospital. This, despite the fact that it was much more reasonable to presume that the unicorn was gone and the eye simply remained along the floor of the cathedral's nave, staring fixedly at the high altar, reporting the monthly accumulations of dust on the chalices and sacred books to the Special Office.

It will be there, he thought. Its image, hard and glistening, swam through the dark interior of his eye socket, immune to the understanding of whatever devices the men in the forest had brought with them.

He saw the unicorn again, the purest embodiment of legend and mystery, moving incomprehensibly through the world, as remote and present as dreams. Ah, he thought, the Special Office's heart may be at one with it. He conceived of the single creature as the underground, guerrilla army of the defeated kingdoms. It would be possible to live in a world where such forces still operated, and it would be necessary for the Special Office to return to protect it.

All through the night, the gun had whispered to itself, conversing with Aden through the wires under his skin, or with the Office over the nonexistent frequencies to Lake Gilbert.

XXXII

Etridge nodded to Anderton. "All right. What are they saying?"

"The upper three traces"—the other man underlined some readings on an oscilloscope with his light pencil—"are using the old Special Office channels. Even the same scramble techniques." Anderton referred to an open notebook with tan and brittle pages. "Now, this one, you can see, is very different. It extends laterally through several spectrums and trails off into places I'd say exist only in a theoretic sense."

"Our unicorn?"

"Its eye, at least. See the similarities in its wave patterns with those of the first two transmissions?"

Etridge did not, but he nodded anyway. "Any directions on them?"

"The first and the third are directed mainly to Lake Gilbert, and the second one is a responding signal."

"You say, mainly."

Anderton hid his embarrassment behind his radiation scars. "Ah, they also contain secondary signals directed toward us."

"Us?" Etridge brought his face closer to the scope. "That might fit in. The Office could hardly resist speaking to one side of its world without hinting to the other that something was going on. Balance. They hold balance very dearly, you know."

"Sir?" Anderton had been concentrating on getting more definition on the signals, but they remained unfocused.

Instantly, all of the screens across the panel were filled with raging light. Anderton started in his chair and braced his hands against the console as if the luminescence carried a physical impact.

Etridge jerked back too, the surfaces of his face closing shut like the armor of the hovercraft. Watch personnel left their stations and nervously circled the room to get a better look.

This was in silence. Over it, Etridge said: "Would that be our unicorn, Mr. Anderton?"

"Yes sir," he whispered through the colors, touching one or two dials to confirm his own words.

"Does he still address us?"

"It's the eye, the eye, sir. It can't be the creature because it has no power without its master."

"No more than the Office which built the eye in the first place." Colors counter-played inside the bridge, drowning the grids and Kessler-graphs in their swirling torrents. Etridge was dressed in his black uniform, standing in the middle of it. His clothes swallowed the colors, and the metallic whiteness of his skin reflected away everything but an occasional flicker of scarlet.

Obscurely terrified by the colors' violent beauty, Anderton stood up and backed away from his scopes and closer to Etridge's rigidly held blackness. The other men, including Stamp, did the same.

The ship's computers whirred in their cabinets, digesting the flood of information they perceived, searching their accumulated records with measured desperation until an appropriate analogue was found for a particular unknown, the resultant hypothesis tested and proven into a postulate.

"Does it, the unicorn—is *that* what it's seeing too?" Tidal rushes of brilliance beat against scope frames that had patent numbers and manufacturers' plaques riveted to them, threatening to burst out into the room.

"Could the . . . ?"

"That is what the Special Office had been watching? Ah, god." Anderton, crooning low, his voice human and unrelated to his own machines for the first time in months. The man sagged within his uniform; his wide shoulders bent, his pity and astonishment crowded the fear from his joints and let him sit down and cover his eyes.

Etridge said nothing at all. He had established a circle of tired, cynical tranquillity around him. The lights had jolted him at first, but his clothes and skin protected him. All the imponderable beauties of the world, he hinted simply by standing there with his hands clasped behind him, staring straight into the scopes, could be shown to be no more, and possibly less than the sum of their component parts. Man, granted his peculiar affliction of mortality, honed and sharpened through his ages of disappointment, would annihilate first the wonders of magic and then the larger mysteries of death and the soul. Beyond that, god might be discovered, cowering in the tumbled ruin of his own failed creation, his measure taken, and the universe shown to be outside of his control. And then, even that would be studied and broken. They would be alone, safe, no longer menaced by mystery and the anxiety of wondering, all the reasons for heartbreak contained and quantified.

That was why Etridge had frightened Stamp; but he had never seen what had driven the man. Isolated by the limits of Anderton's scopes, the colors of the unicorn's perceptions were still worse than any cold and lonely end Etridge might lead them to.

The alienness of what the scopes contained battered him, and set up a reaction that drove him toward Etridge to share his protective despair. The war, Stamp realized, was not nearly over. A specific enemy may have been defeated or driven off, but his weapons remained to be picked up by whatever random god or madman might stumble upon them.

Stamp glanced around the bridge. The colors made the forward part of the room burn with a thousand different fires, and each one was squared and then cubed by each of the succeeding spectrums in which it burned.

Etridge stepped back to Anderton's station. He looked down the rows of screens and then adjusted filter dials, timidly at first and then with more decision.

The computers assisted with more precisely defined parameters. The colors compressed and withdrew from the borders of the screens; they began to fit within their intended limits on the Kessler-graphs. As though pleased with their success, the computers' electric murmuring eased; overload lights switched from red back into blue. The patterns continued to resolve themselves until, while they retained their stunning beauty, they were comprehensible within the experience of men. They no longer threatened the mind but only the heart, and that could be controlled.

"The eye remains," Etridge mentioned needlessly when the colors had gone, and everyone nodded as if he had suddenly made it true. "The unicorn can still see with it, and the Office is still looking."

"Are we undetected?"—Stamp.

Etridge referred to banks of dials on the right side of the cabin. "No. There seem to be various source detections, both reflective from that little display you just saw, and crude spectrum ranging from the highlands to the northwest of us." Anderton nodded in confirmation.

"Target?" Anderton asked upon finding his voice. He stepped back to his position and ran his hand along the rows of toggle switches. Stamp heard the turrets on the hovercraft's topsides moving.

"Not yet." Etridge waved him away and the turrets quieted. "We'll be in there tomorrow. We don't want to be blowing up our own people." He looked at Stamp. "The Office, you know."

"It is our enemy, too?" Stamp asked from far away.

"Not yet," Etridge repeated.

XXXIII

Aden's campfire had burned through the night in three of the nearest spectrums, excluding that of visible light. Discolored leaves and twigs of certain herbs smoldered in the semicircle of rocks. He stamped it out, and made the appropriate gestures through the proper spectrums to fully extinguish it.

It will be good to see again. He looked to the horizon, to the advancing ocean, and chuckled at his pun.

Aden rose, unclipped the scope from the holster and sighted down into the forest. Fountains of infrared light poured upward from the near end of the avenue as the hoverships warmed up their engines. The dawn sun raked across the treetops, shattering a tower of stained glass and another of yellow diamond with the weight of its light.

He chose a shallow drainage which would shield him from unassisted observation and carefully followed it. After half an hour, he encountered a cyclops lying across the trail. From the smell, the thing had been dead for some time, and there was a great scattering of bones and pieces of weapons around it.

The sun moved up, warming the segmented carcass inside its rusting armor. Ants crawled across the empty eye socket of the monster and gnawed at the strands of tendon that locked its hand around a mace.

Aden shifted and noted a movement on the left. He continued turning, more slowly, and saw a dwarf sitting on a rock above him. He was playing noiselessly on a mahogany flute, addressing his songs to the dead cyclops and then to the other bodies around it. He paused and bowed toward each one in turn. By following his gesturing, Aden spotted more and more corpses on either side of the gully until he estimated their numbers in the hundreds.

Aden's surprise quieted. He remembered that it was often the custom of the men of power to commemorate their victories, and sometimes their defeats if they had been at the hand of some particularly worthy foe, with the presence of such a player. Being made of magic, they lived and sang by their graveyards until a newer battle erased them or the power that conjured them was itself erased.

Aden walked through the bodies. The flute player had eyes made of stone and took no notice of him. He passed close to the miniature human, bent near to him and heard a tune he thought he recognized from years ago. If he had the eye back he could have seen into the other spectrums where the song was being played and learn the true meaning of the battle.

The drainage opened onto the plain before the City. He passed by the scenes of other encounters, each without apparent reason or cause but all having been fought only between the adherents of magic. There were no shell casings, no spent cartridges and no chemical residues that the gunsight could discover to show that his world had had a hand in any of them. He found only more dismembered myths of the sort that carpeted the dry lake in front of Joust Mountain after the great battle there, swords engraved with still glowing runes and baroque mottoes written with dragons' blood on the ground beside dead giants.

Each successive battle site had its attendant watcher. They were mostly built along human lines but were invariably dwarfs or stunted, as if their diminished statures could exaggerate the importance of an engagement by contrast. Some played flutes like the first he had seen, while others strummed lyres carved from rosewood and inlaid with pearl, monotonously beat animal skin drums with curved talons dangling over their rims, or just sang wordlessly.

Aden ventured up along the slope of the hill on his left as far as he dared without chancing discovery by the hovercraft and found more of the same. The land was pockmarked with the remains of small, bitterly contested fights, spreading in a rough arc around the walls of the City. There were no great lines which would have indicated the maneuvering of organized companies toward any goal. It was more as if the magicians had emptied all the City's grotesques out onto the foothills, told them the slurs their brothers had committed against their masters' names, and set them upon each other until all were dead.

The gunsight showed that the dead had many different kinds of magic clinging to them, but the memorialists were formed from a single power. The rhyme and measure of their songs, when one could hear them, indicated a common basis.

A sea gull screeched in the air above Aden. It orbited him for a minute and then flew off, back to its ocean to feed on garbage from his world's approaching navies.

Magic, defeated by the examinations of his world, might have sought to affirm its own existence by turning upon itself. The men of power had continued their internecine wars even as they prosecuted their larger offensives against rationality, so it was not inconceivable that their servants had attacked each other as their masters sickened and died. They must have been the last, and the unicorn, alone but for its own servitors, may have created the dwarfs to bear witness to their struggles.

Aden reached the foundations of the road he had left the City on. He was in the open now but at the same elevation on which the hovercraft must approach; the forest would hide him. Steles and pylons, many discolored and snapped in half, bordered it. Everywhere, he conceived, there was commemoration and memorial, projections of thought and alien sentiment that reached through time to connect the observer to the powers that had caused them.

There would be no such monuments raised by the people he had seen last night. They will regard them as signposts whose existences will taunt them and draw them farther along. The unicorn would be sought out for the same reasons.

Aden walked more quickly. Last night he had put together reasons for fearing the arrival of the men. Now he realized that he might be one of them. Though he sought only the eye that had once been his, he was still here. He had used weapons of his own world, the gun and his knowledge of the tank column's analytic web, in destroying both it and the fairy castle.

A hollick the size of a ferret scuttled across the road in front of him. The gun was in his hand instantly. He tracked it until it disappeared into a crumbling tomb on the left.

The gun hummed irritably in his hand. He pointed it to the southeast, to where the forest came closest to the City's walls. High plumes of plasma jetted into the air behind peacock fans of questing radiation. The ships are looking, he whispered to the gun, they are deciphering everything, every deserted altar, corpse, creature, rune and scrap of magical rubbish left behind.

Aden was sweating. His palms glistened when he held them open, and for a moment he feared that their increased conductance would distort the gun's perceptions.

XXXIV

"The old coastline followed this elevation, here." Bock traced a line with his finger. His hands were small and delicate, as was his body, and that was permissible for a cartographer. He had been distrusted by rear echelon people because he had shown some fascination with the nature of the enemy in the way he decorated his maps with fanciful castles and mythic bestiaries. For the same reasons, Etridge valued his presence and his loyalty. "Assuming a steady rate of advance, the ocean should be back to its original borders in four years. After that, I would think intensive dredging can have the harbors ready for deep water traffic in three more."

"Very good, after seven hundred years."

"Better than good," Bock warmed to the subject. "These people never seem to have touched the land. Bauxite, rare earths, pitchblende so rich I'd think that's what makes parts of this country glow at night, copper lodes you hardly need to refine. And all that gold and silver and lapis lazuli they conjured up out of mud is transmuting back into stable nitrogen and phosphorus compounds. The land'll be a garden. It'll be like coming to a new country." Bock looked out the ship's windscreen, fitting his personal mythologies into degrees of latitude and longitude, feeling the earth whole again between his compass and dividers.

They were wrong about the man. He's ours, just infatuated with their stage dressings; it's part of growing up on one's way to attack the godhead. Etridge smiled and Bock thought it was to share his delight in the new land.

"Sir!" the man at the wheel called out to Etridge. "The City!" The trees thinned out as they came onto the plain around the City's walls.

Etridge pushed his hand forward and the engines accelerated in response, blurring the late summer grasses beneath them.

The windows cleared to show the City, long quays and stumps of cranes fronting the skyline of dissolving minarets. Stamp had a notebook open and recited the names of the structures he matched up with old photographs or with the multi-spectrum pictures the unicorn's eye had sent back.

Curving roads faced with marble intersected their path. Grass and weeds had pushed between the paving blocks and were already splitting some of them in two. Piles of skeletons could be observed on either side of the ships; each one had a small creature playing a flute or lyre or other instrument standing beside it. Stamp saw them raise their heads from their playing and stare at the approaching ships.

As they sailed by the players dropped their instruments and expressions of sadness crossed their remotely human faces. Stamp knew the white sides of the hovercraft retained their gleam and polish and speculated as to whether it was the ships or the creatures' own reflections which caused them to look that way.

Anderton reported that the players held no power other than that which sustained their lives; they posed no overt threat. The source of the power itself was identified and traced to the City. Anderton requested permission to hit one of them, but Etridge said it would hardly be worth the trouble.

The City's dimensions sharpened as they approached. The port of Cape St. Vincent had been absorbed by an incredible mass of palaces, guild halls, temples, private fortresses, circuses and baths. They had all seen the reconnaissance photos and the architects' elevations posted for a hundred meters along the main corridors of

Joust Mountain. But they had not been prepared for this. Even Etridge. He judged that the City was already in an advanced state of decay. What could its beauty have been like five or twenty years ago? It was possible, he admitted to himself, that the force of the City's splendor alone could have stopped our missiles in mid-flight and smothered the blast of their warheads.

That was what the Special Office had dealt with every day for three hundred years.

"Ever seen colors like that? Not like last night, no, but look, look . . ."

"Jeez, that dome, to the left of those three towers. You have that map?"

"*H* Town itself. I'd never thought I'd get to see it standing up or even want to."

"Ten, possibly fifteen kilometers."

"Imagine the effort that went into that. Must have taken at least . . ."

The voices rose over the engines.

"And the lot of it falling to pieces like wet paper," Etridge said loudly. "Look at them." He pointed out at the gaping memorialists. "Look how much in love they were with their own power and now with their own death. They were in love with themselves, so deeply they acknowledged nothing else." The ships passed on either side of a tangle of skeletons with its attendant player, and the blast from their supporting air cushions scattered them like jackstraws.

The conversation returned to the normal subjects of range, speed, navigation, energy analysis. Etridge pressed his hands together on the grab bar and permitted his eyes to wander away from the City. If only we were all Andertons and Bocks. He knew that if Stamp now agreed with him it was as much from unacknowledged hatred of the City and the wizards for failing as from any allegiance to him. They had proved themselves weak and vulnerable. However long their threat would linger in the world, it had shown itself capable of defeat and could therefore be feared with a righteousness that hid one's sense of divine betrayal.

Etridge wondered briefly how much of his own thoughts were motivated by loyalty to the world's way of doing things, and how much could be attributed to the wizards for having allowed themselves to be defeated and their dreams with them. Had he seen that, too, at Thorn River?

Stamp waited beside him, referring to the notebook and making corrections on the maps with a pen. Bock was seated to the right of the helmsman; his arms were braced on the control panel as he patiently took photos of their approach. A cable connected the camera to the ranging computers and made it unnecessary to constantly adjust the focus.

"Have you found an opening yet?"

The pilot gestured toward the northern end of the walls that faced them. "Gate Five."

"What did *they* call it?"

"The Teachers' Door," Stamp volunteered; his voice was flat and abstracted.

"Good. After all, we're here to learn. Aren't we, Bock?"

Bock nodded behind his camera. "All we can."

"All there is," Stamp continued in the same tone.

"Anderton. Tell the second unit to find a position up in those hills where they can see as much of the City as possible and still be in range of everything but their smallest stuff. Make sure the area is secure. If they can avoid those musicians and their pet bone heaps, they should. No souvenir hunting. And constant surveillance through all the spectrums as long as we're inside."

"How far in can we take the ship?"

Stamp flipped to an aerial photograph of the City; it was in infrared, so it had the appearance of a negative. "This avenue"—he indicated with his pen—"leads from the Door to a plaza, here. From there we can take either this street or this one into the old section of town. That's where the only real power readings are located."

"The unicorn, do you think?"

"The position is roughly the same as that of the transmission we got last night."

"The eye, too?"

Stamp shrugged. Another enemy blunder. Even he had been able to find it. A year and the poor beast had not caught on to the fact that it was still revealing itself and its master, if he was still around, to the world. "Same position, same power characteristics. Both of them running on identical lines."

Etridge found himself momentarily depressed by the other man's words. Unavoidably, he felt that he had taken the belief from Stamp, rather than having merely shown him how fragile and insubstantial it was. Soon, he thought, the disappointment will break up enough to allow the hatred and contempt to surface; then the desperate intoxication of the pursuit would overtake him. That was the way it had worked after Thorn River.

The other hovercraft fell behind and then glided away from them.

Their ship paralleled the City's western wall. Fragments of vast mosaics depicted the heads and limbs of unimaginable beasts, great armies of gilded warriors and the slaughter of hovercraft such as their own.

Etridge wished that the crew was speaking again, if only in astonishment at the walls. The quiet in the cabin was that of the unbeliever in the cathedral, equally awe and embarrassment, each emotion reflecting back upon the other and magnifying it. There were only a few bodies this close to the walls. There was nothing around which could dilute the size and majesty of the City with its pathetic defeat.

At least there were the engines and the sounds of the scopes and the antenna drives and computers, all of them thoroughly unimpressed with the ruins whose binding forces they had striven for years to untie.

Etridge knew that the application of certain radiant energies would instantly obliterate every mosaic that remained. Others would cause the walls themselves to collapse—which they would do of their own accord within a year. That would be incorrect. He might bury the unicorn before his ships could understand it.

The unicorn was a servant, possibly still serving its master though he had died. He had been the City's greatest magician, if the carefully edited reports of the Special Office could be believed. The lines of power that still connected him to his servant must be found and followed.

There it was. Etridge felt his energy returning. He sensed it growing in Stamp and Bock and Anderton too.

Something at last to occupy the field that had been deserted for the first time in seven hundred years, something overwhelming enough to contain and animate their mortality and rage.

Carefully now, he reminded himself. This too was a spell that could be broken like all the others. He learned how to preserve it at Thorn River when thousands were incinerated while he gently probed and tapped against the skins of their destroyers. "Are we near the gate?"

"One kilometer."

"There should be an approach road. Set it down there, five hundred meters from the Door. We'll wait for the other unit to get established, and then go in tomorrow morning. Stamp and I, and two more men will be on foot. Walking speed, and try to be as careful as you can. I'm sure the museum people will want to see everything as authentically as possible."

"Tourists," Anderton snorted.

"No," Etridge said lightly. "Remember, gentlemen, we are not here. We are hundreds of kilometers to the west, exploring border lands recently vacated by our distinguished adversaries."

"I don't think Lake Gilbert cares where we might be." The desolation remained in Stamp's voice. So many things were being taken from him so quickly: the consequence of having clung to them too long.

"So much the better. We can live with their indifference. If they did want to know where we really were, I think it might be just as much to stop us as help us along." Mutinous talk, even for a commander on the edge of retirement and a continent away from his headquarters.

They drew level with the Teachers' Door, swerved to face it and then settled to the road's surface. Etridge appreciated the drama of the scene and hoped he was not overplaying it.

Anderton leaned over in his chair and touched his sleeve. "Presence on the walls, sir."

XXXV

Below Aden and several hundred meters to the west, the boat-shaped hovercraft waited while an identical unit sped away toward the hills he had just come down from. The purity of their whiteness burned into his eye and made it difficult to distinguish the turrets and antenna domes that pebbled their topsides.

Still only two of them. He looked again and recognized Border Command chevrons on their vertical stabilizers. If the world had chosen to ignore the direction pointed to by the Taritan Valley, the air would have been thick with transports, wind ships and armored helicopters bringing men to bury the dead palaces under linear steel and polymeric roadbeds straight as rifle shots. Instead there were two renegade ships.

He reached the street. Withered, whitened trunks of jewel-maples in onyx planters bordered it, the skeletons of grotesque birds caught in their branches as the sparrows had been in Gedwyn's garden. Aden sat on the edge of one and tried to calm himself. He knew the City. They did not. But they had photos and maps and possibly the image that the eye, *his* eye had sent back to the Special Office. The ships could see through walls. They could probe into solid nuclear masses and listen to the sound of his breathing on the other side.

The wires under his skin were inert. Coldness occupied the empty space where the eye had been. The Special Office was absent this morning. Only its weapon remained, and its eternal humming seemed to be of the same range and frequency as the singing of the memorialists.

That parallel was too close. Both the Office and the men of power had withdrawn and vanished. One left the gun; the others had left the singers lamenting over their remains. The Office has left its own memorialist, too, he thought as he ran his hand over the blinded side of his face: me.

He got up again and found walking surprisingly easy. I am too young, but that is acceptable. I am scarred, but most of the wounds are on the outside and all but the largest two are healed. Though they are Border Command, they cannot know how to deal with real Special Office people. God, Special Office people barely knew how to deal with themselves.

Better, he murmured, and found the skin loosening around his jaw and cheekbones. "These ironies," he began to the passing warehouses, "are not necessarily self-destructive. They can be as amusing as the tricks of your magicians have been. One can hide inside of them, be protected . . . " He cut himself short when he became aware of how loudly he was speaking; they could be listening, through the walls, from kilometers away.

They might not be the only dangers. There was hunger and thirst. His rations of dried meat would be adequate for another week, and there was water for three or four more days. The wells of the City had always been infused with magic (the properties of those in the red light quarter, he remembered distantly, had been renowned through half the kingdoms of magic). Unnameable plasmas, many which he knew to be imperceptible to his gunsight, could fill the spaces between water molecules. The City could abound in mystical booby traps, snares, hair-triggered spells that might have enough power left to them to kill him.

His steps became more certain. Just like the old days. Perhaps one or two of the men of power remained, disguised as homunculi, or statues, or merged into the very person and being of the unicorn and its attendant.

The war, if one's premises were properly phrased within one's mind, might still be on. The awful gateway of death need not yet be entered to meet the nearest enemy.

The sun was going down and the sky over the walls was illuminated by pink and golden clouds spectacular enough to compare with the fraternal wars of the magicians.

If he had the Officer's eye he could carry on the search at night. It was better that he should rest, wait and hope that the ships would be doing the same. He found the town house of a merchant that did not depend on magic to hold its walls together.

He slept on a bed with blue velvet hangings around it, embroidered with the stars the wizards had decreed should hang in the skies of their universe. The room was paneled with oak, carved with bas-reliefs of the commerce of the kingdoms of magic: merchants bartering over spices and rare essences, the trade in slaves (dispirited scientists and soldiers shocked at the irrelevance of their inherent rights and dignity), the dragon-runs where the great beasts were bred and strengthened.

XXXVI

Etridge had personally supervised the placement of the tripods around the ship. There was a moon, so the City was visible in the normal spectrum. The energies that bound it together could be seen through the scopes and sensors, overlaying the walls, rising along with the towers and minarets or running along portions of the avenue that showed through the open Teachers' Door.

"Only the Special Office has seen it like this," Etridge remarked to Stamp as he swung the monocular away from him. "Or like this." The City's jagged outline shone like mercury.

"Until they gave their eyes away." Stamp was intensely depressed.

"I'm sure they kept some for their own. How else could they be able to watch their beloved magicians turn the rest of us into toads?"

"They were not like that."

"No? They were like you, then? Maybe a little more caught up in their own dreams. Enough so they could turn the wizards' crimes into gold and drop their own weapons when they became too powerful and too true for them to handle."

"And *we* are not that way?" Stamp continued, looking at the City and, from the sound of his voice, aging perceptibly.

"Of course not. You've known that for some time," Etridge snorted.

Stamp did not reply, but looked back through the left side windows, up to where the lights of the other ships were bright enough to reveal their colors and keep separate from the stars.

XXXVII

Before he went to sleep, Aden made sure that the room's eastern windows were open and that the bed was positioned in front of them. He was on the fifth floor of a building which was, in turn, set atop a slight rise. The gunsight's infrared range showed that the horizon would be visible over the walls in the morning.

The sun and the morning breeze carried salt air. Gulls circled in front of the windows. Their sharp calls reminded Aden of the morning singing of the City's muezzins when they had come to announce the end of the wizards' testing of each other and that it was safe to honor them again.

Aden awoke quickly. As he had during his first operations for the Office, he waited for his eye to reach through the closed lid and make sure it was safe to move. He had continued doing that after the unicorn had taken the eye, forgotten it and then picked up the habit again in the Taritan Valley, safest and gentlest of all his world's places.

When the engraved eye told him nothing, he opened his own. A thick layer of dust coated the room's furnishings and diffused the sunlight into dream tonalities.

The air muffled the sounds of the City's continuing disintegration and of the gulls singing to the fleets that would follow the ocean to this spot. Aden stretched in the quiet, not wishing to get out from under the blankets.

He swung his feet over the side of the bed, put on his trousers, shirt and boots, and found some dried meat in his pack.

He finished eating and sipped night-cooled wine from his canteen. It comforted him as did the dusty air, and set the various realities that hovered near to him at a bearable distance.

He guessed the hour to be around seven when he reached the street. The sun was coming over the City's walls; it caused the facing buildings and mosaics to flare with stunning radiances. One mosaic, unable to bear the touch of the world's sun, crumbled soundlessly into white dust and drifted down from its supporting wall to the cobblestones.

From Donchak's old store he could orient himself and reach the center of the City. He clipped the holster-stock and the sight onto the pistol. Ranging the nearby streets, he found nothing more than residual energies and lines of force mortaring buildings together or animating decorative statuary.

He could not believe that the City was so deserted. Surely the despair of the magicians could not have infected the common people to the point of suicide too. But a great and fundamental underpinning had been removed from their society. Like the men who had ruled them, they had lived for seven centuries in the demonstrated rightness of a certain universe. Then something had suggested that they were wrong, that the deaths of their sons and fathers had meant nothing, that they had served shadows. The only ones who could have reassured them had discovered the same thing and left. Aden *had* seen the people of the City. They stood dumbly around the imagist in the village park, tried to start farms that would need water and fertilizer, wandering through the mountains seeking gardens where magicians had stopped time.

He walked through the confused streets the wizards had built. At intervals his path was blocked by the rubble of collapsed buildings. His gunsight showed him one heap that was only an illusion of some complexity. This disturbed him for it implied that there might still be some magicians left in the City who could be aware of his presence. Then he examined it more carefully and found that the pile of marble and splintered hardwoods merely represented the decay of an equally imaginary palace.

It had been common to retain a lesser man of power or his assistant to create the illusion of a grander building than that which one really occupied. The practice was much favored by petty merchants and parvenus of all sorts. After all, the City was founded on subjectivity. The power of magic defined reality and such illusions were often appreciated as much as the more respectable mansions built of actual stone and mortar.

Aden stepped into the debris. It offered no resistance, became invisible once he was inside of it and then regained its apparent solidity when he came out on the other side. The comic aspect of the scene was undeniable, and he laughed out loud for the first time since he had left the Taritan.

XXXVIII

Etridge, Stamp knew, was tall and sparely built, and would have passed for a banker or a diplomat in any city of his world. He was also strong for his age, and the unhurried arcs of his movements indicated exceptional reserves of energy and strength.

The City was before them, the sun hidden below its walls. The tapering shadows of domes and spiked minarets pointed their darkness at the foothills to the east. The bones and the other hovercraft shone in the new light as it swept down the hillsides toward them. Stamp moved closer to Etridge, holding his automatic rifle in both hands. If one of the magicians or enough of their power remained, and if he found himself still capable of believing in it, he conceived that it would be a sign to overpower or eliminate Etridge. But if the fraud continued to expose itself and if the City kept dissolving before his world's reality, he also knew that he would need Etridge, as desperately as he had once needed his parents and then a woman named Sarah in the places they had each controlled.

Grant and Halstead were standing in front of the hovercraft, waiting for them. Both looked like younger models of Anderton, stocky, well muscled, unexceptional features; perhaps it was a blandness of spirit that permitted them to stand in front of the Holy City with no detectable emotion. Stamp recalled the emotion Anderton had shown before the lights, and thought that it might also be simple courage. They were good, strong men who wished only to end the force that had produced Thorn River as well as the fairy castles; because they followed Etridge did not necessarily mean that they followed his dreams too.

Their uniforms were scrupulously correct. Packets of electronic equipment studded their tunics. Stamp noticed that their weapons gleamed with cold and constant light when the sun reached them. The mosaics and frescoes on the City's walls remained in shadow, and the contrast between the men and the hovercraft, and the City was startling.

Illusion; it means nothing, he thought, and shielded his eyes. I'm starting to think like him.

Etridge carried a small carbine that looked like a hunting piece. Its stock was made from finely grained wood and the engine turnings on the action lent a softness to the metal. It seemed to be intended more as an insult to the City than a threat to whatever might be left inside its walls.

The sentry pylons had been taken down and stowed inside the ship. As always, it suggested the sea with its canted bow and enclosed superstructure. In a few years the ocean would be back and the true ships would be on it, as they should, rather than floating over deserts and the deserted highways of the enemy.

Again: momentum, convergence, inertia building up in amounts sufficient to overwhelm magic's beauty or the sorrow for its passing, and propel them past anything the men of power had dared to dream or question.

"Ready?" Etridge said to the City. He was distinct and sharply defined before Stamp, as if the sound of his voice had closed the final perceptive circuits necessary for the other man to see the world that stood around him with guns and telescopes in its hands.

"We've got as much as we can right now, sir. There's new activity around the central location." Anderton was commanding the ship. No one questioned the wisdom of Etridge walking outside.

"How so?" Communication would be by voice with the ship following them, watching over their progress.

"Customary variations on existing wavelengths and resonances."

"Anything unusual in that?"

"Only in concentration and variety. It doesn't look like anything we couldn't untangle if we waited."

Etridge considered this for a moment. "No reason to wait. Gentlemen." He glanced at Stamp on his right and at Grant and Halstead back alongside the ship, and stepped forward.

The air was quite still. In between the sounds of the decaying city were those of the men walking, quickly joined by the whistling of the hovership's engines. Stamp looked back and saw the dust clouding out from the inflating plenum skirt. The ship rocked a little and then rose a meter from the road.

Up in the foothills, the sun reflected off the armored surfaces of the other ship. Stamp felt more relaxed than he had thought he would be, neither did he feel desolate as he had before.

Etridge set an easy pace so it took a few minutes to reach the Teachers' Door. It was built from slabs of pale granite that had been fused into a single archway, seventy meters square. Strangely wrought projections of black iron and bronze were spotted along its inner surfaces; they were the physical points on which many of the

Gate's non-corporeal doors were attached. Behind them the two main doors had been left open.

In contrast to the frescoed and mosaiced walls around them, the doors were blank metal, charred like wood along their edges. Anderton informed them over the loudspeaker that the other doors of magic had provided the color and ornamentation the wizards so loved.

Stamp gripped his rifle more tightly to stabilize himself against the sight of the interior City. Its exterior had been unitary, complete, bound together by its muraled walls against their approach. Inside, it fragmented into innumerable parts, as if it were a diadem suddenly hurled against a wall in a fit of anger.

They entered upon an avenue leading directly east, so that it appeared to end in the new sun. On either side its light gilded the rotting buildings. Statues and allegorical figures with the limbs and faces of beasts moved in abbreviated, repetitive gestures.

"See it?" Etridge confided from the side of his mouth. "Just as it was outside the walls with the bone heaps and the singers. Everything devoted to show and ornament." He waved condescendingly at the ruined statues, and several of them obligingly cracked and fell apart as they passed. Etridge had known that they would before they had gone in, but the effect was worthwhile. Grant and Halstead joked to each other and Stamp found himself fighting back a tentative smile.

"The Avenue of Wisdom," Anderton informed them.

"The appropriateness of our path continues, don't you think?" Etridge, again looking straight ahead and speaking conversationally.

Stamp had memorized the aerial views of the City, so he knew the name of the street as it was spoken in the magicians' speech. He also knew, as did Etridge, that many of the triumphal columns and gesturing figures that lined the street commemorated the victories of magic: Heartbreak Ridge, the Third Perimeter, Kells.

If Etridge was as human as he pretended to be, his calculated arrogance might be as much defensiveness as from any intoxication with anticipated discoveries in the ash heaps. Stamp looked about him as he walked, and decided that if it was true, Etridge's capacity for absolutes would render such a distinction meaningless. Etridge could carrying the guilt of a hundred Thorn Rivers inside of himself and still chase his enemies, or their ghosts, or their founding gods until they all dropped from exhaustion.

A dying cyclops limped toward them from a side street. Its single eye was blank and yellowed, and its skin was gray with the mortal rot of Etridge's world. Stamp guessed that it lived because it was too stupid to understand itself. Etridge could understand it and he signaled Grant and Halstead to hold their fire while the ship examined the creature.

It continued to move toward them, obscene, shredded genitals hanging between its legs, the remains of quilted silk and gold mesh armor on its shoulders. Three years ago it had been happily passing its eternal life crushing the enemies of its master; three nights ago, Stamp would have cried to see its ruin so clearly.

Etridge kept walking at his deliberate pace. The sun lit up his face and uncovered a symmetry identical to the hovership's, calm and immovable and ultimately unaware of the strength the cyclops might retain because they were looking through him, using what magic remained to him as a lens that focused the antennas and reflector dishes on the more distant secrets of its dead master.

Anderton said something and Etridge raised his gun. The small weapon hardly bucked and for a second the monster stopped and stood, glaring ridiculously at them. His skin then lightened and granulated like sand drying after a wave. When he was almost white his eye dusted away, the particles falling straight down in the windless air, and then his head, and then the torso, all falling down upon themselves.

Etridge made a point of walking through the powder that was left. Stamp wondered if they might not be going too far out of their way to trample on graves. But that, he remembered from the notebooks, was the idea.

The ship passed over the dust too, and when it was gone the paving stones were clean.

XXXIX

Aden was gratified to find the house so easily. He had taken only two wrong turns before coming upon it. The flags and carpets were gone, so he did not immediately recognize it. But the blue tiled street was the same, as were the perilously overhanging houses and the smell, though all of this was now thickly overlain with rain-clotted dust.

Except for the desertion and neglect, the quarter had survived the wizards' retreat much better than he had first thought. From the hills, the scope had shown him disintegrating roofs and walls, their edges chipped and charred as if a burning rake had been drawn over them. But the walls here were put together with solid stone and cement and faced with marble slabs hung on iron pegs. The statues in front of the more prosperous establishments were respectfully immobile, though they did copy the style and pose of those in front of the magicians' palaces. If the materials were merely physical, their design, the twisting streets and high towers reflected the tastes of magic.

Some of the businessmen of the City had perceived that they could not take it with them, or did not care to go to the places where you could, and so felt no need for memorialists or animated gryphons fanning their grave sites with stone wings, reciting their genealogies until time ended.

Aden struck his hand against his head to drive these thoughts away. The wires were on fire again, the voice of the dead Office leading him on to claim what they had specifically denied him.

The houses leaned over the street. This might have been what Donchak was feeling, he told himself, because this might have been what he was trying to do.

The eye, he repeated to himself, the eye. I must move toward it. If I do not then it may be shown that I am only responding to pressures and stresses imposed by magic, my world, and the Office standing between the two, and that I have no will of my own.

He entered Donchak's house, brushing aside cobwebs and decayed rugs. No power remained in the latter, or at least none that the gunsight could show him. As it had in the merchant's house the dust in the air masked everything in afternoon light, slowing it as if the place had already been removed from present reality and into memory. He asked himself why nothing in his own world had ever seemed so tender and remote. Gedwyn's face rose before him from underneath the Office's healing scars. The sound of his own sharpened breath drove it away.

Aden focused his eye; it seemed more acute in this half-light. He had been in the building one evening, years ago, but still remembered the placement of the furniture, now overturned, the arrangement of the rooms and where Donchak's elaborate tea service had been.

He went over to the serving table, opened the teapot and saw a crust of dried sugar on its bottom. He smelled it and caught a lingering hint of a drug that had been fashionable in polite society when he was last there.

He put down the service and walked into the back room. His orientation, though it was now in daylight instead of by the moon, brought him to the garden in the rear of the building. There were burn stains on the flagstones where the trivial magics Donchak's customers once paid him with had turned from luminous flowers back into the sulfurous compounds from which they had been made.

The wrought iron gate had been blasted off its hinges and lay half-embedded in the stucco wall across the alley.

Aside from the dust, Aden noticed that the ruin was clean. Though deprived of souls, the artificial beings and homunculi the magicians had left behind had still hungered. Apparently, they had fed on the City's garbage while they waited for their masters to order them to war upon themselves. The favorites of the kingdoms fed on year-old fish guts and offal while his world ate sparingly of meat and knowledge, waiting in its air-conditioned bunkers for the screaming and chanting from the east to end.

He stayed in the neighborhoods of the common folk for more time than he should have. The streets continued their turnings with more sensuosity than he recalled, but the course of his progress traced his memory with surprising accuracy. The nondescript contours of the merchants' quarters had impressed themselves as deeply upon one section of his intelligence as the majesty of the City's greater works had on another.

When he reached the square, he found its dimensions as foreign as those of Donchak's building had been reassuringly familiar. The gun came to his shoulder and showed him lemon and saffron plasmas pouring from the fountain. They curled and spurted from the splintered necks and craniums of mermaids; contradictory shadows played over the statuary and the paving blocks around the fountain, blanketing the midmorning light through all the dimensions perceptible to the gun.

The plasmas rose more than a hundred meters and then fell in asymmetrical arcs to the fountain and the square. From there they ran in broad streams that reached to the surrounding buildings before they disappeared into the paving stones or evaporated into a whiskey-colored mist. Through it, twisted homunculi limped, blowing on bone flutes or on bagpipes with bellows made from the scrotal sacs of gryphons.

Aden gasped and ducked back into the alley, as Donchak had made him do ages ago. The memorialists walked past him. None that he had seen on his way into the City had done more than play their instruments or sing; they had never moved from the site they were meant to commemorate. That was their function; that was why they had been created.

Aden felt his heart quicken. Sweat accumulated on his skull and seemed to increase the conductance of his cranial net; it was singing with a volume that threatened to drown out the memorialists. If only he could find some kind of sense in the electric humming, something beyond mere suspicion or feeling to tell him what the Office wanted. If only, for once in its vague centuries, the Office would say something clearly, specifically, definitely, even if it was nothing more than, yes, we still live and exist, and, therefore, so do you. That would be enough. Enough to assure him that the song was not the sympathetic resonances that the hovercrafts' searching radiations struck in the wires.

As he watched, two memorialists came through the opened doors of the cathedral. They were transfixed in the sight's crosshairs, framed by the melted forms of mermen and shrouded by the billowing plasmas. The two circled around the square and passed in front of where he hid; then out of the plaza to an avenue which he remembered to have been named after a woman.

More artificial beings appeared in groups that became loose formations, all dragging themselves out of the cathedral's darkness, down its monumental stairs and across the plaza, each one stumbling along to his own discordant tune, each new group prodding a surprised burst of electric thought from the Office's gun. He felt its weight and texture changing against his cheek as it modified the composition of its ammunition to deal with each successive creature, and then modified its own structure to deal with the recoil and firing of its transmuted bullets.

The gun was a thing of infinite consideration and accommodation, continually adjusting itself to suit both the worlds of science and magic. If the creatures of magic were to be slain, it would be with bullets that were, ultimately, made of magic, rather than its tangible duplication. If the target was from Aden's world, as the tanks had been, the instrument would operate along lines of rigidly defined masses and energies. What, he wondered briefly, painfully, had the gun formulated for Gedwyn.

In its every aspect, the gun was an extension of the Office. Aden wished that its strength would fill the gaps so many years of equivocation and balancing between the absolutes had left in him. There should have been a normal history inside of him where conviction and doubt alternated, as did the feelings of love and hatred, loyalty and deceit, defining a median between the opposing extremes. Instead there was only the attempt at the median itself without supportive feelings on either side.

The magical creatures increased in number and variety. Tall humanoids draped in dignified togas of jet silk marched down the wide steps to the square. In contrast to the memorialists, they neither played nor sang but maintained silence in the one auditory spectrum open to Aden. They carried long tapers that were unlit in the spectrum of visible light, but which his gunsight showed to be blindingly aflame in three others; the fires, gold, turquoise and amethyst, swirled upward around their heads, illuminating their austere and unnaturally drawn features with a startling radiance.

Tame cerberuses paced quietly at their heels. They wore chains of linked and beaded diamonds around each of their three necks.

Other creatures in the shapes of men followed the taper bearers. The gunsight showed them to be made and motivated by simple enchantments; even Aden had some rough idea of the physics upon which the magicians had unconsciously based their lives. They were cast from metal, and the chromium brightness of their skin reflected the noon sun as brilliantly as dragon's hide; the lines of their idealized faces suggested the wounded severity that Aden had observed in some Border fortress commanders.

They were dressed in dark blue velvet knickers and tunics with white hose, trimmed in a lace that was yellow and then ruby in successive spectrums. Each one carried a black cushion upon which rested some crown or decoration or medal.

The gunsight brought the decorations close enough for Aden to marvel at their intricate beauty. Although static and limited, the coronets and medals not only occupied distinct presences along each of the spectrums open to him, but also clearly implied honors that could be understood only through a grasp of all the worlds in which the men of power had held sway.

Understood.

These too, were memorialists. They were deafeningly silent, but they expressed the memory of someone powerful beyond imagining, who had won these tokens of honor and courage in adventures near the borderlines of death and unreality.

So great a man as that, the gun reminded him, was gone. Not killed, or driven into exile, but fled before something more terrible than himself or any power he might dare summon to stand with him against it.

Aden wondered if he could hear the wailing of the hovership over the silence of the creatures. Not yet.

Diamonds, rubies, opals and sapphires that held all the darkness of the ocean the wizards had sent away glimmered on the chains of knightly orders, locked and suspended in filigrees of platinum and iridium, stitched as the memorialists had been in the crosshairs. Their mystery and symbolism should have been unapproachable. Aden whispered: yet I have defined them, calculated their range, atomic weights, compositions, meanings, constructed projectiles to shatter them, and all with a machine that is at least half magical itself and therefore incapable of such complete understanding.

Grave and imperial, twelve ranks of the silver-skinned men walked down the steps of the cathedral. Straggling memorialists scampered around them, baiting the cerberuses, blowing on flutes and pipes, their grating songs emphasizing their silence. It reminded Aden of nothing so much as a funeral.

When the great men of his own world died, either naturally, or by the assaults of magic turning them to stone in their studies or into salt on a battlefield, much was done to mark their passing. Perhaps it had only seemed like a great deal in contrast to the cold, unrelenting rationality his world had adopted in all its other dealings with life and the enemy.

First, there had always been the regiments of foot and horse and their bands playing the slow songs of mourning. The pipers from the highland units were always the most poignant to Aden. They marched with a briefly halting step that seemed to dam up the skirl of their instruments until what reached the listener was an essence of wild sadness.

After that would be chamberlains and other functionaries, displaying the honors of the deceased on velvet pillows. On the dead men's orders and medals, Aden suddenly remembered, there had been dragons and centaurs and all the other mythic creatures that had been driven from his world when they assumed actual, physical reality. But, at these times, they still attended the great, dead men of his world in miniature, surrounded by jewels and mottoes in archaic languages, wrapped about with the music of regimental pipes.

If one continues the parallel, he thought, and if it truly is that creatures of magic serve the men of power in life, but in death shift their allegiance to those of my own world . . . where has their treason occurred, and why? Magic had always been thought of as having been reborn; Gedwyn had told him that. What had drawn the unicorns away from it the first time and convinced them that they should live their fragile, eternal lives on the medals, commemorating the achievements of his own world?

I am personifying again, he muttered through closed jaws. But (always *but*, never *if*, as it had been before the Wizards' War) that was the first hinge of the conflict, that the allegories and metaphors and stories had regained literal truth and power.

But (again), we never lost it. His hand held the gun more tightly. His index finger was pressed painfully against the outside of the trigger guard.

The unicorn emerged onto the cathedral's portico surrounded by solemn black archers and falconers with eagles on their cocked arms. Its attendant, his gleaming body still swarming with the tumult of battle and the hunt, walked blindly at its side. When Aden had first seen him, he had been kneeling toward the altar, looking away from him. Now he could see that he had no face, just an elliptical surface that was reminiscent of the doctor's at the hospital, except that hundreds of tiny cavalrymen charged and retreated across it, then gave way to the coronation pageants of princes that had died long ago. He had no genitals, no fingernails, pores, openings, nothing to imply the flawed and fragmentary life that animated the memorialists.

Aden took out the hilt piece he had picked up near the first bone pile to find a face for the being. The dryad's eyes opened and stared awkwardly to the side until Aden turned it toward the parade. Tear tracks became visible on the carved wooden face, although it did not change expression.

Aden watched and felt its density increase until the fragment was like a lead sinker in his hand and its eyes lost all power of movement or suggestion of life. These acts, he thought, must have drained its last quanta of power. Now it is like the stones of the City and will, in time, transmute into dust.

Last night this would have terrified him or increased the bleakness of his heart. Today, he found that it fit into the center of this City and into the observation of this parade. If the gunsight had been versatile enough he might have been able to perceive the path along which its power fled, discover whether it dissipated into the air or if it was recalled by one of the chamberlains across the square who had decided that the dryad's face would be better suited to the neck chain of the decoration he carried, rather than in the hand of Aden.

The face would not have fit the attendant anyway. Aden put the piece of wood back into his breast pocket and returned his left hand to the bottom of the pistol's magazine.

The crowd of chamberlains, memorialists, lancers mounted on gryphons, archers, taper bearers and falconers made it difficult to keep the unicorn in sight. Still, it was as tall as he remembered it to have been; the arch of its gleaming neck rose above its escort, and the point of its horn was at least four meters from the ground.

They crossed the portico and descended the stairs. From there they moved slowly to their left, following the perimeter of the square and then crossing between him and the fountain. Aden caught the unicorn in the gunsight and tried to determine whether the eye was still there. He found that the creature did not even exist in the fourth spectrum; but that was a place of limited phenomena, and the unicorn's creator apparently had not thought it worthwhile to occupy. The eye, however, did. It floated alone in the air, serene and independent, protectively encircled by lavender wraiths and gryphons.

The wires blazed under his scalp at levels approaching actual pain. The gun hummed so loudly as it digested the incoming radiations from the parade that Aden was afraid one of the passing creatures might hear it.

He dialed the sight to probe the last three spectrums. The unicorn was present in each of these, the beauty of its movements unaffected by the alien lights and presences that surrounded it. In the sixth, the eye was silver and nearly indistinguishable from the ornamentation of the unicorn's chanfron. In the seventh, it was like a faceted diamond, patterned by its interior circuitries, while in the eighth it lost its corporeal substance and evidenced its singularity only by a blue aureole of longwave radiation.

A sound drifted up one of the angled streets that opened onto the square. Aden noted it, but it had to grow from vague indirection to a distinct purring before his conscious mind detached itself from the sight of the unicorn. When it did, he felt his heart and mind suddenly slam against each other and flatten into two dimensions.

He turned back to the parade. Nothing showed that any of them had seen or heard. The main group—where was the catafalque? there should be a gun carriage if this was to be a proper funeral, an ancient caisson with the flag-draped coffin on it—continued at its measured pace. The unicorn itself was within two hundred meters of where he was hiding.

The eye jerked around as he watched, sweeping past him and then aiming at the far end of the square where the first taper bearers were.

"It knows," Aden whispered to the gun and to whoever might be listening to the wires in his skull. "Of course it knows," he went on for himself and for the benefit of the listeners. "How could the eye be there for years and not have it learn how to see with it." Aden's voice rose involuntarily.

A memorialist shaped like a hairless baboon raised his head from his flute and looked directly at Aden. It was thirty meters away, but the gunsight brought it close enough to let its dead, enchanted eyes bracket the vertical line of the crosshairs.

The gun examined the creature, selected its ammunition and fired with a sound no louder than the air at evening. It guarded its muzzle flash as it appeared in all of the spectrums open to it. When the player dropped only the unicorn noticed.

Another memorialist, this one a dwarf in a harlequin's costume, dragged the carcass away from the line of march, obviously concerned that it might cause one of the taper bearers or chamberlains to miss a step. As he took it away, the corpse first turned olive, then tan, and then scattered away as if it were made from leaves.

Aden knew that his finger had stayed on the outside of the trigger guard. This did not trouble him any more than it had when the gun had fired on the tank column.

The unicorn, or at least its eye had seen. It turned its face toward him and Aden found it too beautiful to carry only terror with it. The eye, being a thing of rationality, should have been beyond the reach of anything made so purely of magic. But the creature had found a philosophic bridge, and had possibly translated the information the eye collected from the world around it into terms comprehensible to it. If the eye and the unicorn had become a single thing, they would be as removed from the two enemy worlds as Aden felt himself to be, as the Special Office truly was.

It *is* different, he became convinced. The gun butt was slick and warm in his hand. Its power made it special even before Donchak had taken it and given it to the unicorn. Now it and the unicorn had both become something different. He wavered in his desire and awe of the eye alone.

He felt something like hope for a moment. A synthesis of some kind had been achieved and a middle ground discovered which might be occupied by magic and rationality at the same time. This could be the peace that had eluded the world for seven hundred years.

Weakness came into his joints, and his chest was filled with the wet cotton feeling of fear. Simply because so wondrous a being as the unicorn had combined the antagonistic realities within itself did not mean that its achievement could be shared. And even if it could, if individual human spirits could be made great and strong enough to reconcile the torrents of contradiction that the unicorn's own eye and the Office's must have been reporting, there was no longer anything left to compel his world to accept it. *They* had triumphed. The unicorn's achievement was a bitter joke upon them all.

They are coming in this triumph of theirs, he murmured to the unicorn. They are the hunters again. The duality of your vision cannot protect you any more than it protected Donchak or the Office.

The eye was still centered in the gunsight. The unicorn may have nodded its head in response, or the movement may have been a reflexive jerk caused by the sound of the approaching turbines.

Up and down the parade, various beings slowed and stopped. They turned their heads questioningly, each looking through the one or several spectrums which their creators had allowed to them. Each found a different thing, and so they reacted in different ways, some with what Aden took to be fear, others with indifference, others with eager curiosity. It was difficult to read their expressions.

Whatever emotions the unicorn's face might have revealed were hidden by its chanfron. Only the two eyes showed. The black and golden horn moved like a metronome against the fountain's plasmas.

Again: the caisson? Who among all the millions of things and beings that have died here is all, any of this meant to commemorate?

Aden ducked out of the doorway and darted across the street to the building opposite him. It was made from granite blocks and its stolidity marked it as a former government office. No attempt had been made to decorate it or to disguise its origins despite its prominent location. This meant that Aden would be obvious to anyone that happened to look in that direction. Without any masking powers or presences even the gun would appear as a fire.

That did not matter. The unicorn had already seen him, and it was inconceivable that the ship had not had him under some kind of surveillance since morning. In either event, he was small and of little consequence.

He crept along a columned arcade until he was almost out into the square. From where he stopped, the cathedral was partially blocked by the fountain, but he had a clearer view of the far end of the area.

The ship only seemed to be near to him because of its size and the arrogant clarity of its lines. Four men were walking in front of it. One was dressed in black while the rest were in a gray that matched the building stones around him.

The gun reported them to be human. They existed in the same form and in the same limited way in each of the parallel spectrums. The guns they carried with them were equally simple and unitary, as was the absoluteness of their function.

Conversely, the hovercraft following them was a thing of vast complexity. The sight showed it alternately sucking every scrap of information from the dimensions around it, and then unleashing great torrents of active-probing radiations. In two of the spectrums the hovercraft's antennas aimed such amounts of inquisitory energy at the parade that inexplicable shadows were cast behind the fountain, outlining not only its statuary but also the plasma jets, as if the ship was the sun and the magic of the fountain was a darkness in the world.

Dish and flat panel antennas rotated slowly, carefully on top of the hovercraft. Their pace matched the maddeningly relaxed step of the four men in front of it.

Was this to be the caisson and catafalque? Aden suddenly asked the gun. Could it be that the unicorn had summoned *them,* as it had the sorcerous throng and possibly Aden himself? So many meanings: as if he were in a room roofed and walled with mirrors and prisms, each reflecting a different image and then breaking and commingling light from others, reflecting back on each other, drawing more and more tightly together in an antagonistic circularity that enveloped him completely.

The line of marchers spread out laterally as they hit some invisible barrier twenty meters from the ship.

Though they were turning on curving, bending paths, the beings continued to move forward. Aden saw them stiffen, rise on their twisted spines, drop their instruments and then turn away from the whirling antennas. He adjusted the controls on the scope, as much to find reassurance in their solidity as to sweep the open spectrums. The stone column stayed cool and linear alongside his body.

Despite the alienness of the memorialists' faces, or those of the taper bearers, he thought he could find a common line of knowledge, despair and demoralization. Whether their eyes were made from stones set in ape's skulls, or of sapphires in the faces of godly abstraction, he discovered the same slackening, the same absent redirection downward to the paving stones, the same tentative gestures of their hands or claws toward their heads as if to catch the furious storm of knowledge the antennas were forcing upon them.

The second man from the left nervously ran his hand along the action of his rifle and compressed his eyebrows in fear and mystification at what was happening before him. But that was all. The other three were impassive.

The ship played its high siren wail behind them, rocking on its air bubble. Its guns and rocket launchers stayed fixed and all the motion of its antennas was circular; like the magicians, its greatest power lay in simple gestures made to the accompaniment of certain words, under auspicious alignments of certain stars. The ship had no need for inelegant displays of destructive power.

The men stepped forward. The members of the funeral parade stood in front of them for a second. Then they turned away, facing fully toward Aden again. They had been buried in enough information to suspect from what and how they had been made.

They found, suspended in the simple web of Aden's gunsight, that their heritage and ancestry were in free helium, dust, deuterium, splintered wood and the leavings of dogs.

Others had found that they were nothing more than thoughts, the compacted wave fronts of wizardly imaginations. When they saw this, their own sustaining beliefs in themselves faltered and then crumbled. They dissolved from physical actuality back into the nothing from which they had been formed.

No wonder the servants of magic were often so grand, Aden concluded, when many of them were imaginations made actual. Created thusly, they had never been compelled to make any concessions to either of the real worlds.

Aden examined their faces as they blew away and, unlike the others which were bound, however distantly, to the substance of the world, detected resignation and even contentment.

The rest acknowledged the horror and watched their magnificent clothes, finely wrought weapons and their own limbs rotting through a progression of more stable compounds. They saw this and knew, irrevocably, why it was happening and why nothing else could happen.

All the dreams of glory that they had saved from the departure of the magicians crossed their faces and ended as they walked away from the ship on disintegrating feet, and then on their hands and the stumps of legs turning to sand and sawdust.

Wailing, more terrible than what he remembered from the convoys of refugees fleeing Thorn River, reached him over the ship's engines. He was witnessing a battle being fought completely on the terms of his own world for there were no more men of power left to shape new energies to confound the inductive apparatus of the ship.

The unicorn with its attendant had stopped. Drawn like sleepwalkers, their guard of gryphon-cavalry and archers left them and proceeded cautiously toward the ship. They looked stronger than the taper bearers or chamberlains. Muscles built from essential energy pulsed under the gryphons' golden fur; the riders were armored like knights, protected by terrible charms and talismans.

Their strength would mean nothing. The ship was luring them with its open challenge to their power and to their belief that their own reality was ultimately sacred and therefore beyond knowing.

He considered shooting them. If they died, it would be as whole, functioning beings; their lives' mystery would be translated into the greater mystery of death. They were only the created, not the creators, and so would not know of the possibility of this escape. But they were not the ones he should risk revealing himself for.

The gryphons and their riders ended in the same way the memorialists had. Some vanished so quickly and completely that Aden had trouble being sure if they had existed at all; since they were only thoughts to begin with, their end erased their memory as well as their present physical reality. He recalled them, seconds after they were gone, only in impossibly distant suspicions and flashes of déjà vu.

The rest went more slowly. They reached the twenty-meter line around the ship, stood there a moment, and then faced around to Aden, walking, it appeared, into the earth as their bodies crumbled. The ship had shown them the dark that had always been under their feet. They had been created as lights and beacons against it, but the gulf had been larger than the magicians had suspected.

This kept on for half an hour. Then all of them were gone. Aden estimated that there had been three to four thousand individuals, every one of them fashioned from some kind of magic. Within an hour all their lives had been transformed into formulae, Llwyellan Functions, micro-dots and Henschel profiles.

The four men began walking toward the unicorn, and the ship followed them like an immense pet. Its air cushion kicked up thick clouds of the funeral dust into the air, where a new breeze caught it. The gunsight showed the cloud to be comprised only of static elements, devoid of energy or animation.

The dust fell on his clothes and the gun's barrel. Aden worried for a moment that it might clog the weapon's delicate mechanisms, then decided that it was too late for such thoughts. He leaned out from behind the column. The unicorn and its attendant were where they had stopped when the hovership first came into the square. The dust of their thousands of retainers and protectors also settled on the unicorn's flanks and on the attendant's shoulders, dulling the brilliance of its coverings and tumult of his skin.

The City was empty with shocking finality. Even that morning, there had been the promising threat of lingering magic strong enough to survive the ship. Now the City was a complete ruin, occupied only by its conquerors and its last refugees.

XL

Stamp watched them becoming shrouded in the fog of their own dissolution. They spread out as they came toward the ship, tripping over the ones that had fallen in front of them. He saw them piling up in a wide sweep before him, their colors and hideous forms blurring together, sinking into the paving stones as they milled forward and then away.

Anderton spoke to them from inside the ship. The parade's wailings did not drown him out for he was talking in frequencies the dying could not scream in; the ship adjusted that for him. The effect was comforting, for it lent a feeling of detachment from the horror meters in front of him. It was as if they were only watching a film or hologram of something that had happened long ago.

There had been no sorrow in anything he had seen since they left the forest. Small fractions of pity and curiosity, but little else. The city had proven itself to be as fragile as Etridge accused it of being. The self-destruction of the magicians' servants outside the walls had repelled him. It was a stupid exercise in self-indulgence.

All he had wanted was a gesture worthy of their own myth. Instead he faced the dried-out husks of puppets, phony, impotent monuments to millennial frauds. Everything faded before Etridge and the coldness of his ship.

As they had walked down the Avenue of Wisdom, the ship's radars had discovered an actual magician, locked and embalmed inside an egg of frozen time, in a garden near the square. In a fit of unbidden helpfulness, the computers had come up with the formula explaining how it had been done five seconds after they had charted its location. Two minutes later they produced a formula to crack the spell. Etridge did not think it worth the trouble for the printouts also showed that the magician had died as a consequence of its casting.

Anderton's voice continued, needlessly explaining the mechanics of the ruin occurring in front of them. He noted that the number of creatures was rapidly diminishing, but that the unicorn had not joined in their march; it remained behind, five hundred thirty-two meters from the prow of the ship. Its attendant was with it. It had the eye.

Anderton also noted that the presence they had detected that morning was with them again, hiding in an arcade directly west of where the unicorn was standing. He was human and had been with the Special Office before its official closing. Would Etridge require more?

"No." The parade had destroyed itself. A last memorialist ran back and forth through the dust of his companions, gibbering repulsively. He tripped and fell, exploding into white ash like a dandelion blossom. Etridge raised a set of field glasses, surveyed the square and then motioned them ahead.

Stamp found himself walking easily, taking long, relaxed strides. He could make out the contours of the unicorn and its attendant. Their scale was diminished by the emptiness of the square, and the spaces around them were vacant of any enchantment. There were no memorialists left, no bearers of candles or honors, nothing to block the intrusion of his own world into those spaces, to stop it from extending outward around the isolated unicorn, over the City, over the half of the planet occupied by the men of power, outward too, into the sky and the regions closed to god.

Anderton's voice acquired a relaxed assurance as they crossed the paving stones. The air bubble of the ship kept blowing the creatures' piled dust into the air, lifting it and sending it over them as they walked. At times the dust shoaled thickly, becoming a tan mist that permitted him to stare directly into the sun; it hid the walled horizon and the buildings enclosing the square, suspending the unicorn and its companion like raindrops in a blank sky.

Stamp could not believe that this was what Etridge and the other Border commanders had wanted. All Anderton and Bock wanted was an end. But the commanders must have spent their waking nights expanding strategic maps into tactical diagrams, smothered with continually increasing numbers of arrows: green, brown, silver, black arrows thrusting against the shadow-enemy, enfilading his flanks, blocking his routes of escape, herding him and his enchantments into indestructible, sterile bell jars. And then, more explicitly, the reality of where the arrow points and the shadows interfaced, smeared with fire and lights rocketing back and forth against the parallel spectrums.

This, he thought as he walked through the coarse haze, should have been the time when the ramjet bombers would have finally sought out the aristocratic men, dressed in their splendid robes, attended by legions of fabulous beasts.

He glanced at Etridge, but found that he could not tell if the man had ever conceived of the ending in such a way. Whatever sort of idea Etridge may have saved for this time, it would have been molded by the thought of Thorn River and what he had done there; it could not have helped but act like a lens upon the man's perceptions and dreams. Like the eye of the Special Office, or that of the unicorn, or Joust Mountain itself.

The wind dispersed the dust and the air was clear again. Stamp cradled his rifle in the crook of his left arm and brushed some of it from his sleeves. He did not realize the arrogance of the gesture until he watched Etridge do the same.

Etridge came closer and handed him his binoculars; they had a small gyrostabilizer in them, so they were no problem to use while walking. The man-being did not surprise Stamp. He had seen any number of animated statues and artificial humans as they had traveled through the City, and one more, no matter how wondrously constructed or covered with miniature universes, could not do much more to his senses.

The unicorn, however, touched him across the distance that remained. Like the attendant, it was covered by what might have as easily been its skin as armor, all of it etched with designs of elusive complexity. Its right eye glowed and flickered in its socket, flame like, having no iris or pupil to indicate the direction of its stare. There was a burning in its left eye socket too, but it was dimmer, behind, or possibly inside the jeweled humanness of the Special Office's eye; that one was clearly fixed on them.

Stamp unconsciously slowed, becoming absorbed in the perfection of the unicorn's features and proportions. It was, he conceived with the exaggerated distance of memory, everything he had once thought the kingdoms of magic to be: outwardly magnificent, with an interior reality so foreign to the thinking of his world as to be beyond its mortalities and brutal, knife-edged hungerings.

The eye fit into its lines and presences. In theory, that should have been impossible. The eye should have qualified and flawed the unicorn; instead it strengthened the creature with its knowledge, turning it into something that did not need the magicians.

"We're under attack from them," Anderton reported over the ship's speaker. His voice again sounded harsh and strident without the screaming of the dying underneath it.

Etridge held out his free hand with the palm toward the ground. The three other men and the hovercraft obediently stopped. Stamp heard nothing beyond Anderton and the ship's drag skids.

"Any problems?" Etridge asked conversationally. He motioned again, and Stamp returned the binoculars.

"A bit more than we'd anticipated, sir. Could you come closer to the ship? It'd be easier to protect you here." Grant and Halstead backed up with their rifles raised across their chests. Etridge walked casually back, half turning away from the unicorn.

Stamp reached the ship and pressed his back against the flexible plenum skirt. Air escaping from it felt cool against his ankles. They had been on their feet since they entered the City at the Teachers' Door.

The coolness emphasized the noontime heat in the square. Though it was late summer, the temperature was rising above any possibly normal level. Stamp felt sweat collecting under his arms and dripping down along his ribs. He looked at his watch: 1:00. They had been in the square one hour and five minutes.

The fear building inside of him hinted that this was neither a season of their own world or of magic's, but something new which Etridge might not understand and which, in its understanding of him, could escape, hiding and stalking them through interwoven thickets of magic and rationality.

Stamp knew his mouth and throat were dry. It was inconceivable that the eye would not have been discovered by the men of power without the unicorn participating in the deception.

The centuries of the war had been defined sharply. Betrayal and treason were nothing more than the maintaining of an allegiance for one side while serving the other. Then there was the Special Office, becoming lost to the services and then to itself; now the unicorn. They were *apart* from either world, he thought in his fear; a universe of ungovernable multiplicities suddenly rose before him.

"Signals into the area showing up too." Anderton's voice was disjointed and implied a great deal of preoccupation with the defense against the unicorn.

"From where?" The heat made Etridge's words sound more emotional than they really were.

The pauses between Anderton's replies became longer. "Outside. From home, somewhere. It's very weak and we're only getting it through augmentation with the other unit." A full minute of silence from the ship. "The broadcast . . . This is remarkable! I'd never thought that thing capable of so much new stuff!"

"The broadcast?" Stamp found himself saying ingenuously.

"No, goddammit! The goddamn horse out there!" The loudspeaker roughened Anderton's irritation and turned the rebuke into defensive anger.

Quiet.

"Are we losing?" Etridge inquired mildly. He was looking toward the unicorn and so addressed it, rather than the ship.

"Ah . . . " Voices were undercutting Anderton's. "No. No, I don't think so."

"What about the signal, then?"

"It's to a receiver in this area, using a cross-spectrum wave front. Looks like a variation on what the people at Lake . . . " More delay, more voices from the men away from the speaker mike; " . . . from Lake Gilbert."

"Special Office character?" Etridge's words were melting with the heat and his outward calm could not protect them.

"Yes. Or at least like it. Our man is in the area of reception."

Etridge's face closed its protective planes, muscles bunched under his dry skin and scar lines that had been invisible flamed into redness, spelling out the memory of Thorn River and all the suppressed agonies that revolved around it. He feels the world breaking apart too, Stamp thought; something is thrusting upward, underneath us. "All right. I want it, and the thing beside it if you can get him. Shoot to block its path of travel until we can get some kind of control on it."

Etridge walked through the furnace air. Stamp's palms were still slippery, and he had trouble grasping his rifle when he followed. He raised it tentatively. The unicorn and its rider swam in the space above the iron sights, more insubstantial and equivocal than they had been in the dust.

Streams of perspiration coursed down Etridge's face too. His paleness gleamed like the ship's. But his eyes were almost glowing like the unicorn's right eye: no pupils or irises, just mad illumination and fanatic purpose drilled into sheets of white metal.

Stamp forced his breathing into regular patterns. The effort required him to restrain his fear and to keep walking carefully, one booted foot in front of the other with the same cadence as the ship's antennas.

"Come on. Come on." Etridge, strained and urgent. He was gesturing outward with both hands, the little rifle in his right, motioning Stamp and the other two men to spread out. "Block its exits. Don't let it out of the square."

" . . . the square?" Stamp muttered to himself. "The thing's nearly stopped the ship and he wants us to corral it?" He found this ludicrous, and it gave him a moment of clarity. The City is deserted, yet I feel it to be overrun by unknown presences, secret agencies, madmen, lunatics, spies. He wondered if this was how they had felt on the first day of the Wizards' War.

XLI

Aden could not tell whether it was the heat alone, or if the wires were at last making sense. The net pounded against his mind with a symmetry it had not had before, and which he distantly connected with the days when there was an annunciator connected to it that had allowed the Office to speak directly into his brain with the tone and inflection of his own thoughts.

He looked at the unicorn through the gunsight and saw great, violent sheets of metallic light unfolding from its guarded head and horn, blanketing the spaces perceptible to him and reaching out to smother the ship and the walking men.

There were shields around them that dulled the light and turned it aside. Their composition must have been infinitely complex, shifting without reference to linear time to meet the battering of the unicorn's magic. More than the unicorn, the shields were largely beyond the capabilities of the gunsight.

The men and the ship moved slowly, with obvious pain.

Aden braced himself against the column. He had no shields of his own to stop the heat or block the frightening resonances that he saw through the sight. He thought they were also visible at the edges of his vision, as when one saw faint stars by looking for them with purposeful indirection. That had been the way the Special Office had looked at everything.

The attendant had not moved. Although it was impossible to know, Aden thought that it was the unicorn's own creation. The other possibility that suggested itself was that the giant was the unicorn's master and creator, now enslaved and drained by the creature and the singular vision it had acquired.

But its power, whether the unicorn's own or stolen, did not stop the ship. Its shields expanded against the tiers of light in proportion to the closing distance between them. The undulating walls and wave fronts stiffened, as if they had suddenly dried out, and long, irregular cracks ate at their fluidity. The fissures spread through the unicorn's power like branches of lightning, all twisting angles and lines through which the blueness of the sky shone with jarring tranquillity.

The fabric of the unicorn's power broke against the ship's defenses. Both its eyes began flicking from side to side, briefly snaring Aden where he hid, pleading for help in the casting of its spells, and then jerking back to the advancing ship.

The men staggered under the weight of the enchantments the beast hurled at them. But the heat and the lights that infused all the hidden spectrums only magnified the ship's progress, muffling its irregularities, blurring its halts and hesitations into the semblance of relentless progress.

Aden pressed himself against the stone, frantically asking why he had to watch this.

The unicorn moved for the first time. It shifted its weight from its front hooves to the rear, apparently trying to find better footing on the paving stones.

It wavered, adjusted its stance again, and then took a step backward. The attendant giant stayed where he was. Only the figures on his skin moved.

A shout came from one or two of the men, and a thin hiss of probing electrons and subatomic particles rushed from the ship to fill up the space from which the unicorn had just stepped, studying the nature of the absence it created as thoroughly as other radiations continued to examine its presence.

The men were walking faster, moving more at right angles to the unicorn rather than toward it. Aden looked through the gunsight and saw globes of shimmering light with lines traced upon them, forming within the ship's dish antennas, and then flying outward against the current of the unicorn's magic, toward the center of the square. Thick ropes of energy followed behind them, using them as anchors. Gradually, they contained and enveloped the enemy's world. And if one had been captured, bound in unimaginable chains, imprisoned in a Chinese box of cages-within-cages, each one confining the wizard in each of the spectrums he chose to occupy—what then could one do with him?

Aden guessed. The hideous fantasies and speculations of the preceding nights, and of the entire time since he had left the Taritan flooded back into his mind.

Everything, except the ship, the men flanking it and the unicorn, was held immobile in huge calipers of light and energy. He barely noticed that the City's pace of decay was speeding up around the square, where the near misses of the ship and the unicorn blasted into the walls and buttressed towers.

The gun was locked against his shoulder. He found a shallow border cut into the column and rested the gun barrel against it. With the bracing and the gun's own internal stabilization systems, the image of the unicorn froze in the sight. It wavered only when rolling currents of heated air billowed between them, making it seem as if they were separated by depths of clear water and the ocean had returned and buried them in the middle of their war.

"You!" The voice was far away. "Ad . . . Aden? Aden! Stop him!" Him? The unicorn? Himself?

The wires burned, inflicting visible patterns of light on his consciousness, trying to reassure him with the familiarity of their pain, trying to distract him from the voice with broken snatches of coherency.

Tiny numbers in red lined the bottom of the gunsight; the unicorn's range was exactly thirty-one meters. The gun spoke to itself and reformulated and redefined its ammunition.

At a range of twenty-eight meters he could see that the unicorn's horn was not made of gold and ebony. There was only a single tapering spiral of gold that held an absolute vacuum within it. It was a vacuum of light as well as of air, warmth, energy, life. It was a spear made from the darkness that was supposed to lie behind the throne of god, the night into which even he would, in time, tumble and be lost. It was an absolute, a thing for which there could be no understanding or comprehension. Perhaps. That was how the gryphon-cavalrymen had thought of themselves.

"Stop! Please! Aden, listen to . . . " Engines rising to his left and boots falling rapidly on the paving stones. The ship was pouring immense amounts of energy onto the square, dissolving the fountain and then drowning the attendant where he stood.

The unicorn focused its own eyes and that of the Office on Aden, twenty-two meters away. The cranial net shrieked inside his skull, speaking a single word that he had never heard before.

The gun fired at the command. His senses, heightened by fear, saw the iridescent bulb, electric blue and white, grow from the muzzle, burning away the skin on his knuckles, exposing nerves and old scar tissue, expanding and transmuting into silver and then into the deep chrome that one sees in polished mirrors. The shell was without mass in four of the spectrums perceptible to the gun, infinite in one, and weighing four, five and eight grams, respectively, in the remaining three.

The unicorn faced directly into its flight. The shell drove into its left eye, shattering the artificial one and then the magical one in back of it.

The gun repeated the sequence. This time the bullet struck the right eye, Aden distantly heard more shouting, hysterical and deafening in the abrupt silence of the wires inside his head.

A wall of energy from the ship swept between him and the unicorn. It fell and shoved him laterally down the length of the arcade.

The unicorn died behind the wall. The energies that held it together erupted through the two bullet wounds, and poisoned all of the lands and universes into which it might have tried to flee and carry on the War.

The burning air whipped itself into a storm and then into hurricane circularities around the unicorn. It rose above the sound of the ship's engines and the cursing of the men's voices. Aden could not tell if he was unconscious or buried under debris. Above him, masonry and metal broke apart with thunderous reports. The ground under him quivered as more buildings disintegrated and fell. To maintain the symmetry of its own conception of the world, the dying unicorn was draining all the magic that remained in the City. Sudden gaps were created which could be filled in only one logical way.

Logical. The mode of death was that of his own world, not of the unicorn's.

At the center of the winds, hidden from him by the ship's last screen, Aden envisioned the part of its horn that was the night acting as a dark polar star for the escape of the creature's soul. Its creator had been powerful enough to have imprisoned that on the unicorn's forehead; the creation of a soul so that the unicorn could follow and serve him after its death would have been comparatively simple.

The horn shriveled, and the life of the unicorn fled into it. Behind it, the magical energies of the creature and those which it had torn loose from the City increased, effloresced and blinded Etridge, Stamp, Grant and Halstead.

XLII

They had huddled under the grounded ship for an hour while the unicorn died, unable to move because of the storm it had summoned. While they waited, the winds outside reached four hundred and twenty kilometers an hour and drifting blocks of hard radiation bombarded the ship's armored sides.

It had taken another two hours for the dust to settle. There were no more plasmas spouting from the fountain when they emerged, neither were there any memorialists looking for corpses to eulogize or statues saluting their appearance. The unicorn had taken all the City's magic and hidden it in its own death.

Etridge looked around himself. The afternoon showed them nothing that might have been a recognizable part of a building, so complete was the devastation. Coherency of form remained only in the paving blocks under them and in the ship itself. The cathedral was gone, except for its stairs leading up from the rubble-filled square into blank air. Everything had been crushed and leveled, as if the seven hundred years of war had never happened, as if the wizards had never slaughtered their millions.

Now, Stamp thought, we have only our murderous philosophy and the weapons that articulated it to prove that the enemy had thrown their enchantments against us, or that they ever caused things like Thorn River to have happened.

Anderton reviewed the spectrums. The only thing left was the Special Office man and he directed Etridge to where he lay. Etridge walked stiffly away from the ship.

His initial emotion was self-hatred for not having eliminated the man when he had first been spotted. But he had never thought of the Office as being terribly effective, except in confusing its own personnel—and politicians and theologians when the time was appropriate. The man might have even helped them.

They had intercepted the signals as they were broadcast to the man. The computers had shunted aside any attempt to decode them because it would distract them from their examination of the unicorn, and because they recognized that they were purposely fragmentary and incomplete.

As at Thorn River, Etridge had allowed this Aden to stay, half thinking to see how the energies of magic played against him and the ways they would take him apart. As at Thorn River, he had learned more about the processes of magic than the processes of men. He had discounted the possibilities of Aden's survival and his capacity for action. Being neither committed to his own world nor having fully gone over to the other side, the man obviously existed in a vacuum; nothing lived, Etridge knew, outside of the great counterpositions of rationality and magic, and all the man's actions must therefore be nothing more than futile gestures, deprived of even symbolic meaning.

The man had taken the unicorn from him.

Stamp followed dumbly behind Etridge. They could hear Anderton's voice over the ship's speaker monotonously reciting the absence of extraordinary phenomena in each of the parallel spectrums. The gulls came back over the City, crying to one another, reserving their fishing grounds for when the ocean returned.

Etridge's anger grew inside of him, the rifle glistening where he ran his hands along it. The last gateway had been snatched away from him at the moment of its attainment.

Stamp saw the volcanic light reignited in Etridge's eyes as they neared the man. He was dressed in rags and looked like a beggar from the worst part of any town in either of the enemy worlds.

The air was still thick with powdered masonry and rotted magic, so he could not tell if he smelled as badly as he looked.

"Aden?" Etridge asked with brittle formality.

The man raised his head, looked at them with his one good eye and nodded.

"Special Office?" Etridge went on. Stamp fingered the safety on his rifle uneasily. The cut glass exactitude of his voice indicated shock and insanity.

"I was. It doesn't exist any more." The other man sounded incredibly tired.

"No more than the unicorn does. Now." Etridge bent over, grabbed Aden's filthy tunic with his right hand and easily lifted him to his feet. "But it existed a moment ago. Didn't it? We heard the signals. We saw what this toy of yours did." He let go of the man and grabbed the pistol from his right hand. Etridge stared at it for a second and then hurled it into the rubble. It exploded into gray smoke where it hit.

"The thing is over, sir. We've won." Aden refused to meet their eyes. "Please . . ."

"Name of god I will!" Etridge roared. "You took the unicorn away from me. Blew it up and packed it away in god and history where no one can get it!"

"You couldn't have . . ."

"Then why kill it, Aden?" Etridge had his hand around the man's shirt front again, twisting the cloth and drawing his face closer. "Why the words from your damn Office, or from whatever thing or monster was speaking to you? Why that bastard little gun of yours? Just refugees talking to one another, right? Little, gutless minds the war's used up and thrown away, to bother people like me! That's you, Aden, and your bloody Office! You know that?"

Aden tried to speak but nothing came out. Stamp saw dark recognition spreading over his face, blocking his words. Simultaneously, a mirror image of the same emotion crossed Etridge's face.

Aden tried to tell him about the eye. "The Special Office never was. It closed down . . ."

"It's still open. Just like you. And now that you, all of you've taken the unicorn, I'll tell you what we're going to do!" Etridge paused. He stood there for more than two minutes, looking down into the agent's eye, half of him seeming to wait for some signal to be broadcast to Aden from an antenna at Lake Gilbert or some outpost situated deeply within the terrible regions he wished so passionately to explore and subdue.

"You're so lost in your own language and your precious balancing act between our world and theirs that you're half magic yourselves. That's what you'd want, that's what you'd like, isn't it? *Isn't it?*" Aden nodded stupidly to Etridge. "So we're going to follow *you*. Let you go, all of you, and follow you and your goddamn bleeding Special Office! And when you run from us, when you run in the only ways you've taught yourselves, you're going to lead us to and through all of the secrets that beast took with it." Etridge threw Aden backward into the rubble so violently that he almost lost his balance and fell with him.

"We're going to chase your gang through every spectrum, through every dimension and hiding place you run to. You're cripples, Aden! When we move after you, you and your Office'll run, it'll be in directions that we can anticipate. One chase, one segment at a time. You're going to teach us, everything, until we don't need you any more."

Stamp felt a vicious peace and contentment inside of him; his conversion had not come too soon. This way would take longer, but the understanding and the triumph would inevitably be theirs. He knew that it would, both in his own mind and from the way Aden's face passed through shock into a despair so profound that it could only be a reflection of truth.

AFTERWORD:
Reality of War without End

Gerald Cecil, Professor of Astrophysics
University of North Carolina

Skirmishes over millennia between squabbling survivors of an atomic cataclysm have poisoned lands and broken human spirit. A dwindling cohort roused by prophets of Armageddon to end gloriously Humanity's agonizing death spiral invariably expire without effect. Evil seems for a while to be more competent or at least more creative: it sets up over centuries an interstellar Trojan horse, but ultimately fails. Magic and science coexist in intersecting dimensions, but the reductionists analyze then counteract the magicians to extinction, diminishing the world of the martial victors.

These themes of the Book of Wars trigger darkness on sunny afternoons, a tribute to the young writer's talents. If one reads SF for vistas and planetfalls, starship Victory is potent imagery. But all the credulous workers/ worshippers swept into its mystique don't hold our interest. Rather, we identify with the few who glimpse a plot before an inevitable fatality. The seeming triumph of this machine will stick as a profound betrayal. But from several centuries of perspective on that battle, we learn in Dragon that evil Salasar was vanquished while draining survivors and their lands ever more. Humanity had indeed reached the stars, so Victory was a legitimate tool turned against us. But after its demise, an ultimately futile empathy had drawn the star voyagers home. Entropy got to them, and in Dragon they are using their skills to cannibalize machines for war.

Cassandras are still pointing at our Trojan horse. Fossil fuels underpin our civilization, giving some time away from subsistence farming to read and write. They dispatch our robots into deep space, swelling bodies to the corner grocery, machinery to mine our food, and warriors to stand astride dwindling repositories of ancient sunlight. All species become extinct. But, wouldn't it be grand to clean up our act enough to take it on the interstellar road before closing the show?

The Following is an excerpt from:

STORM FROM THE
SHADOWS

DAVID WEBER

Available from Baen Books
March 2009
hardcover

Chapter One

"Talk to me, John!"

Rear Admiral Michelle Henke's husky contralto came sharp and crisp as the information on her repeater tactical display shifted catastrophically.

"It's still coming in from the Flag, Ma'am," Commander Oliver Manfredi, Battlecruiser Squadron Eighty-One's golden-haired chief of staff, replied for the squadron's operations officer, Lieutenant Commander John Stackpole. Manfredi was standing behind Stackpole, watching the ops section's more detailed displays, and he had considerably more attention to spare for updates at the moment than Stackpole did. "I'm not sure, but it looks—"

Manfredi broke off, and his jaw clenched. Then his nostrils flared and he squeezed Stackpole's shoulder before he turned his head to look at his admiral.

"It would appear the Peeps have taken Her Grace's lessons to heart, Ma'am," he said grimly. "They've arranged a Sidemore all their own for us."

Michelle looked at him for a moment, and her expression tightened.

"Oliver's right, Ma'am," Stackpole said, looking up from his own display as the changing light codes finally restabilized. "They've got us boxed."

"How bad is it?" she asked.

"They've sent in three separate groups," Stackpole replied. "One dead astern of us, one at polar north, and one at polar south. The Flag is designating the in-system force we already knew about as Bogey One. The task group to system north is Bogey Two; the one to system south is Bogey Three; and the one directly astern is Bogey Four. Our velocity relative to Bogey Four is just over twenty-two thousand kilometers per second, but range is less than thirty-one million klicks."

"Understood."

Michelle looked back at her own, smaller display. At the moment, it was configured to show the entire Solon System, which meant, by definition, that it was nowhere as detailed as Stackpole's. There wasn't room for that on a plot small enough to deploy from a command chair—not when it was displaying the volume of something the size of a star system, at any rate. But it was more than detailed enough to confirm what Stackpole had just told her. The Peeps had just duplicated exactly what had happened to *them* at the Battle of Sidemore, and managed to do it on a more sophisticated scale, to boot. Unless something reduced Task Force Eighty-Two's rate of acceleration, none of the three forces which had just dropped out of hyper-space to ambush it could hope to overtake it. Unfortunately, they didn't need to physically overtake the task force in order to engage it—not when current-generation Havenite multidrive missiles had a maximum powered range from rest of over sixty million kilometers.

And, of course, there was always the possibility that there was yet *another* Havenite task group waiting in hyper, prepared to drop back into normal space right in their faces as they approached the system hyper limit. . . .

No, she decided after a moment. *If they had the hulls for a fourth force, it would have already translated in, as well. They'd really have us in a rat trap if they'd been able to box us from four directions. I suppose it's possible that they* do *have another force in reserve—that they decided to double-think us and hold number four until they've had a chance to see which way we run. But that'd be a violation of the KISS principle, and this generation of Peeps doesn't go in much for that sort of thing, damn it.*

She grimaced at the thought, but it was certainly true.

Honor's been warning us all that these *Peeps aren't exactly stupid,* she reflected. *Not that any of us should've needed reminding after what they did to us in Thunderbolt! But I could wish that just this once she'd been wrong.*

Her lips twitched in a humorless smile, but she felt herself coming back on balance mentally, and her brain whirred as tactical possibilities and decision trees spilled through it. Not that the primary responsibility was hers.

No, that weight rested on the shoulders of her best friend, and despite herself, Michelle was grateful that it *wasn't* hers . . . a fact which made her feel more than a little guilty.

One thing was painfully evident. Eighth Fleet's entire operational strategy for the last three and a half months had been dedicated to convincing the numerically superior navy of the Republic of Haven to redeploy, adopt a more defensive stance while the desperately off-balance Manticoran Alliance got its own feet back under it. Judging by the ambush into which the task force had sailed, that strategy was obviously succeeding. In fact, it looked like it was succeeding entirely too well.

It was so much easier when we could keep their command teams pruned back . . . or count on State Security to do it for us. Unfortunately, Saint-Just's not around anymore to shoot any admiral whose initiative might make her dangerous to the régime, is he? Her lips twitched with bitterly sardonic amusement as she recalled the relief with which Manticore's pundits, as well as the woman in the street, had greeted the news of the Committee of Public Safety's final overthrow. *Maybe we were just a little premature about that,* she thought, *since it means that this time around, we don't have anywhere near the same edge in operational experience, and it shows.* This *batch of Peeps actually knows what it's doing. Damn it.*

"Course change from the Flag, Ma'am," Lieutenant Commander Braga, her staff astrogator announced. "Two-niner-three, zero-zero-five, six-point-zero-one KPS squared."

"Understood," Michelle repeated, and nodded approvingly as the new vector projection stretched itself across her plot and she recognized Honor's intention. The task force was breaking to system south at its maximum acceleration on a course that would take it as far away from Bogey Two as possible while maintaining at least the current separation from Bogey Four. Their new course would still take them deep into the missile envelope of Bogey One, the detachment covering the planet Arthur, whose orbital infrastructure had been the task force's original target. But Bogey One consisted of only two superdreadnoughts and seven battlecruisers, supported by less than two hundred LACs, and from their emissions signatures and maneuvers, Bogey One's wallers were pre-pod designs. Compared to the six obviously modern superdreadnoughts and two LAC carriers in each of the three ambush forces, Bogey One's threat was minimal. Even if all nine of its hyper-capable combatants had heavy pod loads on tow, its older ships would lack the fire control to pose a significant threat to Task Force Eighty-Two's missile defenses. Under the circumstances, it was the same option Michelle would have chosen if she'd been in Honor's shoes.

I wonder if they've been able to ID her flagship? Michelle wondered. *It wouldn't have been all that hard, given the news coverage and her "negotiations" in Hera.*

That, too, of course, had been part of the strategy. Putting Admiral Lady Dame Honor Harrington, Duchess and Steadholder Harrington, in command of Eighth Fleet had been a carefully calculated decision on the Admiralty's part. In Michelle's opinion, Honor was obviously the best person for the command anyway, but the appointment had been made in a glare of publicity for the express purpose of letting the Republic of Haven know that "the Salamander" was the person who'd been chosen to systematically demolish its rear-area industry.

One way to make sure they honored the threat, Michelle thought wryly as the task force came to its new heading in obedience to the commands emanating from HMS *Imperator,* Honor's SD(P) flagship. *After all, she's been their personal nightmare ever since Basilisk station! But I wonder if they got a fingerprint on* Imperator *at Hera or Augusta? Probably—they knew which ship she was aboard at Hera, at least. Which probably means they know who it is they've just mousetrapped, too.*

Michelle grimaced at the thought. It was unlikely any Havenite flag officer would have required extra incentive to trash the task force if she could, especially after Eighth Fleet's unbroken string of victories. But knowing whose command they were about to hammer certainly wasn't going to make them any *less* eager to drive home their attack.

"Missile defense Plan Romeo, Ma'am," Stackpole said. "Formation Charlie."

"Defense only?" Michelle asked. "No orders to roll pods?"

"No, Ma'am. Not yet."

"Thank you."

Michelle frown deepened thoughtfully. Her own battlecruisers' pods were loaded with Mark 16 dual-drive missiles. That gave her far more missiles per pod, but Mark 16s were both smaller, with lighter laser heads, and shorter-legged than a ship of the wall's multidrive missiles like the Mark 23s aboard Honor's superdread-noughts. They would have been forced to adopt an attack profile with a lengthy ballistic flight, and the biggest tactical weakness of a pod battlecruiser design was that it simply couldn't carry as many pods as a true capital ship like *Imperator*. It made sense not to waste BCS 81's limited ammunition supply at a range so extended as to guarantee a low percentage of hits, but in Honor's place, Michelle would have been sorely tempted to throw at least a few salvos of all-up MDMs from her two super-dreadnoughts back into Bogey Four's face, if only to keep them honest. On the other hand. . . .

Well, she's the four-star admiral, not me. And I suppose—she smiled again at the tartness of her own mental tone—*that she's demonstrated at least a* modicum *of tactical insight from time to time.*

"Missile separation!" Stackpole announced suddenly. "Multiple missile separations! Estimate eleven hundred—one-one-zero-zero—inbound. Time to attack range seven minutes!"

* * * * * * * * * *

Each of the six Havenite superdreadnoughts in the group which had been designated Bogey Four could roll six pods simultaneously, one pattern every twelve seconds, and each pod contained ten missiles. Given the fact that Havenite fire control systems remained inferior to Manticoran ones, accuracy was going to be poor, to say the least. Which was why the admiral commanding that group had opted to stack six full patterns from each superdreadnought, programmed for staggered launch to bring all of their missiles simultaneously in on their targets. It took seventy-two seconds to deploy them, but then just over a thousand MDMs hurled themselves after Task Force Eighty-Two.

Seventy-two seconds after that, a second, equally massive salvo launched. Then a third. A fourth. In the space of thirteen minutes, the Havenites fired just under twelve thousand missiles—almost a third of Bogey Four's total missile loadout—at the task force's twenty starships.

* * * * * * * * * *

As little as three or four T-years ago, any one of those avalanches of fire would have been lethally effective against so few targets, and Michelle felt her stomach muscles tightening as the tempest swept towards her. But this *wasn't* three or four T-years ago. The Royal Manticoran Navy's missile defense doctrine was in a constant state of evolution, continually revised in the face of new threats and the opportunities of new technology, and it had been vastly improved even in the six months since the Battle of Marsh. The *Katana*-class LACs deployed to cover the task force maneuvered to bring their missile launchers to bear on the incoming fire, but their counter-missiles weren't required yet. Not in an era when the Royal Navy had developed Keyhole and the Mark 31 counter-missile.

Each superdreadnought and battlecruiser deployed two Keyhole control platforms, one through each sidewall, and each of those platforms had sufficient telemetry links to control the fire of *all* of its mother ship's counter-missile launchers simultaneously. Equally important, they allowed the task force's units to roll sideways in space, interposing the impenetrable shields of their impeller wedges against the most dangerous threat axes without compromising their defensive fire control in the least. Each Keyhole also served as a highly sophisticated electronics warfare platform, liberally provided with its own close-in point defense clusters, as well. And as an added bonus, rolling ship gave the platforms sufficient "vertical" separation to see past the interference generated by the impeller wedges of subsequent counter-missile salvos, which made it possible to fire those salvos at far tighter intervals than anyone had ever been able to manage before.

The Havenites hadn't made sufficient allowance for how badly Keyhole's EW capability was going to affect their attack missiles' accuracy. Worse, they'd anticipated no more than five CM launches against each of their salvos, and since they'd anticipated facing only the limited fire control arcs of their fleeing targets' after hammerheads, they'd allowed for an average of only ten counter-missiles per ship per launch. Their fire plans had been based on the assumption that they would face somewhere around a thousand ship-launched counter-missiles, and perhaps another thousand or so Mark 31–based Vipers from the *Katanas*.

Michelle Henke had no way of knowing what the enemy's tactical assumptions might have been, but she was reasonably certain they hadn't expected to see over *seven* thousand counter-missiles from Honor's starships, alone.

* * * * * * * * *

"That's a lot of counter-missiles, Ma'am," Commander Manfredi remarked quietly.

The chief of staff had paused beside Michelle's command chair on his way back to his own command station, and she glanced up at him, one eyebrow quirked.

"I know we've increased our magazine space to accommodate them," he replied to the unspoken question. "Even so, we don't have enough to maintain this volume of defensive fire forever. And they're not exactly inexpensive, either."

Either we're both confident as hell, or else we're certifiable lunatics with nothing better to do than pretend *we are so we can impress each other with our steely nerve,* Michelle thought wryly.

"They may not be cheap," she said out loud, returning her attention to her display, "but they're a hell of a lot less expensive than a new ship would be. Not to mention the cost of replacing our own personal hides."

"There is that, Ma'am," Manfredi agreed with a lopsided smile. "There is that."

"And," Michelle continued with a considerably nastier smile of her own as the leading salvo of Havenite MDMs vanished under the weight of the task force's defensive fire, "I'm willing to bet Mark 31s cost one hell of a lot less than all those *attack* missiles did, too."

The second attack salvo followed the first one into oblivion well short of the inner defensive perimeter. So did the third. And the fourth.

"They've ceased fire, Ma'am," Stackpole announced.

"I'm not surprised," Michelle murmured. Indeed, if anything surprised her, it was that the Havenites hadn't ceased fire even sooner. On the other hand, maybe she wasn't being fair to her opponents. It had taken seven minutes for the first salvo to enter engagement range, long enough for six more salvos to be launched on its heels. And the effectiveness of the task force's defenses had surpassed even BuWeaps' estimates. If it had come as as big a surprise to the bad guys as she rather expected it had, it was probably unreasonable to expect the other side to realize instantly just how hard to penetrate that defensive wall was. And the only way they had to measure its toughness was to actually hammer at it with their missiles, of course. Still, she liked to think that it wouldn't have taken a full additional six minutes for *her* to figure out she was throwing good money after bad.

On the other *other hand, there are those other nine salvos still on the way,* she reminded herself. *Let's not get too carried away with our own self-confidence, Mike! The last few waves will have had at least a little time to adjust to our EW, won't they? And it only takes one leaker in the wrong place to knock out an alpha node . . . or even some overly optimistic rear admiral's command deck.*

"What do you think they're going to try next, Ma'am?" Manfredi asked as the fifth, sixth, and seventh salvos vanished equally ineffectually.

"Well, they've had a chance now to get a feel for just how tough our new doctrine really is," she replied, leaning back in her command chair, eyes still on her tactical repeater. "If it were me over there, I'd be thinking in terms of a really massive salvo. Something big enough to swamp our defenses by literally running us out of control channels for the CMs, no matter how many of them we have."

"But they couldn't possibly control something that big, either," Manfredi protested.

"We don't *think* they could control something that big," Michelle corrected almost absently, watching the eighth and ninth missile waves being wiped away. "Mind you, I think you're probably right, but we don't have any way of knowing that . . . yet. We could be wrong. And even if we aren't, how much accuracy would they really be giving up at this range, even if they completely cut the control links early and let the birds rely on just their onboard sensors? They wouldn't get very good targeting solutions without shipboard guidance to refine them, but they aren't going to get *good* solutions at this range anyway, whatever they do, and enough *bad* solutions to actually break through are likely to be just a bit more useful than perfect solutions that can't get past their targets' defenses, wouldn't you say?"

"Put that way, I suppose it does make sense," Manfredi agreed, but it was apparent to Michelle that her chief of staff's sense of professionalism was offended by the idea of relying on what was essentially unaimed fire. The notion's sheer crudity clearly said volumes about the competence (or lack thereof) of any navy which had to rely upon it, as far as he was concerned.

Michelle started to twit him for it, then paused with a mental frown. Just how much of a blind spot on Manfredi's part—or on her own, for that matter—did that kind of thinking really represent? Manticoran officers were accustomed to looking down their noses at Havenite technology and the crudity of technique its limitations enforced. But there was nothing wrong with a crude technique if it was also an *effective* one. The Republican Navy had already administered several painful demonstrations of that minor fact, and it was about time officers like Oliver Manfredi—or Michelle Henke, for that matter—stopped letting themselves be surprised each time it happened.

"I didn't say it would be pretty, Oliver." She allowed the merest hint of reprimand into her tone. "But we don't get paid for 'pretty,' do we?"

"No, Ma'am," Manfredi said just a bit more crisply.

"Well, neither do they, I feel fairly confident." She smiled, taking the possible sting out of the sentence. "And let's face it, they're still holding the short and smelly end of the hardware stick. Under the circumstances, they've made damned effective use of the capabilities they have this time around. Remember Admiral Bellefeuille? If you don't, *I* certainly do!" She shook her head wryly. "That woman is *devious*, and she certainly made the best use of everything she had. I'm afraid I don't see any reason to assume the rest of their flag officers won't go right on doing the same thing, unfortunately."

"You're right, Ma'am." Manfredi twitched a smile of his own. "I'll try to bear that in mind next time."

" 'Next time,' " Michelle repeated, and chuckled. "I like the implication there, Oliver."

"*Imperator* and *Intolerant* are rolling pods, Ma'am," Stackpole reported.

"Sounds like Her Grace's come to the same conclusion you have, Ma'am," Manfredi observed. "That should be one way to keep them from stacking *too* big a salvo to throw at us!"

"Maybe," Michelle replied.

The great weakness of missile pods was their vulnerability to proximity kills once they were deployed an outside their mother ship's passive defenses, and Manfredi had a point that incoming Manticoran missiles might well be able to wreak havoc on the Havenite pods. On the other hand, they'd already had time to stack quite a few of them, and it would take Honor's missiles almost eight more minutes to reach their targets across the steadily opening range between the task force and Bogey Four. But at least they were on notice that those missiles were coming.

* * * * * * * * * *

The Havenite commander didn't wait for the task force's fire to reach him. In fact, he fired at almost the same instant Honor's first salvo launched against *him*, and whereas Task Force Eighty-Two had fired just under three hundred missiles at him, he fired the next best thing to eleven thousand in reply.

"Damn," Commander Manfredi said almost mildly as the enemy returned more than thirty-six missiles for each one TF 82 had just fired at him, then shook his head and glanced at Michelle. "Under normal circumstances, Ma'am, it's reassuring to work for a boss who's good at reading the other side's mind. Just this once, though, I really wish you'd been wrong."

"You and I, both," Michelle replied. She studied the data sidebars for several seconds, then turned her command chair to face Stackpole.

"Is it my imagination, John, or does their fire control seem just a bit better than it ought to be?"

"I'm afraid you're not imagining things, Ma'am," Stackpole replied grimly. "It's a single salvo, all right, and it's going to come in as a single wave. But they've divided it into several 'clumps,' and the clumps appear to be under tighter control than *I* would have anticipated out of them. If I had to guess, I'd say they've spread them to clear their telemetry paths to each clump and they're using rotating control links, jumping back and forth between each group."

"They'd need a lot more bandwidth than they've shown so far," Manfredi said. It wasn't a disagreement with Stackpole, only thoughtful, and Michelle shrugged.

"Probably," she said. "But maybe not, too. We don't know enough about what they're doing to decide that."

"Without it, they're going to be running the risk of completely dropping control linkages in mid-flight," Manfredi pointed out.

"Probably," Michelle repeated. This was no time, she decided, to mention certain recent missile fire control developments Sonja Hemphill and BuWeaps were pursuing. Besides, Manfredi was right. "On the other hand," she continued, "this salvo is ten times the size of anything they've tried before, isn't it? Even if they dropped twenty-five or thirty percent of them, it would still be a hell of a lot heavier weight of fire."

"Yes, Ma'am," Manfredi agreed, and smiled crookedly. "More of those bad solutions you were talking about before."

"Exactly," Michelle said grimly as the oncoming torrent of Havenite missiles swept into the outermost counter-missile zone.

"It looks like they've decided to target us this time, too, Ma'am," Stackpole said, and she nodded.

* * * * * * * * * *

TF 82's opening missile salvo reached its target first.

Unlike the Havenites, Duchess Harrington had opted to concentrate all of her fire on a single target, and Bogey Four's missile defenses opened fire as the Manticoran MDMs swept towards it. The Manticoran electronic warfare platforms scattered among the attack missiles carried far more effective penetration aids than anything the Republic of Haven had, but Haven's defenses had improved even more radically than Manticore's since the last war. They remained substantially inferior to the Star Kingdom's in absolute terms, but the relative improvement was still enormous, and the gap between TF 82's performance and what *they* could achieve was far narrower than it once would have been. Shannon Foraker's "layered defense" couldn't count on the same sort of accuracy and technological sophistication Manticore could produce, so it depended on sheer weight of fire, instead. And an incredible storm front of counter-missiles raced to meet the threat, fired from the starships' escorting LACs, as well as from the superdreadnoughts themselves. There was so much wedge interference that anything resembling precise control of all that defensive fire was impossible, but with so many counter-missiles in space simultaneously, some of them simply *had* to hit something.

They did. In fact, they hit quite a few "somethings." Of the two hundred and eighty-eight MDMs *Intolerant* and *Imperator* had fired at RHNS *Conquete*, the counter-missiles killed a hundred and thirty-two, and then it was the laser clusters' turn. Each of those clusters had time for only a single shot each, given the missiles' closing speed. At sixty-two percent of light-speed, it took barely half a second from the instant they entered the laser clusters' range for the Manticoran laser heads to reach their own attack range of *Conquete*. But there were literally thousands of those clusters aboard the super-dreadnoughts and their escorting *Cimeterre*-class light attack craft.

Despite everything the superior Manticoran EW could do, Shannon Foraker's defensive doctrine worked. Only eight of TF 82's missiles survived to attack their target. Two of them detonated late, wasting their power on the roof of *Conquetee*'s impenetrable impeller wedge. The other six detonated between fifteen and twenty thousand kilometers off the ship's port bow, and massive bomb-pumped lasers punched brutally through her sidewall.

Alarms screamed aboard the Havenite ship as armor shattered, weapons—and the men and women who manned them—were wiped out of existence, and atmosphere streamed from *Conquetee*'s lacerated flanks. But superdreadnoughts were designed to survive precisely that kind of damage, and the big ship didn't even falter. She maintained her position in Bogey Four's defensive formation, and her counter-missile launchers were already firing against TF 82's second salvo.

* * * * * * * * *

"It looks like we got at least a few through, Ma'am," Stackpole reported, his eyes intent as the studied the reports coming back from the FTL Ghost Rider reconnaissance platforms.

"Good," Michelle replied. Of course, "a few" hits probably hadn't done a lot more than scratch their target's paint, but she could always hope, and some damage was a hell of a lot better than no damage at all. Unfortunately. . . .

"And here comes their reply," Manfredi muttered. Which, Michelle thought, was something of an . . . understatement.

Six hundred of the Havenite MDMs had simply become lost and wandered away, demonstrating the validity of Manfredi's prediction about dropped control links. But that was less than six percent of the total . . . which demonstrated the accuracy of Michelle's counterpoint.

The task force's counter-missiles killed almost nine thousand of the missiles which *didn't* get lost, and the last-ditch fire of the task force's laser clusters and the *Katana*-class LACs killed nine hundred more.

Which left "only" three hundred and seventy-two.

Five of them attacked *Ajax*.

Captain Diego Mikhailovic rolled ship, twisting his command further over onto her side relative to the incoming fire, fighting to interpose the defensive barrier of his wedge, and the sensor reach of his Keyhole platforms gave him a marked maneuver advantage, as well as improving his fire control. He could see threats more clearly and from a greater range, which gave him more time to react to them, and most of the incoming X-ray lasers wasted themselves against the floor of his wedge. One of the attacking missiles managed to avoid that fate, however. It swept past *Ajax* and detonated less than five thousand kilometers from her port sidewall.

The battlecruiser twitched as two of the missile's lasers blasted through that sidewall. By the nature of things, battlecruiser armor was far thinner than superdreadnoughts could carry, and Havenite laser heads were heavier than matching Manticoran weapons as a deliberate compensation for their lower base accuracy. Battle steel shattered and alarms howled. Patches of ominous crimson appeared on the damage control schematics, yet given the original size of that mighty salvo, *Ajax*'s actual damage was remarkably light.

"Two hits, Ma'am," Stackpole announced. "We've lost Graser Five and a couple of point defense clusters, and Medical reports seven wounded."

Michelle nodded. She hoped none of those seven crewmen were badly wounded. No one ever liked to take casualties, but at the same time, only seven—none of them fatal, so far at least—was an almost incredibly light loss rate.

"The rest of the squadron?" she asked sharply.

"Not a scratch, Ma'am!" Manfredi replied jubilantly from his own command station, and Michelle felt herself beginning to smile. But then—

"Multiple hits on both SDs," Stackpole reported in a much grimmer voice, and Michelle's smile died stillborn. "*Imperator*'s lost two or three grasers, but she's essentially intact."

"And *Intolerant*?" Michelle demanded harshly when the ops officer paused.

"Not good," Manfredi replied as the information scrolled across his display from the task force data net. "She must have taken two or three dozen hits . . . and at least one of them blew straight into the missile core.

She's got heavy casualties, Ma'am, including Admiral Morowitz and most of his staff. And it looks like all of her pod rails are down."

"The Flag is terminating the missile engagement, Ma'am," Stackpole said quietly.

He looked up from his display to meet her eyes, and she nodded in bitter understanding. The task force's sustainable long-range firepower had just been cut in half. Not even Manticoran fire control was going to accomplish much at the next best thing to two light-minutes with salvoes the size a single SD(P) could throw, and Honor wasn't going to waste ammunition trying to do the impossible.

Which, unfortunately, leaves the question of just what we are going to do wide open, doesn't it? she thought.

*   *   *   *   *   *   *

Several minutes passed, and Michelle listened to the background flow of clipped, professional voices as her staff officers and their assistants continued refining their assessment of what had just happened. It wasn't getting much better, she reflected, watching the data bars shift as more detailed damage reports flowed in.

As Manfredi had already reported, her own squadron—aside from her flagship—had suffered no damage at all, but it was beginning to look as if Stackpole's initial assessment of HMS *Intolerant*'s damages had actually been optimistic.

"Admiral," Lieutenant Kaminski said suddenly. Michelle turned towards her staff communications officer, one eyebrow raised. "Duchess Harrington wants to speak to you," he said.

"Put her through," Michelle said quickly, and turned back to her own small com screen. A familiar, almond-eyed face appeared upon it almost instantly.

"Mike," Honor Alexander-Harrington began without preamble, her crisp, Sphinxian accent only a shade more pronounced than usual, "*Intolerant*'s in trouble. Her missile defenses are way below par, and we're headed into the planetary pods' envelope. I know *Ajax*'s taken a few licks of her own, but I want your squadron moved out on our flank. I need to interpose your point defense between *Intolerant* and Arthur. Are you in shape for that?"

"Of course we are." Henke nodded vigorously. Putting something as fragile as a battlecruiser between a wounded superdreadnought and a planet surrounded by missile pods wasn't something to be approached lightly. On the other hand, screening ships of the wall was one of the functions battlecruisers had been designed to fulfill, and at least, given the relative dearth of missile pods their scouts had reported in Arthur orbit, they wouldn't be looking at another missile hurricane like the one which had just roared through the task force.

"*Ajax*'s the only one who's been kissed," Michelle continued, "and our damage is all pretty much superficial. None of it'll have any effect on our missile defense."

"Good! Andrea and I will shift the LACs as well, but they've expended a lot of CMs." Honor shook her head. "I didn't think they could stack that many pods without completely saturating their own fire control. It looks like we're going to have to rethink a few things."

"That's the nature of the beast, isn't it?" Michelle responded with a shrug. "We live and learn."

"Those of us fortunate enough to survive," Honor agreed, a bit grimly. "All right, Mike. Get your people moving. Clear."

"Clear," Michelle acknowledged, then turned her chair to face Stackpole and Braga. "You heard the lady," she said. "Let's get them moving."

* * * * * * * * * *

BCS 81 moved out on Task Force Eighty-Two's flank as the Manticoran force continued accelerating steadily away from its pursuers. The final damage reports came in, and Michelle grimaced as she considered how the task force's commanding officer was undoubtedly feeling about those reports. She'd known Honor Harrington since Honor had been a tall, skinny first-form midshipwoman at Saganami Island. It wasn't Honor's fault the Havenites had managed to mousetrap her command, but that wasn't going to matter. Not to Honor Harrington. Those were her ships which had been damaged, her people who had been killed, and at this moment, Michelle Henke knew, she was feeling the hits her task force had taken as if every one of them had landed directly on her.

No, that isn't what she's feeling, Michelle told herself. *What she's doing right now is wishing that every one of them* had *landed on her, and she's not going to forgive herself for walking into this. Not for a long time, if I know her. But she's not going to let it affect her decisions, either.*

She shook her head. It was a pity Honor was so much better at forgiving her subordinates for disasters she knew perfectly well weren't their fault than she was at forgiving herself. Unfortunately, it was too late to change her now.

And, truth to tell, I don't think any of us would want to go screwing around trying *to change her*, Michelle thought wryly.

"We'll be entering the estimated range of Arthur's pods in another thirty seconds, Ma'am," Stackpole said quietly, breaking in on her thoughts.

"Thank you." Michelle shook herself, then settled herself more solidly into her command chair.

"Stand by missile defense," she said.

The seconds trickled by, and then—

"Missile launch!" Stackpole announced. "Multiple missile launches, *multiple sources!*"

His voice sharpened with the last two words, and Michelle's head snapped around.

"Estimate seventeen thousand, Ma'am!"

"Repeat that!" Michelle snapped, certain for an instant that she must have misunderstood him somehow.

"CIC says seventeen thousand, Ma'am," Stackpole told her harshly, turning to look at her. "Time to attack range, seven minutes."

Michelle stared at him while her mind tried to grapple with the impossible numbers. The remote arrays deployed by the task force's pre-attack scout ships had detected barely four hundred pods in orbit around Arthur. That should have meant a maximum of only *four* thousand missiles, so where the hell—?

"We've got at least thirteen thousand coming in from Bogey One," Stackpole said, as if he'd just read her mind. His tone was more than a little incredulous, and her own eyes widened in shock. That was even more preposterous. Two superdreadnoughts and seven battlecruisers couldn't possibly have the fire control for that many missiles, even if they'd all been pod designs!

"How could—?" someone began.

"Those aren't *battlecruisers*," Oliver Manfredi said suddenly. "They're frigging *minelayers!*"

Michelle understood him instantly, and her mouth tightened in agreement. Just like the Royal Manticoran Navy, the Republic of Haven built its fast minelayers on battlecruiser hulls. And Manfredi was undoubtedly correct. Instead of normal loads of mines, those ships had been stuffed to the deckhead with missile pods. The whole time they'd been sitting there, watching the task force flee away from Bogey Four and directly towards *them*, they'd been rolling those pods, stacking them into the horrendous salvo which had just come screaming straight at TF 82.

"Well," she said, hearing the harshness in her own voice, "now we understand how they did it. Which still leaves us with the little problem of what we do *about* it. Execute Hotel, John!"

"Defense Plan Hotel, aye, Ma'am," Stackpole acknowledged, and orders began to stream out from HMS *Ajax* to the rest of her squadron.

Michelle watched her plot. There wasn't time for her to adjust her formation significantly, but she'd already set up for Hotel, even though it had seemed unlikely the Havenites' fire could be heavy enough to require it. Her ships' primary responsibility was to protect *Intolerant*. Looking out for themselves came fairly high on their list of priorities as well, of course, but the superdreadnought represented more combat power—and almost as much total tonnage—as her entire squadron combined. That was why Missile Defense Plan Hotel had stacked her battlecruisers vertically in space, like a mobile wall between the planet Arthur and *Intolerant*. They were perfectly placed to intercept the incoming fire . . . which, unfortunately, meant that they were completely exposed *to* that fire, as well.

"Signal from the Flag, Ma'am," Stackpole said suddenly. "Fire Plan Gamma."

"Acknowledged. Execute Fire Plan Gamma," Michelle said tersely.

"Aye, aye, Ma'am. Executing Fire Plan Gamma," Stackpole said, and Battlecruiser Squadron Eighty-One began to roll pods at last.

It wasn't going to be much of a response compared to the amount of fire coming at the task force, but Michelle felt her lips drawing back from her teeth in satisfaction anyway. The gamma sequence Honor and her tactical staff had worked out months ago was designed to coordinate the battlecruisers' shorter-legged Mark 16s with the superdreadnoughts' MDMs. It would take a Mark 16 over thirteen minutes to reach Bogey One, as compared to the *seven* minutes one of *Imperator*'s Mark 23s would require. Both missiles used fusion-powered impeller drives, but there was no physical way to squeeze three complete drives into the smaller missile's tighter dimensions, which meant it simply could not accelerate as long as its bigger brother.

So, under Fire Plan Gamma *Imperator*'s first half-dozen patterns of pod-launched Mark 23s' drive settings had been stepped down to match those of the *Agamemnons'* less capable missiles. It let the task force put six salvos of almost three hundred mixed Mark 16 and Mark 23 missiles each into space before the superdreadnought began firing hundred-and-twenty-bird salvos at the Mark 23's maximum power settings.

All of which is very fine, Michelle thought grimly, watching the icons of the attack missiles go streaking away from the task force. *Unfortunately, it doesn't do much about the birds they've already launched.*

As if to punctuate her thought, *Ajax* began to quiver with the sharp vibration of outgoing waves of *counter-*missiles as her launchers went to sustained rapid fire.

The Grayson-designed *Katana*-class LACs were firing, as well, sending their own counter-missiles screaming to meet the attack, but no one in her worst nightmare had ever envisioned facing a single salvo this massive.

"It's coming through, Ma'am," Manfredi said quietly.

She looked back up from her plot, and her lips tightened as she saw him standing beside her command chair once more. Given what was headed towards them at the moment, he really ought to have been back in the shock frame and protective armored shell of his own chair. *And he damned well* knows *it, too*, she thought in familiar, sharp-edged irritation. But he'd always been a roamer, and she'd finally given up yelling at him for it. He was one of those people who *needed* to move around to keep their brains running at the maximum possible RPM. Now his voice was too low pitched for anyone else to have heard as he gazed down into her repeater plot with her, but his eyes were bleak.

"Of course it is," she replied, equally quietly. The task force simply didn't have the firepower to stop that many missiles in the time available to it.

"How the *hell* are they managing to control that many birds?" Manfredi continued, never looking away from the plot. "Look at that pattern. Those aren't blind-fired shots; they're under tight control, for now at least. So where in hell did they find that many control channels?"

"Don't have a clue," Michelle admitted, her tone almost absent as she watched the defenders' fire ripping huge holes in the cloud of incoming missiles. "I think we'd better figure it out, though. Don't you?"

"You've got that right, Ma'am," he agreed with a mirthless smile.

* * * * * * * * * *

No one in Task Force Eighty-Two—or anyone in the rest of the Royal Manticoran Navy, for that matter—had ever heard of the control system Shannon Foraker had dubbed "Moriarty" after a pre-space fictional character. If they had, and if they'd understood the reference, they probably would have agreed that it was appropriate, however.

One thing of which no one would ever be able to accuse Foraker was thinking small. Faced with the problem of controlling a big enough missile salvo to break through the steadily improving Manticoran missile defenses, she'd been forced to accept that Havenite ships of the wall, even the latest podnaughts, simply lacked the necessary fire control channels. So, she'd set out to solve the problem. Unable to match the technological capability to shoehorn the control systems she needed into something like Manticore's Keyhole, she'd simply accepted that she had to build something bigger. *Much* bigger. And while she'd been at it, she'd decided, she might as well figure out how to integrate that "something bigger" into an entire star system's defenses.

Moriarty was the answer she'd come up with. It consisted of remotely deployed platforms which existed for the sole purpose of providing telemetry relays and control channels. They were distributed throughout the entire volume of space inside Solon's hyper limit, and every one of them reported to a single control station which was about the size of a heavy cruiser . . . and contained nothing except the very best fire control computers and software the Republic of Haven could build.

She couldn't do anything about the lightspeed limitations of the control channels themselves, but she'd finally found a way to provide enough of those channels to handle truly massive salvos. In fact, although TF 82 had no way of knowing it, the wave of missiles coming at it was less than half of Moriarty's maximum capacity.

Of course, even if the task force's tactical officers had known that, they might have felt less than completely grateful, given the weight of fire which *was* coming at them.

* * * * * * * * * *

Michelle never knew how many of the incoming missiles were destroyed short of their targets, or how many simply got lost, despite all Moriarty could do, and wandered off or acquired targets other than the ones they'd originally been assigned. It was obvious that the task force's defenses managed to stop an enormous percentage them. Unfortunately, it was even more obvious that they hadn't stopped *enough* of them.

Hundreds of them hurled themselves at the LACs—not because anyone had wanted to waste MDMs on something as small as a LAC, but because missiles which had lost their original targets as they spread beyond the reach of Moriarty's lightspeed commands had acquired them, instead. LACs, and especially Manticoran and Grayson LACs, were very difficult for missiles to hit. Which was not to say that they were *impossible* to hit, however, and over two hundred of them were blown out of space as the tornado of missiles ripped into the task force.

Most of the rest of Moriarty's missiles had been targeted on the two superdreadnoughts, and they howled in on their targets like demons. Captain Rafe Cardones maneuvered Honor's flagship as if the stupendous superdreadnought were a heavy cruiser, twisting around to interpose his wedge while jammers and decoys joined with laser clusters in a last-ditch, point-blank defense. *Imperator* shuddered and bucked as laser heads blasted through her sidewalls, but despite grievous wounds, she actually got off lightly. Not even her massive armor was impervious to such a concentrated rain of destruction, but it did its job, preserving her core hull and essential systems intact, and her human casualties were minuscule in proportion to the amount of fire scorching in upon her.

Intolerant was less fortunate.

The earlier damage to *Imperator*'s sister ship was simply too severe. She'd lost both of her Keyholes and all too many of her counter-missile launchers and laser clusters in the last attack. Her sensors had been battered, leaving holes in her own close-in coverage, and her electronic warfare systems were far below par. She was simply the biggest, most visible, most vulnerable target in the entire task force, and despite everything BCS 81 could do, droves of myopic end-of-run Havenite MDMs hurled themselves at the clearest target they could see.

The superdreadnought was trapped at the heart of a maelstrom of detonating laser heads, hurling X-ray lasers like vicious harpoons. They slammed into her again and again and again, ripping and maiming, tearing steadily deeper while the big ship shuddered and bucked in agony. And then, finally, one of those lasers found something fatal and HMS *Intolerant* and her entire company vanished into a glaring fireball of destruction.

Nor did she die alone.

* * * * * * * * * *

HMS *Ajax* heaved indescribably as the universe went mad.

Compared to the torrent of fire streaming in on the two superdreadnoughts, only a handful of missiles attacked the battlecruisers. But that "handful" was still numbered in the hundreds, and they were much more fragile targets. Alarms screamed as deadly lasers ripped deep into far more lightly armored hulls, and the *Agamemnon*-class were podlayers. They had the hollow cores of their type, and that made them even more fragile than other, older battlecruisers little more than half their size. Michelle had always wondered if that aspect of their design was as great a vulnerability as the BC(P)'s critics had always contended.

It looked like they—and she—were about to find out.

Oliver Manfredi was hurled from his feet as *Ajax* lurched, and Michelle felt her command chair's shock frame hammering viciously at her. Urgent voices, high-pitched and distorted despite the professionalism trained bone-deep into their owners, filled the com channels with messages of devastation—announcements of casualties, of destroyed systems, which ended all too often in mid-syllable as death came for the men and women making those reports.

Even through the pounding, Michelle saw the icons of both of her second division's ships—*Priam* and *Patrocles* —disappear abruptly from her plot, and other icons disappeared or flashed critical damage codes throughout the task force's formation. The light cruisers *Fury*, *Buckler*, and *Atum* vanished in glaring flashes of destruction, and the heavy cruisers *Star Ranger* and *Blackstone* were transformed into crippled hulks, coasting onward ballistically without power or impeller wedges. And then—

"Direct hit on the command deck!" one of Stackpole's ratings announced. "No survivors, Sir! Heavy damage to Boat Bay Two, and Boat Bay One's been completely destroyed! Engineering reports—"

Michelle felt it in her own flesh as HMS *Ajax* faltered suddenly.

"We've lost the after ring, Ma'am!" Stackpole said harshly. "*All* of it."

Michelle bit the inside of her lower lip so hard she tasted blood. Solon lay in the heart of a hyper-spac gravity wave. No ship could enter, navigate, or long survive in a gravity wave without both Warshawski sails . . . and without the after impeller ring's alpha nodes, *Ajax* could no longer generate an after sail.